P. (Patrick) Cudmore

The civil government of the states

Constitutional history of the United States

P. (Patrick) Cudmore

The civil government of the states
Constitutional history of the United States

ISBN/EAN: 9783741176432

Manufactured in Europe, USA, Canada, Australia, Japa

Cover: Foto ©Andreas Hilbeck / pixelio.de

Manufactured and distributed by brebook publishing software
(www.brebook.com)

P. (Patrick) Cudmore

The civil government of the states

THE

CIVIL GOVERNMENT

OF THE STATES,

AND THE

CONSTITUTIONAL HISTORY

OF THE

UNITED STATES.

By P. CUDMORE, Esq.,

COUNSELLOR-AT-LAW,

Author of the "Irish Republic," etc., etc.

SECOND EDITION.

NEW YORK:

FOR SALE BY P. J. KENEDY, 5 BARCLAY STREET.

1875.

DEDICATION.

TO THE MEMORY
OF THE
FATHERS OF THE CONSTITUTION OF THE UNITED STATES OF AMERICA,
AND THE
ADVOCATES OF LIBERTY,
THIS VOLUME IS MOST RESPECTFULLY DEDICATED
BY THE
AUTHOR.

PREFACE.

THE object of the author has been to condense into one volume the Colonial, General, and Constitutional History of the United States. This volume is a digest of the writings and speeches of the fathers of the Constitution of the United States, eminent American and foreign Jurists, the journals and annals of Congress, the *Congressional Globe*, the General History of the United States, the Statutes of the several States, the Statutes of the United States, the Decisions of the Supreme Courts of the several States, the Opinions of the Attorneys General of the United States, and the Decisions of the Supreme Court of the United States; of extracts from De Tocqueville, the Madison Papers, the "Federalist," "Elliott's Debates," the writings of Jefferson, Adams, Hamilton, and Vattel, and of extracts from Jefferson, and other eminent authors on parliamentary law. The platforms of political parties are also given. The chapters on Colonial History and Civil Government will be found, at this time especially, instructive and useful. The author most respectfully hopes that this work will be welcomed by the legal profession, the press, and the statesmen of America. The quotations from the several authors are given in the language of the authors themselves. Those who wish to understand the structure of the Government of the United States (State and Federal), will find this volume a useful, reliable, and convenient manual and book of facts and reference.

The causes and consequences of the recent American Civil War are given. The history of Land Grants, the Homestead Law, and the laws pertaining to aliens and naturalization, will be found instructive. The author has studiously endeavored to make this work a useful treatise on our complex form of Government, including Colonial, State, Federal, Territorial, County, Town, and Parish.

For the terms of office of Governors and Members of the State Legislatures mentioned in this book, the reader is referred to the Constitutions of the several States as they were in 1848.

NEW YORK, *July*, 1875.

THE CIVIL GOVERNMENT OF THE STATES,

AND THE

CONSTITUTIONAL HISTORY

OF THE

UNITED STATES.

CHAPTER I.—COLONIAL HISTORY.

The first settlement of Englishmen in North America was attempted in the reign of Queen Elizabeth. Her first patent was issued to Sir Humphrey Gilbert in 1578. An abortive attempt to settle a colony in Virginia was made by Sir Walter Raleigh, in this reign, under a transfer of Gilbert's patent. In the year 1603, one hundred and ten years after the discovery of the *New World*, there was not an Englishman in America. In 1606, the Spaniards had established posts in Florida, and the French had settlements in New France, afterwards named Canada.

James I of England, who succeeded Elizabeth, by an ordinance, April 10, 1606, divided all of North America lying between 34 and 45 degrees of latitude into two districts. The first district was called Southern Virginia; and the second, Northern Virginia (Plymouth Colony) which was changed to New England.

Southern Virginia was granted to the London company in 1607, by James I, and Northern Virginia, (Plymouth Colony) or New England was granted to the Plymouth company November 3,1620, composed " of forty noblemen, knights and gentlemen, called the council," established at Plymouth, in the county of Devon, for the planting, ruling, and governing New England in America, with the Earl of Warwick as head of the corporation.

South Virginia extended from the parallel of 34 to 40 degrees, and from the Atlantic to the Pacific. The first settlement, under the Grant to the London company, was made at Jamestown, Virginia, in 1607. The management of the colony was given to Christopher Newport and Captain John Smith. "The general superintendence of the colonies was vested in a Council, resident in England, named by the king, and subject to all orders and decrees under the sign manual; and the local jurisdiction was intrusted to a Council also named by the king, and subject to his instructions which was to reside in the colonies. Under these auspices, commenced, in 1607, the first permanent settlement in Virginia."—Moore's Int. to the lives of Govs. Ply. & Mass. p. 9. In 1607, a new charter was granted to the company. The colony was to be governed by a governor and council. This was a close corporation. The aristocracy of England, at this period of English history, had little respect for the people. Indeed the idea of a government of the people was repugnant to the aristocracy or wealthy classes of England. The governor was appointed by the Company.—Quackenbos, 73. The people of England had no idea of a Town Meeting as a body politic or a town meeting—"where the people met in their aggregate capacity to elect local officers." For in England, the country was divided into counties, which were represented by Knights elected, generally, by the land owners. There were also certain boroughs represented by burgesses, generally, representing the mercantile interests. The idea of the people meeting in their collective capacity, as in the Republics of Greece, was unknown in England.—Blackstone, vol. i, pp. 159-160. In 1619, the people of Virginia were able to obtain a voice in the government of the colony. Virginia colony was divided into eleven boroughs; and two members from each borough formed the House of Burgesses, in imitation of the British House of Commons. This assembly was the first house of representatives in America.—Quack. 76. As the people were poor and lived in log-cabins they did not think of forming a House of Lords. It might be here remarked that the Southern Colonies followed the institutions and laws of old England which suited their wants and condition. That the people of all the colonies borrowed their laws from the English model, except the Puritans of New England, who followed the laws of Moses — the Bible was the basis of their laws and government.—Moore's Lives Govs. Mass. 77. And as the colonists of Virginia were of the Church of England, they established parishes and maintained the clergy with tithes as in England.

Slaves were brought to Virginia in a Dutch man-of-war. The crown of England became jealous of the extensive powers and territory of the London company. And at last King James I dissolved this great monopoly—this overgrown corporation. The executive powers were in this corporation. King Charles I recognized the authority of the Assembly of Virginia. And as the struggle in England was between Charles and the Parliament—the latter being Puritans, and the former of the Church of England, Virginia took part with the king. The authorities banished all who would not use the liturgy of the Church of England. So Virginians, as well as the Puritans were intolerant—both established church and state.—Quack. 101. We see an antagonism between the South and New England when both held slaves. In 1758, the legislature of Virginia passed an act that the people might commute for the tobacco, in money, a tribute which had to be paid to the ministers of the Church of England. For in the early days of the colony tobacco was the usual currency; for nearly all payments were made in tobacco, as afterwards in the Western States, men had to take what was then called "store pay," that is, an order on a store for goods. Virginia, in a great measure, retained the old English aristocratic customs and prejudices of caste. The land holders, as in the old country, in that age, were the aristocracy. They were called the upper class, and the landless the lower class. The upper class was principally attached to the crown. The people of the South and of New England were dissimilar in politics, religion, manners and customs—they were not of the same race. The Virginians were the descendants of the Normans—"Cavaliers;" and the Puritans of the Saxons, or "Roundheads." The colony of Virginia restricted the right of suffrage to householders; and made the English church the state church. And it compelled attendance at the worship of this church under penalty of twenty pounds. Penal laws were passed against Quakers and Baptists. The colonial legislature and Governor Berkeley were the embodiment of despotism. Berkely is reported to have said, "I thank God that there are no free schools or printing, and

I hope that we shall not have them these hundred years!" This was the status of the colonial legislature of Virginia until Bacon's rebellion, in 1676, when the old intolerant legislature was dissolved and a more liberal one elected. The governors of the colony were appointed by the king.

THE CAROLINAS—NORTH CAROLINA.

The Carolinas were settled under the auspices of Charles II, of England. The colony was granted, in 1668, to Edward Clarendon, Lord Albemarle, the Earl of Shaftesbury and others. The people established a House of Representatives. A short time after this, the colony was divided into North and South Carolina. In 1689, North Carolina banished her proprietary Governor.—Willard, p. 120.

SOUTH CAROLINA.

In 1685, the French Hu-gue-nots, or French Protestants, settled in South Carolina. Governor Colleton was sent over from England, by the proprietors of the colony to govern the people. He was opposed by the Assembly of the people, and finally banished from the colony, in the reign of William and Mary.—Quack. p. 120. So the people of the Carolinas, dressed in "homespun and deer-skins," were considered the "freest of the free." They could not yield to the despotism of the proprietary governors. They wanted to rule themselves. They wanted a home governor.

MARYLAND.

(After the Queen, Henrietta Maria of France.) Maryland, though a part of the territory granted to the London company, was granted to George Calvert, Lord Baltimore, in 1632. Though a Lord, he was democratic in principle. His son Cecil granted liberty of conscience to all men. The first settlement of the colony was made at the village of St. Mary's. "Maryland was the first to proclaim universal suffrage, and to introduce the most democratic forms into the conduct of the government."—De Tocqueville p. 82. Maryland was settled principally by Catholic Irish who granted liberty of conscience to all who believed in Jesus Christ. The majority of the settlers were Irish Catholics. Maryland was a refuge for all who fled from religious persecution from Europe, New England, and Virginia. The people met in one assembly and voted. Every freeman had a vote without religious or property test. The assembly was composed of members chosen by the people. At first the legislature was composed of one house, but afterwards of two houses. The Upper House was chosen by the proprietors, and the Lower House by the people. The Protestants, who flocked from persecution and took refuge in Maryland, soon obtained a majority, and strange to say persecuted the Catholics.

DELAWARE.

The colony of Delaware was founded by Swedes and Fins. It was conquered by the Dutch; and brought under the dominion of New Netherlands, the name given to the Dutch colony in North America. The colonists remained quietly under the Dutch Government and with the Dutch passed under the dominion of England, in 1664.

NEW YORK.

In 1625, Peter Minnets bought the whole Island of Manhattan from the Indians for $24. The Dutch built the city of New Amsterdam, now New York. The Hollanders settled on Long Island, Staten Island, and New

Jersey. The colony was under the control of the home government and
the governors of New York. The Governors of New Netherlands were
military governors; the people had no voice in this military despotism.
The will of the governor of the garrison was supreme. At length deputies from the Dutch villages met in Assembly, and they demanded a
government of the people. The government would not concede to their
demands. The Dutch had no *idea* of a town meeting. In 1664, New
Netherlands fell under the dominion of England, and it was called New
York, in honor of the Duke of York, afterwards King James II, of England. The power of Holland ended in North America.

NEW JERSEY.

In 1664, the region between the Hudson and the Delaware was granted to
Berkeley and Carteret, and was called New Jersey. The people established
a colonial Assembly. The early settlers were Quakers and Dutch.

PENNSYLVANIA.

The Quakers, goaded by persecution in their native England, sought the
wilds of America, and settled in New Jersey, in 1675. The early settlers
of New Jersey were Quakers and Dutch. In 1681, William Penn obtained from
Charles II a tract of land west of the Delaware, which was called Pennsylvania, or the woody land of Penn. Within this territory were settlements
of Dutch and Swedes. The spot where now stands the city of Philadelphia
was purchased by Penn from the Swedes. Penn also purchased the good-
will of the Indians. The people who emigrated to Pennsylvania with Penn
were Englishmen. They followed the institutions of England, so far as
they were suitable to their condition and circumstances. They divided the
colony into counties, the same as in England. Six members were chosen
annually from each county to the Assembly or Legislature. The people
were represented in the Assembly. They had no idea of a town meeting, as
a local government. All freemen had a vote who believed in God and kept
the Lord's day holy. Murder alone was punished with death.—Quackenbos
124. Penn was proprietary governor.

GEORGIA.

In 1732, James Oglethorpe, a member of the British Parliament, obtained
from George II a charter of the country west of the Savannah river.
Oglethorpe was the proprietary governor. In 1752, the trustees resigned
Oglethorpe's charter to the king. The Kings of England were willing
enough, at first, to grant large tracts of country to favorites with a view to
settlement. They allowed their favorites to exercise supreme authority
while the settlements contained but a few persons, who had to contend
with poverty, famine and the savages. But when the colonies became populous and the people had money and property to be taxed, the kings became
jealous and wished to revoke the charters and take the government of the
colonies under their immediate control and authority. Moreover, they
dreaded the *idea of self-government* which was making such rapid strides in
the colonies. They wished to have governors over the colonies chosen by
the crown. From the moment that the Kings of England revoked or compelled the colonies to surrender their charters, we may date the struggle for
independence, which increased in intensity as the colonies acquired wealth,
intelligence and population. The colonists were thrown on their own resources on the wild shores of America, to contend with poverty, famine
and hostile Indians. In the stern school of adversity they learned th

science of self-government. While in their log-cabins, dressed in home-spun and deer-skins, they lost respect for royalty and aristocracy. The youth born and educated in the colonies, in the wilds of the forest, in contact with the "free and independent Redmen," disdained not only the governors sent over by England, but all manner of royalty and aristocracy. Thus, we see that the Southern States were settled by a very different class of Englishmen from those who settled New England, while the inhabitants of the Middle States of New York, New Jersey, Delaware, Pennsylvania, and Maryland differed from both, they being made up of different nationalities and religions.

CHAPTER II.—NEW ENGLAND.

The first settlement of New England was made by the Puritans, a peculiar people, who dissented from the Church of England, "*as by law established*," in 1602, in the reign of James I, King of England. They formed an independent congregation. They elected their own minister. Richard Clifton and James Robinson were chosen.—Moore's Lives Govs. Ply. and Mass. p. 12. Persecution was the order of the times. Archbishop Banchroft and Laud, of Canterbury, persecuted the Puritans with unrelenting severity and cruelty. Exposed to all the rigor of English *penal laws*, which the British government could enforce, the Puritans were compelled to leave their homes in their native land, and seek new homes in foreign countries. Robinson and his congregation fled from the cruel laws of England and took refuge in Holland, in 1609. In consequence of the war between Spain and Holland the Puritans resolved on emigrating to America, where they would be free to retain their religion, laws, customs and language unmolested. They considered themselves in the like situation as the Israelites, and did not want to mix with any other people or religion. They feared that if they should remain in Holland their people would become absorbed in a foreign nation.—*Ibid.* 14. In 1617, Robert Chushman and John Carver were sent to England to negotiate with the London company with a view to settle in Virginia, and also to ascertain if the king would grant liberty of conscience. Though the king promised that he would not molest them, he refused to grant them, by public authority under the seals, liberty of conscience. After some negotiations with the London company of Virginia a patent was obtained under the company's seal, in the name of John Wincomb, who was to accompany the Puritans to America.—Bancroft, vol. i, p. 305. This patent and the proposals of a London merchant, named Thomas Weston, were carried to London, in 1619, for the consideration of the Puritan congregation. November 3, 1620, a territory, extending from 40 to 48 degrees of North latitude and from the Atlantic to the Pacific, was granted to a company of forty persons, with the Earl of Warwick at its head, by James I. This patent is the basis of all subsequent grants, patents or charters of New England.—Moore's Govs. Ply. and Mass. 10. The company had full control over this vast territory, subject to the authority of the king. Meantime, in 1620, Weston went to Leyden, Holland, and the Puritans entered into an agreement with him, that he should supply them with money and shipping to take them to America. The *Speedwell*, commanded by Capt. Reynolds, and the *Mayflower* by Capt. Jones, sailed for America. Both ships had put to sea, but the *Speedwell* was unfit for the voyage, and on September, 1620, the *Mayflower*, with one hundred and' one passengers, besides the ship's officers and crew, sailed for America, with the intention to settle within the jurisdiction of the Virginia Company, on the Hudson river. But they were driven further north by the winds and perils of the sea, and by force of necessity they landed on Plymouth Rock.

As many New England orators and public men claim that their ancestors came over in the *Mayflower*, we give the following for their benefit :

The names of the subscribers are placed in the following order, those who brought wives, marked with a dagger (†), and those who died before the end of the next March, distinguished by an asterisk (*).

1. Mr. John Carver, †	. . . .	8
2. Mr. William Bradford, †	. . . . . .	2
3. Mr. Edward Winslow, †	. . . . . .	5
4. Mr. William Brewster, †	. . . . . .	6
5. Mr. Isaac Allerton, †	. . . . . .	6
6. Capt. Miles Standish, †	. . . . . .	2
7. John Alden,	. . . . . .	1
8. Mr. Samuel Fuller, -	. . . . . .	2
9. * Mr. Christopher Martin, †	. . . . . .	4
10. * Mr. William Mullins, †	. . . . . .	5
11. * Mr. William White, † (1)	. . . . . .	5
12. Mr. Richard Warren, -	. . . . . .	1
13. John Howland, (2)		
14. Mr. Stephen Hopkins, †-	. . . . . .	8
15. * Edward Tilly, †	. . . . . .	4
16. * John Tilly, †	. . . . . .	8
17. Francis Cook,	. . . . . .	2
18. * Thomas Rogers,	. . . . . .	2
19. * Thomas Tinker, †-	. . . . . .	8
20. * John Ridgdale, †	. . . . . .	2
21. * Edward Fuller, †-	. . . . . .	8
22. * John Turner, -	. . . . . .	8
23. Francis Eaton, †	. . . . . .	8
24. * James Chilton, † .	. . . . . .	8
25. * John Crackston, (8)	. . . . . .	2
26. John Billington, †	. . . . . .	4
27. * Moses Fletcher, -	. . . . . .	1
28. * John Goodman, -	. . . . . .	1
29. * Degory Priest, (4)-	. . . . . .	1
30. * Thomas Williams,	. . . . . .	1
31. Gilbert Winslow, -	. . . . . .	1
32. * Edmund Margeson, -	. . . . . .	1
33. Peter Brown,	. . . . . .	1
34. * Richard Britlerige,	. . . . . .	1
35. George Soule, (5)		
36. * Richard Clarke,	. . . . . .	1
37. Richard Gardiner,	. . . . . .	1
38. * John Allerton,	. . . . . .	1
39. * Thomas English,	. . . . . .	1
40. Edward Dotey, (6) -	. . . . . .	
41. Edward Leister, (6)	. . . . . .	

Total persons . . . . . - 101
Of whom were subscribers to the compact - - 41

(1) Besides a son born in Cape Cod Harbor, named Peregrine.
(2) Of Governor Carver's family.
(3) Morton writes his name Craxton.
(4) In Morton, Digery Priest.
(5) Of Governor Winslow's family.
(6) Of Mr. Hopkins' family."
(Moore's lives Gov. Ply. & Mass. page 26.)

The Virginia patent was useless, as they had settled without the jurisdiction of the London company, and within the limits of the Plymouth company. They had no authority from any government or power. They were reduced to a state of nature and could establish a government for themselves. They had no protection from the government of England, but were treated as persons outside the pale of the British laws. Being reduced to a state of nature, they were free to make laws for their own protection and safety. They claimed the right to choose their own government and make their own laws.—*Vide* Vattel's Law of Nations, Book i, chap. 4. pp. 17, 18, 19, 20, 21, 22. Blackstone's Comm. vol. i, page 245; 1 Kent's Comm. pp. 208,209. The emigrants to New England and the other colonies had this advantage that they had "*neither lords* nor common people, neither rich nor poor."

On the voyage one man died, and a boy, the son of Stephen Hopkins, was born—called *Oceanus.* November 10, 1620, the *Mayflower* anchored in the harbor of Cape Cod 42 degrees north latitude, within the territory of New Plymouth. Here the first Englishman, Peregrine White, was born in the colony, on board of the *Mayflower*, in Cape Cod harbor, Nov. 1620. The last survivor of those who came over in the *Mayflower* was Mary Churchman, daughter of Isaac Allerton. The Pilgrims met in the cabin of the *Mayflower* and drew up articles of association. This may be called the first convention in the United States. These articles were a constitution for the government of the colony. At this meeting, they pledged themselves to be governed by the rule of the majority—"to submit to such government and governors, as we should by common consent agree to make and choose." The Puritans were opposed to monarchy, so thought King James I in 1604, when he said of the Puritans, "You are aiming at a Scots presbytery, which agrees with monarchy as well as God with the devil! I will have none of that liberty as to ceremonies."—Bancroft, vol. i, p. 298; Neal, ii, 52; Moore's Lives Govs. Ply & Mass. p. 24, with notes. After this compact was signed, John Carver was elected governor, by a unanimous vote, for one year. This was the first government of the people in America, where the people made their own laws, elected their own officers, civil, military and ecclesiastical, without patent, grant, charter or authority from any king or power in the world. This was establishing a democratic government in the wilds of America. The Puritan clergy were elected by the congregation. The Puritans were a joint-stock company. They mortgaged their labor to London merchants who supplied them with means to emigrate to America. They had to work on the credit system. The London merchants who supplied the Puritans with ships and money had a monopoly of the trade of the colony. They were adventurers. They were also shareholders in the colony. They relinquished all their rights to the colony for £1,800 sterling. There was no oath of office required of John Carver, as he had no patronage. There was no danger of political corruption. The politicians did not get rich on the people's money. The people were poor, frugal, and they possessed a stern and unflinching honesty. They did not want idlers; they despised "a proud heart, a dainty tooth, a beggar's purse, and an idle hand."

From the nature of their compact, being a joint-stock company, they established a community of goods. They planted one field in common with corn; they found the seed in an Indian mound. All had to work, even the governor of the colony. They worked like bees. They had no drones in the hive. Oh, shades of the Puritans!! no Long Branch for the government to live in kingly style!!!

While every man worked in common, the people suffered great privations, and in some instances suffered from famine—at one time they were so far reduced as to live on five grains of parched corn each daily. They would have perished only for the supply of fish. They had to share with the new emigrants who came to the colony. In 1623, Governor Bradford is reported to have said, "By the time our corn is planted, our victuals are spent; not knowing at night where to have a bit in the morning, and have neither bread nor corn for three or four months together."—Moore 68. Such was the state of the colony during the time they had a community of goods. So the colonists, in violation of their agreements with the London adventurers afore-mentioned, in the spring of 1623, agreed that every "family should plant for themselves, on such ground as should be assigned to them by lot."

They had but one boat in the whole colony, and parties of seven men fished in their turn for the benefit of the whole colony; when a deer was killed it was divided among the whole people of the *congregation* or colony. The people, while a community of goods lasted, lived whole days on fish and ground-nuts ! They were in debt and had to pay 30 per cent. per annum for money. But after every man was able to work for himself, industry was encouraged, and the people of the colony, in 1629, were free from the debt they owed the London adventurers, and they were freemen ! So much for communism. There never was a time, since Adam was expelled from Eden, more favorable than this to try the experiment of a community of goods, as the Puritans were all of one nation, religion, manners, customs, and habits and spoke the same language. They were one congregation—all governed by public opinion and religion. They were as one family. Yet, while they were one corporation—all one partnership concern—all possessing a community of goods, they were in a state of starvation. But when every man was for himself, they soon paid off the debt of the colony and sent for their friends to Holland.

The pilgrims followed the example of the Jews—like them they claimed to be the chosen of the Lord. They united church and state. The government of the colony was composed of the church and the congregation.—Moore's lives, Govs. Ply. & Mass, 284, 289, 290, 291, 300, 318. The governor was elected by the people, in town meeting, the same as we now elect Town Officers. The whole body of the people or congregation elected their own officers, and transacted all business pertaining to the church and the state. While Governor Carver lived, the whole people had a vote. Both clergy and congregation, with the governor as chairman, met in one assembly, like the Greek Republics, and made laws and regulations for the colony. The town meeting was both court and legislature. The governor possessed no power but that of a magistrate. He could arrest criminals, but they were tried before the whole body of the people, as judicial and legislative power was then vested in the whole body of the people in town meeting. The governor presided the same as the foreman of a Grand Jury. He was the sole executive officer of the colony. He had no patronage, as he had neither the power to nominate or appoint to office. All officers, civil, religious and military, were elected by the people. The governor was moderator and with his deputies presided at town meetings—voting was by ballot. In time, the franchise was confined to freemen, who had taken a freeman's oath. There was no distinction or exemption from military duty—all had to stand "watch," even the clergy. The highest military officer in the colony was Captain Miles Standish. The town was impaled, and cannon planted on the roof of the church. The people met in town meeting on a common plain. It was an assembly of the sovereign people—for sovereignty was in the people; for they acknowledged no higher law-making power. "They perpetually exercised the rights of sovereignty; they named their magistrates, concluded peace or declared war, made police regulations, and enacted laws as if their allegiance was due only to God."—De Tocqueville, p. 19.

For the English laws were repudiated, in 1636, by the declaration in the cabin of the *Mayflower*. New Plymouth entered upon the record, November 15, 1636, that "*the authority of the English laws, 'at present or to come' is expressly renounced and Parliament denied the right of legislating for the colony.*" This was perfectly right as the Puritans were denied the protection of the King of England. They were reduced to a state of nature, and were free to make laws for themselves.—Vattel's Law of Nations, book i, chapter 4, pp. 17, 18, 19, 20, 21, 22, 23. Kent's Comm., vol. i, pp. 208–9. Blackstone's Comm., vol. i, page 245. Thus the town meeting is the parent of the Colony and the State mass-meetings and constitutional conventions. "The Republic was already established in every township."—De Tocqueville, 28. Governor John Carver was succeeded by William Bradford, in 1621. The first change from the "time-honored town meetings," the fear and dread of kings, a stumbling-block to the Kings of England, and the royal governors sent over to govern New England—or the general court, where the whole people assembled for executive, legislative, and judicial business together, was the appointment of an assistant, or deputy governor. In time, the assistants were increased to five and afterwards to seven. The Puritans had no charter of title either from the king or the Plymouth company. The first patent was taken in the name of John Pierce, and the second in the name of William Bradford, in trust for the colony, in 1629. In 1640, Governor Bradford surrendered this patent to the general court—this title was as good as the crown of England could make it. In 1636, the Puritans declared their "lawful right to their lands in respect of vacancy, donation, and purchase of the natives." In Bradford's patent was granted the right of fishery in Maine, and a tract of land of fifteen miles on each side of the Kennebeck river. In the patent was the following enabling clause to empower the colony to "enact such laws as should most benefit a state in its nonage, not rejecting or omitting to observe such of the laws of their native country as would conduce to their good." The patent granted to William Bradford provided "to frame and make orders, ordinances and constitutions, etc." In 1634, an important change took place in the colony. The governor and assistants were constituted the judicial court, and afterwards the supreme judiciary of the colony. The government was remodelled. The Executive and Judiciary vested in the governor and seven assistants, the town meeting remaining the assembly or general court. In 1639, the first assembly of the colony met. It was composed of four deputies from the *old town of Plymouth*, and two from each of the other towns. In 1649, the legislature or general court was composed of members from each town. These deputies to the general court or legislature were chosen from the freemen of each town.

The towns were governed by town officers called selectmen, who had jurisdiction in civil cases where the amount did not exceed forty shillings, with the right of appeal to the court of *assistants*. In 1649, the qualification of a voter or freeman was that he should be "twenty-one years of age, of a sober and peaceable conversation, orthodox in the fundamentals of religion, and possessed of twenty pounds ratable estate."—Moore's Life of Governor Bradford, p. 75. Prior to 1634, the governor and assistants possessed only the power of magistrates. They could only arrest and bind over criminals to the general court which was the town-meeting—they had no civil jurisdiction. The general court, in 1636, established a body of organic laws for the colony. November 15, 1636, the people met, and promulgated a declaration of independence. This was the first American declaration of independence. Henceforth the British statutes had no force in the colony, except by the authority of the general court. Indeed from this period we may date the time when acts of parliament passed subsequent to the 15 Nov., 1636, ceased to have force or validity in the colony of Plymouth. It is a nice question whether this declaration did not repudiate all acts of parliament in the colony after the promulgation of this order.—Moore's Governors of New Plymouth, 144. I believe that the courts of Massachusetts, after the union of the two colonies of Massachusetts and Plymouth, gave judicial sanction to some acts of parliament, and in time, gave them the force of common law. The clergy of the established church had great authority in the colony. They were the teachers and the expounders of the law—for as there were no lawyers in the colony, the clergy were the only persons who had a knowledge of the law. But they followed the laws of Moses more than the common law of England. Hence, even to this day, the judges of Massachusetts have interwoven the law of the Bible with the common law of England.—Moore's Life of Governor Winslow, 118. The clergy of the established church had great influence. The first settlers were well educated, but their children, who had to work like all those who are raised in a new country,—were not learned. The clergy were supported by private donations, until 1677, when a law was passed compelling the people to support public worship. A law was passed compelling by taxation, without any respect to any particular religion, "the support of the regular congregational ministry," in 1677.— Moore's Lives of Govs. Ply. and Mass., 210. "In 1672, a law was passed establishing the first public school in Plymouth colony."—*Ibid.* p. 209. In 1677, a law was passed, "requiring each town and village, in the colony, to erect, finish, and keep in repair a house for public worship." This was a heavy blow upon the other denominations. The power of the congregational ministry was great. They monopolized the learning of the colony. They held public offices and engaged in business. The Quakers grumbled and were persecuted.

MASSACHUSETTS COLONY.

A colony of Puritans settled at Salem in 1626, where "they resolved to remain as the Sentinels of Puritanism in the Bay of Massachusetts." The settlement of Massachusetts was, at first, a corporation under a royal patent. In 1634, the first assembly of representatives of deputies from the towns met as a legislature. This was the second house of representatives in the New England colonies.—Moore's Life of Gov. Dudley, 285. This legislature was known as the General Court. In 1636, Connecticut was settled by a colony from Massachusetts. A settlement was made in Hartford, in 1637. In Jan. 14, 1639, the people of Windsor, Hartford and Wethersfield met at Hartford, and adopted a constitution for the colony, which was the basis of government for one hundred and fifty years.—Moore's Life of Gov. Haynes, 307. This constitution provided that all civil officers be voted for by ballot, by the whole body of freemen. That two sessions of the general court or legislature should be holden annually. This was the *first formal constitutional* convention in New England. October 7th, 1691, a charter was granted to Massachusetts by William III, which included Plymouth. This union gave great offence to the people of Plymouth. They complained of Massachusetts, thus: "All the frame of heaven moves on one axis, and the whole of New England's interest seems designed to be loaden on one bottom, and her particular motions to be concentric to the Massachusetts tropic." "Few wise men rejoice at their chains."—Moore's Governors of Plymouth and Mass., 224. Massachusetts held a monopoly of the offices, and very few of the old residents of Plymouth, called the old colony, got office in the province of Massachusetts. The Puritans of Massachusetts repudiated the authority of the Church of England. They held that the authority of ordination should not exist in the clergy—that the clergy should be elected. The Governors of Plymouth and Massachusetts, as Justices of the Peace, solemnized marriages. Ministers of the Gospel were not allowed to solemnize marriage until 1692, as they did not want to "bring in the English custom of ministers performing the solemnity of marriage." Governor Winslow was married in Holland by a Dutch magistrate, and Governor Richard Bellingham, in the right of a magistrate, married himself.—Moore's Life Gov. Bellingham, 339. It is strange that the Puritans, who fled from English persecution, should themselves turn persecutors. The Puritans would not suffer the idea of toleration—they banished the Quakers as guilty of divers horrid errors. In 1658, a law was passed that "no Quaker, Ranter or any such corrupt person," should be permitted to be a freeman. All who opposed the Puritans were disabled from holding any office. A vagrant law was passed against Quaker preachers.

The commissioners of the United Colonies of New England, in 1658, issued a recommendation to the several colonies to put the Quakers to death "unless they publicly renounced their accursed errors." In 1637, Massachusetts banished Mrs. Anne Hutchison. In 1644, Massachusetts banished Quakers and made it penal to possess a Quaker book, or to entertain or conceal a Quaker; if banished Quakers returned they were to have their ears cut off; a female concealing or entertaining a Quaker was whipped. If the Quaker came back a second time his tongue was bored with a red-hot iron.—Moore's Governors of Massachusetts, 256. Quakers and members of the Church of England made violent complaints to the government of England against the intolerance of New England. Books and speeches were published in London by both parties. The struggle was kept up by the Puritans. Laws were passed against heresy, in 1646. It was ordered that the Quakers be whipped through the town, tied to a cart, and banished to the nearest town; if they should return, to be branded on the shoulder. Quakers were executed in 1659. So intolerant were the Puritans, that Governor Thomas Prence requested the Governor of Rhode Island to expel the Quakers from that colony. The Governor of Rhode Island answered: "As concerning these Quakers, who are now among us, we have no law among us whereby to punish any one for declaring by words, etc., their minds and understanding concerning things and the ways of God, as to salvation and eternal condition. And we moreover find, that in those places where these people in this colony are most of all suffered to declare themselves freely, and are only opposed by arguments in discourse, there they least of all desire to come." This answer offended the Puritans, and Rhode Island was excluded from the league of 1643.

RHODE ISLAND.

Roger Williams, a minister of Salem, Massachusetts, and 18 others entered into a contract and founded a civil government. They were banished from Massachusetts for religious belief. They established the government of the majority. They held the following principles: "We whose names are under written, do hereby solemnly, in the presence of Jehovah, incorporate ourselves into a body politic, and as He shall help, will submit our persons, lives, and estates, unto our Lord Jesus Christ, the King of kings, and Lord of lords, and to all those perfect and absolute laws of his, given in his Holy Word of truth, to be judged and guided thereby." The Puritans imagined that they were the chosen children of God, and, like the Israelites of old, claimed the divine right to govern, and to banish all from the colony who differed with them in religion or politics. Governor Winthrop said, "It is yourselves who have called us to this office, and being called by you we have an authority from God." They claimed to be brought to the country from England, as the Israelites were brought from Egypt to the Holy Land. All who were not of the Puritan church had no toleration in the colony. "Let men of God in courts and churches watch o'er such as do a toleration hatch." All who did not belong to the established church of the colony of Massachusetts were excluded from office—and were not allowed to vote. Persons of the Church of England petitioned for liberty of conscience, or if that could not be granted, for freedom from taxes and military services. The Puritans held the argument that all men had liberty to do right, but no liberty to do wrong. "The established clergy had supreme control over the colony of Massachusetts and would not tolerate opposition."—Moore's Govs. Mass.,258. At the restoration of Charles II, in 1660, the complaints of the anti-Puritans were heard by the king, and in 1661, he issued his mandamus—"To our trusty and well-beloved John Endecott, Esquire, and to all and every other governor or governors of our plantations of New England, and of all the other colonies thereto belonging, that now are or hereafter shall be, and to all and every the ministers and officers of our plantations and colonies whatsoever within the continent of New England," which writ forbade further persecution of the Quakers. We may here remark that the Puritans derived their persecuting spirit from England.

In 1643, the colonies united against the Indians. One of the greatest delusions of the age, and one which the Puritans inherited from their Anglo-Saxon ancestors, was that of witchcraft. It was one of the sad delusions of ignorance and intolerance. The Puritans in the fulness of their zeal hanged witches for the good of their souls, the glory of God and the glory of the colony. In 1656, a sister of Governor Bellingham was executed in Massachusetts on a charge of witchcraft.—Moore's Govs. Mass., 344. Vide Cudmore's Irish Republic, p. 304. As early as 1634, the government of England wished to establish a general government for all the colonies of New England. Sir Ferdinand Gorges was selected as governor of New England Colonies. But the difficulties of Charles I, in his war in Ireland,—O'Neill's rebellion 1641—prevented this tyrannical act from consummation. Thus this great Irish rebellion prevented Laud from trampling on the chartered rights of New England. So much for Ireland's struggle for independence.—Moore's Life Gov. Winslow, 115-16. In 1674, Sir Edmond Andros was made military governor of the territories, which the crown had granted to the Duke of York. He received possession of New York from the Dutch authorities. He made himself dictator in civil, military and religious matters. He made an attempt to reduce Connecticut under his jurisdiction. Andros would not admit an assembly of the people of New York. The people had no share in the government until 1683, when Governor Dongan came into power, when an assembly of the people was chosen after a struggle of thirty years. In 1691, the supreme court of the colony was established.

In 1685, James II came to the throne. June 3, 1686, he appointed Sir Edmond Andros governor of all New England, except Connecticut. In 1686, Andros landed in Boston and published his commission from the king. He was vested with absolute power. He removed from office the authorities who held under the old charter, and overthrew the most cherished institutions of the old settlers of New England. The last records of the charter government of Massachusetts ended May 12, 1686. Andros was a consummate tyrant. He abolished vote by ballot and suppressed the liberty of the press. He endeavored to blot out every trace of colonial laws, which clashed with the laws of England. He said that the town meetings were too democratic—he said that "there was no such thing as a town in the whole country." He annulled old titles to land, and laughed at the Indian deeds. He said that they were "no better than the scratch of a bear's paw." He laid on a poll-tax. All who did not comply with the tyrant's wishes were fined and imprisoned. He established the English church, Jan. 12, 1687; he dissolved the government of Rhode Island, broke the seal of the colony, and assumed its government. He made a demand on Connecticut while the assembly was in session, Oct. 1687, at Hartford, for a surrender of the charter of the colony. The governor placed the charter on the table, when suddenly the lights were extinguished, and the charter taken from the table and hid in the hollow of an oak tree, ever since known as the "*charter oak.*" October 31, 1687, Andros wrote in the records of Connecticut, "*Finis,*" and assumed the government of the colony. In 1688, New York and New Jersey were added to his jurisdiction. When the news reached the colonies that James was driven from the throne of England, the people of Boston made a prisoner of Andros and established the general court, and recalled Bradstreet as governor. The authorities in England passed over this revolution in silence as they had themselves set the example. King William took from the colonies the right of electing their own governors. England claimed the "unqualified right of binding the colonies in all cases whatever, and specifically of the right of taxing them without their consent. The attempt of the king and parliament to tax by the sword immediately led to the revolution."—Kent's Comm. vol. i, p. 205.

CHAPTER III.—TOWN, SCHOOL, AND PARISH.

The American people had a fair opportunity to establish a Democratic form of government on the model of the Greek Republics, where all the citizens voted in one body in their assemblies. The great mass of the inhabitants were working men, with a few exceptions. "They had neither lords nor common people, neither rich nor poor."—De Tocqueville, p. 14. In the Middle and Southern states grants were made by the crown to great proprietors, and in many instances the governors were appointed by the crown.—De Tocqueville, pp. 18 and 19. New York, under the Dutch government, was no better than a military post. The proprietary governments were established in Maryland, Pennsylvania, Delaware, the Carolinas, the Jerseys, and Georgia. The right of the soil and the establishment of civil government was given to favorites of the crown, who almost exercised royal authority. They appointed the governors and had the right to convene the legislature. The proprietors exercised a veto on the acts of the assemblies. The crown alone had a negative on the acts of the proprietors.—Young's American · Statesman, 30. The New England States had charter governments, which conferred on the colonists all the privileges of natural-born subjects. The only limitation on the colonial legislature of New England was, that no law should conflict with those of England.—Young's American Statesman, p. 22. The proprietary governments were superseded by royal governments, with royal charters which continued until the revolution. They derived their powers from the king, governors held their offices at the pleasure of the king and acted under his instructions. The king appointed the governor and council, and representatives were elected by the people. The governors had a negative on the acts of the legislature. All acts of the legislature had to receive the royal authority. The judges were appointed by the crown. —Young's American Statesman, p. 26. I am of opinion that the town meetings and town laws originated in New England. The New England colonies claimed the right to make all laws for the government of the colonies. They were nearly independent nations. —De Tocqueville, 19. The New England town is older than the counties, the States, or the Federal Union. It answers the purpose of an English parish for supporting the poor, and in colonial times for the support of religion and education—for the support of ministers of the Congregational Church, established by law. For both New England and Virginia established church and state. The New England towns were nearly republics. In Connecticut, in colonial times, parents were obliged to send their children to the parish school or pay a fine.—De Tocqueville, 23, 24. In the towns, the people were sovereign. They were the source of political power. Indeed, the first towns nearly formed independent nations.—De Tocqueville, 47. They gave existence to constitutional conventions. For in New England, the towns exercised more authority than in any other part of the United States. The following are the town officers of Connecticut: Selectmen, town clerk, treasurer, registrar, constables, assessors, surveyors of highways, collectors of town taxes, grand jurors, tythingmen, haywards, gaugers, packers, sealers of weights and measures, weighers, pound-keepers, who serve for one year.—Statutes Conn. p. 101. "The inhabitants of the respective towns, in legal meeting assembled, shall have power to make such orders, rules and regulations for the welfare of the towns, as they may deem expedient, and to enforce them by suitable penalties, if such regulations do not concern matters of a criminal nature, are not repugnant to the laws of the State, and the penalties do not exceed four dollars for any one breach."—Statutes Conn. 102. The town can give a bounty for killing wild cats; may appropriate money for monuments for soldiers and seamen. The selectmen have charge of the poor; may organize a night patrol; may license dealers in junk, etc.; may revoke licenses. The registrars give license to marry; keep records of births, marriages and deaths. "Every town, at its annual meeting for the election of town officers, shall choose not less than two, nor more than six Grand Jurors, to serve for the ensuing year, who shall take the oath prescribed by law."—Statutes Conn. 112. "The civil authority and selectmen of the several towns shall constitute a board of health in their respective towns. The town is a quasi corporation, capable of suing and being sued. Such are the powers of a town that it has control of the internal police of the State; the board of health, in any town, may pass quarantine laws and regulations. The justices of the peace are empowered to summon an inquest, etc. The town has control of the schools."—Statutes Conn. 124. The town officers of Massachusetts, (Statutes, 1836) are: town clerk, asses-

sors, overseers of poor, town treasurer, school committee, surveyors of highways, constables, collectors of taxes, tythingmen, field drivers, fence
viewers, surveyors of lumber, measurers of wood and sealers of leather.
Each town has the charge of the poor and may erect a workhouse. Every
person of the age of eighteen years is liable to keep watch and ward, ministers
of the Gospel, justices, selectmen and sheriffs exempted. We have said that
in colonial times the parish had to support the ministers of the Congregational
Church, but now, it is otherwise. But the Statutes provide "that every
parish or religious society heretofore established is declared to be a body
corporate, with all the powers given to a corporation."—Laws of Mass. 1836.
The town chooses a board of health and may establish quarantine laws.
The town has charge of the schools; and of building schools and hiring
teachers.—Statutes of Mass. 1836. The inhabitants of the town may
divide the town into school districts. The powers and duties of the selectmen nearly similar to the town supervisors of New York, Wisconsin,
Minnesota and other Western States. In Massachusetts the town grants
licenses. The towns in Massachusetts have the capacity to sue and be sued.
They are quasi corporations—they may make by-laws. The school laws of
the several States have been changed nearly every year. In Minnesota, and
other States, the county commissioners divide the counties into
school districts. The school districts are quasi corporations empowered
to sue and be sued; the school officers are a director, treasurer,
and clerk, who are elected annually. In Minnesota, Laws 1873, school
officers are elected for three years. They have general charge of the
schools and school houses in the district—may hire teachers. The qualified voters of the district when assembled at a legal school meeting,
have power to vote a tax on the taxable property of the district for the support of the public school," &c. In some States the
school trustees of each district examine teachers; in others, there is a town
superintendent of schools in each town to examine teachers; and still in
others, the county commissioners of each county appoint a school examiner
for each commissioner district; and still in others the county commissioners appoint a school superintendent of public schools for each county,
whose duty it is to examine teachers and visit and examine schools.—Statutes
Minn. pp. 299-300-1-2-3-4, Ed. 1866. Actions for and against school
districts shall be brought in the name of the school district.—Statutes Minn.
1866, p. 300, sec. 9, and p. 299, sec. 1. Vacancies to be filled by the remaining board of trustees when a vacancy occurs. So, when one of the
trustees resigns, he must tender his resignation to the other two.—Statutes
Minn. 1866, p. 301, sec. 15. So the resignations of school and town officers
depend on the laws of the several States, as well as upon general principles of
law. In Vermont the town officers are, clerk, selectmen, town treasurer, over-
seer of the poor, constables, assessors, auditors, fence viewers, Grand
Jurors, sealers of weights and measures, inspectors of leather, pound-
keepers, surveyors of highways, an agent to prosecute and defend suits in
which the town is interested.—Statutes of Vermont, 1793. The duties of
selectmen nearly similar to those of the supervisors of New York, Wisconsin, Minnesota, and other Western States. In New York, Wisconsin Minnesota (other States), the towns are quasi corporations, and may
"sue and be sued." May make by-laws. Supervisors are elected annually, as
well as clerks, treasurers, assessors, justices of the peace; and constables are
elected for two years, overseers of highways, pound-masters, etc. The towns
are empowered to raise money for town purposes and to defend suits against
their respective towns. In some States the supervisors are fence viewers;
and with the justices of the peace constitute the board of health. In some

States, suits for and against towns are conducted by the supervisors; but the suit must be in the name of the town.—Statutes Minn. 1866, p. 146, sec. 61. Statutes Minn. p. 149. sec. 85, 1866. The papers in a suit must be served on the chairman or in his absence on the town clerk.—Statutes Minn. 1866, p. 149, sec. 87. Each town may pass by-laws. In some States, the supervisors in the several towns have care and superintendence of the roads and bridges in the towns; and may lay out and repair the roads in their respective towns.—Statutes Minn. 1866, p. 190, sec. 1. Overseers of highways must resign to the supervisors.—Statutes Minn. 1866, p. 191, sec. 4, 5. The justices of the peace of each town, and the supervisors, or a majority of them, fill vacancies in the town offices. All town officers must tender their resignation to this board.—Statutes Minn. 1866, p. 144, sec. 45, 46. The powers and duties of the towns and school districts are limited by the statutes, beyond which they can exercise no corporate powers.—Statutes Minn. 1866, p. 140, sec. 9. Wisconsin Rep. vol. 26. See opinion Supreme Court U. S. 21 Howard, 506. Yet, no other officer has control over town officers while acting within the sphere of their respective duties. They may be compelled to perform the duties of their respective offices by mandamus. In some instances, they are liable to pay a fine according to the provisions of the statutes. They are all liable to be indicted for corruption in office, etc. For further on this subject, see the constitutions and statutes of the several States. The courts can reach individual officers both town, school, county, state and federal, for no person in the United States is above the law. The courts by judicial sentence enforce the laws, town, county, state and federal.—De Tocqueville, p. 57. Opinions of the attorneys general of the United States, vol. 1, p. 5.

COUNTY GOVERNMENT.

It has been said that there is no body in New England representing the county as a body politic.—De Tocqueville, p. 51. This was so in the time that De Tocqueville wrote. For then county officers were appointed.—De Tocqueville, p. 48. In Massachusetts, Act of November, 2, 1791, the expenses of the county were voted by the legislature. Until quite recently there was no body in New England representing the county, either directly or indirectly. By the constitution of Vermont, (Constitution, 1793,) "assistant judges of the county court shall be elected by the freemen of their respective counties;" sheriffs, high bailiffs, and state attorneys shall be elected by the freemen of their respective counties. According to the statutes of Vermont (1793,) the county court, which is similar to circuit courts in other states, have jurisdiction in cases of highways on appeals from the selectmen; the county court have the appointment of county clerks, county treasurers, and inspectors of turnpike roads. "The county court in each county shall, by their clerk or an auditor, examine, audit and adjust all accounts against each county, and draw orders on the county treasurer for the same." Certain county officers are appointed by the legislature. —See statutes of Vermont, 1793. The county treasurer has charge of the county buildings. In Massachusetts, under recent laws, "each county shall be a body corporate for the following purpose, to wit: To sue and be sued; to purchase and hold, for the public use of the county lands lying within its own limits and any personal estate, to make all necessary contracts and to do all other necessary acts in relation to the property and concerns of the county."—Mass. Statute, 1836. In 1838, a law was passed in Massachusetts for the election of county commissioners.—Statutes Mass. 1836, p. 161. Their duties are as follows: to erect county buildings; to have charge of the highways; to grant licenses: lay estimate of expenses before the county court, of the sums necessary for county charges; to examine, allow and settle all the accounts of receipts and expenditures of the money of the county, apportion county taxes according to the last State valuation. According to the laws of Connecticut, (Laws 1866), it may be well said that there is no body representing the county. With a few exceptions, county officers are the mere agents of the legislature. In Connecticut the general assembly appoints three county commissioners. . for a term of three years, who shall "*take care* of all the real estate, real and personal property belonging to the county," † "may sell and purchase real estate in behalf of the county," † "all conveyances of real estate in the name of the county treasurer. The county commissioners shall appoint the county treasurer and county surveyors for their respective counties."—Connecticut Statutes, 228, 1866. Powers of the county commissioners limited, as they represent the legislature more than the county. When a tax is necessary for county purposes, the county commissioners call together the representatives, for the time being, of the county of course, chosen to the general assembly. Said meeting shall impose a tax upon the towns in each county, to be collected the same as town taxes and paid to the county treasurer. Suits for or against the county are in the name of the county treasurer.—*Ibid.* 98. By amendments 1838, sheriffs are elected by the people. By the laws of 1850, judges of probate and justices of the peace are elected by the people. New York, Pennsylvania, Ohio and the Western States have a better system of county government, than New England. The several states have changed their system of county government from time to time. In some States, the chairman of the town supervisors for each town represents the county, as the board of county supervisors; in other States, each county is divided into commissioner districts, and each district elects one county commissioner to represent the county. The powers and duties of county supervisors and county commissioners are defined and limited by the laws of the several States. County officers are the creatures of the statutes.—20, Wisconsin, Rep. State *v.* Douglas, p. 428.—Crowell *v.* Lambert 9, Minn. Rep. p. 283, Sanborne *v.* Commissioners of Rice Co., 9 Minn. Rep. 273; 4 Wis. Rep. 167. In New York, Wisconsin, Minnesota and several of the Western states, county officers are elected by the people. In Minnesota and other western states, the county board represents the county. It has power to erect county buildings, to lay out county roads, alter and lay out county roads, to hear appeals from town supervisors on roads; to equalize the taxes of the county; to audit and allow county charges; to select grand and petit jurors; to have care of the county property; to examine the accounts and vouchers of the auditor and treasurer and the funds in the county treasury. The county commissioners "shall have and use the auditor's seal; and papers signed by the chairman and attested by the auditor, with the auditor's seal affixed, shall be evidence of such proceedings in any of the courts of this State."—Minn. Statutes, 1866, p. 117, sec. 96. 97. The county auditor, judge of probate and register of deeds in each county, fill by appointment vacancies in the board of county commissioners. —Statutes of Minn. 1866, p. 116, sec. 95. County commissioners shall tender their resignation to the register of deeds, auditor and judge of probate. The county commissioners fill vacancies in the office of register of deeds. Auditor, Treasurer, Sheriff, County Attorney, County Surveyor. Said officers resign to the county commissioners; vacancies in the offices of the court commissioner and clerk of the court are filled by the judge of the district court. Clerks of the district court and court commissioners should tender their resignation to the judge of the district court. Vacancy in the office of the judge of probate is filled by the governor. The judge of probate should resign to the governor.—See Constitution of Minn. art. 5, sec. 4.

Statutes of Minn. 1866, on resignations, etc. p. 137, sec. 1. Opinions of the Attorneys General of the United States, vol. 1, page 157, and constitution of Minnesota, section 10, art. 6, and 9 Minn. Rep. 283. The Governor may remove from office for malfeasance or nonfeasance of official duty, the clerk of the district court, judge of probate, court commissioner, sheriff, coroner, register of deeds, county attorney, county commissioner, any collector or receiver of public moneys appointed by the legislature, and the Governor.—Minn. Statutes, 1866, pp. 137-8. The laws of the several states in respect to county officers are not the same in all the states —and as there are 38 states and 38 independent legislatures, the powers and duties of county officers and the nature of county governments must, in the nature of things, fluctuate with the wants and wishes of the people— the source of all political power, town, county, state and federal. We have given the general principles which govern the town, parish, school and county organizations, in the United States. Said organizations have capacity to sue and be sued.—The State of Minnesota has a legal capacity to sue.— State v. Grant, 10 Minn. 39. The official acts of the town, school and county officers may be investigated by the Grand Jury of the proper county under the instructions of the presiding judge; for the judicial power of the nation extends to every person and everything in its territory, excepting only such foreigners as enjoy the right of extra territoriality, and who, consequently, are not looked upon as temporary subjects of the State.—Opinions of the Attorneys General United States, vol. 1, p. 5.

CHAPTER IV.—STATE GOVERNMENT.

We have said that the town is the parent of the State. We may further say that the thirteen colonies had different forms of government, which can be seen from the constitutions and charters of the colonies at the time when they adopted the articles of confederation in 1777. On the 4th of July, 1776, the thirteen colonies of North America became independent and sovereign nations or powers, and their legislatures could pass such laws and make such regulations as the welfare of the people demanded, limited by their state constitutions and charters. July 1776, the New England States and the State of New York had no constitutions—nothing more than charters from the crown. The thirteen States adopted their first constitutions, as follows: New Hampshire, 1784; Massachusetts, 1780; Rhode Island, 1842; Connecticut, 1818; New York, 1777; New Jersey, 1776; Pennsylvania, 1776; Delaware, 1776; Maryland, (the first form of government was partly by the proprietors and partly by the people) the first popular constitution was adopted in 1776; Virginia, in 1776; North Carolina, 1776; South Carolina, 1776; Georgia, 1777; Rhode Island and Connecticut acted under their colonial charters after the adoption of the constitution of the United States. The States were not subject to any higher political power, each state being sovereign.—1 Kent Comm. vol. 1, p. 208; Vattel's Law of Nations, book 1, chapter 3, pp. 8, 9, 10, 11. Book 1, chap. 1, pp. 2-8, chap. 4, pp. 12 and 13. 4 Ohio Rep. pp. 294-308. From the above, it will appear that the thirteen colonies or states, though their forms of government differed in some respects, were democratic, for they claimed that the people were the source of all political power. The principle that all political power is inherent in the people was adopted by the several state constitutions. We have said that the forms of government were different in the several colonies at the adoption of the Declaration of Independence; the same can be said of the present state governments. The present state governments are more liberal than they were before the adoption of the constitution of the United States. For before the adoption of the constitution of the United States, all of the States, except Pennsylvania, required a property qualification for the executive office, as well as for members of both houses of the legislature. Under the colonial governments of New Jersey, Maryland, Delaware, and Pennsylvania, the governor was elected by the state legislature. The judiciary of the several States were appointed either by the legislature, the governor and council, or by the governor by and with the consent of the senate and in some States by the governor and assembly and in Virginia, North Carolina, and Georgia by the legislature on joint ballot. Some of the old States still clung to the old system of appointing the judiciary, but New York, Ohio, and Pennsylvania and most of the Western States elect their judges. We have in another place said that New England had established church and state and that religion was supported by the taxes of the people, and that in some States education was compulsory.— De Tocqueville, p. 23. In 1693, the Episcopal religion was established by law in the province of New York.—Constitutions of the States, p. 142. Virginia established the Church of England, and the parsons collected tithes, the same in South Carolina.—Constitutions of States, 266. Naturalization laws were passed by the several states before the adoption of the Constitution of the United States. In Pennsylvania, the act of the British Parliament passed in the 13th year of the reign of George II, Chapter VII, furnished the rule for the naturalization of "all persons being Protestants, etc., who resided for the space of seven years or more within the province by taking the abjuration oath shall be deemed, adjudged, and taken to be the king's natural-born subjects of this province, to all intents." (See Dallas, ed. Penn. Laws, vol. 1. This law excluded the Catholics from the privileges of naturalized citizens or subjects. In New York it was provided that naturalized citizens should take the following oath, to wit: "To abjure and renounce all allegiance and subjugation to all and every foreign king, prince, potentate, and state in all matters, ecclesiastical as well as civil." This, says Chancellor Kent, in his Commentaries, vol. 2, p. 73, was intended to exclude Roman Catholics from the benefits of naturalization, who acknowledged the spiritual supremacy of the pope.—Kent's Com. vol. 2, p. 73. The State of Maryland passed the following act on the subject of naturalization, in July, 1779. "Be it enacted by the general assembly of Maryland, that *every person* who shall hereafter come into this State from any nation, kingdom, or state, and shall repeat and subscribe a declaration of his belief in the Christian religion, and take, repeat, and subscribe the following oath, to wit: 'I do swear that I will hereafter become a subject of the State of Maryland, and will be faithful, and bear true allegiance to said State, and that I do not hold myself bound to yield allegiance or obedience to any king or prince or any state or government,' shall thereafter be adjudged, deemed, and taken to be a natural-*born* subject of this state." By act of the assembly of Georgia, Feb. 7, 1785, an alien "who hath resided at least twelve months in the same, and after the expiration thereof, doth obtain from the Grand Jury of the county where he resided, a certificate, purporting that he hath demeaned himself as an honest man, and a friend of the government of the State," may become a citizen of the State by taking the oath of allegiance provided that no such person (alien-born,) thus made a citizen, shall be a member of the general assembly, or of the executive council, or shall hold any *office of trust or profit*, or vote for

members of the general assembly, for the term of seven years, and until the
legislature shall, by special act for that purpose, enable such person so to do.
And provided also, that all such aliens, or persons aforesaid, shall be subject and liable to pay such alien duties as have been heretofore, or may
hereafter be imposed by the legislature.—See Watkin's Digest Laws of
Georgia, pp. 312–3. It was provided in North Carolina "that every foreigner
who comes to settle in this State, having first taken an oath of allegiance
to the same, may purchase, or, by other just means, acquire, hold, and
transfer land, or other real estate; and after one year's residence, shall be
deemed a free citizen." In Massachusetts, an act was passed, in 1777,
that persons born abroad and coming into the State after 1776, and before
1783, and remaining there voluntarily, were deemed citizens of the
state.—2 Pick. Rep. 394. The supreme court of Connecticut adopted
the same rule without the aid of the legislature. It was held, that a
British soldier, who came over with the British army in 1775 and deserted,
and came and settled in Connecticut, in 1778, and remained there afterwards, became a citizen of the United States.—5, Day's Rep. p. 169. Held
by the Attorney General of the United States, Wm. Wirt, in 1821, that
all free white persons born and residing in the United States are citizens of
the United States.—Opinions of the Attorneys General of the United States
vol. 1, pp. 382, 383, 384.—2 Kent's Comm. p. 1. We insert a few extracts
from the decisions of the courts of Massachusetts on the subject. "An
alien is one born without the allegiance of the commonwealth.—Anslie v.
Martin. 9 Mass. R. p. 459. "A person, born within the territory, of which
the commonwealth of Massachusetts is now sovereign, although he were
born before the Declaration of Independence, cannot be considered an alien
unless he have been expatriated by virtue of some statute judgment at law;
for by his birth he owes allegiance to the commonwealth, as the successor
of the former sovereign, who had abdicated his throne."—Martin v. Woods,
9 Mass. Rep. 377. "A native of Massachusetts, leaving his county after the
commencement of hostilities with Great Britain in 1775, and voluntarily
remaining with the British until after the close of the war, thereby became
an alien."—Palmer v. Downer, 2 Mass. Rep. 179. A person leaving this
country after the commencement of the revolutionary war and going to the
British territories, and residing therein for several years, and afterwards
returning to the United States, before the treaty of peace, without having been
legally disfranchised by judgment of court, retains his right as a citizen of
the United States." Kilham v. Ward & al. II. Mass. R. 236. Gardner v.
Ward & al. II. Mass. R. 244. "The act of April 30, 1779, for confiscating the estates of absentees, does not take away the rights of citizenship
from a person, who has not been prosecuted and convicted under it."—Ibid.
"A person, who resides under the allegiance and protection of a hostile
state, for commercial purposes, is to be considered, to all civil purposes, as
much an alien enemy, as if he were born there."—Hutchinson v. Brock, 9
Mass. R. 119. "Where a person, who was born in the colony of Connecticut, before the commencement of the revolutionary war, removed to the
British dominions, where he remained until after the treaty of peace, he was
considered an alien."—The Inh. Manchester v. Inh. Boston. 16 Mass. 230. "The
statutes of the United States—7 Congr. 1 sess. c. 23, sec. 4. provides that the
children of all such persons, as now are, or have been citizens of the United
States, shall be citizens, whether born within the United States or not."
This provision does not extend to children born of parents, who had quit this
country before the Declaration of Independence; as the term, citizens of the
United States, must be understood to intend those who were citizens of a state,
as much, after the Union had commenced, and the several states had assumed

theirsovereignties."—Inh. Manchester v. Inh. Boston, 16 Mass. R. 230. "An alien can purchase real estate, and can hold against all, except the commonwealth, and can be divested only by office found, and until office found, can convey."—Sheaffe v. O'Neil, 1 Mass. R. 256. Storer v. Boston, 8 Mass. R. 431. Fox v. Southack & al. 12 Mass. R. 143. "An alien, other than a British subject, is not capable of holding and conveying lands.—Commonwealth v. Sheaffe, 6 Mass. R. 441. Opinion of the Justices of the Supreme Judicial District, 7 Mass. 523. "But by the ninth article of the treaty of 1794, which seems to be a stipulation, which cannot be dissolved by any subsequent event, British subjects, who then held lands within the United States, might continue to hold them, according to the nature and tenure of their estates and titles therein; and might grant, sell or devise the same to whom they would, in like manner as if they were natives."—Ainslie v. Martin, 9 Mass. 454, Fox v. Southack & al. 12 Mass. 143. "An alien is liable to taxation; but, by the payment of taxes, he acquires no political right whatever."—Opinion of the Justices of the Sup. Jud. Court, 7 Mass. R. 523. "Thus, if a person, born an alien, be naturalized, he will be placed upon the same ground, as if born a citizen."—Ibid. "So, if a person, born within the allegiance of the King of England, and without the allegiance of the Commonwealth, were an inhabitant of the Commonwealth, at the ratification of the treaty of peace between Great Britain, in 1783, he will be entitled to the privileges of citizenship."—Ibid. "So, if a person be a citizen of some other of the United States, he will be entitled, by the Federal constitution, to the privileges of citizens within the state."—Ibid. "Natural born citizens may inherit and make their titles by descent, from any of their alien ancestors, lineal or collateral."—Palmer v. Downer, 2 Mass. 179. "If an alien be found within this state, he will be liable to be sued in the courts of the state, upon his personal contracts, wherever they may have been made."—Barrett v. Benjamin, 15 Mass. Rep. 354. "The citizens of any of the United States have the same rights and privileges in the courts of this state, which belong to its own citizens.—Ibid. We here give extracts from the rulings of the supreme court of the United States as to who are and who are not aliens.—"One born in England before the year 1775, and who always resided there, and never was in the United States, is an alien, and could not, in 1795, take lands in Maryland by descent from a citizen of the United States."—Dawson's Lessee v. Godfrey, 4 Cranch, 321. 7 Wheaton, 535. Fairfax's Devisee v. Hunter's Lessee, 7 Cranch, 603. "The allegiance which was formerly due from the people of this country to the sovereign of Great Britain, was transferred by the American revolution to the government of their own country. On the 4th of October, 1776, the state of New Jersey being an organized and independent government, had a right to compel the inhabitants of the state to become citizens thereof; and the legislature asserted this right by an act passed on the 4th of June, 1777. A person, therefore, born in New Jersey before the year 1775, and residing there until the year 1777, and then joining the British army, and ever afterwards claiming to be a British subject, may take lands by descent in New Jersey State, that having a right to his allegiance, and the power to compel his services as a citizen."—McIlvaine v. Coxe's Lessee, 4 Cranch, 209. "The treaty of peace of 1783, between the United States and Great Britain did not so operate upon the condition of a person in the above predicament as to make him become an alien to the State of New Jersey, in consequence of his election then made to become a subject of the king, and his subsequent conduct confirming the election; the laws of the state which had made him a citizen being still in full force, and not repealed, or in any manner affected by the treaty."—Ibid. "The concessions in the treaty of peace of 1783, on the part of his Britannic Majesty, amounted to a formal re-nunciation of all claim to the allegiance of the citizens of the United States; but the question, who were at that period citizens, was necessarily left to de-pend upon the laws, of the respective states, who, in their sovereign capacities, had acted authoritatively upon the subject.   It left all such persons in the situation it found them, neither making those citizens who had by the laws of any state been declared aliens, nor releasing from their allegiance any who had become and were claimed as citizens."—*Ibid.*   Persons who, having been born in this country, left it before the Declaration of Inde-pendence and never returned, are aliens, and incapable of taking land by descent.—Inglis *v.* the Trustees of Sailors' Snug Harbor, 3 Peters 99.   "The English and American courts have, however, established different rules as to the time at which American antenati ceased to be British subjects.   The American rule is to take the date of the Declaration of Independence; the English rule is to take the date of the treaty of peace, *prima facie,* and as a general rule, the character in which American ante nati will be con-sidered by our courts, must depend upon the situation of the party, and the election made by him, at the date of the Declaration of Independence. But this general rule must be controlled by special circumstances attending particular cases.   To say that the election must always have been made before, or immediately at the Declaration of Independence, would render the right nugatory."—*Ibid.*   "A person born in the city of New York before the 4th of July, 1776, and remaining there an infant under the custody of his father, during the period of its occupation by the British troops, and who, after the treaty of peace, was carried by his father, an American loy-alist, to England, and never returned to the United States, must be consid-ered as an alien, and incapable of inheriting land in the State of New York." —Inglis *v.* The Trustees of Sailors' Snug Harbor, 3 Peters 99.   "If such per-son had been born after the 4th of July, 1776, and before the 15th of September, when the British troops took possession of the city and adjacent places, his infancy would have incapacitated him from making any election for himself, and his election and character would follow that of his father, subject to the right of disaffirmance in a reasonable time after the termination of his minority."—*Ibid.*   "A. S. was born in South Carolina before the Declaration of Independence: her father at the time, and remaining until his death, in 1782, a citizen of that state, she married J. S., an officer of the British army at that time in possession of Charleston.   Upon the evacuation of this city in 1782, she went with her husband to England, and there remained until her death in 1806.   Her age and death of her father did not appear. Held, that she was capable of taking land by descent from her father in 1782, the time of his death.   If she was under age, she might be deemed under the circumstances of the case, to hold the citizenship of her father; for children born in a country, and continuing while under age in the family of the father partake of his national character.   If she was of age, then her birth and residence might be deemed to constitute her by election a citizen of South Carolina.   The possession of Charleston by the British was not of a character to change the allegiance of its inhabitants; nor could the marri-age of A. S. with an alien produce that effect; marriage changes the civil rights, but does not effect the political character of a feme."—Shanks et als. *v.* Dupont et als. 3 Peters 242.   "The removal of A. S. to England with her husband, after the death of her father, operated as a virtual dis-solution of her allegiance to South Carolina, and fixed her future allegiance to the British Crown by the treaty of peace of 1783.   Being a British sub-ject, at the time of the peace of 1783—at least, within the view of the British Government—she was embraced by the provisions of that treaty, protecting British subjects holding lands in America from the disability of alienage in respect to descents and sales."—3 Peters 242. "It is common learning that an alien has no inheritable blood, and can neither take land himself by descent, nor transmit it by descent to others."—Lessee of Levy et als. v. McCartee, 6 Peters 102.—"At common law an alien cannot acquire by purchase and convey to a vendee a good title to real estate."—Purczell v. Smith 21 Iowa R. 540. The following rule of law has been held by the courts of New York: "*An alien widow of a natural-born citizen cannot be endowed* by reason of her alienism."—Mick v. Mick, 10 Wend R. 379. "Naturalization merely removes the disability of the alien to hold lands, leaving a right in the government to enter if he die without heirs, or leaving alien heirs only." —Sultiff v. Forgey, 1. Cowen 89. "A subject of Great Britain, who emigrated to this country after the Declaration of Independence, is an alien."—Jackson, ex dem. Folliard, v. Wright, 4 Johnson's Rep. 75. "Naturalization has a relation back and confirms the title of the purchaser of land during alienage."—Jackson, ex dem. Calverhouse, v. Beach, I. Johnson's Ch. Rep. 309. "A resident alien is entitled to the benefit of the insolvent laws of the commonwealth."—Judd v. Lawrence, 1. Cush. 531. The courts of Massachusetts and the supreme court of the United States have held that no " person in any way can discharge himself from his allegiance to his native country, unless the protection, which is due to him from the laws, be unjustly denied him." That "the allegiance, which a person owes to the sovereign or government of the country of his birth, cannot be discharged by naturalization in a foreign country; but his duties, arising from his allegiance to his native country, remain unchanged and unimpaired by such naturalization."—Ainslie v. Martin, 9 Mass. R. 454. "The sovereign cannot refuse his protection to any subject, nor discharge him from his allegiance against his consent; but he will remain a subject, unless disfranchised as a punishment for crime."—*Ibid.* Held by the supreme court of the United States that the State of New Jersey before the adoption of the constitution of the United States, had a right to compel the services of a person born in that state; that such person could not renounce his allegiance to the said State of New Jersey.—McIlvaine v. Cox's Lessee, 4 Cranch, 209. The courts of Massachusetts and the supreme court of the United States have held the doctrine of the courts of Great Britain, that a natural-born subject or citizen cannot throw off his allegiance without the consent of the government. The following is the ruling of the supreme court of the United States on the subject. "Allegiance may be dissolved by the mutual consent of the government and its citizens or subjects. This doctrine was recognized in England, in the case of Doe v. Acklman, 2 Barns, Cress. 779; Inglis v. The Trustees of Sailors' Snug Harbor, 3 Peters 99. "The general doctrine is, that no person by any act of his own, without the consent of the government, can put off his allegiance, and become an alien."—Shanks v. Dupont, 3 Peters, 242; 2 Kent, 48. "The right of expatriation was not acknowledged at common law. British subjects, unless specially prohibited by statute, were permitted to seek their fortunes in any country, but always subject to their natural allegiance. Although it has not been regarded as a crime to swear allegiance to a foreign state, yet the British government stands uncommitted as to the embarrassment in which a state of war between the governments of his natural and of his divided allegiance might plunge an individual."—3 Peters, 242.— "There is no natural and inalienable right of expatriation."—*Ibid.*—CI. *American Citizens Abroad*—Declares the right of expatriation; that all naturalized citizens while in foreign states shall receive from this Government the same protection of persons and property that is accorded to native-born citizens in like situations and circumstances; and that when any citizen of the United States has been unjustly deprived of his liberty by any foreign government, it shall be the duty of the President to demand of that government the reasons for such imprisonment, and if it appears to be wrongful and in violation of the rights of American citizenship, the President shall demand the release of such citizen, and if the release is unreasonably delayed or refused, it shall be the duty of the President to use such means, not amounting to acts of war, as he may think necessary to obtain such release. [July 27, 1868.] Held by the attorney general of the United States, that, "white men owing allegiance to the United States, cannot divest themselves of that allegiance by a residence among the Choctaws, nor even by becoming, by adoption, members of the Choctaw nation."—Opinions of the Attorneys Gen. of the United States, vol. 2, p. 985. "By the treaty between the United States and Great Britain of 1794, (art. 9) it is agreed, that British subjects, who then held lands in the territories of the United States, and American citizens who then held lands in the dominion of his Majesty, should continue to hold them according to the nature and tenure of their respective estates and titles therein; and might grant, sell, or devise the same to whom they pleased, in like manner as if they were natives; and that neither they nor their heirs or assigns should, so far as respects the said lands and the legal remedies incident thereto, be considered as aliens."—Jackson v. Clarke, 3 Wheaton 1. The courts of the United States and some of the state courts have ruled as follows as to the common law of England. The old colony at Plymouth, as before mentioned, abolished the common law and statute laws of England, yet Massachusetts and the other New England States have retained the common law by judicial sanction. The following is the doctrine held by Massachusetts on the subject. "Generally, when an English statute has been made in amendment of the common law, it is to be considered as part of our common law."—Com. v. Leach, 1 Mass. 61. Com. v. Knowlton, 2 Mass. 535. "Thus, the statute of Anne, respecting negotiable notes, has been adopted here as part of our common law."—Ibid. "And it is said that the statute of Edward III, respecting the jurisdiction and powers of justices of the peace, have been adopted and practised upon here and are to be considered as a part of our common law.—Ibid. "So, it was said that the statute of 21 Jac. 1, sec. 12, giving double costs to an officer, who sued out of his county, for anything done by him in the execution of his office, being made in amendment of the common law, has been adopted here as part of our common law.—Ibid. The following is the ruling of the supreme court of the United States on the subject: "The common law of England is not to be taken in all respects to be that of America. Our ancestors brought with them its general principles, and claimed it as their birthright; but they brought with them and adopted only that portion which was applicable to their situation."—Van Ness v. Pacard, 2 Peters 137, & Peters Rep. 591. The Town of Pawlett v. Clarke, 9 Cranch 292. "The statutes passed in England before the emigration of our ancestors, which were in amendment of the law, and applicable to our situation, constitute a part of our common law."—Patterson v. Winn. 5 Peters. "There can be no common law of the United States, unless by legislative adoption. The federal government is composed of twenty-four (now 88) sovereign and independent states, each of which may have its local usages, customs, and common law. When, therefore, a common law right is asserted, we must look to the state in which the controversy originated."—Wheaton v. Peters, 8 Peters 591. Rendall v. United States, 12 Peters 524. "The courts of the United States have no jurisdiction, derived from the common law, to define and punish criminal offences.—The United States *v.* Hudson, 7 Cranch 82; United States *v.* Coolidge, 1 Wheaton 416; United States *v.* Bevans 8 Wheaton 336. "The construction which British statutes had received in England at the time of their adoption in this country, indeed, to the time of separation of this country from the British empire may very properly be considered as accompanying the statutes themselves, and forming an integral part of them. But however subsequent decisions may be respected, and certainly they are entitled to great respect, their absolute authority is not admitted. If the English courts vary their construction of a statute which is common to both countries, we do not hold ourselves bound to fluctuate with them.—*Ibid.* We insert the following authority from the father of the constitution of the United States, Mr. Madison, on this subject: "But neither the common, nor the statute law of that, (England) or of any other nation, ought to be a standard for the proceedings of this, unless previously made its own by legislative adoption."—The Federalist, No. 42, p. 228. Several of the states of the Union have retained the English common law practice, in their courts; but New York and some other states have departed from the common law pleadings, and they have adopted, "*the New York Code practice.*" The following states have adopted the common law by constitutional provisions: New York, New Jersey, Delaware, Maryland, Michigan and some other states, have adopted the "common law of England; and all the statutes of Parliament made in aid thereof, prior to the fourth year of the reign of James I, which are of a general nature and not local to the kingdom, were adopted in Virginia by the statute of 1776." Held by the supreme court of Minnesota, on an indictment for conspiracy, "that conspiracy, though not declared a crime by our statute law, is punishable in this state.' Our statutes as to crimes were intended as a modification and not as an entire repeal or abrogation of the common law."—(Berry J., dissenting) State of Minn. *v.* Pulle et al., 12 Minn. R. p. 164. "The common law, by which every man is bound to keep his cattle upon his own land, is in force in Minnesota."—Locke *v.* first division St. Paul & P. R. R. Co. 15 Minn. R. p. 350. It has been decided by the supreme court of the United States, that the decision of the state courts makes a part of the statute law."— Shelly *v.* Grey, 11 Wheaton 361.—"Where a usage is sanctioned by judicial decisions, it becomes the law of the place."—Cookendorfer *v.* Preston, 4 Howard 317. Although the constitutions of the states, before the Federal constitution was adopted, were republican in form, yet they were very dissimilar. The legislatures may be deemed the mouthpieces of the people —they spoke the sovereign will—in colonial times they exercised extraordinary powers, for the executive was elected by the legislature in New Hampshire, New Jersey, Pennsylvania, Delaware, Maryland, Virginia, North Carolina, South Carolina, and Georgia.—Federalist. No. 47, p. 265, 266, 267. If I am not mistaken, and I think I am not, South Carolina and Georgia are the only states in the Union where the legislature elects the executive. The executives are elected by the people in every other state in the Union. The New England States have adopted the principle, that, "where annual elections end, tyranny begins,"—Federalist No. 53, p. 289, by annually electing the executive and legislature. In New York, the governor is elected by the people for 2 years; he shall be a native-born citizen of the United States, 30 years of age, and a resident of the state 5 years. In New Jersey, the executive is elected for three years, he shall be 30 years of age. In Pennsylvania, the executive is elected for 3 years, he shall be 30 years of age. In Maryland, the governor is elected, age 30 years, a citizen of the United States five years, and an inhabitant of the state 5 years. North

Carolina, governor elected for 2 years. South Carolina governor's term of office 2 years, age 30, an inhabitant of the state ten years. Florida, governor elected for 4 years, age 30 years, a citizen of the United States ten years, and an inhabitant of the state 5 years. Alabama. governor elected for 2 years, age 30 years, a native citizen of the United States, and an inhabitant of the state 4 years. Mississippi, governor elected for two years, a citizen of the United States 20 years, and an inhabitant 5 years. Louisiana, governor elected for 4 years, a citizen of the United States 15 years, an inhabitant of the state 15 years. Tennessee, governor elected for 2 years, age 30 years, a citizen of the United States, residence 7 years. Kentucky, governor elected for 4 years, age 35 years, a citizen of the United States, residence 6 years. Ohio, governor elected for 2 years. Indiana, governor elected for 4 years. Illinois, governor elected for 4 years, a citizen of the United States, age 35 years, a citizen of the United States 14 years, a resident 10 years.—Constitutions 1818. In Missouri, (Constitution 1821) the governor elected for 4 years. In Arkansas, the governor is elected for 4 years (Constitution, 1836), he shall be "a native-born of Arkansas, or a native-born citizen of the United States, or a resident of Arkansas ten years previous to the adoption of the constitution," if not a native of the United States." In Texas, the governor is elected for 2 years (Constitution 1845), he shall be "a citizen of the United States, or a citizen of the State of Texas, at the time of the adoption of this constitution." In Iowa the governor is elected for 4 years (Constitution, 1845), he shall be a citizen of the United States, and a resident of the state 2 years. In Wisconsin, the governor is elected for 2 years, he shall be a citizen of the United States. In California, the governor is elected for 2 years, he shall be a citizen of the United States and a resident of the state 2 years. In Minnesota the governor is elected for 2 years, he shall be a citizen of the United States, and a resident of the state one year. The following is the constitutional provision of qualification of members of Minnesota legislature: "Senators and representatives shall be qualified voters of the state, and shall have resided one year in the state, and six months immediately preceding the election in the district from which they are elected." Connecticut has the following in its constitution: "Every person shall be able to read any article of the constitution, or any section of the statutes of this state, before being admitted an elector." Massachusetts has a similar provision in its constitution. Conn. amendment (1855.) In some states the legislature meets annually, and in others biennially. In New Jersey, senators shall be thirty years of age, a citizen of the United States four years, and a resident of the state four years; in Pennsylvania, (Constitution 1838), a senator shall be twenty-five years of age, a citizen of the United States four years, and a resident of the state four years; in Florida, a senator shall be a citizen of the United States two years, and resident of the state two years; in Alabama a senator shall be a white citizen of the United States three years, and a resident of the state two years. In Mississippi, a senator shall be a citizen of the United States four years; in Louisiana, a senator shall be a citizen of the United States ten years, and a resident of the state four years; in Tennessee, senators shall be three years, and a citizen of the United States. The legislative power, in each state, is vested in two houses. The legislature in the states of Massachusetts and New Hampshire is styled the General Court; in Vermont and Rhode Island, the General Assembly; and in Maine, the Legislature; in New York, the Senate and Assembly; New Jersey, Pennsylvania, Delaware, Virginia, North Carolina, South Carolina, Georgia, Florida, Alabama, the General Assembly; Mississippi, the Legislature; in

Michigan, Senate and House of Representatives; in Wisconsin, Senate and Assembly; in California, Senate and Assembly; and in Minnesota, Senate and House of Representatives. In some states the Legislature is styled the Senate and House of Representatives; in others, the Senate and Assembly; in others, the Senate and House of Delegates; and in North Carolina the Senate and House of Commons. The judicial department is elected in Vermont, New York, Maryland, Virginia, Florida, Alabama, Mississippi, Louisiana, Kentucky, Ohio, Indiana, Illinois, Michigan, Wisconsin and Minnesota; and appointed either by the governor, by and with the advice and consent of the Senate or by the legislature in the following states; Maine, New Hampshire, Massachusetts, Rhode Island, Connecticut, New Jersey, Pennsylvania, Delaware, North Carolina, South Carolina, Tennessee, Missouri, Arkansas, and Texas.—Constitutions in 1848. Several states of the Union have provided in their constitutions the following declaration of rights: that all power is inherent in the people; that all men are born free and equal; that the freedom of speech and of the press shall not be abridged; the right of trial by jury; the right to bear arms; the right to assemble and to petition for grievances; that the military shall be subordinate to the civil power; that private property shall not be taken for public use without just compensation; that no tax shall be imposed without the consent of the people, that no soldier, in time of peace, shall be quartered in any house without the consent of the owner, or occupant; that no person shall be subject to martial law, except such as are employed in the army or navy, or in the militia when in actual service, in time of war, or public danger; that the privilege of the writ of *Habeas Corpus* shall not be suspended, unless when in cases of rebellion or invasion the public safety may require it; that the people shall be secure in their persons, houses, and papers against unreasonable searches and seizures; that the legislature shall pass no bill of attainder, *ex post facto* law; that feudal tenures shall be abolished; that no person shall be disfranchised "unless by the law of the land, or the judgment of his peers;" free exercise of religion to all mankind, that all elections shall be free and equal; that no standing army shall be kept up in time of peace. In Pennsylvania and some other states it is provided (Constitution, 1838) that emigration from the state shall not be prohibited. It is provided in Vermont and other states, "that no person shall be liable to be transported out of this state for trial of any offence committed within the same." In Delaware and other states, it is provided that "no power of suspending the laws shall be exercised, but by the authority of the legislature." In Maryland, it is provided that "sanguinary laws ought to be avoided as far as is consistent with the safety of the state;" that a well regulated militia is the proper defence of a free government; that monopolies are odious and contrary to the spirit of a free government. It is provided, in the constitution of Michigan, "that the credit of the state shall not be granted to, or in aid of any person or association.—Constitution, 1836. In Florida, it is provided, that perpetuities and monopolies are contrary to the genius of a free state, and ought not to be allowed." In Alabama— "No human authority ought, in any case whatever, to control or interfere with the rights of conscience." Massachusetts, Virginia and other states have held in their constitutions that the rulers are the servants of the people, that "the idea of a man born a magistrate, lawgiver, or judge, is absurd and unnatural." In Virginia it is held "that all power is vested in, and consequently derived from the people; that magistrates are their *trustees* and *servants*, and at all times amenable to them." The following states have recognized the right of rebellion in their constitutions: New Hampshire, Massachusetts, Pennsylvania, Florida, Alabama, Mississippi, Kentucky,

Arkansas and Texas. New Hampshire has held, " that the doctrine of non-resistance against arbitrary power and oppression, is absurd, slavish, and destructive of the good and happiness of mankind."—*Ibid.* For the right of revolution, see the Federalist, No. 32, p. 168. Kent's Comm. vol. 1, pp. 22, 23, 24, 25, and pp. 208, 209; Vattel's Law of Nations, Book 1, chap. 4, p. 18; and 1 Blackstone, marginal page 245, top page 184 The States of New Hampshire, Vermont, Massachusetts and North Carolina have retained in their constitutions a religious test. We copy the following from the constitution of North Carolina.—Constitution 1776. "No person who shall deny the being of God, or the truth of the Protestant religion, or the divine authority of either the Old or New Testaments, or who shall hold religious principles incompatible with the freedom and safety of the state, shall be capable of holding any office, or place of trust or profit, in the civil department within this state."—*Ibid.* The following provision is in the constitution of North Carolina (Con. 1776): "No clergyman, or preacher of the gospel of any denomination, shall be capable of being a member of either the senate or house of commons, or council of state, while he continues in the exercise of his pastoral function."—*Ibid.* The following is held in Massachusetts; the governor shall "declare himself to be of the Christian religion." The following states have held in their constitutions, that no religious test shall be required as a qualification to any office, or public trust, Delaware, Tennessee, Indiana Illinois.—Constitution 1818. Texas, Iowa, Wisconsin, New Jersey, Alabama, and Minnesota. In some states there is a property qualification for voting and holding office. In Mississippi there is a constitutional provision that "no property qualification for eligibility to office, or for the right of suffrage, shall ever be required by law in this state." This was so in 1848. In Iowa, Wisconsin, California, it is provided, that no distinction shall ever be made by law between resident aliens and citizens, in reference to the possession, enjoyment, or descent of property." The times when the terms of state, county and town officers shall commence are provided in the state and constitutional laws of the several states, as well as the manner of filling vacancies in said offices. So the officer to whom resignation of office shall be tendered depends on the constitutions and laws of the several States. In Minnesota, it is provided in the constitution, that the governor shall fill vacancies "in the office of secretary of state, treasurer, auditor, attorney general, and such other state and district offices as may be hereafter created by law, until next annual election, and until their successors are chosen and qualified."—Sec. 4, Art. 5, Con. Minn. "In case the office of any Judge shall become vacant before the expiration of the regular term for which he was elected, the vacancy shall be filled by appointment by the Governor until a successor is elected and qualified. And such successor shall be elected at the first annual election that occurs more than thirty days after the vacancy shall have happened."—Sec. 10, Art. 6, Con. Minn. 9 Minn. 283. Consequently the above officers shall tender their resignation to the Governor. The following provision is in the constitution of some states: "The Governor shall issue writs of election to fill such vacancies as may occur in either house of the legislature." For certain purposes, a state is a corporation.—Abbot's Digest, vol. 5, p. 76. When a State is sued process shall be served on the "Governor, or chief Executive magistrate, and the Attorney General of such state." Rules and orders of the Supreme Court of the United States, Aug. 12, 1796. From the foregoing commentaries it can be seen that the states can establish any form of government not anti-Republican in form, and not repugnant to the constitution of the United States, and laws of Congress made in pursuance of the constitution of the United States, and the treaties of the United States.—Gibbons *v.* Ogden, 9 Wheaton 1. Worcester *v.* The State of Georgia, 6 Peters 515. The municipal regulations of a state are not binding on the United States.—Palmer *v.* Allen, 7 Cranch 550. The state cannot tax the constitutional means employed by the general government to execute its constitutional powers.—McCulloch *v.* The State of Maryland, 4 Wheaton 316. A state cannot tax the property of the United States. —Opinions Atty. Gen. 1 vol. pp. 101–2; *Ib.* 469.—*Ib.* 486–7. It is provided by act of Congress, in virtue of the Constitution of the United States, that "all the members of the several state legislatures, and all executive and judicial officers of the several states," shall take an oath to support the constitution of the United States, etc.—Brightly's Dig. 700.

THE TERRITORIAL GOVERNMENT.

It has been the policy of the United States to organize new territories out of the vast public domain, by an act of Congress, called the organic act, providing a temporary government for such territory. A governor and secretary are appointed by the President of the United States, for 4 years unless sooner removed by the President of the United States. The legislative power is vested in the governor and "a Legislative Assembly." The assembly is composed of two houses, a Council and House of Representatives. Previous to the first election, the governor orders a census of the inhabitants of the territory. The territorial legislature can pass all acts extending to all rightful subjects of legislation, consistent with the constitution of the United States and the provisions of the organic act.—Minn. Statutes, p. 17. The legislature has power to organize counties and townships. All the laws passed by the legislative assembly and governor shall be submitted to the Congress of the United States, and if disapproved, shall be null and of no effect.—*Ibid.* 17. The judicial power or the territorial government is vested in a Supreme Court, District Courts, Probate Courts, and justices of the peace. The Supreme Court consists of a Chief Justice and two associate justices. The territory is divided into three Judicial Districts. One of the Judges of the Supreme Court shall hold a court in each district. An appeal lies from the district courts to the supreme court of the territory; and an appeal lies from the supreme court of the territory to the supreme court of the United States. An attorney and a marshal are appointed for four years for such territory. Congress provides the manner of taking oath of office by the territorial officers. The governor, secretary, chief justice, and associate justices, attorney and marshal, shall be nominated, and by and with the advice and consent of the Senate, appointed by the President of the United States. The President of the United States is the proper officer to whom the governor and secretary, judges, attorney and marshal shall tender their resignation.—Opinions of the Attorneys General of the United States, vol. 2, pp. 883–4-5-6-7, and vol. 1, pp. 475, 607. A delegate to Congress is elected by the qualified voters entitled to vote for members of the Legislative Assembly. It has been the policy of Congress to pass an act authorizing the inhabitants of a territory to form a state government. It is provided in said act for calling a state convention to form a constitution and state government to be submitted to the people for ratification. The marshal shall take the census of the inhabitants of the proposed state. Said state shall be entitled to one representative to Congress; and such additional representation as the state may be entitled to. Provisions are made in the constitution for the time and manner of electing state officers; the qualification of voters at the first election; and the manner of submitting the constitution to the people for adoption or rejection. It has been the policy of Congress to extend "all the laws of the United States which are not locally inapplicable" to the New States.—5, Statutes at Large, 788. The new constitution is then submitted to Congress when an act of Congress is passed admitting the new state into the "Union on equal footing with the original states.—Opinions of Attorneys General U. S. vol. 2, pp. 14, 19–20, vol. 1, pp. 101–2, and vol. 2, pp. 1006–7–8–9–10. "Foreign-born child. In the absence of any law of the United States governing the particular case, the question, whether one born out of the United States is a citizen, is to be determined by the common law, as it existed, irrespective of English statutes, at the adoption of the Federal constitution."—Court of Appeals, 1863, Ludlam v. Ludlam, 26 N. Y., 356. "If it be conceded that a citizen of the United States can renounce his allegiance without the consent of the government, he cannot do this until he becomes a citizen under some other government, and this he is not competent to do until he arrives at full age."—Ibid. "Therefore, where a citizen of the United States went to Peru at the age of eighteen years, with the intention of indefinite continuance there for the purpose of trading, but took no steps to be naturalized in Peru, or to indicate an intention of a permanent change of domicile, otherwise than as before stated, held that his child born to him in Peru of a wife the native of that country, was a citizen of the United States." Ibid.—Abbott's New York Dig. vol. 7, page 129. "The legislature of this state possesses the whole legislative power of the people, except so far as they are limited by the Constitution. In a judicial sense, and so far as the courts are concerned with its application and construction, their authority is absolute and unlimited, except by the express restrictions of the fundamental law."—Court of appeals, 1863. Bank of Chenango v. Brown, 26, N. Y. 467; Ibid. 529; Supreme court, 1864 Clarke v. Miller, 42 Barb. 255; Luke v. city of Brooklyn, 43 Ibid. 54. "A child of a naturalized alien. By the act of Congress of April 14 1802. minor children of any parent duly naturalized, and who, at the time of such naturalization of the parent, resided within the United States, are entitled to all the privileges of citizens, immediately on attaining majority. —8, Page 443, N. Y. Com. Pleas Special Term, 1861. Matter v. Morrison 22 Howard, Pr. 99.

REGULATION OF COMMERCE.—NAVIGATION.

The power to regulate pilotage is included in the power to regulate commerce conferred upon Congress by the Constitution of the United States.— 9 Wheaton 1, 10 Peters 108; 11 Ibid. 159, 7 Howard U. S. 283; 12 Ibid. 317. And laws and ordinances of a state which conflict with the regulations of an act of Congress, must yield to it.—11 Peters, 158, N. Y. Superior Ct. 1860, Cisco v. Roberts, 6 Bosworth, 494.—Abbotts, N. Y. Dig. vol. 6, p. 117. "Restrictions upon the states, retrospective laws, which do not impair the obligation of contracts, or affect vested rights, or partake of the character of ex post facto laws, are not prohibited by the Constitution."—3 Dall. 386, 36 Me., 9, Supreme Ct. 1862, Bay v. Gage, 36 Barb. 447.

STATES OF THE UNION DEEMED CORPORATIONS.

The individual states having submitted their interfering territorial claim to the judiciary of the United States, are, in respect to those rights, to be deemed to have ceded their sovereignty to the United States, and to be, so far considered as corporations; and the right of a state to grant lands so situate, must be judged by the same rules of common law as the rights of persons; so that a conveyance of the lands, if adversely held, is void.—Ct. of Errors, 1800, Woodworth v. James, 2 Johnson's cases, 417; Supreme Court, 1800, Whitaker v. Cone Ib. 58; Belding v. Pitkin, 2 Caine, 147. "Though the parties of one part to a contract are foreigners, and the contract is made without the state, if it is performed within this state they must be presumed to know the laws of the state, and are in *pari delicto*. There cannot be one rule for the foreigner and an other for the citizen." 5 Selden 53, 3 Comstock, 266, Ct. of Appeals 1858, Dewitt v. Brisbane 16 N. Y. (2 Smith) 508. "Removing from the country, O. and his family, natives of New York, joined the British forces in 1782, and never returned to reside in this country. Held, that having thus elected to continuous allegiance to the British crown, they must be regarded as aliens and not entitled to inherit." 20 Johnson 313, 8 Peters 99. Supreme court 1842, Orser v. Hoag, 3 Hill, 79. " *Citizenship by birth*. L. was born in the city of New York, in 1819, of alien parents, during their temporary sojourn in that city. She returned with them the same year, to their native country, and always resided there afterwards. Held, that she was a citizen of the United States." Lynch v. Clarke, 1 Sandford ch. 583, 638; S. C. 3 N. Y. Leg. obs. 236. "*Alien liable for crime*. That an alien, in whatever manner he may have entered our territory, is, if he commit a crime while here, amenable to our criminal law." Supreme Court 1841.—People v. McLeod, 25 Wend, 483, 573, S. C. 1 Hill, 377. "An alien cannot be admitted as a counsellor of this court, since he cannot take the oath of allegiance, etc.—Supreme Court, April, 1801, case of Mr. Caines, 3 Johnson's cases, 499. "The enlistment of an alien into the army of the United States is valid and binding on the alien enlisted." Supreme Ct. 1843, the United States v. Wyngall, 5 Hill .16. " *Renouncing naturalization*. A naturalized citizen who continues to reside here is liable to be sued in the state courts as a citizen. He cannot make himself an alien by merely taking an oath of allegiance to a foreign power, he must, at least, also change his residence. Supreme Court, 1801, Fish v. Stoughton, 2 Johnson's cases, 407. *Decisions of the Federal courts*. Upon questions arising upon the construction of the Federal constitution, the decisions of the courts of the United States are final and conclusive; and will be followed by the courts of this state, whatever may be their own views upon the question." Ct. Appeals, 1850, McCormick v. Prickering, 4 N. Y. (Comst.), 276. Supreme Court, 1819, Roosevelt v. Cebra, 17 John, 108, Ct. of Errors, 1838, Cochran v. Van Surlay, 20 Wend, 365; Supreme Court 1843, Kunzler v. Kohans, 5 Hill, 317, 3 Cowen, 713. "The Supreme Court is bound, when called upon in due form to do so, to pronounce invalid all acts of the legislature clearly conflicting with the fundamental law of the constitution." Supreme Court 1857, Clarke v. City of Rochester, 24 Borb, 446, S. C.—5 Abbott's Pr. 107, S. C. 14, How, Pr. 193. "It seems, that although the declaration of independence was made by congress on the 4th of July, 1776, and although the convention of delegates of this state adopted the declaration on the 9th, and although we had committees and temporary bodies of men, who took charge of the public safety we (the State of N. Y.) had no executive, legislative, or judicial authority, nor any organized government until the adoption of the Constitution on the 20th of April, 1777. Jackson v. White 20 Johnson 313.

CHAPTER V.—FEDERAL GOVERNMENT OF THE UNITED STATES
OF AMERICA.

It has been held by high authority that the states were sovereign before
the union. Kent. vol. 1, p. 208. Madison and others have held that they
are sovereign under the Constitution of the United States. Federalists,
No. 40, p. 212. Articles of confederation of Nov. 15, 1777. 1 Kent's
Comm. p. 210. Supreme Court United States, McIlvaine vs. Coxe, 4
Cranch, 209. Warren Manufacturing Company, vs. Ætna Insurance
Company, 12 Paine, 501. Buckner v. Finley 12 Peters, 590. Dodge v.
Woolsey, 18 How. 350. Bank of the United States, v. Daniels, 12 Peters.
83 Bank of Austa v. Earle, 13 Peters, 520. Dodge v. Woolsey, 18
How. 350-1. Ohio Life Insurance Company v, Debolt, 16 How. 428.
The thirteen colonies entered into a confederation styled the "confederacy
of the *United States* of America." Arts. Confederation. Art. 1. The
old Congress was composed of delegates annually appointed in such "a
manner as the legislature of each state shall direct." 5. Art. Confed.—Each
state maintained its own delegates.—Art. 5. Confed. Each State had the
right to recall its delegation.—Art. 5. Confed. Each state had but one
vote.—Art. 5. Confed. All disputes between the States were decided
by Congress.—Arts. Confed., 9. It was further provided that no
two or more states should enter into any treaty; that no state
should lay *imposts and duties* or keep vessels of war in time
of peace; that no state should engage in war without the consent
of Congress. Congress had power to regulate the "value of coin
struck by their own authority;" to regulate trade and manage Indian
affairs; to establish post offices; to borrow money. It was also provided
that alterations in the articles of confederation should be confirmed by the
"legislature of every state;" and that the "Union shall be perpetual,"—
Art. 13, confed. The following clause was inserted in the articles of confederation, to prevent the federal government from encroaching on the
rights of the states by the exercise of implied powers. "Art. 2, Each state
retains its own sovereignty, freedom, and independence, and every power,
jurisdiction and right, which is not by the confederation expressly delegated
to the United States in Congress assembled,"—Art. 2, confed. Before the
constitution of the United States went into operation (on the first Wednesday in March 4, 1789, Owings v. Speed, 5 Wheaton 420) all the departments
of government were blended in one mass—1 Kent's Comm. 214, nearly
similar to a state or county convention. The federal form of government remained in force until the 4th day of March, 1789, when the new constitution
went into operation.—Kent's Comm. vol. 1, p. 219, Owings v. Speed, 5
Wheaton, R. 240. The constitution of the United States has divided the
co-ordinate powers of the government into three departments, the
legislative, executive and judicial. Federalist No. 47, pp. 261-2-3-4-5-
6-7. These co-ordinate branches were intended as mutual checks and
balances. The president has a veto on the acts of Congress, but Congress
.can pass a bill by two-thirds of the votes cast over the president's veto.
Again, one house of Congress is a check on the deliberations of the other;
and the judiciary is the final tribunal to settle disputes between the
Congress and the executive; and to decide on the constitutionality of
the laws and treaties of the United States; and to decide on conflicts

between the state governments and the federal government, and controversies between two or more states. Constitution of U. S. Art. 3. sec. 2. The Federalist No. 49, p. 275, Fed. No. 51, p. 281. The United States can exercise no other powers or authority over the states or the inhabitants thereof but such powers as have been delegated to it by the constitution of the United States, expressly, or by necessary implication. Brisco *v.* the Bank of the commonwealth of Kentucky 11 Peters 257. United States *v.* Bailey. 1 McLean 234. Dodge *v.* Woolsey 18 How, 349. It would be as gross usurpation on the part of the Federal government to interfere with *state rights* by an exercise of powers not delegated as it would be for a state to interpose its authority against a law of the Union." Craig *v.* Missouri, 4 Peters, 468. Alabama *v.* Booth, 21 How, 506, Ex parte Milligan, 4 Wallace, 4. Twitchell *v.* The commonwealth, 7 Wallace, 321 (in year 1868) Texas *v.* White, 7, Wallace, 700. Hepburn *v.* Griswold 8 Wallace, 603. United States *v.* Hudson, 7 Cranch, 32. The Supreme Court of the United States has, from time to time, been appealed to for the settlement of boundaries between the states, Rhode Island *v.* Massachusetts, 12 Peters 657. United States *v.* Combes, 12 Peters 72. The Supreme Court have decided that all state laws repugnant to the laws, treaties, and constitution of the United States are void. Amis *v.* Smith, 16 Peters 303. The same court have decided that the government of the United States acts on the people within the scope of the constitution; and that the governments of the states act on the people unless such powers conflict with the constitution of the United States. Rhode Island *v.* the State of Massachusetts 12 Peters 657.

CONGRESS.

The legislative powers of Congress are vested in two houses of Congress; Senate and House of Representatives. The members of the House of Representatives are elected by the people of the several states, by the electors qualified to vote for members of the "most numerous branch of the state legislature," that is, for members of the assembly or House of Representatives. Members of Congress shall be citizens of the United States and of the age of twenty-five years. "Each House shall be judge of the elections, returns, and qualifications of its own members." The House of Representatives elects its own speaker; and with the concurrence of two-thirds, expel a member. The question has been raised whether a Senator or Representative can be impeached, under sec. 4, Art. 2 Constitution of the United States. Held by Judge Story in his Commentaries, vol. 2, pp. 259-262, and by the Supreme Court in the case of Anderson *v.* Dunn. 6 Wheaton 204, that members and senators of Congress cannot be impeached; that though members and senators are not responsible for words spoken in Congress, yet if a member causes his speech to be published he may be indicted for it or sued on a civil action for libel.—Kent's Comm., p. 235, (note). The legislature, under the constitution, provides for the times, places, and manner of holding elections for Senators and Representatives. The Constitution provides for filling vacancies in the House of Representatives, thus, when vacancies happen in the representation from any state, the executive authority thereof shall issue writs of election to fill such vacancies." Con. U. S. sec. 4. Art. 1. So when a member of Congress resigns he should tender his resignation to the House of Representatives and to the executive of his state. Congress shall meet annually on the first Monday in December. The first Congress met under the present constitution on Wednesday,

March 4, 1789. Two years make one Congress, counting from March 4, 1789. The Senate of the United States is composed of two senators from each state. Senators shall be 30 years of age and citizens of the United States. Senators are elected by the state legislature by joint vote or ballot of the two houses.—See Minn. Constitution, Art. 4, sec. 26, and 1 Kent Com. pp. 225-6. The Vice-President of the United States shall be President of the Senate. The Senatecan expel a member by "two-thirds vote of the Senate." The executive of each state issues writs of "election to fill vacancies. When a senator resigns he should tender his resignation to the senate and the executive authority of his state.—1 Kent's Comm. 224. It has been held by high authority that senators are not impeachable, under section 4. Art. 2, of the constitution of the United States.—1 Kent's Comm. p. 235. note.—Anderson v. Dunn.—6 Wheaton, R. p. 204.—Story's Comm. constitution, vol. 2. pp. 259-262. The senate is the high court of impeachment for trying the "President, Vice-President, and all civil officers of the United States, but the House of Representatives" shall have the sole power of impeachment. The Senate tries the case and passes judgment of guilty or not guilty, as the case may be. No person shall be convicted without the concurrence of two-thirds of the members present, judgment extends to "removal from office, and disqualification to hold and enjoy any office of honor, trust, or profit, under the United States. But the party convicted is subject to be indicted. Bills for raising revenue shall originate with the House of Representatives. A majority of each House shall constitute a quorum to do business. 1, Kent's Comm. pp. 235-6. Act of Congress, June 1, 1789, prescribes the oath of office for senators and members of Congress, as follows: "1. The oath or affirmation required by the sixth article of the Constitution of the United States, shall be administered in the following form, to wit: "I, A. B. do *solemnly swear* or affirm (as the case may be) *that I will support the Constitution of the United States.*" 2. At the first session of Congress after every general election of representatives, the oath or affirmation aforesaid shall be administered by any one member of the House of Representatives to the speaker; and by him to all the members present, and to the clerk, previous to entering on any business; and to the members who shall afterwards appear, previous to taking their seats. The president of the senate for the time being shall also administer the said oath or affirmation to each senator who shall hereafter be elected, previous to his taking his seat; and in any future case of a president of the senate, who shall not have taken the said oath or affirmation, the same shall be administered to him by any one of the members of the senate.—Brightly's Digest. The oath of office to be taken by the secretary of the Senate and clerk of the House of Representatives is prescribed by the act of June 1, 1789.—Brightly's Digest, 169. The framers of the Constitution intended that each house should be a check on the other.—1 Kent's Comm. p. 236. For the express powers of Congress, see sec. 8. Art. 1. Constitution of the United States. For the Constitutional restrictions on the powers of the states see sec. 9. Art. 1. Constitution of the United States, Federalist No. 44. pp. 241 2-3-4-5-6. No. 48, p. 236. No. 46, p. 254. Vide Azie v. Moore, 14 Howard, R. 568—345. 20 Curtis Sup. C. R. Smith v. Maryland 18 Howard R. 71. Conway v. Taylor's Ex. 1 Black's R. 603. 20 Howard p. 66. Ableman v. Booth 21 Howard R. p. 506. Bank of Commerce v. New York City. 2 Black's R. p. 620, Cummings v. the State of Missouri 4 Wallace R. p. 227. Crandall v. the State of Nevada, 6 Wallace R. p. 35, Veazie Bank v. Fenno 8 Wallace R. p. 533 Railroad Company v. McClure, 10 Wallace R. p. 511. The Collector v. Day 11 Wallace, R. p. 113. Taylor v. Defrees 11 Wallace,

R. p. 331. United States v. Miller 11 Wallace R. p. 269. and 1 Dillon C. C. R. p. 469. Gibbons v. Ogden, 9 Wheaton 203. The city of New York v. Milner, 11 Peters 102. Groves v. Slaughter, 15 Peters 509. Prigg v. Comm. Pennsylvania, 16 Peters 625; Brouen v. Maryland, 12 Wheaton 438-446. We give from Chancellor Kent the mode of passing laws in the Congress of the United States; "The ordinary mode of passing laws is briefly as follows: one day's notice of a motion for leave to bring in a bill, in cases of a general nature; is required. Every bill must have three readings previous to its being passed, and these readings must be on different days, and no bill can be committed or amended until it has been twice read. Such little checks in the forms of doing business are prudently intended to guard against surprise or imposition. In the House of Representatives, bills, after being twice read, are committed to a committee of the whole House, when the speaker leaves the chair, and takes part in the debates as an ordinary member, and a chairman is appointed to preside in his stead. When a bill has passed one house, it is transmitted to the other, and goes through a similar form; though, in the senate there is less formality, and bills are often committed to a select committee, chosen by ballot. If a bill be altered or amended in the house to which it is transmitted, it is then returned to the house in which it originated, and if the two houses cannot agree, they appoint committees to confer on the subject. When a bill is engrossed, and has passed the sanction of both houses it is transmitted to the President of the United States for his approbation, if he approves of the bill, he signs it. If he does not, it is returned, with his objections, to the house in which it originated, and that house enters the objections at large on its journals and proceeds to reconsider the bill. If after such reconsideration, two-thirds of that house should agree to pass the bill, it is sent, together with the objections, to the other house, by which it is likewise reconsidered, and if approved by two-thirds of that house, it becomes a law," two-thirds of members present.—Kent. p. 239. note. "But, in all such cases, the votes of both houses are determined by yeas and nays, and the names of the persons voting for or against the bill are entered on the journals. If any bill shall not be returned by the President within ten days (Sunday excepted) after it shall have been presented to him, the same becomes a law, equally as if he 'had signed it unless Congress, by adjournment, in the meantime, prevents its return, and then it does not become a law."—1 Kent's Comm. pp. 238-39-40. Jeffer's Manual, and Cushing's Rules of proceedings and debates, etc. Congress cannot control a State legislature. On November 30, 1779, Congress requested the legislature of Massachusetts to stop certain suits then pending in that State, but Massachusetts failed to comply. Opinions of the Attorneys General of the United States, vol. 1, pp. 81-2. Congress cannot abolish Jury trial, unless in cases arising in the Army, Navy, or Militia in time of war. Opinions of the Attorneys General, vol. 1. p. 202. No act can be made an offence against the United States except by act of Congress. The courts of the United States cannot punish for a common law offence. Opinions of the Attorney General of the United States, vol. 1, p. 152. Ibid. 48. It has been held by high authority that a conflict of authority between the Executive and the Judiciary could be avoided by an explanatory act of Congress. Opinions of the Attorney General, U. S. vol. 1, p. 325. Congress have, under the constitution, the right to regulate commerce with foreign nations and among the several states. Under this power Congress can regulate the intercourse between the United States and foreign nations, and between the several states. No state can interdict vessels from entering the harbors of the United States, so long as they conform with the laws and regulations of Congress.

Opinions of the Attorneys General U. States, vol. 1, pp. 492-493. Act of Congress Feb. 25, 1799, provides that the quarantine laws of the states shall be observed by the Federal officers. Brightly's Dig. 810. It has been held that a state could pass quarantine laws. Opin. Atty. Gen, vol. 1, pp. 716-17. Norris v. city of Boston, 4 Metcalf 282, Groves v. Slaughter, 15 Peters' Rep. 509; Prigg v. The commonwealth of Pennsylvania 16 Peter's Rep. 625. 5 Howard, 578, Milne v. New York, 11 Peters' R. 130, Holmes v. Jennison 14 Peters' 568-9 Wheaton 203. When there is any doubt as to the meaning of an act of Congress it can be explained either by the Supreme Court or by an explanatory Act of Congress. Opinions Attys. Gen. U. S. vol. 1, p. 578. Such was the solicitation of the early judges and executives of the United States to avoid a conflict of authority, that in a doubtful case the chief justices recommended an explanatory act of Congress. Congress, under the constitution, have the power to declare war, raise and support armies. Sec. 8, Art. constitution. It has been the rule of Congress to declare war against a public enemy; but "war between the United States and a public enemy may exist without the sanction of Congress—as where an unexpected war is commenced against the United States, and waged before Congress act upon the subject." Opinions Attys. Gen. vol. 2. p. 1168. Congress provides for calling out the Militia of the states; but the mititia officers appointed by the state authorities cannot be ousted by the officers of the United States—"not even by the President himself." Opinions Attys. Gen. vol. 2. pp. 996-7. Kent's Comm. vol. 1, pp. 261-2-3. In July 7, 1838, Congress passed a special act to pay the militia of New York, who were called out by the governor to protect the frontier. Opinions Attys. Gen. U. S. vol. 2, p. 1319. "The powers of Congress extend generally to all subjects of a national nature." Kent's Com. vol. 1, p. 236. The constitution, Art. 2, Sec. 1, provides that the executive power shall be vested in a President, that he shall be thirty-five years of age and a natural-born citizen or a citizen of the United States at the time of the adoption of the constitution, and fourteen years a resident of the United States. He holds his office for four years. On the 23d January, 1845, Congress, by virtue of the constitution Art. 2. Sec. 4. provided for holding elections, for the election of Presidential electors, for the election of President and Vice President, on the Tuesday next after the first Monday in the month of November, in which they are to be appointed. —1 Kent. p. 275, note. It is provided in the constitution—Art. 2, sec. 1, "That the number of electors in each state shall be equal to the whole number of senators and representatives which the state is entitled to send to Congress; and, according to the apportionment of Congress." "And to prevent the person in office, at the time of the election, from having any improper influence on his reëlection, by his ordinary agency in the government, it is provided, that no member of Congress, nor any person holding an office of trust or profit under the United States, shall be an elector; and the Constitution has in no other respect defined the qualifications of the electors."—Art. 2, sec. 1, and Art. 2, sec. 2, 3. "These electors meet in their respective states, at a place appointed by the Legislature thereof, on the first Wednesday in December in every fourth year succeeding the last election, and vote by ballot for President and Vice-President, (for this last officer is elected in the same manner, and for the same time as the President,) and one of whom, at least, shall not be an inhabitant of the same state with the electors. They name in their ballots the person voted for as President, and, in distinct ballots, the person voted for as Vice-President; and they make distinct lists of all persons voted for as President, and of all persons voted for as Vice-President and of the number of votes for each, which lists they sign, and certify, and transmit, sealed, to the seat of the government of the United States, directed to the President of the senate. The act of Congress of 1st of March, 1792, sec. 2, directs, that the certificate of the votes shall be delivered to the President of the senate before the first Wednesday of January next ensuing the election. The President of the senate, on the second Wednesday in February succeeding every meeting of the electors, in the presence of both houses of Congress, opens all the certificates, and the votes are then to be counted. The constitution does not expressly declare *by whom* the votes are to be counted and the results declared. In the case of questionable votes, and a closely contested election, this power may be all-important; and, I presume, in the absence of all legislative provision on the subject, that the president of the senate counts the votes and determines the result, and that the two houses are present only as spectators, to witness the fairness and accuracy of the transaction, and to act only if no choice be made by the electors."—1 Kent's Comm. p. 276. "In determining the result of the election for President in 1841, it was declared by joint resolution of the two houses of Congress, that one person be appointed teller on the part of the senate, and two on the part of the House of Representatives, who were in the presence of the two houses to make a list of the votes as they should be declared, and the result declared to the president of the senate who was the presiding officer, and to announce to the two houses the state of the vote and the person elected. The Vice-President, in this case, broke the seals of the envelopes of the votes and delivered the same over to the tellers to be counted. The tellers having read, counted, and made duplicate lists of the votes, they were delivered over to the Vice-President, and read and he then declared the result, and dissolved the joint meeting of the two houses."—Kent, vol. 1, pp. 276-7. In 1801 and 1824, as no choice was made the House of Representatives retired and voted, and the senate were admitted to be present as spectators. The House of Representatives, in such case, are to choose immediately, though the constitution hold their choice to be valid if made before the fourth of March following. And in the cases of the elections, at the 4th Presidential election, in 1801, Thomas Jefferson and Aaron Burr were the democratic candidates for President and Vice-President. By the electoral returns they had an even number of votes. The election was carried to the House of Representatives. The House was so divided that there was a tie. A contest was carried on for several days, so that sick members were brought to the House on their sick beds. One of Burr's friends withdrew which elected Jefferson by one majority. This occurred on the 36 ballot. This led to the 12 article of amendments to the constitution. The person having the greatest number of votes of the electors for President, is president, if such number be a majority of the whole number of electors appointed; but if no person have such a majority, then, from the person having the highest number, not exceeding three, of the list of those voted for as president, the House of Representatives shall choose immediately by ballot the president. But in choosing the President, the votes shall be taken by states, the representation from each state having one vote. A quorum for this purpose shall consist of a member or members from two-thirds of the states, and a majority of all the states shall be necessary to a choice. If the House of Representatives shall not choose a President, whenever the right of choice shall devolve upon them, before the fourth day of March next following, then the Vice-President shall act as President, as in case of the death or other constitutional disability of the President.—Amendments, Art. 12. The person having the greatest number of votes as Vice-President, is Vice-President, if such number be a majority of the whole number of electors appointed;

and if no person have a majority, then, from the two highest numbers on the list, the senate shall choose the Vice-President; a quorum for the purpose shall consist of two-thirds of the whole number of senators, and a majority of the whole number is necessary to a choice; and no person constitutionally ineligible to the office of President, shall be eligible to that of Vice-President of the United States.—Amendments, Art. 12.—The constitution does not specifically prescribe when or where the senate is to choose a Vice-President, if no choice be made by the electors; and, I presume, the senate may elect by themselves, at any time before the fourth day of March following. "The President and Vice-President are equally to be chosen for the term of four years; and it is provided by law."—Act congress, March 1, 1792, "that the term shall, in all cases, commence on the fourth day of March next succeeding the day on which the votes of the electors shall have been given." "In case of the removal of the President from office, or of his death, resignation or inability to discharge the powers and duties of the office, the same devolve on the Vice-President; and except in cases in which the President is enabled to re-assume the office, the Vice-President acts as President during the remainder of the term for which the President was elected. Congress are authorized to provide, by law, for the case of removal, death, resignation, or inability, both of the President and Vice-President, declaring what officer should then act as President; and the officer so designated is to act until the disability be removed, or a President shall be elected, and who is in that case to be elected on the first Wednesday of the ensuing December, if time will admit of it, and if not, then on the same day in the ensuing year. "And if the office should, by the course of events, devolve on the speaker, of the Congress for which the last speaker was chosen had expired, and before the next meeting of Congress, it might be a question who is to serve, and whether the speaker of the House of Representatives, then extinct, could be deemed the person intended." 1 Kent's Com. 278. Act March 1, 1792,—1 Statutes 239. "The electors shall meet and give their votes on the said first Wednesday in December, at such place in each state as shall be directed, by the legislature thereof; and the electors in each state shall make and sign three certificates of all the votes by them given, and shall seal up the same, certifying on each that a list of the votes of such state for president and vice-president is contained therein, and shall by writing under their hands, or under the hands of a majority of them, appoint a person to take charge of and deliver to the president of the senate at the seat of government, before the first Wednesday in January then next ensuing, one of the said certificates, and the said electors shall forthwith forward by the post office to the president of the senate, at the seat of government, one of the said certificates to be delivered to the judge of that district in which the said electors shall assemble." "The executive authority of each state shall cause three lists of the names of the electors of such state to be made and certified and to be delivered to the electors on or before the said first Wednesday in December, and the said electors shall annex one of the said lists to each of the lists of their votes." 4. If a list of votes, from any state, shall not have been received at the Seat of Government on the said first Wednesday in January, that then the secretary of state shall send a special messenger to the district judge in whose custody such list shall have been lodged, who shall forthwith transmit the same to the seat of government. 5. "Congress shall be in session on the second Wednesday in February 1793, and on the second Wednesday in February succeeding every meeting of the electors, and the said certificates, or so many of them as shall have been received, shall then be opened, the votes counted, and the persons who shall fill the offices of presi dent and vice-president ascertained and declared, agreeably to . the Constitution (see the twelfth amendment to the Constitution which was adopted after the passage of this act.") 6. "In case there shall be no president of the senate at the seat of government on the arrival of the person intrusted with the list of the votes of the electors, then such person shall deliver the lists of votes in their custody into the office of the secretary of state, to be safely kept and delivered over as soon as may be, to the president of the senate." 7. If any person appointed to deliver the votes of the electors to the president of the senate, shall, after accepting of his appointment, neglect to perform the services required of him by this act, he shall forfeit the sum of one thousand dollars." 8. In case of removal, death, resignation, or inability both of the president and vice-president of the United States, the president of the senate *pro tempore*, and in case there shall be no president of the senate, then the speaker of the house of representatives, for the time being, shall act as president of the United States until the disability be removed or a President shall be elected." 9. Whenever the offices of president and vice-president shall both become vacant, the secretary of state shall forthwith cause a notification thereof to be made to the executive of every state, and shall also cause the same to be published in at least one newspaper printed in each state, specifying that electors of the president of the United States shall be appointed or chosen in the several states within thirty-four days preceding the first Wednesday in December then next ensuing; provided, there shall be the space of two months between the date of such notification and the said first Wednesday in December; but if there shall not be the space of two months between the date of such notification and the first Wednesday of December; and if the term for which the president and vice-president last in office were elected shall not expire on the third day of March next ensuing, then the secretary of state shall specify in the notification that the electors shall be appointed or chosen within thirty-four days preceding the first Wednesday in December in the year next ensuing; within which time the electors shall accordingly be appointed or chosen, and the electors shall meet and give their votes on the said first Wednesday in December, and the proceedings and duties of the said electors and others shall be pursuant to the directions prescribed in this act." 10. The only evidence of refusal to accept of a resignation of the office of president or vice-president, shall be an instrument in writing declaring the same, and subscribed by the person refusing to accept or resigning, as the case may be, and delivered into the office of the secretary of state." 11. "The term of four years for which a president and vice-president shall be elected shall in all cases commence on the fourth day of March next succeeding the day on which the votes of the electors shall have been given." 12. "The person appointed by the electors to deliver to the president of the senate, a list of the votes for president and vice-president, shall be allowed, on delivery of said list, twenty-five cents for every mile of the estimated distance, by the most usual rout, from the place of meeting of the electors to the seat of government of the United States, going and returning." 13. "The electors of president and vice-president shall be appointed in each state on the Tuesday next after the first Monday in the month of November of the year in which they are to be appointed; Provided, that each state may by law provide for the filling of any vacancy or vacancies which may occur in its college of electors when such college meets to give its electoral vote: And provided also, when any state shall have held any election for the purpose of choosing electors, and shall fail to make a choice on the day aforesaid, then the electors may be appointed on a subsequent day in such manner as the state shall by law provide. *Ib.* 253–4. 1 Kent's Com. 277, note. The president is commander-in-chief of the army and navy, and of the militia of the several states, when called into the service of the United States. He has the power to grant reprieves and pardons for offences against the United States, except in cases of impeachments. It has been decided by the attorney general of the United States, that the President can pardon conditionally. That the president can pardon before condemnation. Opinions of the Attorneys Gen. U. S. vol. 1, p. 251. The president may pardon for contempt of court. Op. Attys. Gen. U. S. vol. 2, p. 1382. *Ib.* vol. 2, 1034, "There can be no doubt of the power of the President to order a *nolle prose-qui* in any stage of a criminal proceeding in the name of the United States; such an order, however, is never hastily given, because it interferes with the action of an other branch of the government, viz.: the judiciary." Opinions of the Attys. Gen. vol. 1, p. 335, *Ib.* 723–4, 730–732. Now, if the President may order a prosecution begun, to be discontinued, it is evident that he may forbid the commencement. And if, after the seizure of the property, and before it is libelled, he becomes satisfied that it has been wrongfully and improperly seized, he may direct the district attorney not to institute proceeding against it. The president is the proper authority to authorize the agents of the government to settle and adjust claims with the States. Opinions Attys. Gen. United States, vol. 2, p, 983.—Opinions of the attorneys general United States, vol. 2. p. 862.—*Ib.* 1241–2 vol. 1. p. 169, vol. 7 p. 267. The President, by and with the advice and consent of the senate, has power to make treaties with foreign powers and with Indians, provided two-thirds of the senate present concur.—Kent's Com. vol. 1, p. 284. Thus, the President is the constitutional organ of communication with foreign powers. The president is the functionary who acts with foreign nations or powers or their agents and through the law officer of the district informs the judiciary of violations of the law which come under the jurisdiction of the courts.—7 Cranch 116. 2 Dallas 365. The President is vested with that portion of the national power which relates to foreign nations. Opinions Attys. Gen. vol 1. p. 380. International questions with foreign nations usually sent to the secretary of state, who lays such papers before the President. Opinions Attys. Gen. vol. 1, pp. 734–5. The president nominates, and, with the advice and consent of the senate, appoints ambassadors, or public ministers and consuls, the judges of the Supreme Court, and all other officers whose appointments are not otherwise provided for in the constitution; but congress may vest the appointment of inferior officers in the president alone, in the courts of law, or in the heads of departments. The "nomination to the office by the President, confirmation by the senate, signature of the commission, and affixing to it the seal of the United States, are all the acts necessary to render the appointment complete."—United States *v.* La Baron, 19 Howard 73. Kent's Com. p. 287. Judges of the Supreme Court, judges of the District Courts, heads of departments, consuls, ambassadors and public ministers and all other officers who are appointed by the president, under the constitution, or the laws of congress, should tender their resignation to the President. Ex parte Duncan N. Hennen 13 Peters 225, act of Congress Feb. 20, 1863, 12 Statutes at Large 666, Brightly's Dig. 115. For the power of the President to remove officers whose commission shall last *during the pleasure of the President*—see opinions Attys. Gen. vol. 1, p. 157. The President makes all appointments which may occur during the recess of the senate, though the vacancy did occur before the adjournment of the senate.—Opins. Attys. Gen. vol. 1, p. 476, *Ibid.* 326. *Ibid.* 480. The President has the power of appointing such officers, as are established by law.—Op. Attys. Gen. vol. 1, p. 710, see judicial acts 1789–1790. It has been decided by the supreme court of the United States, in the case of ex parte Duncan N. Hennen. 13 Peters 225, that the power of removal is vested in the President. That the power of removal is incident to the power of appointment, ex parte Duncan N. Hennen 13 Peters 225.—1 Kent's Comm. 440, *Ibid.* 309, Federalist No. 77, p. 1. The President, by acts of Congress, is empowered to call the public lands into market; to appoint officers of the land office; to appoint surveyors general and paymasters. He may order the survey of military roads; lease lead-mines, and order the payment of Indians, and regulate Indian affairs. — Act. June 30, 1834. By act 8 March 1853, the President may change the location of land offices; appoint and regulate trade with the Indians; regulate the diplomatic and consular officers; to cause the coast to be surveyed; to cause the erection of additional arsenals; and to direct the sale of unserviceable military stores. Brightly's Digest, 464. The president may employ the public vessels as he may judge expedient in the survey of the coast. Opinions Attys. Gen. vol. 2, p. 1285. The president can instruct the United States marshal to remove intruders from the public lands. Opinions Attys. Gen. vol. 1, p. 353. The president is authorized by act of April 20, 1818, to enforce the neutrality laws. Brightly's Digest, 688. By act of April 20, 1818, the president may compel foreign vessels to depart from the United States. By act of Congress, it is provided that the president appoint officers to hold a general court martial. The sentence to be sent to the secretary of war, to be laid before the president for confirmation or approval or order in the case. Brightly's Digest, 83. Held that an officer cannot be tried by court martial for an offence while he is held on an indictment for the same offence.—That such interference would place the military above the civil power, 16 Wisconsin Rep. 361. Opinions Attys. Gen. vol. 2, pp. 1276–7. We insert the act of February 28, 1795, empowering the president to call out the militia. Act February 28, 1795. "1, In case of an insurrection in any state against the government thereof, it shall be lawful for the President of the United States, on application of the legislature of such state, or of the executive, (when the legislature cannot be convened,) to call forth such number of the militia of any other state or states as may be applied for, as he may judge sufficient to suppress such insurrection." "2. Whenevever the laws of the United States shall be opposed, or the execution thereof obstructed in any state by combinations too powerful to be suppressed by the ordinary course of judicial proceedings, or by the powers vested in the marshals by this act, it shall be lawful for the President of the United States to call forth the militia of such state, or of any other state or states, as may be necessary to suppress such combinations, and to cause the laws to be duly executed ; and the use of militia so to be called forth may be continued, if necessary, until the expiration of thirty days after the commencement of the next session of Congress." 3. "Whenever it may be necessary in the judgment of the president, to use the military force hereby directed to be called forth, the president shall forthwith, by proclamation, command such insurgents to disperse, and retire peaceably to their respective abode, within a limited time. " 4. " In all cases of insurrection or obstruction to the laws, either of the United States, or of any individual state or territory, where it is lawful for the president of the United States to call forth the militia for the purpose of suppressing such insurrection, or of causing the laws to be duly executed, it shall be lawful for him to employ, for the same purposes, such part of the land or naval force of the United States, as shall be judged necessary, having first observed all the prerequisites of the law in that respect"—Brightly's Digest,

440 Act July 27, 1789. "There shall be an executive department, to be denominated the department of foreign affairs; and there shall be a principal officer therein, to be called the secretary for the department of foreign affairs, who shall perform and execute such duties as shall from time to time be enjoined on or intrusted to him by the President of the United States, agreeably to the Constitution, relative to correspondence, commissions, or instructions to or with public ministers or consuls, from the United States, or to negotiation, with public ministers from foreign states or princes, or to memorials or other applications from foreign public ministers or other foreigners, or to such other matters respecting foreign affairs, as the President of the United States shall assign to the said department; and furthermore, the said principal officer shall conduct the business of the said department in such manner as the President of the United States shall from time to time order or instruct." Act Sept. 2, 1789, created the office of secretary of war. Brightly's Digest 879. Act Sept. 9, 1789 created the secretary of the Treasury. Brightly's Digest 879. Attorneys General's office was created by Act Sept. 24. 1789. The office of postmaster-general was created by act of March 8, 1825. The office of secretary of the Navy was created by act of April 30, 1798. The secretary of the Navy shall execute the orders of the President of the United States. Brightly's Digest 680. The office of secretary of the interior was created to perform the duties of the land office. The said secretary of state, secretary of war, secretary of the Treasury, Attorney-General, postmaster general, secretary of the navy, and the secretary of the interior form the President's Cabinet Council. For vacancies in the departments, see Act of Congress Feb. 20, 1863, 12 Statutes 656, Brightly's Digest 115. Act Aug. 3, 1861, empowers the President, by and with the advice and consent of the senate, to appoint an adjutant general and assistant adjutant general and inspector general of the army. Brightly's Digest vol. 2, pp. 10–11. The department of agriculture was established May 15, 1862. A commissioner of agriculture is appointed by the President, by and with the advice and consent of the senate. Brightly's Digest, vol. 2, p. 4. Act of March 8, 1859, provides for the appointment of an assistant Attorney General. Brightly's Digest vol. 2, p. 30. Act June 3, 1864, the President appoints comptroller of the currency. Ibid. 51. The Freedmen's Bureau was established in the war department, to continue for one year after the rebellion. Act March 3, 1865, 13 Statutes 507. Brightly's Dig. 430. Act June 20, 1864, established a bureau of military justice in the war department, with a judge advocate to be appointed by the President, by and with the consent of the senate. Brightly's Dig. vol. 2, p. 26. Act July 4, 1864, empowers the President to appoint Commissioners of Immigration. Brightly's Dig. vol. 2, p. 148.

THE JUDICIARY.

The judiciary is the third department of the Federal Government of the United States. The Supreme Court of the United States is, by virtue of the constitution, the expounder of the constitution, laws and treaties of the United States, from whose decision there is no appeal.—1 Kent's Comm. 313,—1 Kent's Comm. 295. The judicial power of the United States extends to all cases of law, equity, treaties and acts of Congress arising under the constitution; to all cases affecting ambassadors, and other public ministers and consuls; to all cases of admiralty and maritime jurisdiction; to controversies to which the United States shall be a party; to controversies between two or more states; to controversies between a state, when plaintiff, and citizens of another state, or foreign citizens or subjects; to controveries between citizens of different states, and between citizens of the same states claiming lands under grants of different states; and between a state or citizens thereof, and foreign states; and between citizens and foreigners. It has been held by the supreme court, in the case of Chisholm *v.* the State of Georgia, in 1793, that a state was suable by the citizens of another state. The legislature of Georgia defied the Judicial authority, on this question, of the supreme court. To avoid a conflict of authority between the several states and the Federal government Congress, in 1794, proposed an amendment to the constitution, which was subsequently adopted. It was provided by the amendment, that the Judicial power of the United States should not extend to any suit in law or equity against one of the United States by citizens of another state, or by citizens or subjects of any foreign state. The inhibition applies only to citizens or subjects, and does not extend to suits by a state, or by foreign states or powers. "They retain the capacity to sue a state as it was originally granted by the constitution; and the supreme court has original jurisdiction in the case of suits by a foreign state against one of the United States." Commonwealth of Kentucky *v.* Dennison, Governor of Ohio, 24 Howard's Rep. p. 66. 1 Kent's Comm. 297. The supreme court was instituted by the Constitution and the judiciary act of 1789. It has been decided that the Supreme Court has exclusive jurisdiction in civil actions where the state is a party, except that a state cannot be sued by its own citizens or the citizens of other states or by aliens. But it has jurisdiction where the state is plaintiff.—1 Kent's Comm. 298. The judges of the supreme court are judges of the circuit courts. These courts are vested with original jurisdiction, concurrent with the courts of the several states, of all civil actions in law and equity, where the matter in dispute exceeds five hundred dollars, exclusive of costs, where the United States are plaintiffs, or an alien is party, and the suit is between a citizen of the states where the suit is brought, and a citizen of an other state. And no civil action can be brought against an inhabitant of the United States out of his district.—1, Kent's Com. p. 302. The Circuit Courts have original jurisdiction in law and equity of all actions arising under the revenue laws of the United States, and under the laws relating to copy rights or patents.—1 Kent's Com. 302. The District Courts and Circuit Courts derive their power from the provision in the constitution which provides that Congress may "establish courts inferior to the Supreme Court. The district courts have jurisdiction of admiralty and maritime cases, and for penalties and forfeitures incurred for a violation of the laws of the United States. They have concurrent jurisdiction with the state courts of causes where an alien sues for a tort committed in violation of the law of nations, or of a treaty of the United States.—1, Kent's Com. 304. The state courts are invested by acts of Congress with jurisdiction, in certain cases of causes arising under the laws of the United States. "The state courts may, in the exercise of their ordinary, original and rightful jurisdiction incidently take cognizance of laws arising under the constitution and the laws, and treaties of the United States; yet to all these cases the judicial power of the United States extends, by means of its appellate jurisdiction." --1, Kent's Com. 397. But an appeal may be taken from the decision of the state courts to the supreme court of the United States. The supreme court determines what is the supreme law of the land.—1 Kent's Com. p. 313. Held in the case of the United States *v.* Worrall, that the United States could not punish for common law offences.—1, Kent's Com. 309. The Federal courts had no criminal jurisdiction only what they derive from the constitution and acts of Congress. Held by the best of authority that the United States cannot exercise any powers but what are granted in the constitution, given either expressly or by implication.—1 Kent's Com. 312. Thus, all conflicts between the Legislative and the Executive departments of the Federal government, as well as conflicts between the States and the general government, are settled by a judicial decision of the Supreme Court.—Federalist 208-9. Madison, in the Federalist speaking of the Supreme Court, says, Some such tribunal is clearly essential to prevent an appeal to the sword."—Federalist, 208-9. The following is from De Tocqueville. "They have left them," the courts, "at liberty not to apply such laws as may appear to them to be unconstitutional. This fact can only be explained by the principles of the American constitutions." In England, the parliament has an acknowledged right to modify the constitution; as, therefore, the constitution may undergo perpetual changes, it does not in reality exist; the Parliament is at once a legislative and a constitutional assembly, since the Parliament which makes the laws also makes the constitution." De Tocqueville, pp. 80-1. The following is from Wm. Wirt on the coördinate departments of the government. "My opinion is, that the judiciary can no more arrest the Executive in the execution of a constitutional law, than they can arrest the Legislature itself in passing the law. Opinions of the Attorneys General U. S. p. 508. Held that the judiciary cannot arrest by injunction the powers of the executive. Opinions of the Attorneys General, vol. 2, p. 1280, 4 Wisconsin Rep. p. 567. Bashford v Barstow, Ibid. 594. "There is no power in the judiciary to remedy injustice and oppression in a legislative act, except, where in an attempted injustice or oppression, some constitutional provision is violated." Hamilton and Treat v. St. Louis county, 15 Missouri Rep. p. 8. "Before a court will pronounce a law unconstitutional, the court must be free from doubt, and the violation must be palpable. So long as a doubt remains, the legislative act should be enforced,—Armstrong v. Treasurer of Athens Co., 10 Ohio Rep. pp. 235-237." It is the right of the legislature to enact laws, and of the province of the court to construe them. 18 Ohio Rep. 125-127. Act Feb. 24 1855, created a court of claims to hear cases against the United States, and to report their finding in the form of a bill for the action of Congress.—Brightly's Dig. 198. For a conflict between the states and the Federal government on the regulation of commerce and the internal police of the states, see Gibbons v. Ogden 9 Wheaton, 203, the City of New York v. Milne, 11 Peters 102, Brown v. Maryland, 12 Wheaton 438-446, Groves et al. v. Slaughter, 15 Peters, 509. Prigg v. Com. Pennsylvania, 16 Peters 625. 5 Howard, 578 "Being admitted upon a footing of equality with other states, the State of Mississippi had the rightful power to change the channels or courses of rivers within the interior of the state, for the purposes of internal improvement." Withers v. Buckley, 20 Howard R. p. 84. "A state law, granting to an individual an exclusive right to navigate the upper waters of the Penobscot River, lying wholly within the limits of the state, separated from tide water by falls impassable for the purpose of navigation, and not forming a part of any continuous track of commerce between two or more states, or with a foreign country, is not repugnant to the Constitution or any law of the United States." Veazie v. Moore 14. H. 568-345, 20 Curtis Sup. C. R. "The soil below low water-mark in the Chesapeake Bay, within the boundaries of the State of Maryland belongs to the State." Smith v. Maryland 18 Howard R. 71. The decision of a state court not binding on the Supreme Court of the United States in a question of Consti tutional law. Jefferson's Branch Bank v. Skelly, 1 Black's Rep. 436. The authority to establish ferries is not given to the general government, but is reserved to the states. Conway v. Taylor's Ex. 1 Black, R.

603. "In a suit between two states, this court has original jurisdiction, without any further act of Congress regulating the mode and form in which it shall be exercised. Commonwealth of Kentucky v. Dennison, Governor of Ohio. 24 Howard, 66. This was an application to the Supreme Court by the Governor of Kentucky for a mandamus to compel the Governor of Ohio to deliver up a fugitive from justice. Held by the court that: "The act does not provide any means to compel the execution of this duty," delivering up a fugitive, "nor inflict any punishment for neglect or refusal on the part of the Executive of the state; nor is there any clause in the Constitution which arms the government of the United States with this power. Indeed, such a power would place every state under the control and dominion of the general government, even in the administration of its internal concerns and reserved rights. And we think it clear, that the Federal Government, under the Constitution, has no power to impose on a state officer, as such, any duty whatever, and compel him to perform it." 24 Howard, 66. "The process of a state court or judge has no authority beyond the limits of the sovereignty which confers the judicial power." "A habeas corpus, issued by a state judge or court has no authority within the limits of the sovereignty assigned by the Constitution of the United States. The sovereignty of the United States and of a state are distinct and independent of each other, within their respective spheres of action, although both exist and exercise their powers within the same territorial limits. "When a writ of habeas corpus is served on a marshal or other person having a prisoner in custody under the authority of the United States, it is his duty, by a proper return, to make known to the State Judge or Court the authority by which he holds him. But, at the same time, it is his duty not to obey the process of the state authority, but to obey and execute the process of the United States."—21 Howard, R. Ableman v. Booth, 506. A state tax on the loans of the Federal Government is a restriction upon the constitutional power of the United States to borrow money, and if the state had such a right, being in its nature unlimited, it might be so used as to defeat the Federal power altogether. Bank of Commerce v. New York City. 2 Black's R. p. 620. Under the form of creating a qualification or attaching a condition, the state cannot in effect inflict a punishment for a past act which was not punishable at the time it was committed. "Deprivation or suspension of any civil rights for past conduct is punishment for such conduct." A bill of attainder is a legislative act which inflicts punishment without a judicial trial. If the punishment be less than death the act is termed a bill of pains and penalties. Within the meaning of the constitution bills of attainder include bills of pains and penalties. The clauses of the second article of the constitution of Missouri set forth in the statement of the case of Cummings v. The State of Missouri 4 Wallace, pp. 279–281, which requires priests and clergymen, in order that they may continue in the exercise of their professions, and to be allowed to preach and teach, to take and subscribe an oath that they have not committed certain designated acts, some of which were at the time offences with heavy penalties attached, and some of which were at the time acts innocent in themselves, constitute a bill of attainder within the meaning of the provision in the Federal constitution prohibiting the states from passing bills of that character. An *ex post facto law* is one which imposes a punishment for an act which was not punishable at the time it was committed. Cummings v. The State of Missouri 4, Wallace, R. p. 227. "A special tax on a railroad and stage companies for every passenger carried out of the state by them is a tax on the passenger for the privilege of

passing through the state by the ordinary modes of travel, not a simple tax on the business of the companies, and is unconstitutional and void." Crandall *v.* State of Nevada, 6 Wallace, R. 35. "The tax of ten per centum imposed by the act of July 13, 1866, on the notes of state banks paid out after the 1st of August, 1866, is warranted by the Constitution." Veazie Bank *v.* Fenno, 8 Wallace R. p. 533. "Congress has no power to make paper money a legal tender, or lawful money in discharge of private debts which existed in virtue of contracts made prior to its acts attempting to make such paper a legal tender and lawful money for the payment of such debts."—Hepburn *v.* Griswold, 8 Wallace, R. 603. In the above case, Chase, Clifford, Nelson, Field and Grier held as above; dissenting, Miller, Swayne and Davis. Since this decision was rendered Grier resigned, and Grant appointed an attorney of the Pennsylvania Central and Camden and Amboy R. Rs., for the purpose of reversing this decision. This was not enough, for the court was reorganized by appointing another judge friendly to the party in power for the purpose of overruling the above decision; which has been done. The Constitution of a state is a law, within the meaning of that clause of the constitution which ordains that "no state shall pass any law impairing the obligation of contracts. Railroad Company *v.* McClure 10 Wallace R. p. 511." The decision of a state court which simply held that promissory notes, given for the loan of confederate currency together with a mortgage to secure the notes, were nullities, on the ground that the consideration was illegal, according to the law of the state, at the time the contract was entered into, is not a decision repugnant to the Federal constitution.—"Bethel *v.* Demaret, 10 Wallace, R. p. 537." Congress cannot impose a tax upon the salary of a judicial officer of a state." The Collector *v.* Day 11 Wallace, R. 113. "It, (congress) is not deprived of the power to make war, to suppress insurrection, to levy taxes, to make rules concerning captures on land and sea, when the necessity for their exercise is called out by domestic insurrection and internal civil war, instead of by foreign war."—Tyler *v.* Defrees 11 Wallace, R. p. 331. "It can determine what property of public enemies shall be confiscated." United States *v.* Miller 11 Wallace, R. p. 269. "The power of the Federal government to improve public navigable waters, when called into exercise, is not only paramount but exclusive, and cannot lawfully be interfered with to any extent, by or under state authority." United States *v.* Duluth. Dillon, C. C. R. p. 469. "The United States may, in such cases, enjoin illegal interference by state authority." *Ibid.* A court of the United States has no jurisdiction to restrain by injunction, the erection of a bridge over a navigable river lying wholly within the limits of a particular state, where such erection is authorized by the legislature of the state, though a port of entry has been created by Congress above the bridge.—Milnor *v.* New Jersey Railroad Company, 6, American Law R. p. 6, Brightly's Dig. vol. 2, p. 85.

CHAPTER VI.—FOREIGN IMMIGRATION — NATURALIZATION — NATIVE AMERICANS AND KNOW-NOTHINGS.

As early as 1639, Massachusetts passed a law for the removal of foreign paupers. The next step was to require an indemnity bond from the master of vessels. Virginia passed a similar regulation. Pennsylvania had a law for laying a duty on foreigners and Irish servants. Virginia passed a law Nov. 13, 1788, forbidding masters of vessels from landing convicts, under

penalty of fifty pounds.   The same year, similar laws were passed by
Georgia and South Carolina.   New York and Massachusetts passed similar
laws in 1791, and Pennsylvania in 1789.   But this example was never followed by the General Government, except in the case of the *" alien and sedition laws,"* in 1798.   In 1836, the legislature of Massachusetts passed the
following resolution: "Resolved, that it is expedient to instruct our
senators, and request our representatives in Congress to use their endeavors
to obtain the passage of a law to prevent the introduction of foreign paupers
into this country, and to favor any other measures which Congress may be
disposed to adopt, to effect this object."   Congressional Globe 1835-6, vol.
12, part 2, p. 1378.   The following letter from Mayor Clark, will show the
spirit of the anti-foreign policy of the Native Americans:

"Mayor's Office, New York, June 5, 1837.

" Gentlemen of the Common Council:

"The laws of this State require that the captain of every ship or
vessel, landing passengers in this city from a foreign country or *from another
state*, shall report the name, last legal settlement, place of birth, age or occupation of such passengers, to the mayor of the city, within twenty-four
hours after the arrival, under a penalty of $75 for each passenger so neg-
lected to be reported; and that every person not *being a citizen* of the United
States, coming to this city with the intention to reside, shall report himself to the mayor within twenty-four hours after arrival, under a penalty of
$100 for neglecting so to do."   The opinion is entertained that there is a
settled arrangement in some parts of Europe to send their famishing hordes
to our city.   The operations of certain companies have been noticed.   But
contractors are becoming so covetous that they afflict this country with a
pauper population in consideration of receiving from steerage passengers
more than $2 per head extra, for agreeing to land them in New York; in-
stead of which these traders in foreign paupers secretly clear their vessels
for Amboy, in the State of New Jersey, there to land the said passengers, and
thereafter send them to New York by other conveyance, or leave them to
provide for themselves.   Our city is generally the place to which they *contract*
to be carried on leaving Liverpool.   This business is likely to be fiercely
driven through the ensuing year.   Hundreds of thousands of the population of portions of Europe are in a state of poverty, excitement and wretch-
edness—the prospect before them very discouraging. — The old country
has more people than it is convenient to support.   And although many of
them feel no particular anxiety to leave their native land, they see others
depart—they read the mixture of truth and fiction, published by those employed to obtain passengers—they are assured they can easily return if they
are not suited with the country—that certain employment, enormously high
wages, and almost sure wealth await them.   The times being more un-
promising in other countries than in our own, they imagine they
cannot change for the worse, and hither they come.   They cannot
fail to be an *intolerable burthen* to us.   As soon as they arrive within
our limits, many of them begin to suffer and to beg.   Some of those by the
Lockwoods commenced as mendicants on the first day they saw our city, and
some of them on the first night thereafter sought the watch-house for a
shelter; others solicited aid at the commissioner's office, and not a few at
the Mayor's residence.   Nearly 2,000 arrive each week, and it is not likely
that many months will elapse before the number per week will be 3,000.   In
the *Boreas*, which came in on Saturday, there were about 150 steerage passengers.   They were landed from a lighter, near the foot of Rector Street, at

10 A. M. on Sunday. Some of them declared they had not means to obtain one day's storage for a chest. Our streets are filled with the wandering crowds of these passengers—clustering in our city—unacquainted with our climate—without money—without employment—without friends—many not speaking our language—and without any dependence for food, or raiment, or fireside—certain of nothing but hardship and a grave; and to be viewed, of course, with no very ardent sympathy by those native citizens whose immediate ancestors were the saviours of the country in its greatest peril. Besides, many of them scorn to hold opinions in harmony with the true spirit of our government. They drive our native workmen into exile, where they must war again with the savage of the wilderness—encounter again the tomahawk and scalping knife—and meet death beyond the regions of civilization and of home. It is apprehended they will bring disease among us; and if they have it not with them on arrival, they may generate a plague by collecting in crowds within small tenements and foul hovels. What is to become of them ? is a question of serious import. Our whole almshouse department is so full that no more can be received there without manifest hazard to the health of every inmate. Petitions signed by hundreds, asking for work, are presented in vain. Private associations for relief are almost wholly without funds. Thousands must therefore wander to and fro on the face of the earth filling every part of our once happy land with squalid poverty and with profligacy."—"By chapter 50, section 16, of the laws and ordinances of the city of New York, it is enacted, that in all cases where the Mayor shall deem it expedient to commute for alien passengers arriving at this port, instead of requiring indemnity bonds, he is authorized to receive such sum, in lieu of such bonds, as he shall deem adequate, not less than one dollar and not more than ten dollars, for each passenger. I deem it my duty to inform the common council, that it is my intention, hereafter, in all cases where it would not be unreasonable, to require and demand ten dollars for such commutation, from each alien passenger. And on advising with the commissioners of the almshouse as to this intention, I am authorized to say that they approve and unite with me in it; and I am bound to believe that it will receive the sanction of the public. Our city should not, whenever it can be avoided, receive more persons likely to become chargeable. It will be a herculean task to employ and take care of those who are already within our jurisdiction. Our funds appropriated for charitable purposes promise no overplus. Provisions, fuel, and clothing for the almshouse, are still very expensive. Laborers are not sought after, and while we pity the griefs and sorrows of all our fellow-creatures, we cannot deny that a preference, in the distribution of charities, as well as place and employment, is due to the descendants of the soldiers of the revolution, and to the heroes and sufferers of the second war of independence. It was asked by the fathers of American liberty. It has been promised to their sons, it cannot be conceded to aliens without great indignity to our native and adopted citizens; and if foreign paupers and vagrants come here for political purposes, it is proof irresistible that our naturalization laws ought to be immediately revised, and the term of residence greatly extended to qualify them to vote or hold office. Many are, I admit, orderly, well-disposed men, but many of them are of the opposite character. It is believed the action of the common council in the premises is particularly desirable. Our citizens had no serious turn-outs, no riotous parades, no conspiracies against the business and families of quiet, industrious and honest American operatives, until after officious interference by mischievous strangers, and it is melancholy to observe, that in the mad career of some of

these foreigners to destroy our happy system, they have lately recommended to a large meeting of our citizens that they should carry with them deadly weapons of various kinds, to all our future public assemblages. These wild strangers should learn that to do so, is not peaceably to assemble, as provided by the Constitution. Indeed a reason for taking the proper measures to diminish the number of arrivals, is drawn from the fact, that, in addition to the great and grievous expense they would add to the city, should they continue to be numerously thrown upon us, the Common Council will be called upon to provide an armed and a mounted police for both day and night time. Peace cannot be otherwise expected. Many of them come from places where nothing less secures tranquillity.

"AARON CLARK."

A committee of the Common Council made the following report:

"The committee on laws, to whom was referred the message of his honor the Mayor, relative to the quarantine laws and alien passengers beg leave to report in part—That its members have felt a deep interest in the very important matters which the Mayor has so promptly, in the discharge of his official functions, brought before the notice of this board; that upon a proper and discreet settlement of the interesting questions submitted in the communication, depend the peace, prosperity, and good order of this city. The immense numbers of persons arriving at this port, fleeing from the poverty, starvation and oppression of Europe, are calculated, certainly, not only to excite our sympathy for these unfortunate beings, but to create a well founded alarm, as to the results upon our municipal prosperity, as well as the character and morality of our population. The greater number of these immigrants (for there are those who, devoted to agricultural pursuits, and bringing with them some little property and a good reputation, are calculated to add to the resources of the commonwealth), are absolutely penniless and despairing with the accumulated filth, which long confinement on shipboard and an habitual want of cleanliness produce; they almost immediately on their arrival, roam the streets, a band of houseless mendicants, or apply to your alms-houses for succor. Crime succeeds destitution. Your prisons are filled—your hospitals are crowded with them, and your public treasure is spent upon those who never contributed a cent to the general welfare. It is just—it is in accordance with the best feelings of the human heart to commiserate the sufferings of humanity however degraded; but in the opinion of your committee, this city owes a paramount duty to itself and the country of which it is the general emporium. She is bound by wise and efficient laws to prevent the jails and work-houses of Europe, from pouring out on our shores their felons and paupers; to prohibit her from introducing here those whom she is bound by every consideration of justice to support; to prohibit her from disgorging on our people, a population with principles calculated to lower the tone of morals and disorganize the fame of our republican institutions. During the last year 60,541 passengers arrived at this port. The number has greatly increased this season, the average being very nearly 2,000 a week. The alms-house is full, containing, at this moment, 3,074, of which three-fourths are foreigners. In fact, *our public charities are principally for the benefit of these foreigners;* for of 1,200 persons admitted into the hospital at Bellevue, 982 were aliens. The expense of the alms-house establishment and its dependencies, last year, amounted to $205,506. 63. Your committee, therefore, recommend the passage of the following resolutions:

"*Resolved*—That it is the opinion of this board, that the Mayor may be requested to enter into a correspondence with Executives of the States of

New York and New Jersey, and such other persons as to him may seem proper, touching the enforcement of the health laws and passenger act.

"*Resolved*—That this board approve the decision of his honor the Mayor, in raising the amount of commutation money hereafter paid by foreign passengers.

"M. C. PATTERSON, *Chairman.*.
"D. RANDELL."

So much for native Americans. New York and Massachusetts passed laws to discourage emigration by imposing a tax upon passengers. In 1798, during Adams' administration, the Federal party amended the laws on naturalization which required a residence of *fourteen* years as a condition to be admitted to citizenship. So much for the "*blue lights.*"—Thomas Jefferson, in his message to Congress, December, 1801, recommended a change in the naturalization laws:—"I cannot omit recommending a revisal of the laws on the subject of naturalization. Considering the ordinary chances of human life, a denial of citizenship under a residence of fourteen years, is a denial to a great proportion of those who ask it, and controls a policy pursued from their first settlement, by many of those states and still believed of consequence to their prosperity. And shall we refuse to the unhappy fugitives from distress, that hospitality which the savages of the wildernes extended to our fathers on arriving in this land ? Shall oppressed humanity find no asylum on this globe?" So much for Jefferson, the father of democracy, in America ! Annals of Congress, 1801-2, p. 16. An act of congress was passed at the session of 1801-2, admitting to citizenship foreigners after a residence of five years, which is still the law. Annals of Congress of 1801-2, pages 464, 986-88-93, 1132-33-55-57. In 1844, a number of petitions and memorials were presented in both houses of Congress, praying for a change in the naturalization laws requiring that all foreigners should reside twenty-one years in the country before they could be admitted to citizenship. Thomas H. Benton and the democratic party opposed this measure. On the 7th of June, 1844, William S. Archer, of Virginia, spoke on the subject, thus:

"This was a subject which he was sorry to say, had not yet sufficiently attracted the attention of the people of the United States. There was, he thought, a growing combination of circumstances, which furnished ample ground for the conclusion, that the great mass of uneducated foreigners, wholly ignorant of the nature and value of our institutions, annually pouring into our country, could not, within the short period of five years, fixed by the present law, become fit to exercise, with a due sense of their value and responsibility, the rights and privileges of native born citizens." For a *debate* on this subject by Archer, Buchanan, Berrien, and Allen—see Congressional Globe 1843-44, p. 658. On the 31st day of May, 1844, John Quincy Adams presented petitions praying that the "naturalization laws may be changed so as to require a residence of twenty-one years for citizenship."

Mr. Adams moved that the petition be referred to the judiciary committee. Mr. Hammett moved that it be laid upon the table. Mr. Murphy ordered the yeas and nays which resulted as follows:

Yeas—Messrs. Anderson, Arrington, Ashe, Atkinson, Barringer, Benton, Bidlack, Boyd, Brengle, Brinkerhoff, Brodhead, Milton Brown, William J. Brown, Jeremiah Brown, Burke, Caldwell, Sheperd Cary, Carroll Reuben Chapman, Augustus A. Chapman, Clinch Clinton, Coles, Cross, Cullom, Dana, Daniel, Garrett Davis, Richard D. Davis, John W. Davis, Deal, Delet, Dickey, Dillingham, Dromgoole, Dunlap, Ellis, Farlee, Ficklin, Foot,

Foster, French, Goggin, Willis Green, Byram Green, Grider, Hale, Hamlin, Hammett, Hardin, Harper, Henly, Herrick, Hopkins, Houston, Hubard, Hubbell, Hughes, Hungerford, Washington Hunt, James B. Hunt, Charles J. Ingerson, Irvin, Jenks, Cave Johnson, Perly B. Johnson, George W. Jones, Andrew Kennedy, John P. Kennedy, Kirkpatrick, Labrance, Leonard, Lucas, Lumpkin, Maclay, McClelland, McClernand, McConnell, Mc Dowell, McKay, Mosley, Murphy, Ness, Newton, Norris, Owen, Parmenter, Payne, Petit, Peyton, Purdy, Rathbun, Charles M. Reed, David S. Reid, Reding, Relge, Rhett, Ritter, Russell, St. John, Sample, Saunders, Schenck, Senter, Thomas H. Seymour, David L. Seymour, Simons, Slidell, Albert Smith, Thomas Smith, Robert Smith, Steenrod, John Stewart, Stone, Strong, Summer, Sykes, Thomason, Thompson, Tibbetts, Tilden, Tyler, Weller, Wentworth, Wetherard, White, Williams, Woodward, Joseph A. Wright, and Yost—128. *Nays*—Messrs. Abbot, Adams, Causin, Clingman, Collamer, Cranston, Deberry, Giddings, Grinnel, Hudson, Jos. R. Ingersoll, Daniel P. King, McIlvane, Marsh, Morse, Pevnit, Elisha R. Potter, Pratt, Rodney, Rogers, Caleb B. Smith, Spence, Vance, Vinton, Winthrop—26. See further on the subject from the Congressional Globe, 1844-45, pp. 64, 150, and the Appendix Congressional Globe, 1844-45, p. 130. And Smith *v.* Turner and Norris *v.* City Boston. In the case of the Norris *v.* city of Boston, held by the court that: "there is nothing repugnant to the Constitution or law, of the United States in the third section of statute 1837, c. 238, which prohibits the landing of alien passengers who arrive in any vessel at any port or harbor in this state, until the master, owner, consignee or agent of the vessel, shall pay to the regularly appointed boarding officer the sum of two dollars for each passenger, to be appropriated for the support of foreign paupers." 4 Metcalf, p. 282. At the session of Congress 1837-38, the following was offered as an amendment 'to the pre emption law of May 29, 1830, with the object of prohibiting aliens from enjoying the benefit of the pre-emption law:

"That the right of pre-emption granted by this act, or the act hereby revised, shall not accrue to any other person than those who were, on the first day of December, 1837, citizens of the United States; and such citizenship shall in all cases be established by legal and competent testimony, to the satisfaction of the register and receiver of the land district in which the lands may lie, prior to any entry thereof, by virtue of the provisions of this act."

This was a Whig measure. The following is from Thomas H. Benton, on the subject:

"No law had yet excluded aliens from the acquisition of a pre-emption right, and he was entirely opposed to commencing a system of legislation which was to affect the property rights of the aliens who came to our country, to make it their home. Political rights rested on different basis."

Mr. Merrick said:

"I desire, Mr. President, to make a single remark in reply to the honorable senator from Pennsylvania, (Mr. Buchanan.) That Senator, in announcing briefly his opposition to the amendment before the senate, remarked that there seemed to be an extraordinary spirit of opposition to foreigners, manifesting itself in the country. I think on the contrary, there is a morbid affection manifested here and elsewhere for foreigners and aliens."

Henry Clay spoke as follows:

"He wished the senate would go for the interest of the whole Union, as a people, and not so exclusively for the New States. This domain was the public property — the property of the whole people of the United States; and he thanked the senator from Maryland for introducing a proposition for conferring the bounty of the government to our own race, instead of holding out a general invitation to all the paupers of all the European governments to come here, and compete with our own honest poor."

Mr. Clay spoke in reply to Mr. Buchanan thus:

"The honorable senator from Pennsylvania has alluded eulogistically to foreigners. Does he mean to compare the De Kalbs, the Steubens, the La Fayettes, the Pulaskis, with the hordes of foreign paupers that are constantly flooding our shores. There were other foreigners who mingled in our revolutionary struggle, but on the other side, the Hessians."—Mr. Buchanan in reply to Clay, said, "He had observed with regret, that attempts were now extensively making throughout the country, to excite what was called a native American feeling against those who had come from a foreign land to participate in the blessings of our free constitution. Such a feeling was unjust—it was ungrateful. In the darkest days of the revolution, who had assisted us in fighting our battles, and achieving our independence? Foreigners, yes, sir, foreigners. Was it not a fact known to the world, that the immigrants from the Emerald Isle—the land of brave hearts and strong arms had shed their blood freely in the cause of our liberty and independence. Any foreigner from any country under the sun, who, after landing with his family on our Atlantic coast, will make his long and weary way into the forests and prairies of the Mississippi, and there, by patient toil, establish a settlement upon the public lands, whilst he thus manifests his attachment to our institutions, shows that he is worthy of becoming an American citizen. He furnishes us by his conduct, the surest pledge that he will become a citizen the moment that the laws of the country permit. In the meantime, so far as my vote is concerned, he shall continue to stand upon the same footing with citizens, and have his quarter section of land at a minimum price." Mr. Clay subsequently spoke on the subject, thus: "What, he asked, had they seen? A proposition was made by an honorable senator from Maryland, (Mr. Merrick,) to limit the preëmptions to citizens of the United States, native and naturalized; rejected. And could any body say, after that naked vote of the senate, that it had not become the permanent policy of the country to go on inviting all the hordes of Europe to come over and partake of this bounty, derived from our ancestors, and which we should preserve for our posterity?"—Appendix Cong. Globe 1837-38, pp. 128 to 189. The following political creed is from the Boston American Crusader (Native American): 1. Repeal of all naturalization laws. 2. None but Americans for office. 3. A pure American common school system. 4. War to the hilt on Romanism. 5. Opposition, first and last, to the formation of military companies composed of foreigners. 6. The advocacy of a sound, healthy, and safe nationality. 7. Hostility to all papal influences, in whatever form, and whatever name. 8. American institutions and American sentiment. 9. More stringent and effective immigration laws. 10. The amplest protection to Protestant interests. 11. The doctrines of the revered Washington and his compatriots. 12. The sending back of all foreign paupers landed on our shores. 13. The formation of societies to protect all American interests. 14. Eternal enmity to all who attempt to carry out the principles of a foreign or state church. 15. Our country, our whole country, and nothing but our country. 16. And finally, American laws and American legislation; and death to all foreign influences, whether in high places or low!" In consequence of the immense immigration to the United States the following appeared in the public prints and in pamphlets. It went the rounds of the press, as a reason for discouraging foreign influence and foreign immigration: "Because any body and every body may come without let or hinderance, the rogues and vagabonds from London, Paris, Amsterdam, Vienna, Naples,. Hamburg, Berlin, Rome, Genoa, Leghorn, Geneva, etc., may come and do come. The outpourings of alms and work-houses, and prisons and penitentiaries, may come and do come. Monarchies, oligarchies and aristocracies may and do reduce millions of people to poverty and beggary, and compel the most valueless to seek for shelter and a home in the United States of America, and they do so. And what are the consequences? The consequences are that about 400,000 souls from Europe, chiefly Germans, Irish and Dutch are annually arriving in this country and making it their permanent abode. That a vast number of these immigrants come without money, occupation, friends or business. "That go where you will in the United States, you find nearly all the dens of iniquity, taverns, grog shops, beer houses, gambling places," "are kept by foreigners; and that numerous objects of poverty and destitution are to be seen crawling along the streets in every direction. This unlimited and unrestricted admission of foreign immigrants, is a serious injury to the native laboring population socially, morally, religiously, and politically." "But there is an other consequence which is deserving of notice, and it is this: our manufacturers, iron makers, machinists, miners, agriculturists, railway, canal, and other contractors, private families, hotel keepers, and many others, have got into the way of expecting and seeking for cheap labor, through the various supplies of operatives, workmen, laborers, house help, and various kinds of workers, kept up by the indiscriminate and unrestrained admission of immigrants." So much for Native American love for foreigners! The cry, in those days: "America for the Americans."

The following is from a speech from James Cooper of Pennsylvania, in the senate of the United States, January 25, 1855:

"I desire to advert briefly to an other mischief not wholly, but nevertheless, to some extent, the result of admitting into the country the idle and turbulent spirits sent hither in order to relieve their own governments of their dangerous presence. I refer, Mr. President, to the practice now prevalent in the larger cities, of organizing volunteer companies and battalions composed wholly of foreigners, bearing foreign names, wearing foreign uniforms, and parading under foreign colors. In New York, Boston, and elsewhere, you hear of German Jägers, French Chasseurs, Irish Greens, Swiss Guards, &c. I am informed that in the first named city there is a brigade composed entirely of Irishmen, called the Irish brigade. Now, sir, this is all wrong, and would not be tolerated by any other government on the face of the earth." New Hampshire Legislature in Nov. 24, 1798, petitioned Congress to "exclude from a seat in either branch of Congress, any person who shall not have been actually naturalized at the time of making this amendment, and have been a citizen fourteen years at least at the time of his election."

Daniel Webster, in 1844, in a speech before a Whig Meeting in Faneuil Hall, Boston, spoke as follows:--"The result of the recent elections, in several states, has impressed my mind with one deep and strong conviction; that is, that there is an imperative necessity for reforming the naturalization laws of the United States." "But it is not unreasonable that the elective franchise should not be exercised by a person of a foreign birth, until after such length of residence among us, as that he may be supposed to have become, in some good measure, acquainted with our constitution and laws, our social institutions, and the general interest of the country; and to have become an American in feeling, principle, character, and sympathy, as well as by having established his domicile amongst us." "Those already naturalized have, of course, their rights secured: but I can conceive no reasonable objection to the different provisions in regard to future cases." "I avow it, therefore, as my opinion, that it is the duty of us all to endeavor to bring about an efficient reformation of the naturalization laws of the United States."—Nile's Register, vol. 67, p. 172.

So much for the hostility to foreigners by the Federalists, Whigs and Know-Nothings. Foreigners who have held honorable offices from United States senator to municipal offices would be excluded therefrom but for the democratic party!—It is provided by an act of July 17, 1862, that any Alien of the age of twenty-one years and upwards who enlisted in the armies of the United States during the recent rebellion and honorably discharged from the service of the United States, may be admitted to citizenship on proof of one year's residence, upon his petition, without any proof of his declaration to become a citizen of the United States.—Act July 17, 1862.—Brightly's Dig, vol. 2, p. 5.

The reader will understand the present laws on naturalization from the following record of naturalization as adopted by several states, to wit:

"UNITED STATES OF AMERICA.
"State of ——— county of ——— ss.

"Be it remembered that on the —— of March in the year of our Lord one thousand eight hundred and ——, personally appeared before me the Hon. A. G. C. judge of the District court of the county of —— in the eighth Judicial District, and state aforesaid, the same being a court of record having and exercising common law jurisdiction, a seal, and a clerk, and sitting judicially for the despatch of business, at the Court-House in L ——— in the county aforesaid, D. D. an alien born, free, white, male person, above the age of twenty-one years, and applied to the said court, to be admitted to become a naturalized citizen of the United States of America, pursuant to the several acts of Congress heretofore passed on that subject, entitled "An act to establish a uniform rule of naturalization, and to repeal the acts heretofore passed on that subject, approved the 14th day of April, 1802; an act entitled an act in addition to an act entitled an act to establish a uniform rule of naturalization and to repeal the acts heretofore passed on that subject, approved on the 26th day of March, 1804, an act entitled an act supplementary to the acts heretofore passed on the subject, of a uniform rule of naturalization, passed the 30th day of July, 1813; the act relative to evidence in cases of naturalization, passed the 22d day of March, 1816; an act in further addition to an act to establish a uniform rule of naturalization, and to repeal the acts heretofore passed on that subject, passed May 26th, 1824; and the said ——— having thereupon produced to the court record testimony, showing that he has heretofore reported himself and filed his declaration of his intention to become a citizen of the United States, according to the provisions of the said several Acts of Congress, and the court being satisfied as well from the oath of the said D. D. as from the testimony of D. C. and E. F. who are known to be citizens of the United States, that the said D. D. has resided within the limits, and under the jurisdiction of the United States, for at least five years last-past, and at least one year last-past within the state of ———; and that during the whole of that time he has behaved himself as a man of good moral character, attached to the principles contained in the constitution of the United States, and well disposed to the good order, well-being and happiness of the same, and two years and upwards having elapsed since the said D. D. reported himself, and filed his declaration of his intention as aforesaid, It was ordered, that the said D. D. be permitted to take the oath to support the constitution of the United States, and the usual oath whereby he renounced all allegiauce and fidelity to every foreign prince, potentate, state and sovereignty whatever, and more particularly to the ———— of ————, whereof he was heretofore a subject, which said oath, having been administered to the said D. D. by the clerk of said court, it was ordered by the court that the said D. D. be admitted to all and singular the rights, privileges and immunities of a naturalized citizen of the United States, and that the same be certified by the clerk of this court under the seal of said court accordingly.

"In Testimony whereof, the seal of said court is hereto affixed at the clerk's office in L.———— this ———— day of ————A. D. 1875, and of the Independence of the United States, the Ninety ————.

"By order of the Court,

(Attest)   "J. P. H.

[L. S.]   "Clerk of the District Court of L————."

"Under the acts of Congress, children born abroad, not only of citizens by birth, but also of naturalized citizens of the United States, are citizens of the United States. Saspotas v. De la Motta. 10 Richardson Eq. R. 38. —Brightly's Dig. 5. "Allegiance of a naturalized citizen cannot be transferred to another government, by a treaty ceding the territory in which he is domiciled, as in case of a natural born citizen; by such cession he is released from his statutory allegiance and remitted to his original status." Tobin v. Walkingham, 1. McAllister 186. "An alien woman, married to an alien, in a foreign country, and continuing to reside there until her husband's death, does not become a citizen, under the act of 10 February 1855, so as to entitle her to dower, by reasons of her husband's naturalization subsequent to their marriage. Burton v. Burton. 12 American L. R. 425. By the laws of Minnesota all married women are entitled to dower, whether they are citizens or foreigners. Mr. Mahony, an Irishman, ex-editor of the Dubuque Herald and the present editor of the Dubuque Telegraph, when a menber of the Iowa legislature had a similar act passed by the Iowa legislature. "Under the act of 14 April 1802, the residence of an applicant for naturalization within the State, need not have been for the year next preceeding his application. Cummings Petition. 41 New Hamp. 270. "Wilful false swearing, by a person giving material testimony in naturalization proceeding, before a state court, is an offence against the laws of the United States, and punishable only in the Federal Courts. People v. Sweetman 3 Parker C. R. 358 contra Rump v. Commonwealth 6 Casey, 475. "The state courts, in entertaining jurisdiction of cases of naturalization, act exclusively under the laws of the United States, and are to be deemed, quoad hoc, courts of the United States. People v. Sweetman 3 Parker C. R. 358. The inhabitants of a territory ceded to the United States, by treaty, become citizens of the United States, without naturalization under the acts of Congress." Harrold's Case, 2 Penn. L. J. 119. In 1868, the courts of Pennsylvania disfranchised foreign-born naturalized citizens. Foreign-born naturalized citizens, in 1868 were disfranchised in New Orleans, who were naturalized in the district courts. World Almanac 1869, p. 45. Session of

Congress 1868-9, a bill was introduced in Congress providing, that all who had been naturalized since 1867, should give up their naturalization papers and take other papers out of the courts of the United States.

CHAPTER VII.—SOLDIERS' BOUNTY—MILITARY LAND WAR-RANTS—PRE-EMPTION LAW—LAND GRANTS—RAILROAD LANDS—HOMESTEAD LANDS—DECLARATION OF INDE-PENDENCE.

The State Governments and the Federal Government granted bounty lands to the soldiers who fought in the war of the revolution.—Acts of congress 1779 and 1780 gave to each captain in the army of the revolution 400 acres of land. Act March 2, 1807, donated 640 acres of land to each actual settler who occupied them prior to July 1, 1796.—Opinions Attys. Gen. vol. 2. p. 1338. Act of Sept. 28, 1850, sec. 1, page 520, 9 statutes at large, gives land warrants to each of the surviving, their widow or minor children of deceased commissioned and non-commissioned officers, musicians or privates whether of regulars, volunteers, rangers, or militia, who performed military service in any regiment, company or the detachment in the service of the United States in the war with Great Britain, declared by the United States, on the 18th day of June, 1812, or in any of the Indian wars since 1790, and each of the commissioned officers who was employed in the military service of the United States in the late war with Mexico, shall be entitled to lands as follows: Those who engaged to serve twelve months or during the war, and actually served nine months, shall receive one hundred and sixty acres, and these who engaged to serve six months, and actually served four months, shall receive eighty acres, and those who engaged to serve for any or an indefinite period, and actually served one month, shall receive forty acres." Brightly's Dig. 96. Those who received land warrants for military services in the Mexican War should thank Gen. James Shields, an Irishman, who was then a senator from Illinois, and who got the bill passed. He was a true friend of the soldiers, and an honor to Ireland. The eighth section of the act of March 3, 1855, "shall be construed as embracing officers, mariners, seamen and other persons engaged in the naval service of the United States during the revolutionary war." Brightly's Dig. 99. The Democratic party, in the days of Jefferson, Madison and Monroe had scruples about the constitutional powers of Congress to grant lands for internal improvements, but to leave the States donate lands for that purpose. Act 30 April, 1802, Congress appropriated one-twentieth part of the net proceeds of the lands within the said state (Ohio), sold by Congress to be applied in making public roads from the navigable waters emptying into the Atlantic and Ohio, such roads to be laid out under the authority of Congress with the consent of the several states through which the said road shall pass. Brightly's Dig. 708. This was in strict conformity with the Constitution. Congress, from time to time, has granted to the several states formed out of the public domain, a percentage of the net proceeds of. the sale of public lands, for public improvements. Lands have been granted for "county seats," state buildings, seminaries, university buildings. Act Sept. 4, 1841, gives to the States of Minnesota and other new states, lands for internal improvements. 5 Statutes at Large 455. Acts of Congress have given to certain states the swamp lands within the same.—Brightly's Dig. 492. Act Feb. 17, 1855, granted the right of way to the Pacific Telegraph Company.—Brightly's Dig. 862. See act March 12, 1860, which gives swamp lands to Minnesota and Oregon.—12 Statutes 3. Brightly's Dig. vol. 2, p. 291. Several acts of Congress had given the right of pre-emption to actual settlers, residing in the territories before their organization.—Brightly's Dig. 527, 2 Statutes at Large 229. By Act of March 26, 1804, lands were sold at public auction to the highest bidder, the purchaser had the privilege of paying by instalments. —Brightly's Dig. 478. By Act of April 24, 1820, the credit system was abolished, and it was provided that all lands should be first offered at public auction; if not then sold, to be subject to private sale at $1.25 per acre.—Brightly's Dig. 480. The price of lands before the passage of this act was two dollars per acre. Act May 18, 1796. Act March 3, 1803, recognized grants from Spain and England.—Brightly's Dig. 519. Congress granted five per cent of the proceeds of public lands for the building of canals.—Brightly's Dig. 640. Congress granted lands to the State of Mississippi for building the Brandon Railroad. This act passed Sept. 4, 1841.—5 Statutes 457. Act June 25, 1835, Congress granted to a railroad company ten acres of land at the junction of the St. Mark's and Waculla Rivers.—Opinions Attys. Gen. U. S. vol. 2, p. 13—Act of Sept. 27 1850, donates to each actual settler, in Oregon, one-half section of land, and one-quarter section of land was donated to each actual settler in New Mexico.—Brightly's Dig. 575. It was provided that settlers should reside on the land for four years. Act of Congress 1841 gives the right of pre-emption to actual settlers, on the public lands, who are citizens of the United States or who have declared their intentions to become such except those who own 320 acres of land, or who had once pre-empted, or who left his own land to make a pre-emption claim. No person shall pre-empt more than one hundred and sixty acres of land.—Brightly's Dig. 470. $2.50 shall be paid for lands within the limits of land grant railroads. All of the public lands of the United States which shall have been in market for ten years or upwards, prior to the time of application to enter the same under the provisions of this act, and still remaining unsold shall be subject to sale at the price of one dollar per acre; and all of the lands of the United States that shall have been in market for fifteen years or upwards as aforesaid, and still remaining unsold, shall be subject to sale at seventy-five cents per acre; and all of the lands of the United States that shall have been in market for twenty years or upwards as aforesaid, and still remaining unsold, shall be subject to sale at fifty cents per acre; and all of the lands of the United States that shall have been in market for twenty-five years and upwards as aforesaid, and still remaining unsold, shall be subject to sale at twenty-five cents per acre; and all lands of the United States that shall have been in market for thirty years or more, shall be subject to sale at twelve-and-a-half cents per acre." Act Aug. 4. 1854.— Statutes, 10, p. 574. In 1837, public lands were granted to a railroad company in Louisiana, for building a depot. 5 Statutes at Large p. 196. The right of way was granted through the public lands to Carrolton Railroad Company.—Ib. 197. Act June 18, 1838, granted lands to the territory of Wisconsin for constructing a canal. 5 Statutes 245, June 28, 1838, the right of way was granted to a railroad in Florida. 5 Statutes 253. In 1845, lands were granted to the State of Indiana to complete the Wabash and Erie canal to the Ohio River. 5 Statutes 731. So that up to this time, railroad companies were glad to get the right of way over the public lands and a small land grant for depots, etc. But recently they have obtained large land grants in the new states since the advent of the Republican party. The railroad grants have amounted to millions of acres. The whole number of acres would, if located in a body, exceed in extent the States of New York, New Jersey, Ohio, Delaware, Maryland, and Pennsylvania.

THE HOMESTEAD LAW, PASSED MAY 20, 1862.

"Any person who is the head of a family, or who has arrived at the age of twenty-one years, and is a citizen of the United States, or who shall have filed his declaration of intentions to become such, as required by the naturalization laws of the United States, and who has never borne arms against the United States government, or given aid and comfort to its enemies shall, from and after the 1st January, 1863, be entitled to enter one quarter section or a less quantity of unappropriated public lands, upon which said person may have filed a pre-emption claim, or which may, at the time the application is made, be subject to pre-emption at one dollar and twenty-five cents or less per acre; or eighty acres or less of such unappropriated lands, at two dollars and fifty cents per acre, to be located in a body, in conformity to the legal subdivisions of the public lands, and after the same shall have been surveyed; provided, that any person owning and residing on land may, under the provisions of this act, enter other land lying contiguous to his or her said land, which shall not, with the land so already owned and occupied, exceed, in the aggregate one hundred and sixty acres."

"The person applying for the benefit of this act, shall, upon application to the register of the land office in which he or she is about to make such entry, make affidavit before the said register or receiver, that he or she is the head of a family, or is twenty-one years or more of age, or shall have performed services in the army or navy of the United States, and that he has never borne arms against the government of the United States, or given aid or comfort to its enemies, and that such application is made for his or her exclusive use and benefit, and that said entry is made for the purpose of actual settlement and cultivation, and not either directly or indirectly for the use or benefit of any other person or persons whomsoever; and upon filing the said affidavit with the register or receiver, and on payment of ten dollars, he or she shall thereupon be permitted to enter the quantity of land specified; Provided, however, that no certificate shall be given or patent issued therefor, until the expiration of five years from the date of such duty; and if, at the expiration of such time, or at any time within five years thereafter, the person making such entry; or, if he be dead, his widow; or in case of her death, his heirs or devisee; or in case of a widow making such entry, her heirs or devisee, in case of her death; shall prove by two credible witnesses that he, she or they have resided upon or cultivated the same for the term of five years immediately succeeding the time of filing the affidavit aforesaid, and shall make affidavit that no part of said land has been alienated, and that he has borne true allegiance to the government of the United States; then, in such case, he, she, or they, if at that time a citizen of the United States, shall be entitled to a patent, as in other cases provided for by law; And provided further, that in case of the death of both father and mother, leaving an infant child, or children under twenty-one years of age, the right and fee shall issue to the benefit of said infant child or children; and the executor, administrators or guardian may, at any time within two years after the death of the surviving parent, and in accordance with the laws of the state in which such children for the time being have their domicile, sell said land for the benefit of said infants, but for no other purpose; and the purchaser shall acquire the absolute title by the purchase, and be entitled to a patent from the United States, on payment of the office fees and sum of money herein specified." No lands acquired under the provisions of this act shall in any event become liable to the satisfaction of any debt or debts contracted prior to the issuing of the patent therefor." "No individual shall be permitted to acquire title to more than one quarter section under the provision of this act." "Nothing in this act shall be construed as to prevent any person who has availed him or herself of the benefits of the first section of this act, from paying the minimum price, or the price to which the same may have been graduated, for the quantity of land so entered at any time before the expiration of the five years, and obtaining a patent therefor from the government, as in other cases provided by law, on making proof of settlement and cultivation as provided by existing laws granting preëmption rights." "Besides the ten dollars fee exacted by the said act, the homestead applicant shall hereafter pay to the register and receiver each, as commission, at the time of entry, one per centum upon the cash price as fixed by law of the land applied for, and the like commissions when the claim is finally established, and the certificate therefor issued as the basis of a patent."

"In any case hereafter in which the applicant for the benefit of the homestead and whose family or some member thereof is residing on the land which he desires to enter, and upon which a *bona fide* improvement and settlement have been made, is prevented by reason of distance, bodily infirmity or other good cause, from personal attendance at the district land office, it shall and may be lawful for him to make the affidavit required by the original statute before the clerk of the court for the county in which the applicant is an actual resident, and transmit the same with the fee and commissions, to the register and receiver." "If at any time after the filing of the affidavit, as required in the second section of this act, and before the expiration of the five years aforesaid it shall be proven, after due notice to the settler, to the satisfaction of the register of the land office, that the person having filed such affidavit shall have actually changed his or her residence, or abandoned the said land for more than six months at any time, then and in that event the land so entered shall revert to the government." Brightly's Dig. 287-8-9. 42 Cong. 1871-2, the following law was passed for the benefit of soldiers and sailors:

Homesteads for Soldiers and Sailors.—Provides that every honorably discharged private soldier and officer who served in the army during the Rebellion for 90 days or more, including troops mustered into the Service by virtue of the third section of "an Act making appropriations for completing the defences of Washington," &c., approved Feby. 13, 1862, and every seaman, marine and officer who served in the navy or marine corps for 90 days during the rebellion shall, on compliance with the provisions of "an Act to secure homesteads to actual settlers on the public domain," be entitled to a homestead of 160, and shall be allowed six months after locating his homestead to commence his settlement and improvement. But no homestead settler can receive a patent for his land until he shall have resided upon and improved it for at least one year. In case of the death of any person who would be entitled to a homestead under the provisions of this Act, his widow or children may avail of the benefits of the Act. Where a party at the date of his entry of a tract of land, or subsequently thereto, was actually enlisted and employed in the army or navy, his services are to be construed as a residence for the same time upon the tract so entered. Any soldier, sailor or marine, officer or other person coming within the provisions of this Act may enter upon his homestead by an agent if he so elect, provided said claimant in person shall, within the time prescribed, make his actual entry, improvements, etc."

Chap. 114.—*In Relation to Bounties.*—Provides that every volunteer, non-commissioned officer, private, musician and artificer who enlisted into the military service prior to July 22, 1861, under the proclamation of the President, of May, 3, 1861, and was actually mustered before Aug. 6, 1861, into any regiment, company, or battery, which was accepted by the War Department, shall be entitled to $100 bounty.

TREE PLANTING ON WESTERN PRAIRIES.

Chap. 55.—An act to amend the act entitled "An act to encourage the growth of timber on western prairies."—Be it enacted by the Senate and House of Representatives of the United States of America, in Congress assembled, That the act entitled "An act to encourage the growth of timber on western prairies," approved March third, eighteen hundred and seventy-three, be, and the same is hereby, amended so as to read as follows: That any person who is the head of a family or who has arrived at the age of twenty-one years, and is a citizen of the United States, or who shall have filed his declaration of intention to become such, as required by the naturalization laws of the United States, who shall plant, protect, and keep in a healthy, growing condition for eight years, forty acres of timber, the trees thereon not being more than twelve feet apart each way, on any quarter-section of any of the public lands of the United States, or twenty acres on any legal subdivision of eighty acres, or ten acres on any legal subdivision of forty acres, or one-fourth part of any fractional subdivision of land less than forty acres, shall be entitled to a patent for the whole of said quarter-section, or of such legal subdivision of eighty or forty acres, or fractional subdivision of less than forty acres, as the case may be, at the expiration of said eight years, on making proof of such fact by not less than two credible witnesses: *Provided,* That not more than one-quarter of any section shall be thus granted, and that no person shall make more than one entry under the provisions of this act, unless fractional subdivisions of less than forty acres are entered· which, in the aggregate, shall not exceed one quarter-section.

THE DECLARATION OF INDEPENDENCE.

IN CONGRESS, JULY 4, 1776.

THE UNANIMOUS DECLARATION OF THE THIRTEEN UNITED STATES OF AMERICA.

WHEN, in the course of human events, it becomes necessary for one people to dissolve the political bands which have connected them with another, and to assume, among the powers of the earth, the separate and equal station to which the laws of nature and of nature's God entitle them, a decent respect to the opinions of mankind requires that they should declare the causes which impel them to the separation.

We hold these truths to be self-evident: that all men are created equal that they are endowed, by their Creator, with certain unalienable rights that among these are life, liberty, and the pursuit of happiness. That to secure these rights, governments are instituted among men, deriving their just powers from the consent of the governed; that whenever any form of government becomes destructive of these ends, it is the right of the people to alter or to abolish it, and to institute a new government, laying its foundation on such principles, and organizing its powers in such form, as to them shall seem most likely to effect their safety and happiness. Prudence, indeed, will dictate, that governments, long established, should not be changed for light and transient causes; and accordingly all experience hath shown, that mankind are more disposed to suffer, while evils are sufferable, than to right themselves by abolishing the forms to which they are accustomed. But when a long train of abuses and usurpations, pursuing invariably the same object, evinces a design to reduce them under absolute despotism, it is their right, it is their duty, to throw off such government, and to provide new guards for their future security. Such has been the patient sufferance of these colonies; and such is now the necessity which constrains them to alter their former systems of government. The history of the present King of Great Britain is a history of repeated injuries and usurpations, all having in direct object the establishment of an absolute tyranny over these states. To prove this, let facts be submitted to a candid world.

He has refused his assent to laws the most wholesome and necessary for the public good.

He has forbidden his governors to pass laws of immediate and pressing importance, unless suspended in their operation till his assent should be obtained; and when so suspended, he has utterly neglected to attend to them.

He has refused to pass other laws for the accommodation of large districts of people, unless those people would relinquish the right of representation in the legislature; a right inestimable to them, and formidable to tyrants only. He has called together legislative bodies at places unusual, uncomfortable, and distant from the depository of their public records, for the sole purpose of fatiguing them into compliance with his measures.

He has dissolved representative houses repeatedly, for opposing, with manly firmness, his invasions on the rights of the people.

He has refused for a long time, after such dissolutions, to cause others to be elected; whereby the legislative powers, incapable of annihilation, have returned to the people at large for their exercise; the state remaining, in the mean time, exposed to all the dangers of invasion from without, and convulsions within.

He has endeavored to prevent the population of these states; for that purpose obstructing the laws for naturalization of foreigners; refusing to pass others to encourage their migrations hither, and raising the conditions of new appropriations of lands.

He has obstructed the administration of justice, by refusing his assent to laws for establishing judiciary powers.

He has made judges dependent on his will alone, for the tenure of their offices, and the amount and payment of their salaries.

He has erected a multitude of new offices, and sent hither swarms of officers, to harass our people, and eat out their substance.

He has kept among us, in times of peace, standing armies, without the consent of our legislatures.

He has affected to render the military independent of, and superior to, the civil power.

He has combined with others to subject us to a jurisdiction foreign to our constitution, and unacknowledged by our laws; giving his assent to their acts of pretended legislation:

For quartering large bodies of armed troops among us;

For protecting them, by a mock trial, from punishment for any murders which they should commit on the inhabitants of these states;

For cutting off our trade with all parts of the world;

For imposing taxes on us without our consent;

For depriving us, in many cases, of the benefits of trial by jury;

For transporting us beyond seas to be tried for pretended offences;

For abolishing the free system of English laws in a neighboring province, establishing therein an arbitrary government, and enlarging its boundaries, so as to render it at once an example and fit instrument for introducing the same absolute rule into these colonies;

For taking away our charters, abolishing our most valuable laws, and altering fundamentally the forms of our governments;

For suspending our own legislatures, and declaring themselves invested with power to legislate for us in all cases whatsoever.

He has abdicated government here, by declaring us out of his protection, and waging war against us.

He has plundered our seas, ravaged our coasts, burnt our towns, and destroyed the lives of our people.

He is at this time transporting large armies of foreign mercenaries to complete the works of death, desolation, and tyranny, already begun with circumstances of cruelty and perfidy, scarcely paralleled in the most barbarous ages, and totally unworthy the head of a civilized nation.

He has constrained our fellow-citizens, taken captive on the high seas, to bear arms against their country, to become the executioners of their friends and brethren, or to fall themselves by their hands.

He has excited domestic insurrections amongst us, and has endeavored to bring on the inhabitants of our frontiers the merciless Indian savages, whose known rule of warfare is an undistinguished destruction of all ages, sexes, and conditions.

In every stage of these oppressions we have petitioned for redress in the most humble terms. Our repeated petitions have been answered only by repeated injury. A prince, whose character is thus marked by every act which may define a tyrant, is unfit to be the ruler of a free people.

Nor have we been wanting in attentions to our British brethren. We have warned them, from time to time, of attempts by their legislature to extend an unwarrantable jurisdiction over us. We have reminded them of the circumstances of our emigration and settlement here. We have appealed to their native justice and magnanimity, and we have conjured them by the ties of our common kindred to disavow these usurpations, which would inevitably interrupt our connections and correspondence. They too have been deaf to the voice of justice and of consanguinity. We must, therefore, acquiesce in the necessity which denounces our separation, and hold them, as we hold the rest of mankind, enemies in war, in peace friends.

We, therefore, the representatives of the UNITED STATES OF AMERICA, in general congress assembled, appealing to the Supreme Judge of the world for the rectitude of our intentions, do, in the name, and by authority of the good people of these colonies, solemnly publish and declare that these United Colonies are, and of right ought to be, FREE and INDEPENDENT STATES; that they are absolved from all allegiance to the British crown, and that all political connection between them and the state of Great Britain is, and ought to be, totally dissolved; and that, as FREE AND INDEPENDENT STATES, they have full power to levy war, conclude peace, contract alliances, establish commerce, and to do all other acts and things which INDEPENDENT STATES may of right do. And for the support of this declaration, with a firm reliance on the protection of DIVINE PROVIDENCE, we mutually pledge to each other our lives, our fortunes, and our sacred honor.

JOHN HANCOCK,
President, and Delegate from Massachusetts Bay.

New Hampshire—Josiah Bartlett, William Whipple, Matthew Thornton.
Massachusetts Bay—Samuel Adams, John Adams, Robert Treat Paine, Elbridge Gerry.
Rhode Island, &c.—Stephen Hopkins, William Ellery.
Connecticut.—Roger Sherman, Samuel Huntington, William Williams, Oliver Wolcott.
New York.—William Floyd, Philip Livingston, Francis Lewis, Lewis Morris.
New Jersey.—Richard Stockton, John Witherspoon, Francis Hopkinson, John Hart, Abraham Clark.
Pennsylvania.—Robert Morris, Benjamin Rush, Benjamin Franklin, John Morton, George Clymer, James Smith, George Taylor, James Wilson, George Ross.
Delaware.—Cæsar Rodney, George Read, Thomas M'Kean.
Maryland.—Samuel Chase, William Paca, Thomas Stone, Charles Carroll of Carrollton.
Virginia.—George Wythe, Richard Henry Lee, Thomas Jefferson, Benjamin Harrison, Thomas Nelson, Jun., Francis Lightfoot Lee, Carter Braxton.
North Carolina.—William Hooper, Joseph Hewes, John Penn.
South Carolina.—Edward Rutledge, Thomas Hayward, Jun., Thomas Lynch, Jun., Arthur Middleton.
Georgia.—Button Gwinnett, Lyman Hall, George Walton.

The following is from eminent authorities on the right of revolution; "But when the injustices are manifest and atrocious, when a prince, without any apparent reason, attempts to deprive us of life, or of those things the loss of which would render life irksome, who can dispute our rights to resist him? Self-preservation is not only a natural right, but an obligation imposed by nature, and no man can entirely and absolutely renounce it. And though he might give it up, can he be considered as having done it by his political engagements, since he entered into society only to establish his own safety upon a more solid basis? The welfare of society does not require such a sacrifice; and, as Barbeyrac well observes in his notes on Grotius; 'If the public interest requires that those who obey should suffer some inconvenience, it is no less for the public interest that those who command should be afraid of driving their patience to the utmost extremity. The prince who violates all laws, who no longer observes any measures, and who would in his transport of fury take away the life of an innocent person, divests himself of his character, and is no longer to be considered in any other light than that of an unjust and outrageous enemy, against whom his people are allowed to defend themselves."—Vattel's Law of Nations, Book 1, Chap. 4, p. 22. "If the representatives of the people betray their constituents, there is then no resource left but in the exertion of that original right of self-defence, which is paramount to all positive forms of government; which against the usurpation of the national rulers, may be exerted with an infinitely better prospect of success than against those of the rulers of an individual state."—Federalist, No. 29, p. 146.

"This memorable declaration, in imitation of that published by the Netherlands on a similar occasion, recapitulated the oppressions of the British King, asserted it to be the natural right of every people to withdraw from tyranny, and, with the dignity and the fortitude of conscious rectitude, it contained a solemn appeal to mankind, in vindication of the necessity of the measure. By this declaration, made in the name, and by the authority of the people, the colonies were absolved from all allegiance to the British crown and all political connection between them and Great Britain was totally dissolved. The principle of self-preservation, and the right of every community to freedom and happiness, gave sanction to this separation. When the government established over any people becomes incompetent to fulfil its purpose, or destructive to the essential ends for which it was instituted, it is the right of that people, founded on the law of nature and the reason of mankind, and supported by the soundest authority, and some very illustrious precedents, to throw off such government, and provide new guards for their future security."—Kent's Comm. vol. 1, pp. 208–9.

Webster on revolution:

"The inherent right of the people to reform their government, I do not deny; and they have another right, and that is, to resist unconstitutional laws, without overturning the government. I admit that there is an ultimate violent remedy, above the Constitution and in defiance of the Constitution, which may be resorted to when a revolution is to be justified."—Debate between Webster and Hayne.

Jackson on revolution:

"That a state, or any other great portion of the people, suffering under long and intolerable oppression, may have a natural right to appeal to the last resort, need not, on the present occasion, be denied."—Jackson's Nullification Proclamation. "If therefore any future prince should endeavor to subvert the Constitution by breaking the original contract between king and people, should violate the fundamental laws, and should withdraw himself out of the kingdom; we are now authorized to declare that this conjunction would amount to an abdication, and the throne would be thereby vacant." "In these cases" the learned author leaves "to future generations" to decide "whenever the necessity and safety of the whole people shall require it" (the right to resist the king or Executive or government), "the exertion of those inherent, though latent powers of society, which no climate, no time, no constitution, no contract, can ever destroy or diminish."—1 Blackstone's Comm. p. 245 (Marginal p.)

CHAPTER VIII. — CONTINENTAL CONGRESS — REVOLUTION AND INDEPENDENCE—CONSTITUTIONAL CONVENTION— FEDERALISTS.

The people of the colonies of New England, who left the Mother Country, in consequence of the oppression of the government and the established church, were jealous of their rights, civil and political. They wished to breathe the pure air of freedom in the wilds of America, and feared every encroachment of the despotic power of the British Crown. To avoid the encroachment of the British government the first Continental Congress was held, in 1634, composed of delegates from the four colonies of Massachusetts, Plymouth, New Haven and Connecticut, styled the "United Colonies of New England." This union lasted for forty years. The object of the union was to resist the tyranny of England, for annulling the charter of Massachusetts, in 1634; for Massachusetts had set up a system of church and state of her own, and had boldly refused to comply with the discipline of the Church of England. The British authorities had grave fears that the people of Massachusetts would separate from the mother country and form an independent government. A Congress met at New York, May 1, 1691, for the purpose of guarding the frontiers against the ravages of the Indians and French. Congresses educated the people to unite against the common enemy and to prepare them for self-government. A Congress composed of delegates from the New England states, New York, Pennsylvania and Maryland met at Albany, July 4th, 1754, when a plan of confederation was drawn up by Dr. Franklin, but was rejected by both England and America. In consequence of an attempt of Great Britain to tax the colonies, without their consent and without representation in making laws; and other odious, tyrannical and oppressive measures, the people of the colonies resolved to strike for freedom, and to rid themselves and posterity from the thraldom of British misrule and despotism. Finding that England was becoming more and more despotic, the brave people of the colonies raised the standard of freedom, and nobly avowed resistance to British rule and unjust and oppressive taxation ! The first Continental Congress of the colonies met at Philadelphia, at Carpenter's Hall, September 4th, 1774. There were in attendance delegates from New Hampshire, Massachusetts, Rhode Island, and Providence Plantations, Connecticut, New York, New Jersey, Pennsylvania, Delaware, Maryland, Virginia, North Carolina, and South Carolina. Georgia had no delegates. Each colony had an equal voice in the Congress, which appears from a resolution of September 6th, 1774 : "*Resolved*—That, in determining questions in this Congress, each colony or province shall have one vote; the Congress not being possessed of, or at present able to procure, materials for ascertaining the importance of each colony."—Madison Papers, 181. The first opposition to the authority of the congress came from Vermont. The authorities of Vermont resisted the authorities of New York, and seceded from that State, and set up an independent government. The Continental Congress, March 18th, 1780, called upon Vermont to submit to the authority of New York. On the 27th November, 1782, it was solemnly declared in congress that the traitorous intentions between the inhabitants of Vermont and the public enemy should be suppressed. The delegates from New Jersey were opposed to using force against the authorities of Vermont. But this was done under instructions from the Legislature of that State. Vermont had nullified a resolution of Congress of 1799, which called upon her to make restitution to those whom she had driven from their homes. — Madison papers, 8–9. It was also declared in Congress that the authorities of Vermont were perfidiously devoted to the British interest. The only state which stood by Vermont in her secession, nullification, and treasonable conduct, was Rhode Island, (which was interested in Vermont lands), and the state of New Jersey, which acted under instructions from her legislature. Thus, we find Rhode Island justifying treason, secession, and nullification for a mere consideration — for filthy lucre. Thus sacrificing liberty, union, and patriotism for self-interest.— Madison papers, p. 10. After the peace of 1783, the monarchy-men wrote to Washington intimating to him that the best and most desirable form of government for the colonies, was a monarchy, and that he was the most suitable and popular person for a king. But the noble patriot and father of his country looked upon such scheme with disdain and detestation! The Tories and monarchy-men thought to use the name and popularity of the Father of his country to establish monarchy in America—to entail on the colonies the fatal curse of domestic monarchy! This would be only exchanging a foreign for a domestic tyrant—foreign slavery for local and domestic slavery—this would be throwing away all the blessings of liberty! sacrificing the noble boon for which the heroes of 1776 fought and bled and conquered! Jefferson speaks thus, of the designs of the monarchy-men: "Delegates in different places had actually had consultations on the subject of seizing on the powers of a government, and establishing them by force, had correspondence with one another, and had sent a deputy to General Washington to solicit his co-operation. He refused to join them." "The final passage and adoption of the constitution completely defeated the views of the combination, and saved us from an attempt to establish a government over us by force."—Jefferson's Works, vol. 9, p. 188. The monarchy-men being thus foiled in their unholy attempt to establish a government by force and usurpation, the next plan was to form the society of "*Cincinnati*" with Alex. Hamilton as grand master: with the intention to incorporate monarchical and aristocratical principles on the new government. Jefferson wrote to Washington to have him use his influence in abolishing the "*Cincinnati*" society, which he partially effected; but the members refused to discontinue it during the lives of the members. They were the more unwilling to abolish the society, as Major La Infant had just returned from France with the eagles for the society, as well as letters of leave from the French King to the French soldiers in America, to accept of the order of the society. The monarchy-men, failing to incorporate the favorite principles of this secret society on the government, embarrassed the deliberations of the convention, called by the Middle States, so that nothing could be done. They wanted that the convention would break up without accomplishing anything — so that they would make their way from anarchy to monarchy. Madison seeing the designs of the monarchy-men, moved a resolution for calling a general convention at Philadelphia, which was adopted notwithstanding the strenuous opposition from the monarchy-men. The commissioners recommended that the States should send delegates to the Philadelphia convention to amend the old articles of confederation. The convention met at Philadelphia, May 14, 1787, with closed doors; members were not allowed to communicate the proceedings of the convention to the public. It was found that the delegates had conflicting opinions, on the theory of the government itself; local interests, and opinions arising from prejudice and private ambition, which pervaded the deliberations of the convention. The monarchy-men contended strenuously for the annihilation of the state governments, and for the adoption of the British constitution, with Kings, lords, and commons, together with its bribing policy and corruption, as the best model of government in the world.

Mr. Dickinson said:

"A limited monarchy he considered as one of the best governments in the world."—Madison Papers 148.

Mr. Gerry said:

"If the reasoning of Mr. Madison were just, and we suppose a limited monarchy the best form in itself, we ought to recommend it, though the genius of the people was decidedly adverse to it."—Madison Papers, 184.

We give Madison's opinion of the monarchy-men. "It was known that there were individuals who had betrayed a bias towards monarchy and there had always been some not unfavorable to a partition of the union into several confederacies, either from a better chance of figuring on a sectional theatre, or that the sections would require stronger governments, or by their hostile conflicts, lead to a monarchical consolidation." Madison Papers 120.

We insert Hamilton's opinion of the British constitution. "This progress of the public mind led him to anticipate the time, when others as well as himself would join in the praise bestowed by Mr. Neckar on the British Constitution—namely, that it is the only government in the world, which unites public strength with individual security. . . . . Their House of Lords is a most noble institution." . . . "The English model was the only good one on the subject. The hereditary interest of the king was so interwoven with that of the nation, and his personal emolument so great, that he was placed above the danger of being corrupted abroad; and at the same time was both sufficiently independent and sufficiently controlled to answer the purpose of the institution at home."—Madison Papers, pp. 202–203.

Hamilton further showed that he was in favor of adopting the British constitution, with its secret service and corruption system. He speaks thus: "It was known that one of the ablest politicians (Mr. Hume) had pronounced all that influence on the side of the crown, which went under the name of corruption, an essential part of the weight which maintained the equilibrium of the constitution."—Madison Papers 229. The second party proposed what was called the Jersey plan: to retain to the *thirteen* states their sovereignty, independence, and equality in full force and enjoyment. To have one house of congress where all the states should be equally represented. To amend the old Federal government so as to enlarge the powers of congress for collecting the revenue and paying the debts of the states—for the protection of the states from foreign and domestic violence. To grant such powers to the Federal Government as was necessary for the public good. The third plan was that proposed by Virginia, giving to the populous states of Pennsylvania, Virginia, and Massachussetts a preponderance in the Government over the smaller and less populous states—which would give to these three states thirteen senators out of twenty-eight, wealth and numbers to be the basis of representation. To form a government part Federal and part national —to run a line between the Jersey plan (a confederation of the states) and the consolidation of the states and a national government. The monarchy-men finding themselves in a minority with the convention and the people, and finding that they could not then carry their schemes through, and apprehensive that they could not establish a monarchy on the basis of a government which derived its existence and power from the State legislatures. That while the government acted only on the states, as states, and not on the people as individuals, they could never consolidate the states and establish a monarchy. For the state legislatures would be found a check on any attempt to usurp power or to favor a monarchy or a military despotism! Hamilton finding that he could not establish a monarchy, and wishing to defeat the Jersey plan proposed a compromise: To divide the United States into districts, composed of one or more states; and to elect a president and senate by the people, to hold office during good behavior; to elect a House of Representatives for two years. To appoint the courts and state governments by Congress. Hamilton wanted to abolish the state governments and to make the power of Congress supreme. To have the army, navy, and state militia, under the exclusive control of the national government. To give Congress a negative on state laws. But this plan did not receive much support; so the monarchy-men joined the advocates of the Virginia plan and defeated the Jersey plan. Hamilton speaks in favor of electing officers for life thus:

"Let one branch of the legislature hold their places for life, or at least during good behavior. Let the executive, also, be for life."—Madison Papers 203. Beware of a third term!

Madison speaks of the attempt of Hamilton to abolish the state legislatures; "One gentleman (Col. Hamilton) in his animadversions on the plan of New Jersey, boldly and decisively contended for an abolition of the state governments."—Madison Papers, 220.

Unfortunately for liberty, there was a large party in the convention, that viewed everything pertaining to government through the medium of the British Constitution and British laws. The monarchists imagined that British statesmen were the wisest of men and the British government the very height of human perfection. They despised the power of the states and the people. They wanted a strong consolidated government which in time would abolish the state governments and end in monarchy. They were in favor of a limited monarchy. They hated democracy and the power of the people! The Jersey-men, at the beginning of the convention, were called Federalists, as they were in favor of a Federal confederation of the states. Those who opposed the Jersey plan were, then, called anti-Federalists. During the progress of the convention, as the Jersey plan was defeated the Virginia plan was called a Federal government, which received some support from the monarchy-men. The monarchy-men, the better to hide their ultimate views and plans, assumed the name of Federalists, and those in favor of state rights were called anti-Federalists. The state-rights men now assumed an opposition to consolidation and monarchy. The Federalists were in favor of putting supreme power in the national government and reducing the states to counties!

Mr. Picking offered the following resolution enlarging the powers of Congress: "to negative all laws passed by the several states interfering, in the opinion of the legislature," for they spoke of the Congress by this name in the convention, "with the general interests and harmony of the Union, provided that two-thirds of the members of each house assent to the same."

Mr. Rutledge said on this occasion:

"If nothing else, this alone would damn, and ought to damn, the constitution. Will any state ever agree to be bound hand and foot in this manner? It is worse than making mere corporations of them, whose by-laws would not be subject to this shackle." Madison papers 468. If the fathers of the constitution had lived until now, what would they think of the usurpation of the Congress and the Radical party? What would they think of the military despotism wielded over the south? What would they think of reducing states to mere military departments, to be governed by the whim of some military dictator, acting under the dictatorship of Congress! Did they dream that the whites of eleven states would be reduced to such an abject servitude, as to be under the dominion of the "Anglo African!!" Oh! shades of the mighty dead!!

Hamilton speaks in favor of the abolishment of the states, thus:

"By an abolition of the states, he meant that no boundary can be drawn between the national and state legislature; that the former must therefore have indefinite authority. If it were limited at all, the rivalship of the states would gradually subvert it. Even a corporation the extent of some of them, as Virginia, Massachusetts, &c., would be formidable. As states, he thought they ought to be abolished."—Madison Papers, 212.

Again, he says: "He acknowleged himself not to think favorably of Republican government; but addressed his remarks to those who did think favorably of it, in order to prevail on them to tone the government as high as possible."—Madison Papers, 244.

Gouverneur Morris said in a speech in the convention on uniting and consolidating the states, thus:

"This country must be united. If persuasion does not unite it, the sword will."—Madison Papers, 276. Was this prophecy? How faithfully the Radicals have followed in the footprints of the "blue-light Federalists." Indeed the present Radicals derive all their arguments from the Tories and Federalists. Yea, even from the Parliamentarians of England and the Red Republicans of France and from the theories of despotic governments ancient and modern! Again, this same Gouverneur Morris speaks further of the abolition of the states:—

"State attachments, and state importance, have been the bane of this country. We cannot annihilate, but we may perhaps take out the teeth of the serpent."—Madison Papers, 277. Oh, shade of Federalism! how perseveringly the Radicals have, since their advent into power, worked to annihilate the state governments. Oh, admirable Stevens, Sumner, Butler and Wade, you have been apt disciples of the "*blue-light Federalist*"—you have faithfully and religiously followed the political teachings of John Adams and Alexander Hamilton. But though you did not completely succeed in establishing monarchy, you made a bold and vigorous attempt. Though you attempted the annihilation of the southern states, by your infamous re-construction bills, yet you did not establish monarchy; but you made vast and rapid strides! Though you trampled the constitution under foot, yet you did not attain your darling object, the establishment of the British Constitution with Kings, Lords, and Commons on the ruins of the Constitution of Washington! It is true that though you failed to establish a monarchy, you succeeded in establishing a dictator!! Your power is gone!! The Federalists in the convention and through the states wanted to make wealth and education a test of qualification for citizenship and for holding office.

Mr. Mason moved: "That the committee of detail be instructed to receive a clause, requiring certain qualifications of landed property, and citizens of the United States, in members of the national legislature; and disqualifying persons having unsettled accounts with, or being indebted to, the United States from being members of the national legislature."

"Col. Mason mentioned the parliamentary qualification adopted in the reign of Queen Anne, which, he said, had met with universal approbation."—Madison Papers, p. 370.

The following is from a speech of Gouverneur Morris on the qualification of voters.

"Give the votes to people who have no property, and they will sell them to the rich, who will be able to buy them. We should not confine our attention to the present moment. The time is not distant when this country will abound with mechanics and manufacturers, who will receive their bread from their employers? Will such men be the secure and faithful guardians of liberty? Will they be the impregnable barrier against aristocracy? He was as little duped by the association of the words 'taxation and representation.' The man who does not give his vote freely, is not represented.. It is the man who dictates the vote."—Madison Papers 386. Madison moved to strike out the word "landed" before the word "qualification." "Landed possessions were no certain evidence of real wealth, many enjoyed them to a great extent who were more in debt than they were worth. The unjust laws of the states had proceeded more from this class of men than any others."—Madison Papers, 371.

"The right of suffrage is certainly one of the fundamental articles of republican government, and ought not to be left to be regulated by the legislature. The gradual abridgment of this right has been the mode in which aristrocacies have been built on the ruins of popular forms."—Madison Papers, 387.

Mr. Pinckney said:

"It was prudent, when such great powers were to be trusted, to connect the tie of property with that of representation in securing a faithful administration. The legislature would have the fate of the nation put into their hands. The president would also have a very great influence on it. The judges would not only have important causes between citizens, but also where foreigners are concerned. They will even be the umpires between the United States and individual states, as well as between one state and another. Were he to fix the quantum of property which should be required, he should not think of less than one hundred thousand dollars for the president, half that sum for each of the judges, and in like proportion for the members of the National Legislature."—Madison Papers, 403.

Dr. Franklin said in reply, that he "expressed his dislike to everything that tended to debase the spirit of the common people. If honesty was often the companion of wealth, and if poverty was exposed to peculiar temptations, it was not less true that the possession of property increased the desire of more property. Some of the greatest rogues he was ever acquainted with were the rich rogues."—Madison Papers, 403.

The Radicals of Massachusetts and Connecticut have followed faithfully the example of their Federal ancestors, by excluding all from the ballot-box, who cannot read and write the English language. The radicals of Rhode Island have gone still further by making property a qualification for citizenship. We have many Radicals in other states who are wishing for an opportunity to make education and property a qualification for citizenship in all the states. The Federalists wanted to exclude foreigners from participation in the government. They wanted Americans to rule America—to reduce the foreigners to vile servitude—mere hewers of wood and drawers of water. Gouverneur Morris moved to insert fourteen instead of four years' citizenship, as a qualification for senators; urging the danger of admitting strangers into our public councils."—Madison Papers, 398.

Butler said that he "was decidedly opposed to the admission of foreigners without a long residence in the country. They bring with them, not only attachments to other countries, but ideas of government so distinct from ours, that in every point of view they are dangerous." "He mentioned the great strictness observed in Great Britain on this subject."—Madison Papers, 399.

Gouverneur Morris again said: "Run over the privileges which emigrants would enjoy among us, though they should be deprived of being eligible to the great offices of government; observing that they exceeded the privileges allowed to foreigners in any part of the world; and that as every society, from a great nation down to a club, had the right of declaring the conditions on which new members should be admitted, there could be no room for complaint. As to those philosophical gentlemen, those citizens of the world, as they call themselves, he owned, he did not wish to see any of them in our public councils. "He would not trust them. The men who can shake off their attachment to their own country can never love any other." "Admit a Frenchman into your Senate, and he will study to increase the commerce of France."—Madison Papers, 400.

Mr. Williamson said:

"He wished this country to acquire, as fast as possible, national habits. Wealthy emigrants do more harm, by their luxurious example, than good by the money they bring with them."—Madison Papers, 411.

Mr. Madison said:

"He wished to invite foreigners of merit and republican principles among us. America was indebted to emigrants for her settlement and prosperity. That part of America which has encouraged them most had advanced most rapidly in population, agriculture, and the arts." "Instances were rare of a foreigner being elected by the people within any short space after his coming among us. If bribery was to be practised by foreign powers, it would not be attempted among the electors, but among the elected, and among natives having full confidence of the people, not among strangers, who would be regarded with a jealous eye."—Madison Papers, 412.

Franklin said:

"We found in the course of the revolution that many strangers served us faithfully, and that many natives took part against their country. When foreigners, often looking about for some other country in which they can obtain more happiness, give a preference to ours, it is a proof of attachment which ought to excite our confidence and affection."—Madison papers 399. Thus, we see that the Federalists showed their hostility to foreigners. Native Americans and Know-Nothings have religiously followed in the footpaths of the Tories and Federalists. Oh, what ingratitude to foreigners, who had shed their blood in the cause of American independence! It appears that all parties who have opposed the democratic party, were the enemies of foreigners. Know-Nothing principles can be traced back to the very convention, that framed the constitution. Yea, before the bodies of those patriotic foreigners who died in the cause of American freedom, had moldered into clay! What ingratitude—"*No Irish need apply.*" This vile attempt of the monarchy-men to establish a monarchy, an aristocracy, or a consolidation of the states, on the ruins of. the states and American liberty, alarmed the friends of state-rights and popular government both in the convention and throughout the country. Some delegates left the convention and went home and never returned, for they claimed that the states had sent them to amend the Federal constitution, and not to form a national government. That the states would never send delegates to the convention, if they thought that the deliberations of the convention would turn on the consolidation of the states or a national government. The Federalists and the friends of a strong government were in favor of giving congress the power to "*emit bills of credit*," to abolish slavery; to incorporate banks; to pass laws for the encouragement of commerce, manufactures and agriculture, they wanted to clothe the government with discretionary powers! It is from this source that Federalists, Know-Nothings, Republicans and Radicals have derived their principles, prejudices and bigotry. The state rightsmen did not want to trust the government with the purse and the sword, or with discretionary power of taxation, and with the power of raising men without any limitation. They argued that if the Federal government were invested with discretionary power over the resources of the states, the people would be ground between the upper and nether millstone; that there would be nothing left to support the state governments. That the Federal government would centralize the power of the country, which, in time, would annihilate the state governments; and end in the establishment of a military government or a monarchy! It appears from *Madison Papers*, and Elliott's debates, that the southern people were jealous of their rights, particularly, on the tariff and slavery questions; that they would never have entered into a union, if they thought that either of these rights would be invaded! Indeed, the constitution would never have been formed or adopted, only for the conciliatory and compromising spirit of the *Fathers and Founders* of the constitution and the Union.—Greeley's Amer. Conflict, vol. 1, p. 46. They yielded their own private and public views for the public good! From the history of the country, the debates and journals of the convention, and the opinions of the "Fathers," we find that the *Federal Union* is the creature of the states, deriving its power and existence therefrom. That all powers not granted to the Federal government is reserved to the states. Immediately after the adoption of the constitution, the advocates of a strong government, the Federalists, sought by implication and inference to give the Federal government the very same powers they failed to ingraft on the constitution, in the convention. They claimed to give to the constitution a latitudinous construction, adding inference upon inference from "earth to heaven, like Jacob's ladder."

We quote the following from Thomas Jefferson on the objects and plans of the Federalists, in construing the government into a monarchy:

"I have stated the above, that the original objects of the Federalists were, 1st, to warp our government more to the form and principles of monarchy, and, 2d, to weaken the barriers of the state government as co-ordinate powers. In the first they have been so completely foiled by the universal spirit of the nation, that they have abandoned the enterprise, shrunk from the odium of their appellation, taken to themselves a participation of ours, and under the Pseudo-Republican mask, are now aiming at the second object, and strengthened by unsuspecting or apostate recruits from our ranks, are advancing fast towards an ascendency."—Jefferson's Works, vol. 7, p. 293. Well, if the Federalists did not gain an ascendency, in the time of Jefferson, their followers, under false colors of a Republican name, used under false pretense to get into power, like a pirate, hoisted the *black flag* of Federalism at their mast head, and by the aid of *military necessity*, they have committed the most glaring usurpations and wielded a military despotism which Jefferson never dreamt of. If they did not establish a monarchy in name they wielded a military despotism and trampled the constitution of the United States, and the constitutions and laws of several States under foot.

Jefferson further speaks of the opinions and principles of the Federalists:

"Federalism, stripped as it now nearly is, of its landed and laboring support, is monarchism, Anglicism; and whenever our own dissensions shall let them in upon us, the last ray of free government closes on the horizon of the world."

Oh, how prophetic of the despotism of the so-called Republican party, since the election of Lincoln! for the Republican party is the faithful successor of the Federalist. It has made a vast and rapid stride towards monarchy.

Again, Jefferson says:

"Among that section of our citizens called Federalists, there are shades of opinion. Distinguished between the leaders and the people who compose it, the leaders consider the *English Constitution* as a model of perfection, some with a correction of its views, others, with all its corruptions and abuses. This last was Alexander Hamilton's opinion."—Jefferson's Works, vol. 6, p. 95.

"This government they wished to have established here, and only complied and held part, at first, to the present constitution, as a stepping-stone to the final establishment of the final model. This party has therefore always clung to England as their prototype, and great auxiliary in promoting and effecting this change."—Jefferson's Works, vol. 6, p. 95.

How faithfully the Radicals have followed the teachings of Alex. Hamilton and the "blue-light Federalists," since their advent into power. Had the people followed them in their mad career, they would have established a monarchy on the ruins of the constitution and free government.

CHAPTER IX.

The new constitution went into operation, on March 4th 1789, with Washington as President. He formed his cabinet of Federalists and Democrats; Thomas Jefferson, Secretary of State, and Alexander Hamilton, Secretary of the Treasury. The democratic party and Thomas Jefferson, as their *leader*, contended for a strict construction of the constitution. They held that the exercise of doubtful or discretionary powers, by the executive or Congress, were not warranted by the constitution. That the general government should exercise only such powers as were given by the letter of the constitution, or such as were absolutely necessary for carrying those powers into force—that the assumption of doubtful powers were null and void—a palpable usurpation of power, destructive of popular liberty; the rights of the states and the liberty of the people. Those were the principles of the democratic party then, and are its principles now. If the democratic party should ever abandon its principles, then will end the hopes of popular government, not only on this continent, but all over the world! Hamilton formed his political and financial system, so as to control Congress, consolidate the states and form a monarchy! "His financial system had two objects: 1st as a puzzle, to exclude popular understanding and inquiry, 2d as a machine for the corruption of the legislature; for he avowed the opinion, that man could be governed by one of two motives only, force and interest. Force, he observed, in this country was out of the question, and interest, therefore of the members must be laid hold of, to keep the legislature in unison with the executive."—Jefferson's Works vol. 9, p. 91. How faithfully the Congress and the Radical state legislatures have yielded to the motives of interest—the lobby-men could tell—the various rings in the United States could reveal it. The great overgrown monopolies could tell of your wholesale venality. Hamilton used the funding system as a means to corrupt the Congress and to bring to his aid the vile speculators and the '*Stock-jobbing*' herd, who made vast fortunes by Hamilton's scheme of finance. Such has *been the policy of the Radicals towards the bondholders of our time!* For Federalists and Radicals are, in principle, identically the same! The Eastern States made threats of seceding from the Congress and of dissolving the union, if Congress did not assume the state debts.—Thus, New England was the first to raise the standard of secession, if the Federal government refused to assume the debts of the states. As a compromise the Federal government assumed twenty millions of the state debts; on receiving this *bonus* New England remained in the union!! The next step of the monocrats was to establish a money power, or *United States Bank*, as a permanent institution for centralization and corruption; as a *stepping-stone to Monarchy*." The bank was located at Philadelphia, the then Capital, which made Congress a sink-hole of venality, bribery, and corruption. Members of both houses of Congress were directors of the bank, who together with speculators and friends of the bank and *Stock-jobbers gave* Hamilton a majority. This violent and corrupt course of Hamilton caused an opposition to the administration. The following is from Jefferson, the leader of the opposition:

"Here then were the real grounds of opposition, which was made to the course of the administration—its object was to preserve the legislature pure and independent of the executive, to restrain the administration to republican forms and principles, not permit the constitution to be construed into a monarchy, and to be warped in practice, into all the principles and pollutions of their favorite English model. Nor was this an opposition to General Washington. He was true to the Republican charge confided to him, and has solemnly and repeatedly protested to me, in our conversations, that he would lose the last drop of his blood in the support of it; and he did this the oftener and with the more earnestness, because he knew my suspicions of Hamilton's designs against it, and wished to quiet them. For Hamilton's great argument in favor of a national bank was that it was necessary for the public credit and to prosecute the Indian wars.

Jefferson opposed the national bank and gave a written opinion of its unconstitutionality. Hamilton and his party were for copying everything from England—government, banks, paper money, and corruption. They showed great favor to England and hostility to France, the former ally of America. This was gratitude with a vengeance!

During the X. Y. Z. Congress, the Federalists were in favor of making war on France, so as to aid England. "The government was well apprised of the predominancy of the British interest in the United States; that they considered Colonel Hamilton, Mr. King, Mr. William Smith of South Carolina as the main support of that interest: that particularly, they considered Colonel Hamilton, and not Mr. Hammond, as their effective minister here; that if the anti-federal interest (that was his term), at the head of which they considered Mr. Jefferson to be, should prevail, these gentlemen had secured an asylum to themselves in England."—Jefferson's Works, vol. 9, p. 145.

"The Federalists wished for everything which would approach our new government to a monarchy." Jefferson's Works vol. 9, p. 480.

Jefferson gives the following account of the origin of parties, thus: "We broke into two parties; each wishing to give the government a different direction; the one to strengthen the most popular branch, the other the more permanent branches and to extend their permanency." Jefferson's Work's vol. 6, pp. 143-4.

Jefferson further speaks of the usurpation of the Federal party, thus:

"Giving a little to-day and a little to-morrow; advancing its noiseless steps like a thief, over the field of jurisdiction until all shall be usurped from the states, and the government of all be consolidated into one. To this I am opposed; because, when all government, domestic and foreign, in little as in great things, shall be drawn to Washington as the centre of all power, it will render powerless the checks provided of one government on the other, and will become as venal and oppressive as the government from which we separated."—Jefferson's Works, vol. 7, p. 216. Hamilton said that the general government must swallow up the state governments.— Greeley's Am. Conf. vol. 1, p. 82.

Well, how faithfully the Republicans have carried out this programme of their prototypes, the Federalists, for since their advent into power they have been more corrupt and venal than any government in the world, ancient or modern. They have stolen into power under false colors. They have centralized all power in the authorities at Washington; trampled on the constitution of the United States and the Constitutions of several states. They have incarcerated all who claim constitutional law, whenever they felt so disposed.

John Adams, a federalist, succeeded Washington, as President of the United States and his party were in favor of monarchy, as appears from the following authorities:

"In 1793," said Cobot, a Federalist, "things will never go right, till you have a President for life, and an hereditary senate."—Jefferson's Works, vol. 9, p. 184.

In 1797, Adams said: "Damn 'em, damn 'em, damn 'em! You see that an elective government will not do. "Republicanism must be discarded." Hamilton said, "for my part I avow myself a monarchist. I have no objection to a trial being made of this thing of a Republic."—Jefferson's Works, vol. 9, p. 187.

"Oh!" said Hamilton, "say the Federal monarchy. Let us call things by their right names, for a monarchy it is."—Jefferson's Works, vol. 9, p. 191.

"Hamilton declared openly, that there was no stability, no security in any kind of government but a monarchy.—Jefferson's Works, vol. 9, p. 126.

We give Adams' opinion on the British constitution, thus:

"After the cloth was removed, and our questions agreed and this dismissed, conversation began on other matters, and by some circumstance, was led to the British constitution, on which Mr. Adams observed: Purge that constitution of its corruption, and give to its popular branch equality of representation, and it would be the most perfect constitution ever devised by the wit of man. Hamilton paused and said: "Purge it of its corruption, and give to its popular branches equality of representation, and it would become an *impracticable* government; as it stands at present, with all its supposed defects, it is the most perfect government which ever existed. And this was assuredly the exact line which separated the political creeds of these two gentlemen. The one was for two hereditary branches and an honest elective one; the other for an hereditary King, with a House of Lords and Commons corrupted to his will, and standing between him and the people."—Jefferson's Works. vol. 9, p. 96.

Again, we find that John Adams and his party were enemies of the Union, and anticipated its dissolution. On a petition being presented to John Adams, while President of the United States, for a donation, for a College, in Tennessee, he said; "He saw no possibility of continuing the union of the states, that their dissolution must necessarily take place: that he therefore saw no propriety in recommending to New England men to promote a literary institution in the south; that it was in fact giving strength to those who were to be their enemies; and, therefore, he would have nothing to do with it." Jefferson's Works vol. 9, pp. 203, 204. Goodhue, a Federalist, said in 1798: "I'll tell you what, I have made up my mind on the subject; I would rather the old ship should go down than not" (meaning the union of the States).—Jefferson's Works, vol. 9, p. 189.

Hamilton treated the people with disdain, for he said himself: "And it is long since I have learned to hold the popular opinion of no value."—Hamilton's Works, vol. 5, p. 52.

John Adams' opinion of the British Constitution:

"I only contended that the English Constitution is, in theory, both for the adjustment of the balance and the prevention of its vibrations, the most stupendous fabric of human invention; and that Americans ought to be applauded instead of censured, for imitating it as far as they have done. Not the formation of languages, not the whole art of navigation and shipbuilding does more honor to the human understanding than this system of government.—Adams' Works vol. 4, pp. 358–9.

"For, instead of the trite saying, no bishop, no king, it would be much more exact and important truth to say, no people, no King, and no King, no people."—Adams' Works, vol. 4, p. 371.

This shows that Adams and Hamilton and their party were only waiting for an opportunity to abolish the Constitution and Union and to establish a monarchy. If they did not succeed, Butler, Stevens, Sumner, Stanton, Wade disregarded the Constitution of the United States and established a military despotism!!

Again, Adams says of the British Constitution:

"We shall have reason to exult, if we make our comparison with England and the English Constitution."—Adams' Works, vol. 4, p. 382.

Again, Adams says: "A Republican government is little better than a government of devils."—Adams' Works, vol. 2, p. 469.

"This is the true reason, why all civilized free nations have found, by experience, the necessity of separating from the body of the people, and even from the legislature, the distribution of honors, and conferring it on the executive authority of the government. When the emulation of all the citizens looks up to one point, like the rays of a circle from all points of the circumference, meeting and uniting in the centre, you may hope for uniformity, consistency and subordination; but when they look up to different individuals, or assemblies, or councils, you may expect all the deformity, eccentricities, and confusion of the Polemic system."—Adams' Works vol. 6, p. 256.

Again, he makes a comparison between the nobles and the people: "But on the other hand, the nobles have been essential parties in the preservation of liberty. The people pretended to nothing but to be villains, vassals, and retainers to the Kings or the nobles."—Adams' Works vol. 6, pp. 417–8. In the time of John Adams the Federalists attempted to make democracy unpopular in America, by holding them responsible for the acts of the Red Republicans of France. The democracy sympathized with France, and held that the people were able to govern themselves, that all just and good governments reflect the will of the people.

Jefferson's views on the power of the people are most forcibly expressed in the following words:

"Governments are Republican only in proportion as they embody the will of the people, and execute it."—Jefferson's Works, vol. 7, p. 9.

He also held that free government would last so long as the people remained virtuous. That great monopolies and the concentration of wealth and power in a few were dangerous to the safety and stability of a republic.

Jefferson speaks of moneyed monopolies, thus:

"Raising up a moneyed aristocracy in our own country, which has already set the government at defiance."—Jefferson's Works vol. 7, p. 64.

The democrats held that the government should be built in the affections of the people. That each branch of the government should be confined within the pale of the Constitution. Jefferson speaks of the evil of the Federal government usurping the powers and rights of the states, thus:

"Can any good be effected by taking from the states the moral rule of their citizens, and subordinating it to the general authority, or to one of their corporations, which may justify forcing the meaning of words, hunting after possible construction, and hanging inference on inference from heaven to earth like Jacob's ladder? Such an intention was impossible, and such a licentiousness of construction and inference, if exercised by both governments, as may be done with equal right, would equally authorize both to claim all power, general and particular, and break up the foundations of the Union."—Jefferson's Works, vol. 7, pp. 297–8.   Jefferson held that state-rights were a necessary check on the general government.

"I believe the states can best govern our home concerns, and the general government our foreign ones. I wish, therefore, to see maintained that wholesome distribution of powers established by the constitution for the limitation of both, and never to see all offices transferred to Washington, where further withdrawn from the eyes of the people, they may more secretly be bought and sold at market."—Jefferson's Works vol. 7, pp. 297–8.

Jefferson further held that equal encouragement should be given to agri-culture, commerce, and manufacture. That doubtful and discretionary power should not be exercised by Congress or the executive. That the constitution should be strictly construed. That the Federal government should not usurp the rights of the states.—I see, as you do, and with the deepest affliction, the rapid strides with which the Federal branch of our government is advancing towards the usurpation of all the rights reserved to the states, and the consolidation in itself of all powers foreign and domestic: and that too by construction, which if legitimate, leaves no limit to their power."—Jefferson's Works vol. 7, p. 426.

Again Jefferson says:

"Yet although I have little hope that the torrent of consolidation can be withstood, I should not be for giving up the ship without effort to save her."—Jefferson's Works vol. 7, p. 430.   The Federalists held that Congress pos-sessed discretionary powers. They claimed a latitudinous construction for the constitution. After the French revolution, in 1789, French refugees came over to the United States and naturally joined the democratic party; whose principles rested on the theory that "a man is a man"—that man should be governed by reason and the laws of nature. That the people are capable of self-government. That the toiling millions should not be taxed to feed the pampered few. That the condition of the people should be im-proved. That labor should be respected and rewarded. That all offices of trust and honor and emolument should be open to the people. Equality for all branches of industry: no fostering monopolies for any! Jefferson speaks of a government of reason thus: "It is our sacred duty to suppress passions among ourselves, and not to blast the confidence we have inspired of the proof that a government of reason is better than one of force."—Jefferson's Works vol. 7, p. 183.

The Federal party and John Adams were very jealous of foreigners, and passed a law extending the time of naturalization to fourteen years. They passed laws to muzzle the press and to suppress the freedom of speech: to prevent native American democrats from denouncing the tyranny and extravagance of the Federal administration; they passed the sedition law to silence the native democrats and to banish foreigners, who may not support the policy of the administration! The Federal party had the President, John Adams, the supreme court, and both houses of Congress. After the Irish rebellion of 1798, a number of Irish patriots (rebels so called) came over to the United States, who joined the democratic party and opposed the Federalists, who were friends of England and monarchy! The Federalists were the enemies of all foreigners, but particularly the Irish—indeed, they showed the same hostility to foreigners, that their disciples, the Native American party and Radicals display to-day! The darling policy of the Federalists was to exclude the Irish and French from participation in the government; just as we find the same exclusive policy practised by the Native Americans, Know-Nothings, Wide-a-wakes, and Union Leaguers of our time—to exclude foreigners from office. The alien law was passed, in

1798, which gave John Adams power to compel all foreigners to depart out of the territory of the United States, all such aliens as he should judge dangerous to the peace and safety of the United States. The sedition law inflicted a fine not exceeding two thousand dollars, and imprisonment not exceeding two years, for writing, publishing, and printing any false, scandalous, or malicious writing, or writings against the government of the United States, or either house of Congress of the United States, with or without intent to defame the said government or either house of said Congress, or the President, or to bring them, or either of them into contempt or disrepute; or to excite against them, or either or any of them the hatred of the good people of the United States. The following will show the violent opposition of the Federalists to forcigners, especially towards Irishmen during the time the Federalists were in power, which is practised by their disciples, the Radicals at the present day. King, the Federal minister to England wrote home, thus:

"In Ireland, though for some months there will be partial and unimportant risings, the force of the insurrection is broken, and the danger nearly over, The chiefs have been without much character and without intellect." —Hamilton's Works vol. 6, pp. 308-9. "In Ireland the rebellion is suspended, and our government will, I hope, have the power and inclination to exclude those disaffected characters, who will be suffered to seek an asylum among us."—Hamilton's Works vol. 6, p. 315.

"You will see that I have prevented the sending to you of about fifty Irish State prisoners, who were at the head of the rebellion in Ireland, and closely connected with the Directory at Paris. Probably our patriots will think my conduct presumptive. In the present posture of affairs, I could have no hesitation!"—Hamilton's Works. I ask, in all sincerity, is it to be wondered that the Irish should vote the democratic ticket?

The above quotations from the works of Hamilton, should satisfy any reasonable man. The Irish are democrats in self-defence, as well as from principle!

We give further evidence of the intention of the Federalists to subvert the constitution and to establish on its ruins their model government the British Constitution. The following is from John Adams:

"That as to trusting to a popular assembly for the preservation of our liberties, it was the merest chimera imaginable; they never had any rule of decision, but their own will."—Jefferson's Works vol. 9, p. 190.

Dexter, a Federalist, said:

"'I suppose you would prefer an election by districts.' 'Yes,' "said Nicholas," I think it would be best, but would nevertheless agree to any other consistent with the constitution.' "Dexter said he did not know what might be the opinion of his state, but his own was, that no mode of election would answer any good purpose; that he should prefer one for life." Beware of a third term.—Jefferson's Works vol. 9, p. 196.

"The St. Andrew's Club of New York, (all Scotch tories) gave a public dinner lately. Among other guests, Alexander Hamilton was one. After dinner, the first toast was the President of the United States. It was drunk without any particular opposition. The next was, 'George the Third.' Hamilton started upon his feet, and insisted on a bumper and three cheers. The whole company accordingly rose and gave three cheers."—Jefferson's Works vol. 9, p. 197.

In consequence of those hateful and odious principles of the Federalists, as well as the enactment of the alien and sedition laws, and the tyranny and oppression of the Federalists in both Houses of Congress, the democratic members in both Houses of Congress resigned, and went home, excepting Thomas Jefferson, who remained in the senate, as Vice-President, and Gallatin in the House, (the speaker) Madison and other democrats, who left Congress, got elected to their State legislatures. As a check on the usurpation of the Federalists, the Democrats passed the celebrated Virginia and Kentucky resolutions of 1798. They denounced the alien and sedition laws as unconstitutional, and as a violation of the rights of the States and the citizens of the States. Massachusetts, then at the head of the Federal party, through her legislature, pronounced, "the alien and sedition laws, not only constitutional, but expedient and necessary." That the constitution did not make the legislature the judges of the acts or measures of the general government. The alien and sedition laws became so obnoxious to the people that the Federal party became odious and was defeated. This paved the way for the election of Thomas Jefferson, the father of democracy, as President of the United States. Such was the popular indignation of the American people towards the Federalists that Jefferson was succeeded by two patriotic democrats, Madison and Monroe. The Federalists became rebels and traitors to the Constitution, the Union, and liberty! They were the mere instruments of the English government. They would bear all manner of insults from the British government so long as they made money by English commerce. During Jefferson's administration Louisiana was purchased by treaty from France. Jefferson was an honest man and an extreme stickler for the Constitution.—Greeley's American Conflict, vol. 1, p. 84.

During the war of 1812, the Federal party aided England and threatened to secede from the Union and to divide the states. The New England clergy of the Federal school were violent supporters of England and the most hostile enemies of the administration and the Union. The Blue-light Federalists of New England not only opposed the war with England, but resisted the President in calling out the militia to resist a foreign and invading foe. The Federalists were the friends of England, and the Democrats the friends of France.—Greeley's American Conflict, vol. 1, p. 55. The Federalists of Connecticut passed the following resolution:

"Resolved, that the conduct of his excellency, the governor, in refusing to order the militia of this state, on the requisition of the secretary of war and Major-general Dearborn, must meet with the entire approbation of this assembly." President Madison informed Congress, in his message in 1812, that the governors of Massachusetts and Connecticut had refused to furnish their quota of militia. They not only opposed the United States government until the end of the war, but also refused the government the use of the jails to confine prisoners of war. "The city Council of Hartford determined to put what obstacles in the way of it (recruiting,) they legally might, enacted a local ordinance forbidding the marching and parading of troops, the beating of drums and displaying of flags, in fine, the opening of any recruiting station, except within ce:tain limits excluding the most populous parts of the towns." Hildreth's History of the United States vol. 3, page 46. On the 18th of Oct. 1814, the legislature of Massachusetts called for a convention of the New England states, alleging for a reason for this treasonable design against the government, at a moment when the country was at war with the most formidable enemy in the world, that "*the constitution of the United States, under the administration of those now in power, had failed to secure to Massachusetts and New England generally, those equal rights and benefits, the great object of its promotion, and which could not be relinquished without ruin.*" This shows that the supposed grievances of the New England Federalists were that they did not get hold of the power and patronage of the Federal government, the almighty dollar! The legislature of Connecticut denounced the President's war measures, as unconstitutional, intolerable; barbarous, and oppressive. The infamous, odious, and treasonable Hartford convention proposed the following amendments to the constitution:

1st. "To provide that slaves should not be counted as a basis of representation; but that free negroes should be counted."

2d. "That no state should be admitted into the Union without the concurrence of two-thirds of both houses of Congress."

3d. "That Congress should not have power to lay any embargo on the ships of citizens, for more than sixty days."

4th. "That Congress should not have power to prohibit intercourse between the United States and any foreign nation."

5th. "Requiring a two-third vote of Congress to declare war, except for defence, in case of actual invasion."

6th. "That no foreigner thereafter naturalized should hold any civil office under the United States."

7th. "That the same person should not be elected President a second time—or two successive Presidents be taken from the same state."

The following resolution was also passed: "The power of compelling the militia and other citizens of the United States, by forcible draft or conscription, to serve in the regular armies as proposed in the late official letter from the secretary of war, is not delegated to Congress by the constitution, and the exercise of it could be not less dangerous to the liberties than hostile to the sovereignty of the states."

A town meeting of the citizens of Boston assembled to oppose the enforcement of the embargo acts, and passed the following resolution:

"*Resolved*—Not voluntary to assist in carrying into execution the embargo act; and that all who should do so ought to be considered as enemies of the State of Massachusetts, and hostile to the liberties of the people."

This nullification ordinance was vetoed by the democratic Governor of Massachusetts. Thus: nullification, treason, meditated secession, final separation and the dissolution of the Union were fostered in New England! New England Federalists proclaimed the doctrine of secession during the war of 1812. Greeley says that Josiah Quincy was the first secessionist—that he made a secession speech at Boston, 1811.—Greeley's Am. Conf. vol. 1. p. 86.

John Quincy Adams, twenty years afterward said in writing:

This object was, and had been for several years, a dissolution of the Union. He knew (he said) from incontrovertible evidence, though not provable in a court of law, that in the case of civil war the aid of Great Britain to effect the purpose would be as surely resorted to, as it would be indispensably necessary to the design. . . That if force should be resorted to by the government to quell that resistance (the resistance organizing in Massachusetts) it would produce a civil war, and in that event he had no doubt that the leader of the party would receive the co-operation of Great Britain."

Massachusetts, in 1809, resolved, that "on such occasions, passive obedience," (to the laws of Congress) "would on the part of the people, be a breach of their allegiance, and, on our part, treachery and perjury."

The following is an address of the Federalists on this occasion:

"Choose, then, fellow citizens, between the condition of citizens of free states, possessing its equal weight and influence in the national government or that of a colony, free in name but, in fact, enslaved by sister states." The legislature of Massachusetts further resolved, that the war originated and was to be ascribed to the influence of worthless foreigners over the press and the cabinet, and Congress."—"Such was the true reason of the war. The freedom of commerce and the rights of seamen, was a pretence." Massachusetts, not satisfied with resisting the lawful requisition of the President for troops; nullifying the laws of Congress; bidding defiance to the government, by armed resistance; the raising of state funds and troops to intimidate the government; claiming it as a matter of conscience to oppose the government of the United States, passed a law denying the use of her prisons to the Federal government to confine British prisoners of war, or deserters from the American army, and to compel, by law, jailers to discharge all British officers, as prisoners of war, held by the United States authority in custody! And all of this diabolical treason was preached by the '*higher law clergy*' and politicians of New England, who held that resistance to the general government was loyalty to *God*.

"The victory of New Orleans, and the peace of *Ghent*, broke the power of the Federal party, and brought both the name and party into odium, which compelled them to change their party name. They claimed that the action of the convention was justifiable." Jefferson, in a letter to General La Fayette, Feb. 14, 1815, speaks of the Hartford convention:

"Their fear of Republican France being now done away, they are directing to Republican America, and they are playing the same game for disorganization here which they played in your country. The Murats, the Dantons, and the Robespierres of Massachusetts are in the same pay, under the same orders and making the same efforts to anarchize us, that their prototypes in France did there."

In a letter to General Dearborn, March, 17, 1815, Jefferson said:

"Oh, Massachusetts! how I have lamented the degradation of your apostasy! Massachusetts, with whom I went with pride, in 1776, whose vote was my vote on every public question, and whose principles were then the standard of whatever was free and fearless. But then she was under the control of the two Adams, while Strong, her present leader, was promoting petitions for submission to British usurpation."

The Federalists and Whigs during the administrations of Monroe and John Quincy Adams, divided the country between the advocates of a *strict and literal interpretation of the constitution* and the strict adherence to fundamental principles and state rights on the one hand; and those who advocated the creation of local monopolies by Congress; the investing of Congress with supreme powers; the creation of a national bank; the improvements of rivers and harbors by the Federal government, and a high protective tariff. The democrats advocated the former, and the Federalists and Whigs the latter.

CHAPTER X.

In the Congress of 1820-21, the country was alarmed on the slavery ques tion in Congress, which ended in what is called the Missouri compromise, prohibiting slavery north of 36 deg. 30 min. "During the Missouri struggle both Jefferson and Madison gave their influence with the south." Yet Greeley, at page 39-40 of his American Conflict, claims Jefferson as Anti-slavery. How conflicting? But Greeley's logic was not of the best.—Greeley's American Conflict vol. 1, p. 75.

During the sessions of 1820-24, commenced the debates on the tariff, which led to South Carolina nullification — *which threatened the Union, in* 1832. The first tariff act was passed in 1789, for the sole purpose of raising a *revenue* for the support of the government; so as not to resort to a direct tax—it was not intended as a protection to manufactures, but simply as an incident to revenue. Clay was the great champion of the tariff, in 1824. He was opposed by Webster, who said in his great speech: "Society is full of excitement. Competition comes in place of monopoly, and intelligence and industry ask only for fair play and an open field." But, when New England became a manufacturing country, Webster changed his mind, and became an advocate for a high tariff.—Greeley's Am. Confl., vol. 1, pp. 90–91. John Quincy Adams, in his inaugural, recommended internal improvements by the Federal government and a high protective tariff. This was the dividing line between Adams and the Democrats, for the Democrats held that the Constitution did not give the Federal government power to spend money for internal improvements — the improvement of rivers and harbors. That a tariff for any other object than as an incident to its *revenue* was unauthorized by the Constitution. In 1828, Adams recommended a high protective tariff which was opposed by the Democrats, as unconstitutional, sectional, and unjust, and as being oppressive to the rights and interest of the agricultural portion of the country. This protective tariff scheme originated with the Federalists, in 1816. For after their defeat on the odious *Alien and sedition laws*, as well as their defeat after the Hartford Convention, they attempted to make a *high protective* tariff a *ladder to climb into power*.—Hence protection to manufactures became the main plank in the Whig platforms. But the Morrill tariff bill, in 1861, capped the climax, and so offended European powers, who, in consequence, threatened to recognize the Southern Confederacy. Jackson assailed the United States bank — declared it unconstitutional, and opposed its re-chartering. The friends and advocates of monopoly, with Clay at their head, in Congress and in the state legislatures, assailed the President both from the rostrum, the stump, and through the press. The session of Congress of 1831–32, is famous in our political history for the great party conflict for the rechartering of the United States banks. The first charter was obtained by Hamilton, in 1791. The second charter was granted in 1816. The charter of 1816 was opposed by President Madison, who said: "That the genius of the British Monarchy favored the concentration of wealth and power; in America, the genius of the government required the diffusion of wealth and power." The act for the rechartering of the bank passed both Houses of Congress, for the friends of the bank had a majority in the Congress of 1832, but was vetoed by the President. On the appearance of the veto Message, the President was denounced by labored speeches, by Webster Clay and other friends of the bank, among whom were many apostate democrats (the Stantons and Butlers of the time,) who voted for the bank for a consideration.

Thus Jackson had to fight the Whigs and the combined moneyed power of the country together with the *hired press!* The bank and the moneyed power of the country brought on a financial crisis, which crippled all branches of industry, for the sole purpose of having something to charge the President with—for they claimed that the President's veto caused the "hard times." Distress meetings were held all over the country to defeat Jackson's re-election! But though the *bank* and other monopolies expended large sums of money in the Presidential Campaign, Jackson was triumphantly elected over Clay. A bill was passed, which provided for the removal of the deposits from the United States bank, and for depositing them in local banks. The friends of the *bank* concentrated their power by contracting credit—deranging the currency, to ruin merchants and farmers to create a money panic, and to compel the President to replace the deposits in the United States bank. Meetings were called all over the country and Jackson was denounced in the most violent terms, as the author of the "distress of the country." This brought about the general money panic of 1834.

A bill was passed for the equalization of gold and silver, and for making gold and silver of foreign coin a legal tender. This caused gold and silver, which paper had banished to foreign countries, to flow back in the usual course of commerce and customs. This caused manufacture, agriculture, and commerce to prosper, and with this general prosperity came the downfall of the bank. Thus, did the sagacity, patriotism, and firmness of Jackson and the democratic party save the Union from the power, oppression and dominion of a "moneyed king." In 1832, the Whigs, with Clay at their head, introduced their favorite system of a "*high protective tariff.*" Jackson, in his message, recommended the abolition of duties on articles of comfort and necessity. Clay threatened a dissolution of the Union, if his favorite bill for a "*high tariff*" was not passed. Calhoun and his friends threatened a dissolution of the Union on the passage of a "*high protective tariff.*"

South Carolina, grieved by the passage of this high tariff bill, on the 24th of Nov. 1832, issued her nullification ordinance declaring the tariff of 1828 and 1832, unconstitutional, null and void, and declaring it unlawful to "enforce the payment of duties imposed by the said act *within the limits of this state.*" That if the general government attempted to collect said duties they would proceed to organize a separate government and "do all other acts and things which sovereign and independent states may of right do." Calhoun resigned the Vice-Presidency and was chosen United States Senator. Jackson issued his famous proclamation against nullification; and sent a message to Congress recommending a reduction of the tariff as a compromise. This shows that Jackson, as well as the Democratic party, always considered a tariff as a mere incident to revenue and not for the fostering of monopolies. Clay offered a compromise on the tariff, and in a speech, Feb. 12, 1833, he said: "I behold a torch about being applied to a favorite edifice, and I should save it if possible, before it was wrapt in flames, or at least preserve the precious furniture which it contains." Calhoun accepted Clay's tariff compromise and gave it his support; thus, compromise saved the Union then. Oh, that we had Jackson as President in 1861, he could have averted a civil war ! On the heads of the Radicals, rests their part of that awful responsibility. "The democrats have, on all occasions, tried to quiet the prejudices and fears of the people by compromise. They have adhered to the constitution and constitutional laws, justice and equal political rights. They have always endeavored to prevent a conflict between the Jurisdiction of the states and the Federal Government, by moderation and conciliatory measures. Their mottoes have been liberty, equality and fraternity. They have respected the rights of the citizens of the Union without respect to Geographical lines—No North, no South, no East, no West. Our government rests on three massive columns, liberty, equality and fraternity. Destroy any one of them; and then we may cry, alas for civil glory !"

Mr. Van Buren in his inaugural, March 4th, 1837, indicated that the policy of his administration would be a strict adherence to the principles of Thomas Jefferson—a compliance with the expressed provisions of the constitution. That the administration should give the constitution a strict construction—a strict economy in the administration of the government. The democrats held that it was dangerous for Congress to interfere with

Slavery, but to leave that question with the states that were interested. That Congress had no power to abolish slavery in the district of Columbia, or in the territories; or to interfere with it in the states. The abolitionists held that the government has been built on anti-slavery principles. The national bank failed to pay and tried to have the President sanction its re-charter. Vermont, in 1837-8, sent a memorial to Congress against the annexation of Texas, for the Whigs of the *North* were now becoming abolitionized. They had assumed a sectional aspect. They did not want Texas as they knew she would become a democratic state and would increase the power of the South in the Councils of the nation. For they preferred their party to the glory and prosperity of the nation. This movement of the abolitionists of Vermont was followed by petitions from the *North* praying for the abolition of slavery, in the territories and in the District of Columbia; and against the annexation of Texas, as they knew she would be a Slave State. The whigs and abolitionists were opposed to the acquisition of Florida, Louisiana and Texas. Greeley's Am. Conf. vol. 1, pp. 149 to 178 inclusive. This agitation of the abolitionists grew from year to year until it ended in blood, in 1861. For notwithstanding what the Radical writers may say, the slavery agitation in Congress created a sectional party which kept on increasing in power until the election of Lincoln on a sectional platform which led to secession and rebellion!! This will be the verdict of posterity. Had the American people wisely followed the admonition of Washington in his farewell address, and avoided a sectional party, there would be no rebellion. The democratic party frequently appealed to the abolitionists to keep the slavery agitation out of the halls of Congress. On this occasion Clay offered the following resolution: "That the interference by Citizens of any of the States, with the view to the abolition of slavery in the District of Columbia is endangering the rights and security of the people of the district; and any act or measure of the Congress designed to abolish slavery in the district, would be a violation of the faith implied in the cessions by the states of Virginia and Maryland—a just cause of alarm to the people of the slaveholding states— and have a direct and inevitable tendency to disturb and endanger the Union."—Benton.

This resolution passed, yeas 340, nays 8. Second resolution:
"*Resolved*—That every attempt of the Congress to abolish slavery in the territories, in which it exists would create serious alarm and just apprehension in the states that sustain that domestic institution, and would be a violation of good faith towards the inhabitants of every such territory, who have been permitted to settle with, and hold, slaves therein; and because, when any such territory shall be admitted into the Union as a state, the people thereof shall be entitled to decide that question exclusively for themselves." The vote stood yeas 36, nays 8.—Benton.

This was the doctrine of Statesmen, during Van Buren's administration—to let the people of the territories decide for themselves on the question of slavery. This agitation was carried to the House, which claimed the southern members. The slavery agitation in Congress now became permanent, and entered into the debates of Congress, gradually widening the gulf between the North and South, until it finally culminated in blood— until it brought on the most terrific rebellion known in the annals of the world! We give a brief sketch of emancipation in the North. All of the Colonies held slaves, except Massachusetts, before the revolution. The Puritans held Indian and Negro slaves. But slavery was not profitable in New England—slaves were kept as a mark of family distinction and aristocracy.—Greeley's Am. Conf. vol. i, pp. 30, 35, 36. Massachusetts claimed that the constitution of 1780 abolished slavery. Pennsylvania passed gradual emancipation in 1780; Vermont abolished slavery in 1777; New Hampshire 1783; Rhode Island 1784; Connecticut 1784; New York 1799, and New Jersey 1804.

A bill was introduced in Congress to graduate the price of the public lands and passed the senate, but was lost in the House. The Whigs moved to amend the bill confining its provisions to citizens of the United States, only which amendment was opposed by the democracy! Let foreigners never forget that were it not for the democrats this bill would have passed which would have excluded thousands of foreigners from the public lands who would be compelled to purchase lands from speculators.

After a violent struggle between the administration of Van Buren and the Whigs the government revenue was divorced from the bank; and the government funds placed in the custody of the government officers! This measure is known as the Subtreasury Act. In 1839, the banks failed and created another money panic, as a means of defeating the democracy and electing a whig President who would favor a rechartering of the United States Bank. In the campaign of 1840, the Whigs dropped Clay and nominated General Harrison, who was elected with the promises of "*roast beef and two dollars a day*," the corruption of the money power, "*Coon-skins,*" "*hard-cider,*" and *log cabins.*" In 1839, the abolitionists held a convention at Warsaw, New York, November 13. The convention nominated James G. Birney, of New York, for President, and Francis J. Lemoyne, of Pennsylvania for Vice-President. They received a total vote of 7,609. Thus, the abolitionists could poll but this paltry vote, 1840. Yet, in 1860, after twenty years, they were able to elect Abraham Lincoln on an anti-slavery platform! In 1853, on the political suicide of the whig party, the abolitionists fused with the Whigs, Native Americans and apostate democrats and raised the standard of anti-slavery. In the halls of Congress, in the state legislatures, through the press and from the pulpit and the Stump, private and public gatherings, nothing was heard from this fusion party but denunciation of slavery, until it finally succeeded in electing Lincoln as its standard-bearer, who in a speech, in 1858, said that the country could not exist half free and half slave. That the country could not rest secure until slavery should be ultimately abolished in the states. Greeley says the first abolition society was formed in Penn. 1774; New York Manumission society, 1785: that of Rhode Island 1786; Maryland 1789; Virginia 1791; and New Jersey 1792.—Greeley's American Conflict vol. 1, p. 107. The American Colonization society was established 1816. The society and colonization were opposed and condemned by the abolitionists—Greeley, Garrison, and Wendell Phillips.—Greeley vol. 1, p. 73. The first abolition convention was held in Philadelphia, 1824.—Greeley, p. 113. William Lloyd Garrison and other abolitionists had for their motto, "Our country is the world—our countrymen all mankind"—"No union with slaveholders "—The Constitution is a covenant with death and an agreement with hell."—Greeley's American Conflict vol. 1, p. 110. The Garrisonians were stanch supporters of women's rights. In 1776, the Quakers were opposed to slavery.—*Ibid* 118. The apostates of the old abolition school were "infidels."—Greeley vol. 1, p. 121. But the modern Abolitionists were professed churchmen.—*Ibid.* The mails, in 1835, were loaded with abolition documents. Such was the feeling against abolitionists, in 1835, Garrison was led through the streets of Boston with a rope around his body.—*Ibid.* 127. England liberated her West Indian slaves to embarrass the south and finally to bring about a dissolution of the Union, lavished her gold on English and American abolitionists to attain her ends. For this purpose she sent over, in 1838, one

George Thompson an eminent English Abolitionist to promote abolitionism in this country and finally a dissolution of the Union. After Harrison's election, he called an extra session of Congress; but died before it met. The duties of the office of President devolved on John Tyler, the Vice-President.

On the meetings of Congress, Clay submitted the following resolution:

Resolved—As the opinion of the Senate, that at the present session of Congress no business ought to be transacted, but such as being of an important or urgent nature, may be supposed to have influenced the extraordinary convention of Congress, and such as that the postponement of it might be materially detrimental to the public interest."

The Whigs passed a bill, entitled A bill for incorporating a United States bank, which was vetoed by the President, John Tyler, who was once a democrat but went over to the Whigs. The President was now denounced by Clay, in the senate, who charged him with bad faith towards the Whigs. A second bill passed and was vetoed by the president. Such was the violence and mortification of the Whigs and the friends of the bank that they hissed the veto message in the galleries of the senate. This was only eclipsed by the Radicals hissing in the galleries of the senate on the impeachment trial of President Johnson because he was acquitted !!

Such was the chagrin and disappointment of the Whigs, that immediately after the second veto, the cabinet who were Whigs, resigned, with the exception of Webster, the Secretary of State; who exclaimed "where shall I go?" The President was denounced by the Whigs. A final separation took place between the President and the Whigs about the close of this session of Congress. The United States bank after a vigorous struggle with the democratic party expired and became an "*obsolete idea;*" until the Federalists, under the guise of a Republican party name got into power in 1860, and as soon as they found the country disturbed by a stupendous rebellion, they established, not only a United States bank, but banks, until now, their name is legion ! An attempt to annex Texas during Tyler's administration failed. The annexation of Texas was made an important issue in the election of James K. Polk. John Quincy Adams and others said, in 1843, that an annexation of Texas would justify a dissolution of the Union.—Greeley, vol. 1, p. 160. Clay was opposed to the annexation of Texas without the consent of Mexico.—*Ibid.* 164. Greeley and the abolitionists opposed the annexation of Texas—*Ibid.* 168–9. The abolitionists renewed the agitation of slavery in Congress. On 12 August 1846, Mr. Wilmot, of Pennsylvania, offered his famous proviso, as a condition of the annexation of Texas.

" That no part of the *territory to be acquired should be open to the institution of slavery.* This proviso formed the nucleus for the *Free soil party,* in 1848, and for the fusion party in 1853–4. This sectional party had but *one idea* —Hostility to slavery, the abolition of slavery, no more slave states. The democrats held that congress had "*no power to legislate upon slavery in the territories.*"

This doctrine of " *non-intervention,*" got the name of squatter sovereignty from John C. Calhoun, in 1848, for the extremists north and south were opposed to non-intervention. The abolitionists claimed that Congress had the right of excluding slavery in the territories, while the Calhoun party claimed that Congress had power to protect slavery in the territories, the same as other property, while the friends of non-intervention held that the people of the territories were the best judges whether they wanted slavery or not, so that Congress should leave the whole subject of slavery with the people of the territories who could vote slavery up or down. Texas was annexed to the Union during Polk's administration, which led to the Mexican war.

CHAPTER XI.

The Democratic party met in convention, at Baltimore, in 1848. Two sets of delegates presented themselves from the State of New York, one set in favor of the nomination of General Cass; the other of Martin Van Buren. The convention rejected both, leaving the great State of New York unrepresented which had voted for a democratic President, since the organization of the party by Thomas Jefferson. General Cass was the regular nominee of the democratic party. The disappointed Van Buren party met at Utica, and afterwards at Buffalo and nominated Martin Van Buren for President. The Buffalo platform consisted of one *idea*—hostility to slavery—the negro hobby for politicians to ride into power. It held that it was the duty of the Federal government to abolish slavery, whenever it could be done, under the constitution, that in the states wherein slavery existed, the people thereof had the exclusive right to interfere with it. That Congress alone had the right and power to abolish slavery in the territories. This *"free soil* or *Barn-burners"* opposed General Cass and though Van Buren did not carry a single state, yet, by this division they defeated Cass and elected General Taylor, the Whig candidate. The popular vote of 1848: Taylor and Fillmore 1,360,752; Cass and Butler 1,219,962; Van Buren and Adams 291,342. Thus we see that the Van Buren split defeated the democratic party in 1848, (*Ib.*193.) The party catchwords of the *free soil* party were *"free speech," "free labor," "free soil"* and *"free men;"* which were afterwards taken up by the so-called Republican party. Seward, in 1848, held that slavery (speech at Cleveland, Ohio, Oct. 26, 1848) was the great living issue which divided the national parties, (*Ib.* 199-200). Henceforth the Whig party became abolitionists. The slavery question threatened a dissolution of the Union in 1850. The cry of disunion resounded from one end of the country to the other. The conservative Whigs and democrats of the *North,* forgetting their mutual political differences, saved the Union by compromise and conciliation! The compromise measures were denounced by the abolitionists of the North and by the extreme agitators of the South. The abolitionists were dissatisfied on account of the fugitive slave law, and the extremists of the South because the Missouri compromise line was not extended to the Pacific ocean. Jefferson Davis said that he would take nothing less than the Missouri line to the Pacific.—*Ibid.* 204-5. Clay in a speech said:

If the citizens of the territories choose to establish slavery, and if they come here with a constitution establishing slavery, I am for admitting them with such proviso in their constitution; but then it will be their own work, and not ours, and posterity will have to reproach them and not us, for forming constitutions allowing the institution of slavery to exist among them; and I care not how extensively or universally they are known." Clay said, "That the great principle, which lies at the foundation of all free governments is, that the majority must govern; from which there is or can be no appeal but the sword.—Clay's Speeches vol. 2, p. 47. Had the policy of Clay been adhered to, the Union could never be disturbed. Had the slavery agitation been excluded from the halls of Congress we would not have had the recent war—we would not have sacrificed thou-sands of lives—leaving thousands of destitute widows and orphans—we would not have created a mountain of debt—we would not have to groan under eternal taxation! The compromise measures met with the universal approbation of the union - loving people *north* and south, and restored peace and harmony all over the country. The people thought that the slavery question was finally banished from the halls of Congress forever. But this confidence of the people was soon disturbed. For the abolitionists at the North, who opposed the compromise measures in and out of Congress, while under debate, now, through their partisan press, assailed the Fugitive Slave law. Societies were organized, at the north, to nullify the *Fugitive* slave law, state *legislatures* passed *personal liberty bills* to prevent the execution of the fugitive slave law. Mobs at the north broke prisons and rescued fugitive slaves from the Federal authorities. But the great *masses* of the people north and south were satisfied with these compromise measures except the extremists. Senators Mason, Hunter, Butler, Barnwell, Pierre Saule, Jefferson Davis, Atchison, Morton, and Youlee offered a protest to the admission of California and to the passage of the compromise measures, which they signed and requested to have it spread on the journal; which was refused. Thus, the compromise measures were opposed by the abolitionists of the north and by the Calhoun school of southern politicians. The southern members opposed to the compromise measures, met at Nashville, in convention, and passed resolutions against the compromise measures; only the two states of South Carolina and Mississippi were represented. The compromise measures were approved by both whigs and democrats, in the Presidential Campaign of 1852, and the country became pacified on the slavery question, as was then supposed, forever! The Federal party, resurrected, under the name of abolitionists, was now only waiting for any opportunity to spring the slavery question in the halls of Congress, as a ladder to climb into power. For as the Federalists or Whigs were defeated on the bank question and high tariff, their only hope of getting into power was on the slavery question. Indeed some of the leaders of the so-called Republican party, John P. Hale, S. P. Chase, and William H. Seward voted, in 1850, for a dissolution of the Union! The Federalists, now the abolitionists, assumed a violent opposition to the fugitive slave law—mobs in Massachusetts, New Jersey, Ohio, and Wisconsin broke jails and rescued fugitive slaves from the custody of the Federal authorities—and denounced the democrats, as "*Slave Catchers.*" States nullified the act of Congress and the Constitution of the United States by opposing the fugitive slave law by force. Clay said, "that the white man must govern the black man, or the black must govern the white." Clay's Speeches vol. 2, p. 367.

At the session of Congress of 1854, the Federal party again sprung the slavery question in Congress. It is true that they did not call themselves Federalists as that name had become odious. They found it necessary to come under an assumed name; but still they were the advocates of Federal principles. "Whence cometh Smyth, albe he Knight or Squire, But from the smith that smiteth at the fire."

We find the Radicals possessing the *ear marks* of Federalism! We quote the following from Jefferson, which is as applicable to Republicans as it was to the Federalists.

"The Hartford Convention, the victory of Orleans, the peace of Ghent, prostrated the name of Federalism. Its votaries abandoned it through shame and mortification; and called themselves Republicans. But the name alone is changed, the principles are the same. On the eclipse of Federalism with us, although not its extension, its leaders got up the Missouri question, under the false front of lessening the measure of slavery, but with the real view of producing geographical divisions of parties which might insure them the next President."—Jefferson's Works vol. 7, pp. 325–6.

This is a fair picture of the so-called Republicans. Their aim was to secure the next President, in 1860 and when once in power, then to establish Federal principles at the cannon's mouth and the point of the bayonet. On the 23d May, 1854, the Missouri compromise was repealed and the Kansas and Nebraska bill passed. This was what the Federalists, or abolitionists desired, as it gave them an opportunity to form a sectional party opposed to the institution of slavery everywhere. This broke up old party lines. The *Northern Whigs*, with a few exceptions, abandoned the Southern Whigs and joined the abolitionists (Federalists,) to form a *new party*, called at first the "Anti-Nebraska party." They used this name to get apostate democratic politicians to join them. Many democrats who were opposed to the repeal of the Missouri compromise left the democratic party and joined the anti-Nebraska party. The democrats joined this new sectional party in hopes of riding into office on the slavery question, and on the troubled waters of excitement and popular change. Strange to say those apostate democrats still claimed to be democrats ; asserting that the old Democrats had abandoned their old landmarks and had sold themselves to the Southern oligarchy. So intense was the indignation of the abolitionists, that they burned Senator Douglas in effigy. He was denounced by an abolition mob on his way from Washington to Chicago. At Chicago he was threatened with violence by the mob, at a public meeting; where he attempted to explain his position and the nature of the Kansas and Nebraska bill. Party excitement grew intense; the Republican party held that Congress had power to abolish slavery in the territories by virtue of the ordinance of 1787, and article 4, section 3, part 2 of the constitution of the United States. This perversion of the constitution led to the election of Lincoln and brought on the rebellion in 1861. For the people would never interfere with slavery in the territories were they not persuaded that the constitution gave them that right ; for before the election of Lincoln the people held the constitution in great reverence and no party dared to advocate an unconstitutional act or measure. Clay said, that "the free states have no more right to interfere with institutions in the slave states, confined to the exclusive jurisdiction of those states, than they would have to interfere with institutions existing in any foreign country."—Clay's Speeches vol. 2, p. 336.

Such was the indignation raised by this new-fangled fusion party against the Nebraska bill, that it was the favorite theme of New England preachers from their pulpits. Assaults on the slave power were poured forth from the stump, the pulpit and through the press. Many New England ministers of the gospel ceased to preach "*Christ and he crucified*"—but devoted their Sunday services and sermons to the denunciation of democrats, the slave power and the Nebraska bill. They excluded the gospel from their churches and turned political stump speakers.— By such means the democrats were defeated this year, only *thirteen* democrats were elected to the House from the North, and even four of them were from Missouri. The opponents of the Kansas and Nebraska bill appealed to the passions of the people of the North, through the press, the pulpit, and public meetings to contribute money, clothing and *Sharp's rifles*, and to aid in sending emigrants to Kansas to prevent Kansas from becoming a Slave State ; and to commence a war between the North and South,—which in due time would give them an opportunity to abolish slavery everywhere. For this purpose emigrant aid societies were immediately organized in New England, New York and other Northern States, which furnished money, clothing, and *Sharp's rifles* to emigrants, who were sent to Kansas to defeat the Kansas and Nebraska act. Plymouth church, Brooklyn (H. W. Beecher's) raised a subscription to supply families going to Kansas with a *bible* and a rifle.—Men of the Times by Harriet Beecher Stowe, p. 555. Those emigrants marched through Chicago, on their way to Kansas, with streaming banners, with emblazoned mottoes, denouncing Douglas, the Kansas bill and the democratic party. They marched through Missouri with their banners, causing great excitement; which provoked a counter opposition on the part of Missourians. This armed emigration caused civil war in Kansas, which was what the Republicans wanted. The cry of *"bleeding Kansas"* resounded from the soil of Kansas, to the halls of Congress and the State legislatures, as well as from the pulpits, the stump, and through the press. The name of "border ruffians" was given to all democrats North, South, East and West. The Republicans charged the Democrats with trying to force Kansas into the Union as a slave State. This falsehood reiterated daily through the press, from the pulpits, and by public meetings, alienated thousands from the old democratic party who were led bound hand and foot into the "Republican" camp. Thousands thought that the old time honored democratic party was annihilated forever. That it had shared the fate of the Whig party!! Another enemy to democracy made its appearance. This was the Know-Nothing party, which was only a revival of the Native American party. It was a revival of the Federal party of the alien and sedition laws notoriety. Their platform was hostility to Catholic foreigners. This party carried the election in New England, Maryland, and California, in 1854. In 1855, Massachusetts, Connecticut, New Hampshire, elected Know-Nothing governors and a large part of the state legislatures. California elected a Know-Nothing governor and a majority of the legislature. Thus, the democratic party had to fight both the Republicans and the Know-Nothings. In 1856, the Know-Nothings ran ex-President Fillmore for President on the Know-Nothing platform. The Republicans ran John C. Fremont, as a sectional candidate for the Presidency. The platform of the Republican party was *the abolition of slavery in the District of Columbia; the repeal of the fugitive slave law; opposition to the acquisition of any more slave territory; opposition to the admission of any more slave states into the Union.* In 1856, the Republicans hoisted on their banner only sixteen states, to show that they wanted to sever the Union. Both the Republicans and Know-Nothings took their candidates from the Free states to show their anti-slavery feelings. They said that they would not hold faith with slaveholders. That they would either abolish slavery in the south or else let the south go. That the constitution was anti-slavery. That they wanted an "anti-slavery bible," an anti-slavery God and an anti-slavery government. In their speeches and debates they showed their hostility to slavery even in the states, where it then existed. Their cry was, down with the slave power. Both Know-Nothings and Republicans were defeated and James Buchanan was elected democratic President. After this defeat the Know-Nothings fused with the Republicans, on condition of getting a share of the public plunder! The democrats lost every northern state, except Illinois, Indiana, California, and Pennsylvania, and got every slave state, except Maryland, which went Know-Nothing.

The Republican party was now composed of Anti-Nebraska Democrats, Abolitionists, *free soilers*, Whigs, and Know-Nothings. This party swept the country like wild fire. The Know-Nothing party fell into bad odor, so much so, that in 1859, no one would own that he had ever been a member of the Know-Nothing party. Presidential vote of 1856: Buchanan,

Democrat, 1,838,169 ; Fremont, Rep. 1,341,264 ; Fillmore, Know-Nothing, 874, 534. Greeley Am. Conf. vol. 1, 284. A combination between Fremont and Fillmore would have defeated Buchanan. In 1857, the Dred Scott case came before the Supreme Court, when it was decided that a Negro was not a citizen of the United States. That Congress had no power to legislate on slavery in the territories. This opinion was denounced by the Republicans; the opinion was given to the public, through the Republican papers in a garbled manner. The Republicans denounced Chief Justice Taney as a traitor! The Dred Scott decision formed materials for Republican speeches and newspaper articles in the election campaigns. Unfortunately for the country a rupture took place between Douglas and President Buchanan on what is known as the Le Compton Constitution, which was sprung in Congress, at the session of 1857-8. This division divided the democracy at a time when the Republicans and Know-Nothings were united. This breach came to a crisis, in 1860. The Republicans held various and conflicting opinions to suit the public mind and to make votes. For they had no principles but to get into power, by some means fair or foul. They had one grand and controlling *idea*, the "Irrepressible conflict," which was formally announced by Seward, in his famous Rochester Speech, Oct. 25, 1858. In 1858, Lincoln said:

"In my opinion it will not cease until a crisis shall have been reached and passed." A house divided against itself cannot stand ! I believe the government cannot endure permanently half slave and half free. I do not expect the Union to be divided—I do not expect the house to fall—but, I do expect it will cease to be divided. It will become all one thing or all the other. Either the opponents of slavery will arrest the further spread of it, and place it where the public mind shall rest in the belief that it is in the course of ultimate extension." Lincoln's Speech, Springfield June 17, 1858. Seward's Speech at Rochester Oct. 25, 1858, on the irrepressible conflict.

This doctrine of Seward and Lincoln became the corner-stone of the Republican edifice! This doctrine alarmed the southern people when they saw a party coming into power with the avowed intention of finally abolishing slavery everywhere. The doctrine of the irrepressible conflict "was advocated by the Republicans from the pulpit, through the press, from the Halls of Congress, and the state legislatures. The *ultimate abolishment of slavery* was their favorite topic all over the North.

CHAPTER XII.

December 14, 1859, a resolution was adopted in the senate, inquiring into the cause which led to the invasion of the state of Virginia, and the seizure of the United States arsenal and armory by a band of armed men, under the lead of John Brown, as follows: "Whether the same was attended by armed resistance to the authorities and public force of the United States, and by the murder of any of the citizens of Virginia, or of any troops sent there to protect the public property: "Whether such invasion and seizure was made under color of any organization intended to subvert the government of any of the states of the Union; what was the character and extent of such organization; and whether any citizens of the United States not present were implicated therein, or accessary thereto, by

contributions of money, arms, munitions, or otherwise. "What was the
character and extent of the military equipment in the hands or under the
control of said armed band; and where and how and when the same was
obtained and transported to the place so invaded. "That said committee
report whether any and what legislation may, in their opinion, be necessary
on the part of the United States for the future preservation of the peace of
the country, or for the safety of the public property; and that the said committee have power to send for persons and papers."

It appears from the evidence taken before the committee of the senate,
that John Brown, in the winter of 1857-8, had organized a party in Kansas
for the purpose of making war on Slavery. He organized a military school
at Springdale, in Iowa. In 1858, he went to Canada and called a convention at Chatham, and formed a provisional government as a preliminary step
to the invasion of the Slave States.—Greeley's American Conf. vol. 1, p. 287.

John Brown had received money, clothing, and arms from "Massachusetts State Kansas Committee," and from the "National Kansas Aid Committee, and from several persons of wealth and influence in New England.
Pikes were manufactured for him in Connecticut and other places, and put
into his hands to be used for anti-slavery purposes. He was present at
several of the anti-slavery meetings, where he received pecuniary aid. It was
well known that Brown would use force against the Slave States. He
had arms sent to him to Chambersburg, Pennsylvania. He had them then
removed to Harper's Ferry and concealed. They consisted of arms for 1,500
men besides 200 Sharp's rifles, 200 revolvers, and 1,000 pikes with
ammunition and clothing. He had supposed that if he appeared in any of
the Slave States and put arms in the hands of the slaves that they would
flock to his standard and inaugurate servile war, and overthrow
the states government and establish a provisional government. With
this object in view he, with about 18 others, on the night of
October 16, 1859, entered the village of Harper's Ferry and took possession of the United States arsenal and armory. He made a futile attempt
to arouse the Negroes and incite them to insurrection and confined
many of the citizens in the Engine-house of the armory. He was captured
by Colonel Robert E. Lee, who commanded the United States marines; but
not until the engine-house was taken by storm. In this encounter between
the John Brown party and the United States troops 14 were either killed
or wounded. This, indeed, was the beginning of the war, for it so alarmed
the southern people that they were sure that the object of the Republicans,
if they should get into power, was to free the slaves. The following from
the writings of Jefferson will show that the people of the South had for a
number of years a dread of a servile insurrection. "What does the Holy
alliance in and out of Congress mean to do with us on the Missouri question? And this, by the by, is but the name of the case, that it is only the
John Doe or Richard Roe of the ejectment, the real question, Are slaves to be
presented with freedom and a dagger? For if Congress has power to regulate the condition of the inhabitants of the states, within the states it will be
but another exercise of that power, to declare that all shall be free. Are we
then to see again Athenian and Lacedemonian Confederacies? To wage another
Peloponnesian war to settle the ascendency between them, or is this the
tocsin of merely a servile war? That remains to be seen; but not, I hope,
by you or me. Surely, they will parley a while, and give us time to get
out of the way. What a bedlamite is man!"—Jefferson's Works vol. 7, p. 200.

We see what an alarm the slavery question had raised then—it had kept
on increasing until John Brown's raid had alarmed the southern people and
filled their minds with the dread of a servile war. John Brown was aided

at the north, with money, clothing, and arms; and many of the influential parties, at the north, approved of the John Brown raid.　George L. Stearns, Chairman of the Massachusetts State Kansas Committee, said under oath before the senate Committee that he "believed John Brown to be the representative man of this century, as Washington was of the last.　The Harper's Ferry affair, and the capacity shown by the Italians for self-government the great events of this age.　One will free Europe, and the other America." Brown's execution called forth from the Republicans, a stream of vile abuse on the slave power.　Songs were sang to the tune of John Brown's "Soul, marching on" through the ethereal realms of space. Greeley said: Let no one doubt that history will accord an honorable niche to old John Brown." Youth's History of the War, p. 62.　In 1860, Lincoln was nominated by the Republicans.　He ran on the Chicago platform.　The Chicago Republican convention met May 11, 1860.　This was purely an anti-slavery convention, for David Wilmot was temporary President—and Giddings of Ohio was a leading spirit.　Greeley, vol. 1, pp. 819-321.　The Democrats split in fragments and nominated two candidates.—It will now be admitted by the impartial reader that if the people had elected Douglas we would not have been cursed with a civil war.　If the principles of popular sovereignty had been adopted we would not have been plunged into the most cruel, stupendous and devastating rebellion known in history !!　Lincoln was not elected by the popular vote but by the constitution—for he lacked 980,170 of a popular majority.　If Douglas, Breckinridge and Bell men fused they could have elected Douglas and defeated Lincoln. Greeley, Am. Confl. vol. 1, p. 328. Had the people of the North followed Washington's Councils and had they not established a sectional party, arraying one section of the country against the other we would not have been plunged into the vortex of revolution; we would not have to pass through a reign of terror; we would not have a mountain of debt on our backs—we would not be ground to powder by eternal taxation—our substance would not be taken to feed a legion of United States tax-gatherers !!　And the bread would not be taken from the mouth of labor to feed a few pampered bondholders, and the industry of the country would not be taken to support monopolies.　The Republicans can never exculpate themselves from their responsibility in fomenting the rebellion.　Greeley, Seward, Phillips, Garrison, Wade, Wilson, Chandler and the other leaders of the Republican party are as responsible for the rebellion and its consequences as the Fire-eaters of the South.　Seward, in 1853, formed a sectional party on the principles of hostility to slavery and its ultimate extinction in all the states.　He then laid the mine which exploded in rebellion.　For the extremists North and South, Republicans and Fire-Eaters had mutually fed and fostered one another.　The speeches of the Northern fanatics were published and circulated South to "fire the Southern heart," and the speeches of the Fire-Eaters were published in Northern newspapers to increase Northern hostility to the "slave power." Greeley showed some consistency in "bailing Jeff Davis" for their mutual teachings helped to plunge the country into war.　The Republicans said that the fathers of the Constitution were abolitionists—speeches were made to show that Washington, Jefferson, Madison, Franklin, Henry, and Clay, were anti-slavery men.—Globe 1859-60, pp. 1028-1854-5.

Seward said in his Rochester speech, Oct. 25th, 1858:

"So resistance to slavery and devotion to freedom, the popular element now actively working for the Republican party among the people must and will be the resources for its ever renewing strength and constant invigoration."—Globe, 1859-60, p. 154.　This manifesto from Seward, who was considered the leading spirit of the Republican party, together with the speeches of Phillips—the onslaught of the Republican press—the numerous anti-slavery tracts of the Sabbath schools, the Helper book had created a reign of terror at the south—the dread of servile war—the Republican orators "played on a harp of a thousand strings"—in some places they claimed to be Democrats—that the Democracy committed political heresy in 1854.—Globe, 1859-60, p. 1027.   They claimed that the Republican party now held the principles of the fathers. During the session of Congress for 1859-60, a great deal of time was taken up with the slavery question, John Brown speeches—Seward's irrepressible conflict—the Dred Scott case—and slavery in the territories.   This session was wasted in making political Capital.   Seward said in his place in Congress, in 1858:

"Free labor has at last apprehended its rights, its interests, its power, and its destiny, and is organizing itself to assume the government of the Republic.   It will henceforth meet you boldly and resolutely here; it will meet you everywhere, in the Territories or out of them, wherever you may go to extend slavery. It has driven you back in California and in Kansas; it will invade your soil." In Delaware, Maryland, Virginia, Missouri, and Texas.   It will meet you in Arizona, in Central America, and even in Cuba. The invasion will be not merely harmless, but beneficent, if you yield seasonably to its just and moderate demands."—Globe 1859-60. p. 37.

Geddings had said:

"I look forward to a day when I shall see a servile insurrection in the South—when the black men, supplied with bayonets, shall wage a war of extermination against the whites—when the master shall see his dwelling in flames and his hearth polluted; and though I may not mock at their calamity, and laugh when their fear cometh, yet I shall hail it as the dawn of political millennium."—Youth's History of the War, p. 60.

This was, indeed, a declaration of war.   This shows that the object of the war was the annihilation of slavery.

This struggle finally came to a crisis on the defeat of Douglas and the election of Lincoln.   Had not the abolitionists made the abolition of slavery an issue the Fire-Eaters of the south could never have succeeded in their secession plans—for the great masses of the people were religiously attached to the Union—nothing but the alarm of a servile war, fomented by abolition speakers and writers, could induce the people of the south to revolt!! Southern Statesmen, in their speeches, said that they were afraid of the growing strength and power of the abolitionists.   The Fire-Eaters quoted the speeches of the abolitionists to show the growing sentiment and hostility of the anti-slavery party.—The Republicans rejoiced in the success of the Fire-Eaters, in the southern elections.   The Fire-Eaters threatened to secede on the election of Lincoln; which threat was met with derision and defiance by the Republicans.

The Republicans told the people of the North that the southern threat was mere gasconade—mere idle threats of intimidation.   That after election the southern mind would become calm, and the political excitement would subside: that the cry of dissolution, having been used so often, was nothing but a mere electioneering trick.   It is certain that the Radical Republicans hoped that the South would plunge the country into rebellion, so that, having the power of the government in their hands—the purse and the sword—they could, in the turmoil of war, abolish slavery in the South, and establish the equality of races.   The Federalist wing of the Republican party prayed for war, so that they could abolish the state governments, and establish a consolidated government, and, finally, a military despotism, as a stepping-stone to monarchy, and their darling idol the British Constitution!

In vain did the Douglas democrats appeal to the people warning them of the imminent danger of the country. In vain did they warn them of the fearful calamity of civil war. The people, led by blind and fanatical zeal were led captive into the abolition camp. They committed themselves to the guidance of blind leaders; they voted against Douglas; they left the old democratic party, and followed the lead of the Republicans, who were Federalists under false colors; whose ambition was to plunge the country into war; their motto was rule or ruin!! The Republicans said that if the southern people should leave the Union, they would, like the prodigal son, be glad to come back. That the north could whip them back in sixty days.

CHAPTER XIII.

After the election of Lincoln, December 20, 1860, South Carolina passed an ordinance of secession. On the 26th of December Major Anderson evacuated Fort Moultrie, spiking his guns, and occupied Fort Sumter. The withdrawal of South Carolina from the Union was treated by northern Republican papers with derision. They said that at the approach of the first regiment in Charleston harbor secession cockades would be found as scarce as cherries in the snow. But the New York *Tribune* said encouragingly, "let the prodigal go," for the leading Republican papers and politicians wished for war so that they could wipe out slavery and establish a reign of terror and govern their enemies by military forces!! Yet in a few months afterwards the *Tribune* said, that the southern cities should be laid in ashes and their soil sown with blood. That the "rebels" returning home would find their wives and children cowering in rags, and famine sitting at their fireside.—*Tribune* Nov. 26 and December 17, 1860.

The same paper said, May 1, 1861: "The whole coast of the South from the Delaware to the Rio Grande, must be a solitude."—Again, it said: "When a portion of this Union, large enough to form an independent self-sustaining nation shall see fit to say authoritatively to the residue, we want to go away from you, we shall say—and we trust with self-respect, if not regard for principles of self-government, will restrain the residue of the American people to say go!"

In the *interim* between the secession of South Carolina and the meeting of Congress, in December, 1860, the democratic party hoped that some compromise would be effected which would avert the impending danger and effusion of fraternal blood!

Greeley said that the Chicago platform was worth nine Unions—the Federalists never did love the constitution; they denounced it as a league with hell and covenant with death. They had often denounced Washington— they poured out the vials of their wrath and intensified indignation on the fathers of the constitution for not establishing the British monarchy with its corruption and vile despotism. They preached from time to time "to let the Union slide." They wanted to plunge the country into civil war, so that they could march from military despotism to their favorite goal, a monarchy after the model of the British constitution." During the war the Radicals could write or speak against the Union and constitution without danger or molestation from the authorities at Washington. But woe to the unfortunate democrat who had the temerity to find fault with the blind policy of the administration. The most intense excitement pervaded the public mind, north and south—various and conflicting opinions were entertained as to the policy which Lincoln would pursue, on assuming the control of the government.

The New York *Herald* and other papers called on the President elect to quiet the public mind by disclosing, in plain, candid, and manly terms the policy and course he would pursue, in regard to the threatened secession of the southern states, when the reins of government came into his hands. But he (who was under the control of the abolitionists), said that it was time enough when he got into power. That it would do no good to disclose his policy. He adhered to this determination to the hour of his death—when hard set he could ward off all such inquiries by a timely old joke.

Had he told the people that he would not interfere with slavery, it would have calmed the over-excited minds of the Southern people; and the leaders of secession would be unable to incite a rebellion. For the people of the South loved and cherished the Union and nothing could have induced them to secede but their fears of a servile insurrection. Lincoln did not want to sacrifice the Chicago platform. Had he followed the example of Washington, in the Pennsylvania Whiskey rebellion, or of Jackson in the South Carolina nullification difficulty, we would not have been plunged into a fratricidal war, we would not have sacrificed thousands of precious lives to the God of battles—we would not have erected a monument of bonds to perpetuate the reign of Radical tyranny—we would not have to groan under a mountain of taxation—we would not have desecrated the temples of Religion — we would not have suppressed the freedom of speech and of the press, in the name of liberty—we would not have seen the constitution trampled under foot, in the name of law and order— we would not have seen sovereign states reduced to territories, the ballot-box discarded and loyalty pronounced by the lips of treason. The Halls of Congress would not have been polluted by the most infamous venality, corruption, and bribery unparalleled in the annals of history! Those who wish to contrast the honesty of the democratic party with the Republican party should ponder on the Evidence of Horace Greeley in his charge against Democrats for annexing Texas and for paying that state ten millions of dollars as a consideration for the relinquishing of her claim to certain territories.

"By this article, the public debt of Texas, previously worth in market but twenty to thirty per cent. of its face was suddenly raised nearly or quite to par, to the entire satisfaction of its holders—many of them members of Congress, or their very intimate friends. Corruption, thinly disguised, haunted the purlieus and stalked through the halls of the Capitol; and numbers, hitherto in needy circumstances, suddenly found themselves rich. The great majority, of course, were impervious to such influences; but the controlling and controllable minority were not. This was probably the first instance in which measures of vital consequence to the country were carried or defeated in Congress under the direct spur of pecuniary interest.—*Ibid.* 208-9. See what Benton says: This charge is wanton and not supported by authority. But even taking it as true, it proves that Congress was free from all pecuniary corruption until the advent of the Republican party into power; for this is the only charge of corruption made by Greeley against the democratic party to this time.' Lincoln knew that there would be war even before he got into office, notwithstanding his "*nobody hurt.*" For he knew that Frank Blair had organized, in secret regiments of Wide-Awakes, in St. Louis. That he had organized in St. Louis a Committee of safety. That Blair had intended to hold St. Louis if Missouri left the Union.—

Life of Seymour and Blair pp. 328–9, 331–335–6. Blair called on Lincoln at his home in Springfield and told him the above facts.—*Ibid.*

All of the slave states, except South Carolina, were represented in the session of Congress of 1860–61. The leading Southerns wanted to save the Union by such a compromise, as would exclude the slavery question from the halls of Congress. Those who passed the Missouri compromise and the compromise of 1850, wished to exclude the agitation of slavery from the Halls of Congress. But neither Lincoln nor the Republicans would yield the Chicago platform, as it would virtually be recognizing slavery. They boldly announced that the days of compromise were gone. For they well knew that if they abandoned the Chicago platform it would annihilate their party. This they would not do, for their ultra leaders were imbibed with Federal principles and beheld the long wished for opportunity to lay violent hands on the constitution, which stood in their way on their forward march towards centralization of power, the annihilation of the states, and the establishment of monarchy! Moreover the Republicans, composed of the fag-end of all parties, held together by the cohesive power of corruption and public plunder, who saw glittering before their visions the long coveted booty, the spoils of the victor, feared that if they made terms with the "*slave power*" their abolition allies would secede from the republican camp, and join the democrats. For many abolitionists frankly told the Republicans that if they should yield to the "slave power," they, (the abolitionists,) would join the democrats and crush the Republicans. Lincoln and his party feared, that if they would compromise with the South and abandon the Chicago platform the democrats would again get into power. So they sacrificed their country to save their party. For rather than compromise they would "*let the Union slide.*" The New York *Tribune* said on November 26, 1800:

"If the cotton states unitedly and earnestly wished to withdraw peacefully from the Union, we think they should and would be allowed to do so. Any attempt to compel them by force to remain would be contrary to the principles enunciated in the immortal Declaration of Independence—contrary to the fundamental ideas on which human liberty is based."

From the *Tribune* of December 17, 1860:

"If it (the Declaration of Independence) justified the secession from the British Empire of three millions of colonists in 1776, we do not see why it would not justify the secession of five millions of southerners from the Union in 1861." The same paper again said, February 23, 1861:

"Whenever it shall be clear that the great body of the southern people have become conclusively alienated from the Union, and anxious to escape from it WE WILL DO OUR BEST TO FORWARD THEIR VIEWS. The New York *Tribune* in an article two days after Lincoln's election was for letting the South go. Greeley's Am. Conf. vol. 1, p. 358. Thus, we find the leading Republican papers of the North encouraging secession!

The southern members in Congress said that if the "*Arizona Bill*" was not passed that they would leave the Union in sixty days. But the leading Republicans told them, that as the North had more men and money they would whip the South back—yea starve them into submission, by making them eat their own cotton. That they could whip them back in three months! That the country wanted some "blood-letting." Members from Pennsylvania, on the floor of Congress, boasted that Pennsylvania could whip the South. Members from Ohio proposed to take a contract for putting down the Rebellion!

The southern members said that they wanted some guarantee for slavery; as the North had passed personal liberty bills to prevent the rendition of fugitive slaves to their owners. They also said that the election of a President on a sectional and abolition platform was the forerunner of Negro emancipation. That if they did not get some guarantee for slavery they would secede from the Union, peaceably if they could, if not, by force. That they wanted that Congress would guarantee that the general government would not interfere with slavery.

The Southern people, particularly the women, feared that if the Republicans got control of the Federal government they would abolish slavery in the states, and turn the South into a second San Domingo. In the midst of this excitement they were made to believe, that France and England would become Southern allies, that Northern commerce and manufactures would be crippled, and that the Southern army would make New York and Boston its headquarters. By such arguments the people of the South were seduced into rebellion. "All know the immediate cause of it" (the war). "The North and South were at length arrayed against each other, in two great political parties on the question of slavery.—Thus the breach between the North and South gradually widened, till without some radical change, it became apparent that a separation or attempted separation was inevitable. Scenes were enacted in every Congress that did not tend to allay excitement and even gradually became more hostile in feeling and sentiment than any two entirely separate nations, in the civilized world. In this emergency, some Whigs of its old leaders cast about for something on which to organize a new party, and seeing how deep and widespread was the anti-slavery sentiment of the North, determined to make it in some form its platform. This was the first great step towards placing the North and South face to face to each other in a struggle for the control of the government." Headley vol. 1, p. 37. The Republicans of the North held out to the deluded followers the hope that there would be no war at all,—that after the South had made a few secession speeches in Congress that the excitement would die out, and peace would reign in Mosco! But the leaders well knew that there would be war, but they were waiting for an opportunity to precipitate it. They knew well that the people would have to support the authorities right or wrong! The people were led into war before they were aware of its frightful dimensions. Thousands thought that it would be over in thirty days! Indeed, the Republicans wished to plunge the country into war. They spoke of impeaching President Buchanan. They spoke of Cromwell's triumph over Charles the First, and of the Red Republicans of France over Louis XVI. They depicted in vivid colors the American reign of terror, as effectually as if they knew the bloody programme that was about to deluge the country with human gore. While the extremists North and South were endeavoring to precipitate the country into internecine war, the Douglas democrats appealed to both extremists North and South to settle the troubles of the country by compromise. In the midst of this posture of affairs the patriot John C. Crittenden offered his famous compromise measures 18 December, 1860, to save the Union, by restoring the Missouri compromise, which would have placed the question of slavery out of the reach and control of the Federal government. "But the party clamor at the north by the Republican party drowned all patriots. Headley vol. 1. p. 46.—Crittenden Compromise. Globe, 1860-61. p. 114. The Republican press and politicians, a few weeks previous, when South Carolina left the Union, said let the South go in peace, as a wayward sister;—that a union held together by bayonets was a despotism; that the union should not be held together by force now; they said that the "days of compromises were gone by;" that they would make no more compromises with slavery. They denounced the Crittenden Compromise. All who advocated a compromise were branded as traitors, who were in league with the Southern rebels, or as sympathizers, giving them aid and comfort. They proclaimed in the Halls of Congress, and through the leading press, that they would let the Union slide rather than the Chicago platform. So the Republicans preferred their party platform to peace. Jeff Davis said that if the compromise came from the north, the south would not leave the Union; but the Republicans would not compromise.—Greeley, Am. Conf. vol. 1, p. 883. Indeed, they showed a want of sincerity in not adopting the Crittenden Compromise; as they gained strength from the democratic ranks by the clamor raised after the repeal of the Missouri compromise. Now, they refused to restore it, as they voted against extending it to the Pacific, in 1850. Indeed, it was the repeal of the Missouri compromise which gave power to the abolitionists as they were able to fuse with all parties opposed to the Kansas and Nebraska act and the repeal of the Missouri compromise. The responsibility of secession and rebellion must be divided between the fanatics of the North and the Fire-Eaters of the South, who for years had labored to bring about a dissolution of the Union. The majority of the southern people were deceived and believed they were in danger of subjugation and that they would have to contend with an insurrection of the slaves after emancipation." Headley vol. 1, p. 48.

December, 1860, Mr. Adrian offered a resolution in Congress, the purport of which was that Congress should abandon the doctrine of interference with slavery in the territories.—Cong. Globe 1860, p. 77. That the personal liberty bills in the states interfering with slavery should be repealed. That the fugitive slave law should be obeyed and that the states should faithfully adhere to the compromises of the constitution. This resolution was opposed by the Republicans as being in conflict with their platform. They said that they would not abandon the Chicago platform if the heavens should fall! December 1860, Mr. Mallory offered a resolution to protect slavery south of the line of 30 deg. 30 min.—Cong. Globe, 1860–61 p. 78. So far were the Republicans from conceding to these new demands of the South that Mr. Kilgore offered a resolution December 12, 1860, that the right of trial by Jury should be allowed to fugitive slaves which would in many of the northern states amount to a substantial repeal of the fugitive slave law.—Cong. Globe 1860–61, p. 78.

Wade said, on the 17th day of December, 1860:—

"If I know myself I am the last man that would be the advocate of any law or any act that would humiliate or dishonor any section of this country, or any individual in it: and, on the other hand, let me tell these gentlemen I am exceedingly sensitive upon that same point. Whatever they may think about it, I would rather sustain an injury than an insult or dishonor; and I would be as unwilling to inflict it upon others as I would be to submit to it myself. I never will do either the one or the other if I know it."—Cong. Globe 1860–61, p. 100.

Seward said to Mr. Adams, United States minister to London: "For these reasons he (Mr. Lincoln) would not be disposed to reject a cardinal dogma of theirs (the secessionists) namely, that the Federal government could not reduce the seceding states to obedience by conquest, even although he were disposed to question that position, but in fact the President willingly accepts it as true, only an imperial or despotic government could subjugate thoroughly disaffected and insurrectionary members of the state. This Federal Republican system of ours is of all forms of government the very one most unfitted for such labor."

Was this the true sentiment of the leading Republicans, or was it a delusion and a snare to blind the people, by making them think that there would be no war? Was not this a mere sham to prevent and defeat compromise; to delude the people into the belief that everything would be all right and that peace would reign in Warsaw? Their object being delay until the Republican party was in an attitude to make war and then to dictate their own terms at the point of the bayonet. The conclusion drawn from the after acts of the Republican drama is irresistible that they were not sincere in their professions of peace.

On the 17th January, 1861, Florida seceded from the Union: Mississippi on January the 9th, 1861: Alabama January 11, 1861: Georgia January 20, 1861: Louisiana January 26, 1861, and Texas February 1, 1861. Thus, in three months after Lincoln's election, all the cotton states had seceded from the Union and seized the New Orleans mint, they had secured all the forts and arsenals except Sumter and Fort Pickens.

Resolutions were offered in Congress calling for a national convention, but they were defeated by the Republicans.—Globe 1860-61, pp. 114-17 316. Buchanan's message, Dec. 8, 1860:

"The different sections of the Union are now arrayed against each other, and the time has arrived, so much dreaded by the father of his country when hostile geographical parties have been formed. I have long foreseen and often forewarned my countrymen of the now impending danger."

"Violent agitation of the slavery question throughout the North for the last quarter of a century has at length produced its malign influence on the slaves, and inspired them with vague notions of freedom. Hence a sense of security no longer existed around the family altar. This feeling of peace at home has given place to apprehensions of servile insurrection. Many a matron throughout the South retires at night in dread of what may befall herself and her children before the morning. Should this apprehension of domestic danger, whether real or imaginary, extend and intensify itself until it shall pervade the masses of the southern people, then disunion will become inevitable." "It cannot be denied that, for five and twenty years, the agitation at the North against slavery in the South has been incessant. In 1835, pictorial handbills and inflammatory appeals were circulated extensively throughout the South, of a character to excite the passions of the slaves; and, in the language of General Jackson, to stimulate them to insurrections, and produce all the horrors of a servile war. This agitation has ever since been continued by the public press, by the proceedings of state and county conventions, and by abolition sermons and lectures. The time of Congress has been occupied in violent speeches on this never-ending subject; and appeals in pamphlet and other forms, indorsed by distinguished names, have been sent forth from this central point, and spread broadcast over the Union.

"How easy would it be for the American people to settle the slavery question forever." All that is necessary to accomplish the object, and all for which the slave states have ever contended, is to be let alone, and permitted to manage their domestic institutions in their own way."

"The most palpable violations of constitutional duty which have yet been committed consist in the acts of different State Legislatures to defeat the execution of the fugitive slave law."

"In order to justify secession as a constitutional remedy, it must be on the principle that the Federal government is a mere voluntary association of states, to be dissolved at pleasure by any one of the contracting parties If this be so, the confederacy is a mere rope of sand, to be penetrated and dissolved by the first adverse wave of public opinion in any of the states "

"The question fairly stated is: Has the constitution delegated to Congress the power to coerce a state into submission which is attempting to withdraw or has actually withdrawn from the Confederacy? If answered in the affirmative, it must be on the principle that the power has been conferred upon Congress to declare and to make war against a state. After much serious reflection I have arrived at the conclusion that no such power has been delegated to Congress or to any other department of the Federal Government. It is manifest upon an inspection of the constitution, that this is not among the specific and enumerated powers granted to Congress; and it is equally apparent that its exercise is not necessary and proper for carrying into execution any one of these powers. So far from this power having been delegated to Congress, it was expressly refused by the Convention which framed the constitution.

"It appears, from the proceedings of that body, that on the 31st May, 1787, the Clause *authorizing an exertion of the force of the whole against a delinquent State* came up for consideration. Mr. Madison opposed it in a brief but powerful speech, from which I shall extract but a single sentence. He observed: The use of force against a state would look more like a declaration of war than an infliction of punishment; and would probably be considered by the party attacked as a dissolution of all previous compacts by which it might be bound!"

"Upon this motion the clause was unanimously postponed, and was never I believe again presented. Soon afterwards, on the 8th June, 1787, when incidentally adverting to the same subject he said: Any government for the United States, formed on the supposed practicability of using force against the unconstitutional proceedings of the States, would prove as visionary and fallacious as the Government of Congress: evidently meaning the then existing Congress of the old confederation.

Without descending to particulars, it may be safely asserted, that the power to make war against a state is at variance with the whole spirit and intent of the Constitution. Suppose such a war should result in the conquest of a state; how are we to govern it afterwards? Shall we hold it as a province, and govern it by despotic power? In the nature of things we could not by physical force, control the will of the people, and compel them to elect senators and representatives to Congress."

"The fact is, that our union rests upon public opinion, and can never be cemented by the blood of its citizens shed in civil war. If it cannot live in the affections of the people, it must one day perish. Congress possesses many means of preserving it by conciliation; but the sword was not placed in their hands to preserve it by force."

This message caused great excitement among the Republicans. Buchanan was openly denounced as a traitor. He was blamed for not sending troops into South Carolina—for making any mention of compromise or reconciliation. The majority of the people north and south were of the opinion that there was no power in Congress to coerce a state. The leading Republicans, such as Greeley of the New York *Tribune*, held this doctrine. But nearly all except the leading politicians and their fanatical dupes shuddered at the idea of bloodshed. And if a convention of all the states in the union had assembled they would be adverse to bloodshed and would yield to the compromise measures. But the Radicals did not want any compromise which would oust the slavery question from Congress and politics. Buchanan was in favor of a compromise, for he said:

"The explanatory amendment might be confined to the final settlement of the true construction of the constitution on three special points:

1. "An express recognition of the right of property in slaves in the states where it now exists or may afterwards exist.

2. "The duty of protecting this right in all the common Territories throughout their territorial existence, and until they shall be admitted as states into the Union, with or without slavery, as the constitutions may prescribe.

3. "A like recognition of the right of the Master to have his slaves, who had escaped from one state to another, restored and 'delivered up' to him, and of the validity of the fugitive slave law enacted for this purpose, together with a declaration that all state laws impairing or defeating this right are violations of the constitution, and are consequently null and void." This would be adopting both the Dred Scott decision and the recent Breckinridge platform and ingrafting them on the constitution.—The Republicans denounced it and said before they would submit to such an amendment of the constitution they would let the Union slide.—It would in substance swallow up the Chicago platform. Greeley said he would let nine Unions slide before he would give up the Chicago platform.

The border states now appealed to the cotton states and to the northern Republicans, to compromise and avert civil war. They said that the border states had suffered more from the intermeddling abolitionists of the north, than the cotton states. That their slaves were stolen and sent north by the "underground railroad," while the cotton states had lost but very few slaves. That in the event of war between the north and south, all the fighting would be done on the soil of the border states. That they would be continually losing their slaves and other property, by the ravages of war on their soil. That the tide of war passing over their states would desolate their plantations, towns, and cities. That during such war their slaves would easily run away and cross over the line to Pennsylvania, Ohio, Indiana, and Illinois. That after the war was over, should the south gain her independence, yet, their slaves would run over to the free states. That the border states would have to maintain a chain of forts and bristling cannon along the border line to guard against raids from the Free-States. The Republican party refused to pass the Arizona Bill, or the Crittenden compromise, referred to, and the cotton states seceded, not by submitting the question of union or disunion to the people, but by a convention of the seceding states. There was a large union party south, and if encouraged by the Republican party, to compromise secession would be impossible! The border states of Delaware, Maryland, Virginia, North Carolina, Kentucky, Arkansas, Tennessee, and Missouri were adverse to a dissolution of the union. Virginia, the mother of states and statesmen, now entered the lists as a mediator between the north and the cotton states. She thought that she could effect such compromise measures, as would keep the border states in the union. That after some time the cotton states would come back again into the Union. For this purpose, she called on all the states to send delegates to a peace Congress, to be holden at the city of Washington.

This Congress met, with ex-President Tyler as chairman. The States of Michigan, Maine, and Minnesota refused to send Delegates to this Congress. For the Republicans had from time to time declared that they would not pass any compromise that would conflict with the Chicago platform. Numerous petitions were sent to Congress to compromise and save the country from the effusion of blood. North Carolina recommended the adoption of the Crittenden compromise. The Peace Congress broke up without accomplishing anything. This was the second time that the Republicans refused to compromise; preferring the *Chicago platform* to the peace and welfare of the country, the Constitution and the Union. They were willing to accept the horrors of civil war! The Republicans said that the advocates of compromise were traitors! That they would never compromise with the slave power. That they would rather let the Union slide than compromise with slavery. In 1861, Jefferson Davis, Fitzpatrick, Clay, Youlee, and Mallory resigned their seats in the United States Senate. Delegates from the six seceded states met at Montgomery, Alabama, on the 4th day of February, 1861, for the purpose of organizing a provisional government. This body adopted a Constitution for the confederate states on the 8th of February. On the 9th of February 1861, Congress elected Jefferson Davis President and Alexander H. Stevens vice-President. (Lost Cause p. 90.)

The Constitution adopted by the Confederate States was nearly the same as the old Constitution of the United States, with only a few exceptions. It prohibited bounties to any branch of business. The President held his office for six years; he was re-eligible to the same office. It provided for the right to take slave property into the territories.

Feb. 9th, 1861, the democratic convention of Ohio had sent a resolution to Congress to have that body "do something definite and practical to avert the terrible evils of civil war."—Cong. Globe 1861, p. 820. During this session of Congress a hope of pacification was entertained *north and south*. But the leading Republicans said that no concession would be yielded, that an issue of arms was more to be desired than otherwise. All propositions to compromise were voted down by the Republicans. Hale and several other senators said that they would not agree to any compromise whatsoever.—Cong. Globe 1860–61, p. 116. Feb. 27, 1801, a joint resolution from a select committee of *thirty-three*, to amend the constitution so that slavery should never be abolished in the slave states was defeated.—Cong. Globe 1861 p. 1264.

At this critical time the people of the *North* looked to Mr. Lincoln as an oracle, who was to decide the destinies of the country and calm the excitement of the public mind. This was no idle expectation, for Mr. Lincoln could by his proclamation keep the border states in the union by proposing peace measures on the principle of the Crittenden compromise. But instead of meeting the question as Washington did the "*Whiskey Rebellion*," in a plain, candid, frank, and unequivocal manner, he merely said, on his way to Washington, that *no body was hurt. That all things would be right.* —That the rebellion was only an artificial excitement.—Headley vol. 1, p. 49. Though he well knew that seven states had seceded from the union, he feigned to treat the whole matter lightly. He said it was no more than ·a mere riot. Notwithstanding he went disguised in a Scotch cloak and cap to Washington, and was the first President, who called on the army to furnish him with a body-guard. He went to the Capitol to be inaugurated, guarded by bristling steel! This was the first step towards a military despotism!

The seceded states told the border states that they did not want to break up the Union, but that they wanted to go out to get further guarantees for their property. That they wanted to get amendments to the Constitution guaranteeing their rights now or never.—Headley, vol. 1, p. 52.

Mr. Lincoln's inaugural was susceptible of different constructions. It was got up as a puzzle to impose on the people, so that it might be construed by those in favor of peace, as a peace measure; and by those in favor of abolition as an abolition measure; and by those in favor of war as a war measure. Indeed, it was the embodiment of a Non-Committal of his policy, which he did not want to disclose, until he was firmly established in the Presidential chair surrounded by a large army! He wished to feel his way slowly at first. When he secured an inch he was preparing to take a rod!

He wanted to keep his policy in the dark until Congress would enlarge his powers. He did not want to propose any plan, which would conflict with the Chicago platform; or the wishes of his party, even to save the Union! He was afraid of the wrath of the abolitionists, who threatened him with vengeance, as they did afterwards President Johnson, if he dared not to comply with their wishes. They even went so far as to say that they wanted a more active man to put down the rebellion.

During the session of Congress of 1860–61, the Republican party in Congress refused to let Judge Douglas and the Democratic party know what policy they intended to pursue to settle the difficulties of the country, whether by peace or war. This was the fatal rock on which the Republican party wrecked the constitution. Had Lincoln discarded the Radicals, who by their preaching, had brought the country to the awful precipice of "Civil War," he could have summoned to his aid the conservatives, loyal, and patriotic men of the country and having proposed compromise in his inaugural and in his message to Congress, he would have the support of the Democrats and conservative Republicans, the border statesmen and the Union men of the south. The cotton states would then be glad to return to the Union, as soon as a general amnesty bill would be passed in regard to acts of secession! But the Republicans, as already stated, denounced all propositions for compromise and conciliation and preferred to plunge the country into the fatal maelstrom of civil war rather than give up the Chicago platform! The extremists both north and south had control of the state Legislatures, and failed to pass acts for submitting the question of war or peace to a vote of the people, who would have voted for compromise to save the country from war.

The majority of the people thought that Lincoln would withdraw the troops from South Carolina. The New York Tribune and other Republican papers said "let the South go in peace." The President hesitated to reinforce Fort Sumter. Some discussion took place in the cabinet about the surrender of Fort Sumter. Chase was in favor of withdrawing the troops from Sumter. Greeley's Am. Conflict vol. 1, pp. 440–42.

The administration ordered a fleet to sail to reinforce Fort Sumter: which arrived outside of Charleston harbor and bar about the time that Beauregard was bombarding Fort Sumter. Immediately on the fall of Sumter the whole North was seized with a frenzy. Republican mobs raised the "flag excitement" and all persons who were known to be leading democrats were visited by mobs and compelled to "hoist the flags" over their buildings. Those who merely disapproved of the war, were denounced as traitors, rebels, or rebel sympathizers. To oppose or even speak against the war policy was considered treason. Such papers as opposed or even disapproved of the war policy were suppressed, either by mobs or the authorities and the proprietors and editors sent to Fort La Fayette and other forts. Meantime the President issued his proclamation, April 1861, declaring the cotton states in a state of rebellion and calling out 75,000 men, for three months, to protect the capital, and to repossess the public property. He declared the ports of the cotton states closed to the commerce of the world, as also the Mississippi River. He called a special session of Congress to meet on the 4th of July, 1861. The border states, through their executives, refused to respond to the call of the President for troops—declaring his acts calling out 75,000 men and closing the ports unconstitutional. Virginia, who before this proclamation, voted down in convention, secession by a majority of 70 for the Union—App. Globe, 1861–62, p. 13, now said they would not let the Federal troops invade the "Sacred soil of Virginia." The state of Kentucky declared that she would remain neutral. That she would not allow either the Federal or Confederate troops to invade the state! North Carolina had voted down secession before Lincoln's proclamation. Arkansas had postponed her convention until full in hopes of compromise which was hoped would be passed to save the Union. Now, these states declared that they would secede from the Union as all hope of pacific adjustment was lost. West Virginia seceded from the old State of Virginia, and set up a government of its own and sent representives to Congress, who were admitted to seats. This was a palpable violation of the constitution! This Congress sanctioned secession and a violation of the constitution, This shows the bad faith of the Republicans. They showed that they were always ready to violate the constitution whenever it answered their party purposes.—For they had always preferred party and public plunder to their country, the Union, and the constitution! Two days after the interview of the commissioners with Mr. Lincoln, Virginia joined the confederates. North Carolina, Tennessee and Arkansas followed Virginia, and the President occupied Maryland with troops; citizens were disarmed in Maryland and Missouri—many arrests were made—the writ of Habeas Corpus was suspended and the country put under a reign of terror! Tennessee was divided between the union men and the confederates. Indeed, there was a strong union element in every one of the seceded states before the President issued his proclamation. They were forced into rebellion when they beheld the reign of terror inaugurated by the Radicals, for the Radicals trampled under foot both free speech and free press! The Radicals called it treason to speak either in favor of peace or compromise, or even to say that the war would last long and that we would have to pay an enormous debt and eternal taxation! In Missouri, Governor Jackson and the other state officers were deposed by a state convention and new state officers elected. The state of Maryland attempted to secede. Congress met July 4th 1861, and the Republicans in their 4th of July orations told the people that there should be but one party, and that the Republican party. That opposition to Lincoln's administration was treason! They called upon the President to abolish slavery by proclamation. They said there could be but one party in the country. Those who were loyal and those who were disloyal. Those who differed with the President were either mobbed or bastiled! At this session of Congress (in 1861,) a resolution was passed prohibiting the transaction of any business but what pertained to war and for putting down the rebellion. This was done to exclude the passage of peace measures; for the Republicans did not want peace. They preferred war so as to have an opportunity to establish their Federal principles at the cannon's mouth and the point of the bayonet! But to lull the people into confidence in the policy of the administration as well as to get volunteers, congressmen said that the war would be over in three months. That they could cut off the southern people from the commerce of the world and starve them into submission. That the northern blockade squadron would prevent them from selling their cotton, and as they would have neither money nor provisions that they could not carry on the war for three months. The President made a great mistake in not calling Congress together sooner before the secessionists had time to discipline their armies. This delay cost the country thousands of lives, and millions of dollars!

The states of Maryland, Delaware, and the quasi state of West Virginia, Tennessee, Missouri, and Kentucky, sent representatives to Congress, still hoping to avert war by some compromise: but all compromises were read out of order, as the Republicans had passed a resolution the first day of the session, as already mentioned, that Congress should pass no act but what was necessary as a war measure; and to clothe the President with powers to put down the rebellion. By this foolish act the Republicans repudiated all accommodation or compromise with the South and left the question to be decided by the God of battles. Congress passed an act enlarging the powers of the President, so that he could, on his own motion, declare any part of the country in rebellion and blockade its ports, and seize on vessels of the citizens of said rebellious district found in any of the ports of the United States. Congress also ratified the acts of the President, just as if Congress had the right to abolish or violate the constitution or to absolve the President for violating it. Congress claimed and has ever since claimed the right to govern the country by the sword. For it fell back on the old Federal docrines of Hamilton and Adams, and the public law of imperial Rome. The republicans denounced as traitors all who spoke of preserving the constitution!

"Chief Justice Taney held that the President could not suspend the writ of Habeas Corpus by mere proclamation. But the Republicans having a majority in Congress, as well as a majority of the Northern governors and state Legislatures, set the opinion of the Chief Justice at defiance. They held that the mere will of the President and the Congress was the supreme power to which all should submit. The Chief Justice said, that if the liberty of the citizen were subject to the whim, caprice, or tyranny of military men the people would be reduced to abject slavery. This was prophetic. The President got an opinion from his Attorney General Bates, who held that the President, as a "*military necessity,*" could suspend the Writ of Habeas Corpus, close the ports and call out 75,000 men to suppress the rebellion. This opinion was weak and unfounded in law.

"At the beginning of the present Presidential term, four months ago, the functions of the Federal Government were found to be generally suspended within the several states of South Carolina, Georgia, Alabama, Mississippi, Louisiana, and Florida, excepting only those of the Post Office Department."

"Finding this condition of things, and believing it to be an imperative duty upon the incoming Executive to prevent, if possible, the consummation of such attempt to destroy the Federal Union, a choice of means to that end became indispensable. This choice was made, and war declared in the inaugural address. The policy chosen looked to the exhaustion of all peaceful measures, before a resort to any strong ones. It sought only to hold the public places and property not already wrested from the government, and to collect the revenue, relying for the rest on time, discussion, and the ballot-box."

Here was a pledge from the President of the United States to the people of the North and of the border states that the resort to arms was merely to recover the public property for the Constitution and the Union. This was done to induce the Democrats of the North and the Union men of the South to join the Union army. How he kept his promise—how he redeemed his pledge, his word, is now known to the world. Thousands of men North and South who joined the Union army and fought for the old flag would not do so if they knew that they would be used as a means for subjugation, for establishing a military despotism both North and South, but they were induced to join by means of this promise of the President. But in a few months he violated his promises and pledges! The same message shows Lincoln's policy on the evacuation of Sumter and on the practicability of reinforcing the same:

"On the 5th of March, (the present incumbent's first full day in office,) a letter of Major Anderson, commanding at Fort Sumter written on the 28th, of February signed at the war department on the 4th of March, was by that department placed in his hands. This letter expressed the professional opinion of the writer, that reinforcements could not be thrown into that fort within the time for his relief, rendered necessary by the limited supply of provisions, and with a view of holding possession of the same, with a force less than twenty thousand good and well disciplined men." * * "The whole was laid before Lieutenant General Scott, who at once concurred with Major Anderson in opinion." * * "He also stated at the same time that no such sufficient force was then at the control of the government."* * "In a purely military point of view, this reduced the duty of the administration in the case, to the mere matter of getting the garrison safely out of the fort. It was believed, however, that to abandon that position, under the circumstances, would be utterly ruinous."

CHAPTER XIV.

The next attempt was to send a fleet to garrison Fort Pickens, and to evacuate Fort Sumter as a military necessity. But it was found difficult to reinforce Fort Pickens. In the meantime a fleet was fitted out to relieve Fort Sumter. The Governor of South Carolina was notified that Fort Sumter would be provisioned, and if an attempt would be made to prevent the same—then the fort would be reinforced. South Carolina had offered to supply the fort with provisions herself.—This was the state of affairs when the Federal fleet appeared off Charleston harbor—when the Confederates fired upon Sumter. The president held a correspondence with the authorities of South Carolina about provisioning Sumter. This is what the leaders wanted, for they did not want to evacuate the fort and they wanted the South to fire the first gun.—To commence the rebellion—this was Seward's policy, for they well knew that this would arouse and unite the North against the South. Indeed, many Republicans had a few days before this expressed the opinion openly that they were willing to let the South go in peace. So said Greeley and other leaders of the Republican party!

The President further said in his message on the evacuation of Fort Sumter:

"This government desired to keep the garrison in the Fort, not to assail them, but merely to maintain visible possession, and thus to preserve the Union from actual and immediate dissolution—trusting, as herein before stated, to time, discussion, and the ballot-box, for final adjustment." How soon he abandoned this position when he had an army at his control. Many of his political opponents were made to believe that the war was for no other purpose than for the constitution, the Union, and the supremacy of the laws. It was necessary for the President and his party to keep their ultimate object in the background—for even in the border states the majority were for the Union. Here is what the President said: "The border states, so called, were not uniform in their action, some of them being almost for the Union, while in others—as Virginia, North Carolina, Tennessee, and Arkansas the Union sentiment was nearly repressed and silenced." The fear that the war would be used for ultimate abolition was the cause of this. The people were not certain that Mr. Lincoln would keep his word. Many persons both North and South said that the Republicans would, when able, use the war power for the Emancipation of the slaves. The Republicans denied this and denounced the democrats as traitors and copperheads. But time shows that the Democrats were right!

The President in his message claimed the right to suspend the writ of habeas corpus—to call out the militia, to close the ports, and to declare the blockade. He said whether legal or not they "were ventured upon under what appeared to be a popular demand and a public necessity, and trusting then as now that Congress would readily ratify them."

Now, why did not the President call Congress together sooner? Certainly he could convene Congress sooner—why wait from the 4th of March, to the 4th of July—while the country was in the midst of revolution? It was done so that he could inaugurate the war before Congress assembled, so as to cut off all debates on compromise. How did he know that Congress would ratify his actions? had he an express promise from the leading Republicans? Compromise would have saved the union—would have prevented blood. Hear what he further says in his message on this subject:

"It may well be questioned whether there is, to-day a majority of the legally-qualified voters of any state, except perhaps South Carolina, in favor of disunion.

"It is ventured to affirm this even of Virginia and Tennesee; for the result of an election held in military camps, where the bayonets are all on one side of the question voted upon, can scarcely be considered as demonstrating popular sentiment. At such an election, all that large class who are at once for the union, and against coercion, would be coerced to vote against the union."

It was to get the union men to support the Lincoln policy that the following part of the message was addressed, as to the future policy of his administration: "Lest there be some uneasiness in the minds of candid men as to what is to be the course of the government towards the southern states after the rebellion shall have been suppressed, the executive deems it proper to say, it will be his purpose then, as ever, to be guided by the constitution and the laws; and that he probably will have no different understanding of the powers and duties of the Federal government relatively to the rights of the states and the people, under the constitution, than that expressed in the inaugural address."

Many democrats north and south believed that Mr. Lincoln would keep his word and conduct the war merely for constitutional purposes. But he did not mean to abandon either the platform of his party or his own principles—that the country could not last "half slave and half free." He had the emancipation of the slaves before his mind day and night, as can be seen from his future messages. It was with the deepest regret that the executive found the duty of employing the war power in defence of the government forced upon him. He could but perform this duty, or surrender the existence of the government. No compromise by public servants could in this case be a cure; not that compromises are not often proper, but that no popular government can long survive a marked precedent that those who carry an election can only save the government from immediate destruction by giving up the main point upon which the people gave the election." Now, it may be asked what vital question was before the people, in the election of 1860? It was the slavery question as set forth formally in the Chicago platform. That was the *main point* that elected Mr. Lincoln. This is what he did not want to compromise, for he would be the political death of his party.

Lincoln did not offer any plan of compromise. He was willing that the American people should engage in a cruel and bloody war—father against son—brother against brother—neighbor against neighbor. He was willing to behold the burning of cities—the desolation, carnage, and misery of fraternal war—the agonies and moans of the widows—the tears of the orphans—

a mountain of debt—eternal taxation—yea, and even military despotism, and military prisons. And what for ?—to support the Chicago platform—to uphold a mere political party.

The Republican papers now raised the war cry—that the Capital was in danger. That the flag should not be trampled upon. They denounced all who spoke of liberty or the Constitution. In the name of loyalty they denounced Democrats and all who spoke of peace. Evidently the Republicans wished to plunge the country into war as they saw an opportunity of making money, as army contractors and speculators; others wished for the titles of captains, majors, colonels and generals—they saw before their visions crowns, stars, and garters; which filled their imaginations with ambitious views of future greatness! Those, who, on the contrary, beheld that the war would bring national calamity, misery, and eternal taxation, and who saw before them a long and bloody war, were denounced as sympathizers with the rebellion. Many were thus driven into silence and others into prison, or mobbed;--the Radicals had things their own way.

To impose on the people and to cover up the arbitrary proceedings of the administration and the Republican party, the cry was raised that the war would not last long. This was done for an other object, to encourage the enlistment of volunteers, so that France and England would not recognize the southern confederacy by representing that those states were merely disturbed by a local and insignificant insurrection !

Mr. Seward instructed Mr. Dayton, minister to France, to have him impress on the French government that there was no idea of a dissolution of the union. On this occasion, the New York *Tribune*, which a few months previous was in favor of letting the south go, now said: "That Jefferson Davis & Co. would be swinging from the battlements at Washington, at least by the 4th of July."

The New York *Times* said, "We have only to send a column of twenty-five thousand men across the Potomac to Richmond, and burn out the rats there; another column of twenty-five thousand to Cairo seizing the cotton ports of the Mississippi; and retaining the remaining twenty-five thousand included in Mr. Lincoln's call for seventy-five thousand men, at Washington, not because there is need for them there, but because we do not require their services elsewhere." The Philadelphia *Press* said; "no man of sense could, for a moment doubt that this much ado about nothing would end in about a month. The "Chicago *Tribune* said: That Illinois could whip the south herself."—Lost Cause p. 126-7-8. The loyal governors of Ohio, Indiana, Pennsylvania, Massachusetts and New York offered men to suppress the rebellion. Several northern merchants offered money to the government to suppress the rebellion. This shows that there was a great party in the north in favor of war as they were made to believe that it would last but a few months. Though the authorities knew better as Congress had empowered the President to take possession of Railroads and Telegraphs. Acts were passed for increasing the army and navy.

The leaders of the rebellion wished also to delude the people, and induce them to go to war. The Southern orators told their people that there would be no war. That they would be willing to drink all the blood that would be shed.—Lost Cause, p. 129.

They said "the Yankees would not fight; that cotton was king; that France and England could not exist without cotton; that they would have to aid the South."—Lost Cause, p. 133. So the leaders, both North and South held out a cheap termination of the war—both deluded the people. On the 24th May, the Federal Army occupied Alexandria and the Rebels fell back upon Manassas Junction. The Radical politicians wanted to hurry on the war. They even charged Lincoln and his cabinet and General Scott with conniving with the "Rebels." In the meantime Scott got a large army on the Potomac. General Beauregard, with much bravado, said they could easily whip the Yankees—that Scott's army on the Potomac was an armed mob.—Lost Cause 138–9.

General Butler, who commanded in Maryland, held that all fugitive slaves, who came within his lines were "contraband of war," and declared them free; this was a step towards emancipation.

The Northern press now assumed the right to dictate the manner of conducting the war. They claimed the right to dictate to General Scott and General McClellan, the latter being in command of West Virginia. On the 22d June, 1861, Pierpont called the new constitutional Legislature of West Virginia. On the 23d June, 1861, General McClellan issued his proclamation announcing the course he would pursue towards the loyal and those who were found in arms.—Headley vol. 1, p. 92. The Radicals raised the cry of "on to Richmond" and forced the army to move south. The Union army was defeated at the battle of Bull Run. The defeat at Bull Run was caused by the Radical press and Congressmen dictating to generals in the field. Many Congressmen left Washington to see the fun but they were forced to make a hasty retreat back to Washington. At the battle of Bull Run, the N. Y. 69th Reg. (Irish) under Col. Corcoran showed the world what Irish soldiers can do on the field of battle.' They proved to the world that the valor of Irishmen on the battle field, all over the world, is a historical fact. The 1st Reg. Minn. Vols. commanded by Col. W. A. Gorman fought well. Yet, notwithstanding the bravery of Shields, Mulligan, Corcoran and Meagher, and W. A. Gorman and of the thousands of Irish soldiers who fought in the Union army, the Radicals did not want to promote Irishmen. No Irish need apply ! They wanted all for their own party, civil and military ! Had the secretary of war sent troops which were kept around Washington to the aid of McDowell he would have driven the Confederates from Manassas. The leading "rebels" would have been taken and the back bone of rebellion broken. Then by timely conciliation and compromise and a general amnesty the war would have been ended, but the Radicals did not want peace. They did not want the constitution and Union of Washington. They wanted a Union and constitution without slavery—for they had for years denounced the constitution and the Union as a "league with death and a covenant with hell."

The New York *Tribune* said, January 26th, 1862:

"The nation is fighting for life—though all the paper constitutions on earth be scattered to the winds we can honestly say that, for the old Union, which was kept in existence by southern menaces and northern concessions, we have no regrets, and no wish for its reconstruction. Who wants any Union which can only be preserved by systematic wrong and organized political blunders ? Who wants any Union which is nothing but a sentiment to decorate Fourth of July orations with ?

Now that the Radicals had the power of the President, the Congress and the army and the navy at their backs, they were determined to throw off the mask and display their true characters. They said there could be tolerated but one party and that was the party that supported Lincoln; all others were to be put down by force. They told the country that the rebellion could be put down in sixty days by means of the great Anaconda, with its head at Fortress Monroe and its tail at Winchester, that this great monster could soon annihilate the rebellion. That there were thousands of union men south watching for the advance of the union forces to join the north! That we would have a united north and a divided south. That all who opposed

them should be denounced, persecuted, and imprisoned—two thousand
were kept in duress vile without a charge being preferred against them!
On the 26th July, 1861, McClellan was called to Washington to take command
of the army of the Potomac. About this time Fremont had returned from
Europe with arms, and was put in command of the western department, with
headquarters at St. Louis. When McClellan took command of the army
he found the troops around Washington in a state of perfect demoralization
—it was an armed mob. The bar rooms in Washington and other cities
were crowded with officers in full uniform without the least idea of military
discipline. The idea of military subordination seemed a disgrace to those
who volunteered. They could not appreciate such a thing as a military
superior,—this feeling was displayed and shared by the soldiers. (Headley
vol. 1, p. 125.) General Fremont assumed command of the western department. He appeared with the pomp and power of an Eastern Satrap.
On the 10th of August 1861, he issued a proclamation declaring martial law
in Missouri: asserting that his lines extended from Leavenworth to Cape
Girardeau on the Mississippi. That the property real and personal of all
those who took up arms against the United States should be confiscated and
their slaves set free. This measure was prompted by the abolitionists as a
feeler to find if the people were ready for emancipation. For the administration was careful to keep back their real object until the minds of the
people were prepared by northern orators and the press for final emancipation. This move of Fremont was premature, as the bulk of the northern
people thought that the war was for the Union and not for the abolition of
slavery. The administration was not yet prepared for Fremont's proclamation; so his proclamation was disavowed and overruled. Fremont
showed his utter unfitness for his military command. He had refused to
reinforce Colonel Mulligan, though he had a large force at his command,
but he let him be captured at Lexington, Missouri, by a superior force. Yet
Mulligan fought with great bravery. When called upon to surrender, he said:
"If you want us you must take us."—Lost Cause 163-4-5. Fremont proved
a complete military failure in Missouri, and orders were sent from Washington for his removal and for the appointment of Hunter in his place.
Fremont did not want to obey-this order for his removal; but finding himself unsupported by Sigel and Ashboth he had to yield to the authority of
the administration.—Lost Cause pp. 166, 167, 168.

Congress had appointed a committee to clear the public offices on charges
of treason. Men in every part of the North found themselves suddenly
arrested, and without the form of trial hurried to prison. No writ of
Habeas Corpus could reach them. The bayonet was stronger than the order
of the court. Men began to look aghast, and began to speak of the Star-
chamber, *lettres de cachet* of France. Secret informers lurked everywhere,
newspapers were suppressed and a reign of terror and of despotism inaugurated. The confiscation of rebel property was proclaimed through the
press. The government was not disposed to exchange prisoners of war.
But Davis told them he would imprison man for man and that he would
hang man for man. The Lincoln administration had to yield and exchange
prisoners. This was a recognition of the confederacy as a "*belligerent
power.*" The Republican newspapers lauded McClellan to the skies. They
called him "the young Napoleon." On the 26th of August, 1861, an expedition sailed from Fortress Monroe, and on the 28th arrived before Hatteras,
and that fort fell into the hands of the union army. This was considered
by the North as a great victory over the "rebels." France and England
were very sensitive under the blockade and it was thought that they would
demand its abandonment the next spring.

On the 8th of November 1861, Captain Wilkes of the United States sloop-of-war San Jacinto, overhauled the English Mail steamer Trent and demanded the surrender of two confederates, Mason and Slidell, who were on an embassy to the courts of England and France. They were taken by force from the steamer. England displayed her usual bluster and demanded of the authorities at Washington prompt reparation. Earl Derby notified the English vessels that war with America was probable. The government of England made rigorous preparation for war—reinforcements were sent to Canada and the country fortified along the frontiers.

Meantime Captain Wilkes received due praise from the Secretary of the navy. He received public thanks from Congress. Gov. Andrews of Massachusetts said "that that was one of the most illustrious services that had rendered the war memorable." "The New York *Times* said, "consecrate an other 4th of July to him." It was thought that war with England was inevitable. But neither Lincoln nor Seward had back-bone enough to go to war, and after all this bluster of Congress and the press, Mason and Slidell were given up to England. Oh, if we had then a Jackson! Great indignation was felt, when it was announced that the Nashville had arrived in England, with the crew of the Harvey Birch, an American merchant ship which the Nashville had burnt at sea. The English authorities would not allow the Tuscarora which had pursued the Nashville to sail the same time as the latter, but was delayed by British authorities, until the Nashville had 24 hours the start of her. Many Americans wished for peace at home, that they might have an opportunity to make war on England.—Headley vol. 1. pp. 210–11.

LINCOLN'S MESSAGE, DECEMBER 3, 1861.

The following is an extract from Lincoln's message, December 3, 1861, on his policy on the Slavery Question and the object of the war.

Confiscation of Rebel Property.

"Under and by virtue of the act of Congress entitled, "An act to confiscate property used for insurrectionary purposes," approved Aug. 6, 1861, the legal claims of certain persons to the labor and service of certain other persons have become forfeited. and numbers of the latter, thus liberated, are already dependent on the United States, and must be provided for in some way. Besides this, it is not impossible that some of the states will pass similar enactments for their own benefit respectively, and by operation of which persons of the same class will be thrown upon them for disposal. In such case I recommended that Congress provide for accepting such persons from such states according to some mode of valuation, in lieu *pro tanto*, of direct taxes, or upon some other plan to be agreed on with such states respectively: that such persons, on such acceptance by the general government, be at once deemed free, and that, in any event, steps be taken for colonizing both classes (or the one first mentioned, if the other shall not be brought into existence,) at some place, or places, in a climate congenial to them. It might be well to consider, too, whether the free colored people already in the United States could not, so far as individuals may desire, be included in such colonization." We see that Mr. Lincoln changed his policy in the short time from the 4th of July to the 3d day of December. He said in his message in July that the object of the war was for the Constitution and the Union. Was there any thing in the Constitution justifying Mr. Lincoln to accept human beings in lieu of direct taxes? Nothing, whatever. It was this message, as well as the last, that extinguished the embers of hope which still lingered in the hearts of the Union men of the south. Now they saw that the war would be used for confiscation and emancipation—consequently thousands who were good Southern men joined the Confederate army. In the North many of the Democrats got dissatisfied with Lincoln's policy and refused to volunteer. The cry was, "the Republicans have begun the war —they have refused to compromise with the South, let them do the fighting themselves. Hence the fierce opposition to Mr. Lincoln. But the Republicans denounced all who refused to endorse Mr. Lincoln and his party. He had a divided North and a divided South. Many of the Northern Democrats when they enlisted in 1861, thought that it would be a good thing to colonize the Africans. That the agitation of slavery had been the cause of trouble and excitement, and in order to get it out of politics and for the peace of the country they were willing to have the Negro in some country by himself. The soldiers caught up the same idea and were willing to violate the Constitution on this point alone. So Mr. Lincoln found favor with many, as they did not dream that he would go so far as to issue a wholesale proclamation for the emancipation of all the slaves in the South. He carried out his policy by "a little to-day and a little to-morrow." He kept up pace with public opinion; and if he found that he had got ahead of public opinion he took the back track until the times changed. In the meantime the press of the country, of the Republican stripe, was busy moulding public opinion in favor of Emancipation, paper money, high tariff, and monopoly. The Republicans did not care for the welfare of the Negro as they did to weaken the power of the people of the South, who always were for free trade. The Republicans with great force made it a point to impress on the minds of the people that Lincoln was honest. That his motives were pure. This was believed by many, even by democrats. But, still he was for his party first and last.

Mr. Lincoln in his message, never mentioned peace, for he well knew that the Republicans did not want peace, for they wanted to enrich themselves by the war and the misfortunes of the country—they were willing to sell their country for gold and office. Radicals in Congress at the session of 1860–61, passed resolutions that the war was to be prosecuted for the union and constitution alone; that the administration did not want to interfere with slavery in the states; now having a large army and navy they said that the "Rebels" had lost all rights by their rebellious acts. That slavery should be abolished and if necessary the Southern States should be reduced to territories, to be settled by Northern immigrants. That South Carolina should be made a Colony for freedmen. At this session of Congress the Republicans passed a bill for abolishing slavery in the District of Columbia and in the territories. They appropriated $100,000,000, to be put in the hands of the President to compensate the owners of slaves in the District of Columbia. Some of the western members, when they arrived in Washington, were loud in their denunciation of McClellan, for not moving on the enemy—they denounced what they called his "masterly inactivity." It seemed certain that the Radicals were forming a party against him for he would not adopt the Lincoln policy. McClellan's friends asserted that wherever he moved his army that his plans were divulged to the enemy. Suspicion fell on persons in high station—on the authorities. The secretary of war was also blamed, and not without good cause for he wanted to defeat every democratic general.—Headley vol. 1, pp. 210–11. He feared that McClellan would take Richmond and that the democratic party would get into power. The Republicans had a *mania* for office and plunder. They would not give up power, cost what it would, for the abolitionists never before had control of the government, and now having control they had no scruples to prevent them from trampling on the constitution which they had always denounced as a "covenant with hell." And as for the Federalists of the Republican party they had opposed the constitution from the beginning, and only wanted an opportunity to abolish it and adopt the British Constitution, so-called. At the session of Congress 1861-62, the Radicals held that as slavery was the cause of the war it should be abolished. The politicians were so much exasperated against McClellan that nothing but "unqualified victory" could save him from ruin.

The administration resorted to the most extraordinary modes of warfare for putting down the rebellion. A number of old vessels loaded with stone, were sunk in Charleston harbor, to make the blockade more complete. England remonstrated, but Mr. Seward informed the British authorities that the English blockade runners with contraband goods on board, had entered Charleston harbor since the sinking of the stone fleet.—Headley vol. 1, pp. 226-7.—The members from the border states, in Congress wished to maintain the Union and put down the rebellion; but they differed materially from the Republican party in the manner of putting it down. For they did not want to interfere with Slavery, but to let it alone and to put down the rebellion by force of arms—to maintain the constitution and the Union unimpaired. But the Radicals insisted that slavery should be destroyed, that the abolition of slavery should keep pace with the advance of the army.

Lincoln sent a message to Congress making a proposition to the border states for purchasing their slaves. He said that if they did not accept his proposition that they would have to lose their slaves. This strengthened the power of Jeff Davis as the union men of the south saw that the object of the war was the abolition of slavery. This proposition weakened the power of the authorities at Washington. The old Federalists who, from the days of John Adams and Hamilton, were trying to mould the government after the model of the British constitution, now had an opportunity to indulge in their favorite scheme of copying from England. This Congress passed an income tax. Acts for issuing United States notes and bonds were passed. Congress made these notes "legal tender," in violation of the constitution which provides for the payment of debts in gold and silver. A. S. Johnson with a rebel force occupied Kentucky with his right wing at Bowling Green and his left at Columbus. The Richmond papers urged him to cross the Ohio and capture Cincinnati and carry the war into Africa. A large force of Federals had been collected at Paducah, at the mouth of the Tennessee river, which penetrated into Alabama and Tennessee with nothing to protect it but Fort Henry. The Cumberland river was still more important as the avenue to Nashville. But the capture of Fort Donelson compelled the Confederates to fall back from Bowling Green to Murfreesboro, abandoning both Nashville and the Cumberland river.

The South was doomed to experience the fall of island No. 10, and the northern generals with the gunboats had command of the upper Mississippi. The fall of Shiloah or Pittsburg landing still contracted the rebel lines. But the southern leaders held that this only gave them strength as it weakened the northern forces by running them farther from their base of supplies. The southern press endeavored to make the people of the south think that every defeat was a victory. But the fall of New Orleans, the great commercial city of the south filled the southern mind with gloom and despair. This could not be called a contraction of lines or a change of base. It was a sad affair for the south; for the people north and south knew that this was a vital point. They remembered that the British made a great effort to capture it in the war of 1812. That the defeat of Pakenham had immortalized General Jackson. That the battle of New

Orleans had been celebrated the same as the fourth of July. So that the ingenuity of the Confederates could not satisfy the people of the south that the fall of New Orleans was a military stratagem. This broke the rebel power in Louisiana, Texas, and the Gulf States—closed the access to the grain and cattle country of the south. This gave the Union army a new base of operation and had the effect to shake the confidence of European powers in the fortunes of the confederacy. It closed the port and prevented them from shipping off their cotton and getting supplies. General Burnside captured Roanoke island, January 1862, with a fleet of sixty vessels. This capture was the first to create public censure towards the Richmond authorities.—Lost Cause p. 213. The rebels fell back on all sides—an actual invasion of the :"sacred soil" had taken place.—Lost Cause p. 215. Immediately after these great victories the abolitionists threw off the mask and through the press commenced to pave the way for the attainment of their favorite idol, the abolition of slavery.

Mr. Seward said, in the senate, before Lincoln's inauguration. "Experience in public affairs has confirmed my opinion that domestic slavery existing in any state is wisely left by the constitution of the United States, exclusively, to the care, management and disposition of the states, and if it were in my power I would not alter the constitution in this respect." But he did not mean this; he was not sincere; for the Republicans did not want to disclose their ultra plans of final abolition in the states. The army had obtained several important victories in the field. Although the President had nullified Fremont's proclamation freeing slaves in Missouri now as public opinion had favored General Hunter's proclamation, proclaiming martial law in Georgia, South Carolina, and Florida and freeing the slaves therein which Lincoln also nullified, for he wished to crush the rebellion first and slavery afterwards.—Headley vol. 1, p. 232. Even, in 1861, the leading abolitionists showed that they intended to abolish slavery when clothed with power, for in 1861, Lovejoy offered a resolution in Congress "that it was no part of the duty of a soldier to capture and return fugitive slaves. An act was passed confiscating slaves found in arms against the government. In 1862, Senator Bright of Indiana, was expelled in a most shameful manner from the senate. The Republicans, having now a two-third vote, in consequence of the southern members leaving the Halls of Congress, determined to inaugurate a reign of terror and expel democrats from Congress, who opposed their revolutionary schemes or who commented on the gross system of frauds, corruption, and plunder.

Lincoln now disclosed his plan for emancipation—his friends in Congress passed a resolution declaring that the United States would co-operate with such States as would gradually abolish slavery (Act March 6, 1862) by giving them pecuniary aid, August 28, 1862. Greeley addressed a letter to Lincoln, through the *Tribune*, to abolish slavery; that if the rebellion was crushed out to-morrow, within a year it would be in full vigor if slavery was not abolished. Greeley vol. 2, p. 249. Lincoln held back his emancipation proclamation for some time for fear that the 50,000 soldiers in the Union army from the border states would go to the South. Greeley vol. 2, p. 252. On the 22d day of September 1862, he issued a proclamation that the slaves of all rebels would be emancipated Jan. 1, 1863. He wanted the success of the Union army before issuing his proclamation; he wanted also to wait the result of the fall election. Lincoln's war policy and the ill treatment of McClellan gave the Democracy majorities in New York, and New Jersey. The Republicans lost strength in Penn., Ohio, Indiana, Michigan and Wisconsin.—*Ib.* 254–5. The majority at the North was opposed to changing the war for the Union into a war for the Negro.

A majority was in favor of peace and compromise and against emancipation.—Greeley vol. 2, p. 254–5.

The Confederate Congress passed a conscription law April 16, 1862. It drew all citizens between the ages of Eighteen and Thirty-five from state control and put them under the Confederate authorities.—Lost Cause 220–21. This seems strange of the southern leaders, who had for years, denounced all who interfered with state-rights. They seceded from the Union because they asserted that Lincoln would violate state rights by abolishing slavery: now they themselves struck down the most sacred of state rights for they took from the states all control over the state militia.

Lincoln knew that the people were attached to state-rights. That they would not like to see them violated. For this purpose he said in his message that the people should not be too scrupulous about "*state-rights*," as the union was older than the states. That the union made the states. He intimated that the state governments might be abolished to save the union. This was done to pave the way for future Radical reconstruction! For a long time before the election of Lincoln the Republicans quoted Jefferson for the purpose of gaining recruits from the Democrats. Now, when they wanted to violate the constitution, they claimed the right to put down the rebellion by the right of conquest. They quoted from Vattel, and other writers on the law of nations. They considered the rebels in the union for the purpose of reducing them under the jurisdiction of the Federal authorities, and outside of the union and constitution for the purpose of confiscating their property by the laws of war; in the same breath they treated them as citizens of the United States and alien public enemies. They now held that the President could dispense with the constitution and govern the country by the laws of war and the law of nations. The Republicans violated every sacred guarantee of the constitution, both in the rebellious and free states. A great battle was fought between the *Merrimac* and the *Monitor* which revolutionized the naval affairs of the world. The "rebel" *Merrimac* would have sunk many of the nothern vessels if she had got to sea, which was only prevented by the timely arrival of the little *Monitor*. Complaints were made against the secretary of the navy for not providing against the *Merrimac*. For the government knew all winter that she was building a month before she made her appearance. Some French officers who visited her had pronounced her formidable. This great conflict between the *Merrimac* and *Monitor* produced a profound sensation in Europe, especially in England. Her wooden walls vanished in a day.—Headley vol. 1. p. 300–1.

Grant failed in his Belmont expedition. He also failed in not coming up to reinforce Rosecrans at the battle of Iuka. Had he rendered the necessary aid to Rosecrans at that time he could have captured the rebels. But he failed to come up until next day; and Price was able to escape and fall back into the interior.—Headley vol. 2, p. 95. Grant made another blunder at the battle of Pittsburg Landing; he failed to be on the field of battle in time to form his men. The Union army would have been driven into the Tennessee River only for the death of the confederate general Johnson, and the bravery of General Sherman and the timely arrival of General Buell.

General Grant made a great mistake in marching his army on the west side of the Tennessee River before he formed a junction with Buell's corps, which was crossing the country from Nashville, while Johnson was at Corinth, having water and rail communication with New Orleans and Mobile and the entire south to reinforce him. On the 4th of April, Johnson moved his entire army to attack Grant on Saturday, but in consequence of the muddy roads he was not able until Sunday morning. The Union army was surprised and Prentiss with 3000 men taken prisoner, and the whole army would have been driven panic-stricken into the river but for the bravery of Gen. Sherman.

There was no one on the field of battle to form a line—each general had as much as he could do to take care of his own division, as Grant was at this time at Savannah several miles down the river, when the battle begun. This was a stupid blunder. Had any Democrat, who was not friendly to Lincoln's administration or war policy, committed such a blunder he would have been court-martialed. The Union army which stretched, in the morning, in a semi-circle of over six miles, was in the evening compressed within a circle of half a mile,—one more push would drive them into the Tennessee River. "Oh! that Buell or night would come!" was the most earnest wish of the Union officers. The whole army was on the brink of ruin and annihilation, when Buell's cavalry appeared on the opposite brink of the Tennessee River. Buell's presence turned defeat into victory. The Union army now became triumphant and the whole Mississippi valley was saved from falling into the hands of the Confederates! Headley vol. 1, pp. 339–40–41–2–3–4–5–6–7–8–9; 350–1–2.

Grant's stupendous blunder was unpardonable in moving his army across the Tennessee River before he had formed a junction with Buell as he might have known that Johnson would move his army on him from Corinth. As we have said before, he would have been able to attack Grant on Saturday but for the muddy roads, and he would have defeated him before Buell could come up. What a stupid act this was for Grant to remain behind at Savannah. But thanks to Sherman and Buell for the Union victory of Shiloh. Yet we find that the Radicals persecuted the same Buell who saved the Union soldiers from meeting a watery grave in the blue waters of the Tennessee River. And what for?—because he was a Democrat and would not worship Lincoln's policy;" for Lincoln and his administration were intent on sacrificing one way or an other all generals who differed with them or who would not yield to their sole opinion. Grant kept his mind to himself, so that he might be able to please both parties. Corinth was evacuated on the 30th of May, 1862, and on the 7th of June the Confederates fell back on Tupelo.—Lost Cause, 820–21. After the fall of Corinth the Confederates evacuated Memphis.

While the country was deluged in blood, Butler had a fine harvest of "spoons," in New Orleans. He reigned more like a monarch than a general of a Republican army. He practised with some show of success the example of the Mexican Generals. He issued orders to his soldiers to insult southern women, citizens were arrested and cruelly confined with ball and chain. Mayor Monroe was confined in Fort Jackson—a woman was confined at Ship Island for laughing while a soldier's funeral was passing. While Butler was in New Orleans hurling orders at women he could have captured Port Hudson and Vicksburg—saving thousand of lives and millions of dollars. He was so covetous for money that his brother traded with the rebels for cotton—thus making his own brother his agent.

Butler had created such a reign of terror in New Orleans, that he was obliged to be always surrounded by his body guards. Such was the reign of terror inaugurated by the *beast* that the Louisiana soldiers went into battle shouting "remember Butler."—Butler had a sign in his office in the St. Charles Hotel, with the following inscription: "A she-adder bites worse than a male-adder."—Youth's Historical War, p. 184. See Youth's History of the Civil War, pp. 182–3.—Greeley's Am. Conf. vol. 2, pp. 105–6. The misfortunes and defeats of the Confederates were somewhat alleviated by the great victories of Stonewall Jackson in the valley. He made himself famous by his victories in Virginia; he defeated Banks, captured all his commissary stores and ordnance.

CHAPTER XV.

Congress now held that the constitution was played out; that there should be no other power but the will of "the powers that be," at Washington! General Halleck was appointed commander-in-chief of the army of the United States; he was only a mere *Lawyer*, who had no experience in military affairs. Lincoln's cabinet had no men of military experience.— Greeley's Am. Conf. vol. 1, 501. He was not competent to drill a company of soldiers, but he was a strong supporter of Lincoln's policy. If any one wanted promotion in the army it was necessary to coincide with "Lincoln's policy;" any democratic general who was firm enough to oppose "Lincoln's policy," was sacrificed. Such was the case with Buell, McClellan, Porter, Rosecrans and Shields. General Shields, the Sarsfield of America, was the only man who whipped Stonewall Jackson: he was an old veteran, who won immortal fame on the battle fields of Mexico, and in the war in Florida under General Jackson, fighting against the Indians.—But he was not a Lincoln man—that was enough! The Republicans claimed that the constitution was played out; indeed military governors were appointed for North Carolina, Tennessee and Texas, July 21, 1862. John S. Phelps was appointed military governor of Arkansas. A Bill was passed confiscating rebel property, July 17, 1862. Another act was passed to suppress insurrection and to punish treason and rebellion. At this session the Writ of Habeas Corpus was suspended. A bill was introduced for the employment of Negro soldiers. Indeed very little was done at this session of Congress but legislating against slavery; passing tariff laws; and increasing the war power of the President. July 1, 1862, Congress passed a revenue law which greatly added to the power and patronage of the party by creating an army of officials. On May 20, 1862, an act was passed increasing the powers of the secretary of war. May 21, 1862, an act was passed for the education of colored children of the district of Columbia. This act caused great excitement at the north; for it could not be called a military necessity. For it was not pretended that it helped to put down the rebellion. It was evident that Congress had now assumed unlimited powers—not controlled by the constitution or the traditions of the founders and fathers of the constitution.

June 5, 1862, an act was passed to appoint a minister to Hayti. This was the first time that the Federal government had recognized the government of that island. This caused great displeasure North and South. In the North all unconstitutional acts weakened the power of the authorities of Washington: while at the South it drove thousands of union men into the confederate ranks.

June 7, 1862, an act was passed for collecting taxes in the rebel states. June 19, 1862 an act was passed for abolishing slavery in the territories. This was the old bone of contention. For this question had agitated the country for years. It was the great issue in 1860.

Feb. 25th, 1862, an act was passed for issuing notes and for the funding of the public debt.

An act was passed March 6th, 1862, requiring an oath of allegiance and to support the constitution of the United States to be administered to the masters of American vessels.

May 15, 1862, Congress passed an act for the establishment of the department of agriculture. The Radicals intoxicated with power, became wild and reckless. They were not restrained by the constitution of the United States nor the welfare of their common country; they were ready to sacrifice all patriotism and the welfare of their country on the altar of party politics. Every thing was sacrificed for the Chicago platform. For some time, they had been, with great ingenuity, construing the constitution by implication and intendment, but now they openly declared that the constitution was "played out." They fell back on the law of nations and the laws of war. They even said that they would trample under foot the constitution ! They said that they wanted a strong government. Indeed, all the old arguments of the Federalists were resounded in the ears of the people. "Have we a government or not," was the cry ! The Republicans, as already stated, were determined to defeat McClellan for fear that if he should take Richmond he would become so popular that he would be made President. That the democratic party would get into power; that the Republicans would lose for ever their darling object of abolishing slavery everywhere. McClellan had to delay for many causes. He had to discipline his army, which, when he took command, he found in a demoralized state. He would be able to move sooner only for the intermeddling of the authorities at Washington, who wanted to thwart all his movements for party purposes, although when the war broke out they pledged themselves to the democrats that all parties should be merged in the patriots. That there should be but one party and that that party should crush out rebellion and maintain the constitution and the Union. But this was all a delusion and a snare to gull patriotic democrats to enlist. This delay of McClellan gave an opportunity to the confederates to recruit their forces and to fortify their position.

Although the Confederates had lost many strongholds, that they held from Vicksburg to Richmond, Stonewall Jackson held the valley, and Lee was formidable at Richmond, with an army for offensive operation; besides the Confederates had a large Trans-Mississippi army and many strongholds on the coast. Charleston and Sumter were well fortified and well garrisoned. McClellan's plan was to send an army to Charleston; an other to Texas and another force to sail up the Mississippi from New Orleans to form a junction with an army which was to move down the Mississippi from Cairo; another army was to move through Kentucky, Tennessee and Georgia to the sea; while his own army was to move on Richmond by way of the James. See report of Gen. McClellan to the Secretary of war. This was an admirable plan and the one after several blunders, which was adopted by Grant. But these plans were marred by the authorities at Washington, for they wanted to defeat him. He had to disclose his plans to the Washington officials, who had now assumed the complete control of the movements of the army. These plans were made known through the Northern press. The Confederates profited by this information; as they were apprised of all McClellan's movements. Lincoln ordered McClellan to advance on the 22d of Sep., 1862. His army was divided into five army corps and a mountain department, under Fremont, in western Virginia. The President virtually assumed the duties and responsibilities of the Commander-in-chief. McClellan called a Council of war. All but four generals pronounced the movement unwise. But the President overruled their decision and ordered McClellan to move at once. By this act Lincoln

and his Secretary of war took the grave responsibility of breaking up the
well matured plans of General McClellan and his officers, disregarding the
counsels of these officers, whom he had put at the head of military affairs,
who ought to know more about the movements of an army than mere civilians and political generals who could not drill a company—who were from
their education unfit to judge of military matters, as well as officers learned
in the science and arts of war. For McClellan had experience in military
matters from his education, as well as from his experience in the Mexican
war, and his knowledge of European warfare, as he was one of the officers
detailed by the United States to inspect the mode of warfare practiced by
the French, English, Russians, and Turks at the siege of Sebastopol,
while Lincoln, Stanton, and Halleck had no experience excepting what
Lincoln had in the Black Hawk war among the western savages.

McClellan was defeated in consequence of the blunder of Stanton in not
sending McDowell to McClellan to close up his right wing. By this
blunder Stonewall Jackson got into his rear and McClellan was forced
to fall back on his gunboats. Had McClellan had his own way of
conducting the war he could have taken Richmond and could have
crushed the rebellion. But the Radicals did not want the war over, for
they were making vast fortunes by it, and as we have said before, they did
not want to see the Democrats get into power. For they would sooner see
the south out of the union than see McClellan President of the United
States. Greeley blamed McClellan for favoring war with England, on the
Trent affair.—Greeley Am. Conf. vol. 1, 628. Lincoln took ten thousand
men from McClellan's command and sent them to Fremont in the mountains
of Virginia where they were not wanted.—Youth's History of the Civil War,
pp. 193-4-5. Lincoln feared for his own safety at Washington. McClellan
frequently wrote to him and Stanton for reinforcements. He told them
that he would have to fight a superior force. Lincoln and Stanton, who were
lawyers without military education or experience, assumed to fight the
battles of the country from their desks.—See McClellan's report to the
Secretary of war. They failed to send the desired reinforcements. Jackson slipped from Banks and Fremont and got by McDowell into McClellan's
rear. Lee called on the available troops of Virginia commanded by Stonewall Jackson, Jeff Davis, Longstreet, Magruder, Hill and Ewell.—Greeley,
vol. 2. pp. 132 to 154.

Immediately after McClellan's defeat on the Potomac, caused by the
blunder of the traitor and villain Stanton in not reinforcing him, the President called out 600,000 men. Why did not the President call out 600,000
men before the defeat at Richmond ? The people now began to realize the
effects of the war; real estates depreciated 50 per cent and all the necessaries
of life rose one hundred per cent. The people now awoke as from a dream
to behold the huge dimensions of the war which was brought on by the
Radicals and Fire-eaters ! The opposition to the administration increased,
for it was soon found that 600,000 men could not be raised by volunteering,
so Congress passed an act giving additional bounties. Towns, cities and
counties gave bounties. Congress passed an act for drafting if the states
should fail to fill up their quotas. Now the Radicals said that they would
not sustain the war if the Union was restored with slavery ! Greeley and
the governor of Massachusetts told the President that if he would issue a
proclamation for the emancipation of the slaves, " that in such an event the
roads from Boston to Washington would be black with union soldiers.
This made the war one for the abolition of slavery !

In order to put down all opposition, and to trample free speech under
foot and to inaugurate a reign of terror, the Radicals put the country North

and South under martial-law. It was made penal to discourage enlistments and persons were prevented from leaving the country without a passport. The Provost Marshals reigned as petty despots and in some instances persons were forced into the ranks of the army or drugged and then forced. Secretary Seward had, some time previous, issued his order for the purpose of preventing persons from leaving the United States without a passport. In short, the administration became despotic; in a few months the United States Government which before Lincoln's election was the freest and best in the world, now became the most despotic in the world—no person was safe—private suspicion and party malice consigned thousands to prison, in the free states alone without charge or trial!

After the battle of Richmond, Pope superseded McClellan. Pope arrested citizens for refusing to take an oath of allegiance. He banished thousands from their homes for refusing to take an oath unauthorized by the Constitution on mere frivolous complaints—even on mere suspicion. In 1862, the Republicans were elated by means of the victories of the Union Army, and now that the war spirit was on the increase at the north, they could drown all opposition by the cry of "*rebel sympathizers*." The war Democrats in the army, having become accustomed to look upon every person south outside of the union picket lines, as an enemy, were willing that anything might be done to put down the rebellion—so that they could go home to their families and friends. They gradually began to abate their love for their southern brethren. They did not forget the Charleston Convention nor the defeat of Douglas—for the Southerners by running three candidates helped to elect Lincoln. Many Democrats in the army now became indifferent to the rights of the South, and did not care if the "peculiar institution" was abolished—moreover military commands, by general orders from the war department, were allowed to forage in Virginia, Georgia, Florida, Alabama, South Carolina, Mississippi, Louisiana, Texas, and Arkansas, so from taking the property of "rebels" in one instance they did not object to see the Negro set free.

The word abolitionists, which a few years before, was considered by democrats as something infamous, was now treated with indifference. This was what the Republicans wanted. This was what Seward, Greeley, and Lincoln wanted. Having prepared the minds of the army for the ultimate abolition of slavery, strong party lines were now drawn in Congress. The democratic party still claiming that the object of the war should be the suppression of the rebellion and the maintenance of the constitution and the union. Meantime the Republicans threw off all disguise and set themselves to work to free the slaves in the southern states, while the war extermination was at fever heat. As early as March 13, 1862, Congress passed an act prohibiting the employment of union troops in returning fugitives from labor to their owners. This was a violation of the old fugitive slave law, which the Republican party never intended should be enforced, for they had time and again mobbed those who claimed their fugitive slaves. Even before the war, they went so far as to break jails and take those fugitives from the custody of the United States authorities.—See act 1862.

The object of this act was to prepare the minds of the Democrats in the army to sanction the abolition of slavery.

On the 22d September, 1862, Lincoln issued his first emancipation proclamation which was not to go into effect until January 1st. 1863. For he did not know what the people would think of it at the fall elections. Indeed, Lincoln's policy was condemned at the fall elections: Seymour was elected governor of New York. The tyranny of the administration was

condemned, and New York, New Jersey, Pennsylvania, Ohio, Indiana repudiated the unconstitutional acts of the administration by electing
Democrats!

The defeat of the Radicals was sorely felt—Seward, Blair and Smith were
in favor of withdrawing the emancipation proclamation, but Chase said that
the abolitionists, who had control of Congress, would not prosecute the
war if the Union was reconstructed with slavery. That they would sooner
let the Union slide. He said that he had a letter from Sumner, Wade, Wilson, Fessenden, and Lovejoy to that effect. That the issue was war for the
abolition of slavery!

This caused a bitter feeling at the north and the Republicans backed up
the policy with the sword. Lincoln now traded off fat offices, both civil
and military, to all who supported his policy: several leading apostate Democrats joined Lincoln for offices and army contracts. The age of corruption
and tyranny now assumed gigantic proportions. The administration had
recourse to the old Hamiltonian principles of bribery and corruption and the
hideous system of spies and informers. The Republicans copied every thing
that was wicked from England. The people who were now smarting under
hard times and taxation—having to pay one hundred per cent more
for clothing and other necessaries of life than before the war—were indignant at the weakness and failure of the administration in putting down the
Rebellion by this policy. They saw that the army was controlled by the
administration, composed of men who were ignorant of all military affairs;
as well as the mere "paper officers" greedy, ignorant, and inefficient who
were to lead thousands of Union soldiers to be butchered! The administration
and Congress had their favorites and political friends in positions where they
filled their pockets as speculators and contractors.

Lincoln, knowing that colonization was even popular with the Whigs and
many Democrats, offered colonization as a step towards universal emancipation—it was indeed, a great stroke of policy.

An extract from President Lincoln's message December 1st, 1862, on the
subject of the colonization of free Africans: "Applications have been made
to me by many free Americans of African descent to favor their emigration
with a view to such colonization as was contemplated in recent acts of
Congress. Several of the Spanish American Republics have protested
against the sending of such colonies to their respective territories. Under
these circumstances, I have declined to move any such colony to any state,
without first obtaining the consent of its government. Liberia and Hayti
are, as yet, the only countries to which colonies of African descent from
here could go with certainty of being received and adopted as citizens; and
I regret to say such persons contemplating colonization do not seem so
willing to emigrate to those countries as to some others, nor so willing as I
think their interests demand." He held the following opinion on the
currency, which shows how much the Radical party has drifted from the
principles held by Mr. Lincoln, in 1862.

"A return to specie payments, however, at the earliest period compatible
with due regard to all interests concerned, should ever be kept in view.
Fluctuations in the value of currency are always injurious."

He then referred to his emancipation proclamation of 22d September,
1862, and of the resolution for "compensated emancipation."

"The proposed emancipation would shorten the war, perpetuate peace,
insure the increase of population, and proportionally the wealth of the
country. With these, we should pay all that emancipation would cost,
together with our other debt, easier than we should pay one other debt,
without it."

"The plan is proposed as permanent Constitutional law. It cannot become such without the concurrence of, first, two-thirds of Congress, and afterwards, three-fourths of the states."

"In giving freedom to the slave we assure freedom to the free honorable alike in what we give and what we preserve. We shall nobly save, or meanly lose the last, best .hope of earth. Other means may succeed; this could not fail."

Comment is unnecessary. Before the war, the complaint of the South was that the Lincoln party wanted to free the slaves, whenever it got into power. The President said that they should take the last opportunity oñ earth to abolish slavery—this, indeed, is the key-note of the opposition of the peace democrats to the policy of the administration in conducting the war for the abolition of slavery, and not for the Union. Hence the grumbling. of that portion of the democracy called copperheads. They wanted the war for the support of the constitution and the union!

We here find an issue between the Republicans and the democrats on the war policy. The former wanted to use the war power for the abolition of slavery, and the latter for the suppression of the rebellion, and the maintenance of the Constitution and the Union. This was the gulf which divided the two parties. The Republicans denounced all who did not accept this policy as traitors and copperheads. This even broke up the Democrats into two factions, the war and peace Democrats.

December 16, 1862, Vallandigham, of Ohio, offered the following amendment:

"*Resolved*—1. That the Union as it was, must be restored and maintained forever under the constitution as it is—the fifth article providing for amendments included.

"2. That no final treaty of peace ending the present civil war can be permitted to be made by the Executive, or any other person in the civil or military service of the United States, on any other basis than the integrity and entirety of the Federal Union, and of the States composing the same, as at the beginning of hostilities, and upon that basis peace ought immediately to be made.

"3. That the government can never permit armed or hostile intervention by any foreign power in regard to the present civil war.

"4. That the unhappy civil war in which we are engaged was waged, in the beginning, professedly," not in any spirit of oppression, or for any purpose of conquest, or subjugation, or purpose of overthrowing or interfering with the rights or the established institutions of the states, but to defend and maintain the supremacy of the constitution, and to preserve the Union with all the dignity, equality, and rights of the several states unimpaired," and was so understood and accepted by the people, and especially by the Army and Navy of the United States; and that, therefore, whoever shall pervert, or attempt to pervert, the same to a war of conquest and subjugation, or for the overthrowing or interfering with the rights or established institutions of any of the states, and to abolish slavery therein, or for the purpose of destroying or impairing the dignity, equality, or rights of any of the states, will be guilty of a flagrant breach of public faith, and of a high crime against the constitution and the Union.

"5. That whoever shall propose, by Federal authority, to extinguish any of the states of the Union, or to declare any of them extinguished, and to establish territorial governments or permanent military governments within the same, will be deserving of the censure of this House and of the country.

"6. That whoever shall attempt to establish a dictatorship in the United States, thereby superseding or suspending the constitutional authorities of the Union, or to clothe the President or any other officer, civil or military, with dictatorial or arbitrary power, will be guilty of a high crime against the constitution and the Union and public liberty.—Cong. Globe 1862–63, p. 104.

December 22, 1862, Mr. Vallandigham offered this resolution to restore peace.

"*Resolved*—That this House does earnestly desire that the most speedy and effectual measures be taken for restoring peace in America, and that no time may be lost in proposing an immediate cessation of hostilities, in order to the speedy final settlement of the unhappy controversies which brought about the unnecessary and injurious civil war, by just and adequate security against the return of the like calamities in times to come; and this House desires to offer the most earnest assurances to the country that they will, in due time, cheerfully coöperate with the executive and the states for the restoration of the Union by such explicit and most solemn amendments and provisions of the constitution as may be found necessary for securing the rights of the several states and sections within the Union under the constitution."—Cong. Globe 1862–63, p. 165.

For these resolutions and his speeches he was denounced as a traitor and a copperhead. His name was known in the land as the leader of what was then called copperheads. Any democrat who would either vote or speak for him was called, in the army, a rebel. Indeed, any one who spoke of any other peace but final and unconditional surrender, was called a traitor. Anything short of the rebels giving up their leaders and submitting at discretion was then called, by the Republicans, treason to the government ! To vote the democratic ticket was called treason !

December 9th, 1862. The bill to indemnify the President and other persons for suspending the writ of habeas corpus being before the House, the following debate took place.

Mr. Bayard:

"The President of the United States has asserted the right to dispense with the law which requires the habeas corpus to be issued in any case of judicial arrest. He has claimed that right; he has exercised that right. He has openly, through the Secretary of war, issued a proclamation which virtually subverts this government, if carried out in practice; because the secretary of war is authorized to appoint an indefinite number of men, constituting a corps of provost marshals, who are to have the right, in addition to their military duties, to arrest any citizen throughout the country for indefinite charges, and to call in military aid to sustain their action; and they are to report to the central authority at Washington, and hold the party in custody subject to the orders of that central authority.

"If the judiciary attempt to intervene, as in the case of the prisoner at Fort Warren, the bayonet of the soldier rejects the service of the writ upon the military commandant who has possession of the prisoner. The judiciary, then, are powerless for redress; and under this asserted right on the part of the President, that the judicial department of the government being powerless to redress individual wrong, if the legislative branch, which is equally powerful with the executive, are not to interpose by calling for the information, the facts, and by the expression of their opinion, if it be necessary, when facts are returned to them, what protection has the citizen against the aggression of executive power ? How can the government be a free government, where, when the judiciary is put at defiance, the legislative unites in saying to the citizen, "you shall have no investigation; you may be arrested by officers unknown to the law, indefinite in numbers, on offences unknown to the laws, not described, for disloyal practices, which may mean anything that an executive officer pleases. You may be arrested not only by the order of a functionary at Washington, who, from his position, may be supposed to have ability to exercise some discretion, but you may be arrested at the discretion of any one of his subordinate deputies, and an investigation is not to be made by any other tribunal than by an *ex parte* return made in your absence, and without any power of investigation on your part, to the central authority at Washington. If the proclamation of the 26th of September be carried out, and taking the general facts that have occurred as matters of history, that is the state of things and the power claimed by the executive. Sir, I consider that power a subversion of this government."

"Clearly, it has nothing whatever to do with the war; it can have no possible connection with the war, when we ask the President for the evidence on which a man has been committed to prison."

"If we abandon our functions here of calling for evidence on which this is done—this government is no longer a free goverment, it is simply a despotism in the hands of a bureau aristocracy at Washington."

Mr. Clark:

"I hope that this resolution will be laid on the table. I hope that this resolution, and all resolutions of a similar character, offered in this one body or in the other, will not receive the sanction of either House of Congress."

Saulsbury:

"I am not here to offer any excuse for any man who has raised his hand against the constitution or government of the United States."

If any of the citizens of Delaware so act, let them be arrested according to law, tried according to law, convicted according to law, and punished according to law. But, sir, if citizens of a state are arrested and are placed in the forts of your country, without any knowledge on their part, or on the part of their friends, of the causes of their arrests, shall no voice be raised in their behalf?"—Cong. Globe, 1862–63, pp. 26–7–8–9.

Mr. Trumbull:

"My own views upon this subject have been expressed to the senate. I have thought that these arrests, in the manner in which they have been made, have been unfortunate and impolitic, to say nothing about the question whether they were legal or illegal. Upon that question there is a great diversity of opinion in the country. The better opinion, as has been stated here to-day, among judges, and lawyers, and constitutional commentators, surely is, that the writ of habeas corpus was never intended by the constitution to be suspended except in pursuance of an act of Congress. The courts have so held, judges have so stated, commentators have so written, and not a commentator can be found, who has written on the constitution before this rebellion, who ever disputed that proposition."—Cong. Globe, 1862–63, p. 31.

Doolittle:

"Does not the senator from Kentucky know that we are at war; that the whole country is at war, that the law of war is in operation in Wisconsin as well as in Kentucky, in New York as well as in Mississippi?"

Mr. Powell:

"The oath which has been required from many of these persons is not simply an oath of allegiance but is far wider than that. I repeat again, if I were arrested for an offence I would not purge myself by an oath."

"I thought I understood what the laws of war were. All the laws of war we have in this country are the Articles of war, which are statute passed by the Congress of the United States for the government of the army, and those who are not in the land or naval service are not subject to those laws and articles of war."

McDougall:

"The military power of the government has required not only the oath of fealty but also a special oath something in this nature: the party solemnly swears that he will not hold the persons arresting him responsible for civil damages at any future time." Mr. Doolittle. "I have never heard of such a thing."

Mr. McDougall: "I will say then to the senator I am, I think, well-advised that by direction of the war department such an oath was administered to a gentleman who was a candidate for representative from Iowa, who was discharged. (His name, I think, is Mahony.) Mr. Mahony was an Irishman, the editor of the Dubuque *Herald*. He was arrested because the administration feared that he would be elected to Congress—he was a Democrat. They required that oath of him, and I am advised they required the same oath of others. I am well advised that the evidence of it is in the war department."

Mr. Saulsbury:

"A gentleman residing in the town in which I live was arrested by military authority and carried to Cambridge, Maryland; there the affidavits were examined and he was released; and he informed me that he was required to take an oath that he would not prosecute the persons who arrested him."—Cong. Globe 1862-63, pp. 35, 36, 37.

Mr. Davis:

"The President of the United States has promulgated three of the most extraordinary and startling edicts that ever originated with any man who occupied the position of the chief Magistrate of a free people. They are in the form of proclamations, dated the 22d and 24th of September, 1862, and the 1st of January 1863; and he comes at length to profess to issue them by virtue of the power vested in him by the constitution, as commander-in-chief of the Army and Navy of the United States, as a fit and necessary war measure to suppress the rebellion."—Cong. Globe 1862-63, p. 529.

It was said by senators and members of Congress and the leading Republicans, in and out of Congress, that those who were arrested on suspicion would have the prison door open if they took the oath of allegiance. The Republicans appealed to the passions of those who had friends in the union army that all those who complained of false arrests were disloyal, in sympathy with traitors—that it was no hardship for loyal men to take the oath of allegiance. Although those who were arrested had to swear that they would not prosecute those who arrested them. That the President should be supported, that it would not do to arraign him for his acts, so long as he was putting down the rebellion. That the arrests were done under the war measure.

December 1st, 1862, Mr. Powell introduced the following joint resolution in relation to illegal arrests in the United States.

Whereas, many citizens of the United States have been seized by persons acting, or pretending to be acting, under the authority of the United States, and have been carried out of the jurisdiction of the states of their residence and imprisoned in the military prisons and camps of the United States without any public charge being preferred against them, and without any opportunity being allowed to learn or disprove the charges made or alleged to be made against them; and whereas, it is the sacred right of every citizen that he shall not be deprived of life or liberty without due process of law, and when arrested shall have a speedy public trial by an impartial jury. Therefore be it resolved, by the senate and House of Representatives of the United States of America in Congress assembled, that all such arrests are unwarranted by the Constitution and the laws of the United States, and a usurpation of power never given by the people to the President or any other official. All such arrests are hereby condemned and declared palpable violations of the Constitution of the United States; and it is hereby demanded that all such arrests shall hereafter cease and that all persons so arrested and yet held should have a prompt and speedy public trial according to the provisions of the Constitution, or should be immediately released." Mr. Collamer: "Let it lie over."— 1862–63, p. 3.

December 10th, 1862, Mr. Saulsbury offered the following resolution. "*Resolved*, That the secretary of war be, and he is hereby, directed to inform the senate whether Dr. John Laus and Whiteley Meredith, or either of them, citizens of the State of Delaware, have been arrested and imprisoned in Fort Delaware; when they were arrested and so imprisoned; the charges against them; by whom made; by whose orders they were arrested and imprisoned; and that he communicate to the senate all papers relating to their arrest and imprisonment."—Cong. Globe 1862–3, p. 17.

Saulsbury:

"From time to time, numbers of the citizens of that state have been arrested, I believe generally by the Maryland home guards; whether it has been done by authority of the department of war, I do not know. They have been carried off and confined in military forts. I have not, however, proposed to go into any general inquiry in reference to the arrests in that state; but as to these two gentlemen, one of whom resides in my own county and the other not far off in the adjoining county, they are known to me personally, and have been for a number of years, and as their friends do not know of any just cause why they should be imprisoned in Fort Delaware or elsewhere, I have felt it my duty to call for this information. I hope the senate will not perceive any reason for refusing to comply with this request. If they are there properly, if they have been guilty of any attempt to subvert the government, if they have acted traitorously in any respect, their friends do not know it; I do not know it, I do not believe it. They have been in Fort Delaware now for some time, and neither themselves nor their friends have been apprised of any cause for their arrest, or of the reason for which the arrests were made. I hope the senate therefore will adopt the resolution.

Mr. Wilson of Massachusetts:

"I feel constrained to oppose the adoption of the resolution. I believe that instead of the few hundred arrests we have had, we ought to have had several thousands."

"I know the government of this country has forborne a great deal. Adopting this resolution at this time looks to me as a sort of arraignment of the government of the Country for making these arrests."—Mr. Bayard: "Mr. President, I had supposed, previous to the events of the last year or two, that in this country we lived under a free government, though we were at war. I always supposed that the great value of this government consisted in the fact that it afforded, beyond all other governments, the best guardianship to the liberty of the individual citizen.

The honorable senator from Massachusetts tells us that, in his opinion, the government have forborne.

"At Fort Warren in which the soldiers of the United States refused to allow the writ of habeas corpus, issued by a judge of the supreme court itself, to be served."

"In the State of Delaware there has been neither insurrection—revolt, nor contemplated revolt, by any citizen of the state against the government or its authority. The state has been perfectly peaceable. I suppose it is not disloyal to oppose an existing administration, to differ from it in opinion, to believe that the question of emancipation had better be left to be dealt with in the future, as it has been in the past, by individual states."

"Loyalty is attachment to the laws and the Constitution of the country, and tested by that, I claim that the people of Delaware were what their natural position would make them, eminently Union men." "Why should citizens of Delaware have been arrested, and we be told that we are not entitled to inquire into it ?" . "The doctrine of secession, the right of secession, has never been advocated in the state of Delaware." "They were arrested on that day at the place of election, as I understood, by order of Colonel Wallace, a commander of the home-guards of Maryland." "These men were arrested and have been held in confinement since the 7th day of October. Their friends have been unable to ascertain what they are confined for. No hearing has been allowed them; no means of judicial application to test the ground of their arrest. "If the government persist in this system of arrests by discretion—it comes back to that—if the law of the land which the judiciary are bound to execute is put at defiance by the military power of the government, and if Congress will not, in the case of arrests, even call for the testimony and inform their own judgments," or whether this is a proper case for holding men in imprisonment for an indefinite period of time, then of course we are living under just as despotic a government as existed in France in the time of Louis XIV."

Mr. Doolittle:

"There has been some complaint, and with more reason, perhaps, made against the government because it has been notoriously engaged, in sympathy and in act, too, with the traitors against the government; and the complaint has been, not because suspected parties have been arrested, but because the guilty have not been shot or hung."—Cong. Globe 1862–63. pp. 18.

Saulsbury:

"These two are not the only men who have been arrested. Men from the adjoining state of Maryland, who, I understand, refused to go out of their own state to fight the battles of the country, are in the habit of coming over into my state and dragging off peaceable, quiet citizens from their homes. It has not been two months since two of the citizens of my county came in the hour of night to my house to know how they could escape from the oppression of these Maryland home guards. The house of one of them was attacked, and a young man occupying his store was assaulted. Another was compelled to flee from his own house to escape—what ? the Maryland home guards." "But, sir, I tell the senate that at our last general election armed soldiery were sent to every voting place in the lower counties of the State of Delaware. When I went to vote myself, I had to walk between drawn sabres in order to deposit my ballot. Peaceable, quiet citizens, saying not a word, on their way to the polls, and before they had got to the election ground, were arrested and dragged out of their wagons and carried away. Peaceable, quiet citizens were assaulted at the polls." Mr. Powell: "Judge Duff, in one instance, in Illinois, was arrested by the Marshal and taken from his court where he was administering the laws, and lodged in the old Capitol prison here." Cong. Globe 1862–3. p. 1191.

General Grant's expulsion of the Jews, December 17, 1862. General Grant issued an order for the expulsion of the Jews in twenty-four hours.

Mr. Powell offered the following resolution:

"And whereas, by virtue of said order, the Jews, as a class, who claim to be loyal citizens of the United States, have been expelled from the city of Paducah, Kentucky, and have been driven from their business and homes by the military authority, without any specific charges having been made against them, or any opportunity given them to meet the vague and general charges set forth in said order: Therefore,

Resolved by the senate of the United States, That the said order of Major-General Grant, expelling the Jews, as a class, from the department of which he is in command, is condemned as illegal, tyrannical, cruel, and unjust, and the President is requested to countermand the same." "I have in my possession documents that go to establish the fact beyond the possibility of a doubt that the Jews, residents of the city of Paducah, Kentucky, some thirty gentlemen in number, were driven from their homes and their business by virtue of this order of General Grant, only having the short notice of four and twenty hours; that the Jewish women and children of that city were expelled under that order; that there was not a Jew left, man, woman, or child, except two women who were prostrate on beds of sickness." "These people are represented by the most respectable citizens of Paducah to be loyal men. Many of them are men who were not engaged in commerce. They were mechanics, attending to their daily avocations, at their homes." Let General Grant and all other military commanders know that they are not to encroach upon the rights and privileges of the peaceable loyal citizens of this country." "Many of these Jews, who were expelled from Paducah were known to me for many years as highly honorable and loyal citizens. This order expels them as a class from that entire department, and prevents their having a pass to approach his person to ask a redress of grievances."

Mr. Hale and Mr. Sumner: "Why not table it?"—Cong. Globe 1862-63, pp. 245-6.

Vallandigham in his speech Feb. 23, 1863, said:

"Sir, not many months ago, this administration in its great and tender mercy towards the six hundred and forty prisoners of State was a lad of fifteen, a newsboy upon the Ohio river, whose only offence proved, upon inquiry, to be that he owed fifteen cents the unpaid balance of a debt due to his washer-woman." "For four weary months the lad had lain in that foul and most loathsome prison, under military charge."—Cong. Globe 1862-63, App. p. 176.

Nov. 1862, France made a proposition to Russia and England to have these powers use their influence with the Washington and Confederate authorities for an armistice and peace. Peace and even foreign intervention had many advocates. Although the draft had been postponed several times, it was put in force—it was resisted in Wisconsin, in the fall of 1862. The rioters were arrested and were discharged on a writ of Habeas Corpus by the supreme court of the United States which pronounced it unconstitutional for the President to suppress the Writ of Habeas Corpus! The Republican party had from time to time called upon the President to remove every Democratic general who was opposed to "Lincoln's policy." Laboring under this pressure, General Buell was removed from command, on October 1862, although General Thomas had telegraphed to the authorities at Washington to reverse their action.—Headley vol. 2, p. 104. On the 5th November, 1862, General McClellan was relieved by Burnside. The authorities at Washington and the Republican party who had suffered a

defeat at the recent elections, did not want a political opponent to hold the
chief command of the army!

Burnside found the army of the Potomac in three grand divisions under
Sumner, Hooker, and Franklin. The army was indignant at the loss of its
chief, and so was Burnside, who did not wish for the position and who
openly declared that McClellan was the man fit for the command of the
Potomac army or to match Lee.—Headley vol. 2, pp. 118-19-20. Burnside's
plan was to advance on Richmond by Fredericksburg.—Lost Cause 340.
The country was indignant for the base treatment of McClellan. But the
fact of it was, the Republican party did not want any man, who was a Democrat and who did not adopt "Lincoln's policy," to be in command of the
army. Lincoln said that the party who elected a President could put down
the rebellion. Burnside was completely defeated at Fredericksburg by
Lee. He walked into a trap. The country was greatly excited on hearing
of the fatal disaster; but Lincoln and Stanton would not give up the control
of the army to generals in the field but persistently marred their matured
and well laid plans. The peace Democrats denounced the administration.
They raised their voice against arbitrary and irresponsible arrests; they
complained of the small success of the war party; they protested against
emancipation; they reminded Mr. Seward of the declarations made in 1862
in his letter to Mr. Adams that such a measure "would re-invigorate the
declining insurrection in every state of the south."—Lost Cause 361. The
opposition to the administration can be gathered from Vallandigham's
speech of January 14, 1863.

"It is now two years, Sir, since Congress assembled soon after the
Presidential election. A sectional anti-slavery party had been chosen
upon a platform of avowed hostility to an institution peculiar to nearly one
half of the States of the Union, and who had himself proclaimed that there
was an irrepressible conflict because of that institution between the States;
and that the Union could not endure "part slave and part free." Congress
met therefore in the midst of the profoundest agitation, not here only but
throughout the entire South. Revolution glared upon us. Repeated efforts
for conciliation and compromise were attempted in Congress and out
of it. All were rejected by the party just coming into power, except only
the promise in the last hours of the session, and that, too, against the
consent of the majority of that party both in the senate and House; that
Congress nor the executive should never be authorized to abolish or
interfere with slavery in the states where it existed. South Carolina seceded;
Georgia, Alabama, Florida, Mississippi, Louisiana, and Texas, speedily followed. The Confederate Government was established. The other slave
states held back, Virginia demanded a peace Congress. The commissioners
met, and after some time, agreed upon terms of final adjustment. But
neither in the senate nor the House were they allowed even a respectful
consideration.

The President elect left his home in February, and journeyed towards
this capital, jesting as he came; proclaiming that the crisis was only artificial, and that "nobody was hurt." He entered this city under cover of
night and in disguise. On the 4th of March he was inaugurated, surrounded by soldiery; and, swearing to support the Constitution of the United
States announced in the same breath that the platform of his party should
be law unto him.

From that moment all hope of peaceable adjustment fled. But for a little while, either with unsteadfast sincerity or in premeditated deceit, the
policy of peace was proclaimed, even the evacuation of Sumter and the
other Federal forts and arsenals in the seceded states. Why that policy

was suddenly abandoned, time will disclose. But just after the spring elections, and the secret meeting in this city, of the governors of several
northern and western states, a fleet carrying a large number of men was
sent down ostensibly to provision Fort Sumter.   The authorities of South
Carolina eagerly accepted the challenge, and bombarded the fort into surrender, while the fleet fired not a gun, but, just as soon as the flag was
struck, bore away and returned to the North.   It was Sunday, the 14th of
April, 1861, and that day the President in fatal haste and without the
advice or consent of Congress, issued his proclamation, dated the next day,
calling out seventy-five thousand militia for three months to repossess the
forts, places, and property seized from the United States, and commanding
the insurgents to disperse in twenty days.   Again the gage was taken up
by the South, and thus the flames of Civil war, the grandest, bloodiest, and
saddest in history, lighted up the whole heavens. Virginia forthwith seceded; North Carolina, Tennessee, and Arkansas followed; Delaware, Maryland, Kentucky, and Missouri were in a blaze of agitation, and within a
week from the proclamation, the line of the Confederate States was
transferred from the cotton states to the Potomac, and almost to the Ohio
and Missouri, and their population and fighting-men doubled.

In the North and West, too, the storm raged with the fury of a hurricane.
Never in history was any thing equal to it.   Men, women, and children,
native and foreign born, church and state, clergy and layman, were all
swept along with the current.   Distinction of age, sex, station, party perished in an instant.   Thousands bent before the tempest; and here and
there only was one found bold enough, foolhardy enough it may have been,
to bend not, and him it smote—fell as a consuming fire.   The spirit of persecution for opinion's sake, almost extinct in the old world, now, by some
mysterious transmigration, appeared incarnate in the New; Social relations
were dissolved; friendships broken up; the ties of family and kindred
snapped asunder. Stripes and hangings were everywhere threatened, some-
times executed. Assassination was invoked; slander sharpened his tooth;
falsehood crushed truth to the earth; reason fled; madness reigned. Not
justice only escaped to the skies, but peace returned to the bosom of God,
whence she came. The gospel of love perished, hate sat enthroned, and
the sacrifices of blood smoked upon every altar.

But the reign of the mob was inaugurated only to be supplanted by the
iron domination of arbitrary power.

Constitutional limitation was broken down: habeas corpus fell; liberty of
the press, of speech, of the person, of mails, of travel, of one's own house,
and of religion; the right to bear arms, due process of law, judicial trial,
trial by jury, trial at all; every badge and muniment of freedom in Republican government or kingly government—all went down at a blow, and the
chief law officers of the crown—I beg pardon, sir, but it is easy now to fall
into this courtly language—the Attorney General, first of all men, proclaimed
in the United States the maxim of Roman servility; *whatever pleases the
President, that is law !* Prisoners of state were then first heard of here. Midnight and arbitrary arrests commenced; travel was interdicted; trade em-
bargoed; passports demanded; bastiles were introduced; strange oaths invented; a secret police organized; "piping" began; informers multiplied;
spies now first appeared in America. The right to declare war, to raise and
support armies, and to provide and maintain a navy was usurped by the
Executive; and in a little more than two months a land and naval force of
over three hundred thousand men was in the field or upon the sea. An army
of public plunderers followed, and corruption struggled with power in
friendly strife for the mastery at home.

On the 4th of July Congress met, not to seek peace; not to rebuke usurpation not to restrain power; not certainly to deliberate; not even to legislate, but to register and ratify the edicts and acts of the Executive; and in your language, sir, upon the first day of the sessions, to invoke a universal baptism of fire and blood amid the roar of cannon and the din of battle. Free speech was had only at the risk of a prison; possibly life. Opposition was silenced by the fierce clamor of "disloyalty." All business not of war was voted out of order.

"In twenty, at most in sixty days, the rebellion was to be crushed out To doubt it was treason. Abject submission was deemed. Lay down your arms, sue for peace, surrender your leaders—forfeiture, death—this was the only language heard on the floor. The galleries responded; the corridors echoed; and contractors and placemen and other venal patriots everywhere frowned upon the friends of peace as they passed by. In five weeks seventy-eight public and private acts and joint resolutions, with declaratory resolutions, in the Senate and House, quite as numerous, all full of slaughter, were hurried through without delay and almost without debate."

And now pardon me, sir, if I pause here a moment to define my own position at this time upon this great question, "Sir, I am one of the number who have opposed abolitionism, or the political development of the anti-slavery sentiment of the north and west, from the beginning, in school, at college, at the bar, in public assemblies, in the legislature, in Congress, boy and man as a private citizen and in public life, in time of peace, and in time of war." "But there was not an hour from the beginning when it did not seem to me as clear as the sun at broad noon, that the agitation in any form in the North and West of the slavery question must sooner or later end in disunion and civil war."

"It was only a question of time, and short time. Such was its strength, indeed, that I do not believe that the Union of the Democratic party in 1860, on any candidate, even though he had been supported also by the entire so-called conservative or anti-Lincoln vote of the country, would have availed to defeat it; and if it had, the success of the abolition party would only have been postponed four years longer."

"The doctrine of the "irrepressible conflict" had been taught too long and accepted too widely and earnestly to die out, until it should culminate in secession and disunion; and, if coercion were resorted to, then in civil war. I believed from the first that it was the purpose of some of the apostles of the doctrine to force a collision between the North and South, either to bring about a separation or to find a vain but bloody pretext for abolishing slavery in the states. In any event, I knew, or thought I knew, that the end was certain collision, and death to the Union."

"The Candidate of the Republican party was chosen President, secession began, civil war was imminent. It was no petty insurrection, no temporary combination to obstruct the execution of the laws in certain states: but a revolution, systematic, deliberate, determined, and with the consent of a majority of the people of each state which seceded."

"It was disunion at last. The wolf had come. But civil war had not yet followed. In my deliberate and most solemn judgment there was but one wise and masterly mode of dealing with it. Non-coercion would avert civil war and compromise crush out both abolitionism and secession. The parent and the child would thus both perish. But a resort to force would at once precipitate war, hasten secession, extend disunion, and while it lasted, utterly cut off all hope of compromise. I believed that war, if long enough continued, would be final, eternal disunion."

" But that party, most disastrously for the country, refused all compromise. How, indeed, could they accept, that which the South demanded and the Democratic and conservative parties of the North and West were willing to grant, and which alone could avail to keep the peace and save the Union, to inflict a surrender of the sole vital element of the party and its platform; of the very principles, in fact, upon which it had just won the contest for the Presidency?" Sir, the crime, the "high crime," of the Republican party was not so much its refusal to compromise, as its original organization upon a basis and doctrine wholly inconsistent with the stability of the constitution and the peace of the Union."

"Sometime in March it was announced that the President had resolved to continue the policy of his predecessors and even go a step further, and evacuate Sumter and the other Federal forts and arsenals in the seceded states. His own party acquiesced, the whole country rejoiced."

"I did not support the war, and to day I bless God that not the smell of so much as one drop of its blood is upon my garments."

"The country was at war; and I belonged to the school of politics which teaches that when we are at war, the government—I do not mean the executive alone, but the government—is entitled to demand and have, without resistance, such number of men, and such amount of money and supplies generally, as may be necessary for the war, until an appeal can be had to the people."

"I meant that, without opposition, the President might take all the men and all the money he should demand, and then to hold him to a strict accountability before the people for the results. Not believing the soldiers responsible for the war, or its purposes, or its consequences, I have never withheld my vote where their separate interests were concerned. But I have denounced from the beginning the usurpations and the infractions, one and all, of law and constitution, by the President and those under him, their repeated and persistent arbitrary arrests, their suspension of Habeas Corpus, the violation of freedom of the mails, of private houses, of the press and of speech and all other multiplied wrongs and outrages upon public liberty and private rights, which have made this country one of the worst despotisms on earth for the past twenty months; and I will continue to rebuke and denounce them to the end."

"And did not the party of the Executive control the entire Federal Government, every state government, every county, every city, town and village in the North and West? Was it patronage? All belonged to it. Was it influence? What more? Did not the school, the college, the church, the press, the secret orders, the Municipality, the corporations, railroads, telegraphs, express companies, the voluntary associations, all, all yielded it to the utmost." Was it unanimity? Never was an administration so supported in England or America. Five men and half a score of newspapers made up the opposition. Was it enthusiasm? The enthusiasm was fanatical. There has been nothing like it since the Crusades. Was it confidence? Sir, the faith of the people exceeded that of the patriarchs. They gave up constitution, law, right, liberty, all, at your demand for arbitrary power that the rebellion might, as you promised, be crushed out in three months and the Union restored." * *

"But in the beginning, the Roundhead outwitted the Cavalier, and by the skilful use of Slavery and the Negro united all, New England first, and afterwards the entire North and West, and finally sent out to battle against him Celt and Saxon, German and Knickerbocker, Catholic and Episcopalian, and even a part of his own household and of the descendants of his own stock." * * But we, also, of the North and West, in every state and by thousands, who have dared so much as to question the principles and policy, or doubt the honesty, of this administration and its party, have suffered everything that the worst despotism could inflict, except only loss of life itself upon the scaffold. Some even have died for the cause by the hand of the assassin."

Shall we destroy the government because usurping tyrants have held possession and perverted it to the most cruel oppressions?

"Stop fighting. Make an armistice—no formal treaty. Withdraw your army from the seceded states. Reduce both armies to a fair and sufficient peace establishment. Declare absolute free trade between the North and South. Buy and sell. Recall your fleets. Break up your blockade. Reduce your navy. Restore travel. Open railroads. No more monitors and iron-clads, but set your friendly steamers and steamships again in motion. Visit the North and West. Vist 'the South. Exchange newspapers. Migrate, intermarry. Let slavery alone." Congressional Globe 1862–63. App. pp. 52–3, 4, 5, 6, 7, 8, 9.

This was the the position taken by Mr. Vallandigham, which gave the Administration so much trouble; which caused him to be arrested and sent across the lines into the southern confederacy. These principles were adopted by many of the peace Democrats. History will give Mr. Vallandigham credit for his honesty and candor, but as to his mode of settling the war question merely by an armistice, will lead to some grave and serious differences of opinion. Indeed in 1863, the South had gone so far that nothing would satisfy Jeff Davis short of independence—he wanted the South recognized as a separate government.

Feb. 23, 1863, Mr. Vallandigham spoke against the conscription bill.

"Sir, what are the bills which have passed, or are still before the House? The bill to give the President entire control of the currency—the purse of the country. A tax bill to clothe him with power over the whole property of the country. A bill to put all power in his hands over the personal liberties of the people. A bill to indemnify him, and all under him for every act of oppression and outrage already consummated. A bill to enable him to suspend the Writ of Habeas Corpus, in order to justify or protect him, and every minion of his, in the arrests which he or they may choose to make—arrests too, for mere opinion's sake. And now, to-day, for opinions on questions political, under a free government, in a country whose liberties were purchased by our fathers by seven years' outpouring of blood and expenditure of treasures, we have lived to see men, the born heirs of this precious inheritance, subjected to arrests and cruel imprisonment at the caprice of a President or a secretary or a constable. And, as if that were not enough, a bill is introduced here to-day, and pressed forward to a vote, with the right to debate, indeed—extorted from you by the minority—but without the right to amend, with no more than the mere privilege of protest—a bill which enables the President to bring under his power, as commander-in-chief, every man in the United States between the ages of twenty and forty-five—three millions of men. And as if not satisfied with that, this bill provides, further, that every other citizen, man, woman, and child, under twenty years of age and even forty-five, including those that may be exempt between these ages, shall be also at the mercy—so far as his personal liberty is concerned — of some miserable "provost marshal," with the rank of captain of cavalry, who is never to see service in the field, and every Congressional district in the United States is to be governed—yes, governed—by this petty Satrap—this military eunuch —this Baba—and he even may be black—who is to do the bidding of your sultan."

What is it, sir, but a bill to abrogate the constitution, to repeal all existing laws, to destroy all rights, to strike down the judiciary, and erect upon the ruins of civil and political liberty a stupendous superstructure of despotism? And for what? To enforce the law? No, sir. It is admitted now by the legislation of Congress, and by the two proclamations of the President, it is admitted by common consent, that the war is for the abolition of Negro slavery, but others openly and candidly confess that the purpose of the prosecution of the war is to abolish slavery." The freedom of the Negro is to be purchased, under this bill, at the sacrifice of every right of the white men of the United States. "Sir, I have done now with my objections to this bill. I have spoken as though the constitution survived, and was still the supreme law of the land." "Give us known and fixed laws, give us the judiciary; arrest us only upon due process of law; give us presentment and indictment by grand juries; speedy and public trial; trial by jury;" secure us in our persons, our houses, our papers, and our effects;" give us free speech and a free press, free and undisturbed elections and the ballot; take our sons, take our money, our property.—Cong. Globe 1862-63. App. pp. 172-3-4-5-6-7. The Republican papers all over the land denounced Vallandigham for this speech as a traitor. They said that he was aiding the Rebels by opposing and discouraging enlistments. The peace Democracy hailed this speech with applause.

January 1, 1863, the President issued the emancipation proclamation. It was opposed by the conservatives of the north, but hailed with joy by the Radicals. This measure drove the south to desperation—it drove the southern union men into the Confederate army by thousands. This made the Confederates fight with desperation at Fredericksburg, Murfreesboro, and Vicksburg. Jeff Davis issued his proclamation (as an offset to Lincoln's emancipation proclamation), threatening to hang all northern officers who aided slaves to escape. This proclamation of President Lincoln, with other acts of his administration, was worth to the south more than a million of men!!

Northern papers said, that in consequence of the President's emancipation proclamation, making the war an anti-slavery one—the corruption and inefficacy of the administration, that there was a great feeling throughout the country to sever the Middle and Western States from New England. The army became greatly demoralized in consequence of the war taking an abolition turn; the removal of McClellan; the defeat of Burnside at Fredericksburg; defeat of the union army at Murfreesboro; the corruption of vile contractors—an other cause of grievance was that the soldiers were many months without pay: while their families were in want, while, at the same time, officers and contractors, who had big pay, were promptly paid! In the army of the Potomac, alone, as many as 350 officers were absent at one time—absentees from the northern army were about 100 per day, desertion was also very large; as many of the volunteers were sick of the war when they saw that it was the "rich man's war and the poor man's fight!"

May 5, 1863, Vallandigham was arrested by order of General Burnside, at his residence, in Dayton, Ohio. The office of the Dayton *Journal* was destroyed by a Radical mob.

May 11, 1863, the Buell court of inquiry adjourned, after a session of 165 days. May 25, 1863, Mr. Vallandigham was delivered over to the rebels, at Murfreesboro, Tennessee. This was a most stupendous outrage and stretch of despotic power. This was a relic of barbarism and in full keeping with the odious alien and sedition laws, which made the name of John Adams hateful to the American people. But the administration was now prepared for any measure which would crush all opposition. For this purpose it trampled under foot every particle of American liberty. Republicans copied from the Cromwellians and the Red Republicans of France! General Lovell, after the fall of New Orleans, ordered the defence of Vicksburg, And to Van Dorn, in the summer of 1862, was assigned the defence of Vicksburg. This was a great blunder on the part of General Butler, for immediately after the fall of New Orleans he could have captured Vicksburg and Port Hudson. But he wasted his time in the "spoon business" in New Orleans and in amassing a large fortune. He preferred himself to his country—indeed the Republicans were more for themselves than for their country. His god was his ambition. For he would be either a Democrat, Republican or rebel as it suited his ambitious views. This was characteristic of the Butler family, even in Ireland!

The "Beast" would be Jew, Turk, Christian or Heathen, as it might suit the times! If Jefferson Davis could subvert the Union and erect on its ruins an empire, Butler would be his instrument of imperial oppression. He was a curse to the Union cause—for had he shown as much patriotism, as he displayed a greed for the accumulation of filthy lucre, he would have captured Port Hudson and the works of Vicksburg. By such means he could have saved the lives of thousands and he could have saved millions of dollars afterwards lost in the capture of these places. But though Butler was fond of fame, his love of gold drowned every other impulse! The acquisition of wealth was his leading aim—his great passion and moral weakness.

We have said that Butler could have taken Port Hudson and Vicksburg before they were fortified. Porter had advised the government at Washington, of the necessity of fortifying these strongholds. That the Confederates were fortifying them. He urged the necessity of stopping them. He even offered with a thousand men and his gunboats to hold and occupy these places. "But the year 1862 was a year of blunders on the part of the war department and of great disasters in the field. The army of the Potomac had been driven from Richmond, on one hand, and from the Rapidan, on the other and shattered into fragments on the heights of Fredericksburg: Buell had been forced back from Chattanooga to Nashville and Morgan compelled to evacuate Cumberland Gap; and to close up the sad record, Port Hudson had been allowed to become wellnigh impregnable.—Headley vol. 2, p. 149. The campaign of 1863 was resumed early, as Lincoln was apprehensive that the Democrats would gain further strength as they had in the fall elections in consequence of the multitudinous blunders of the administration. He was now preparing for the presidential campaign of 1864. He knew that it was necessary to gain some decisive success. To gain the support and confidence of the people success was necessary, as the term of service of many of the Union soldiers would soon expire. General Hooker was raised from corps-commander to that of general-in-chief. "Fighting Joe Hooker made himself famous in the newspapers by his criticism of McClellan's campaign. He said he would capture Richmond if in McClellan's place. Fighting Joe Hooker, having by this idle bravado obtained the command of the Potomac army, crossed the Rappahannock and was, notwithstanding his previous boasting, most beautifully whipped at the battle of Chancellorsville, though he had boasted that Lee's army was the legitimate property of the army of the Potomac."—Headley vol. 2, p. 186. Lee with an army of sixty thousand whipped Hooker, who had under his command one hundred and fifty thousand men.—Headley vol. 2, p. 189. Grant spent weeks digging a canal, to turn the Mississippi from its old course so as to leave Vicksburg high and dry. Although the Republicans ridiculed McClellan for digging in the swamps of the Chickahominy, yet they lauded Grant to the skies although he had spent time and money with his army in digging a canal which proved a total failure and a monument of human folly. Yet, there was neither censure nor criticism from the Radical press. On the contrary, they called it a great stroke of military strategy. The people heard with impatience for weeks 'digging still.' After a display of military ignorance and stupidity Grant found his novel plan of turning the Mississippi into a canal a failure and a stupendous blunder I As he had no 'policy of his own' he had the support of the Radicals, who branded as copperheads and traitors and rebel sympathizers all who found fault with Grant's military blunders. This canal might be called 'Grant's folly.'— Headley vol. 2, p. 149–50.

On the failure of diverting the floods of the "great father of water" into the "grant Canal," Grant attempted, by the aid of Porter's fleet, to capture Vicksburg, by going up the Yazoo River and capturing Haines Bluff and by this means get into the rear of Vicksburg. He failed in this project, as completely, as at Belmont, in his famous Canal business: so after much labor he had to abandon this project. He also failed to get in the rear of Vicksburg by way of the " Black Bayou."—Headley vol. 2, p. 187.

Failing in these attempts to capture Vicksburg, Grant was forced to adopt the McClellan plan, so much condemned by the Republican press, and so much condemned and ridiculed by Pope and Hooker, to build *Corduroy* bridges over the Swamps on the west side of the Mississippi, and by the cooperation of Admiral Porter's gunboats, got his transports past the batteries of Vicksburg while the forces passed by land. Porter with his gunboats ran the transports past the rebel batteries and Grant got his army in the rear of Vicksburg.

He took Vicksburg after a long and bloody siege. The country around Vicksburg as far as Jackson was made one vast graveyard. Vast numbers of lives would have been saved but for the stupidity of General Butler, who preferred reaping a rich harvest of gold and silver at New Orleans; and thus neglected to take Port Hudson and Vicksburg, which Porter said could be taken by his gunboats and a thousand men; so that Stanton, Halleck, and Butler are responsible for the lives of thousands of brave Union soldiers, who fell in the memorable siege of Vicksburg. They made by their wicked and culpable negligence, widows and orphans, by thousands, and brought desolation and woe to thousands of families I The fall of Vicksburg now opened the Mississippi to the Union army. The Union Steamboats had control of the river, cutting the Confederacy in two. The fall of Vicksburg and the defeat at Gettysburg, hastened the overthrow of the Confederacy.

CHAPTER XVI.

The south had now suffered from the depreciation of her currency. The amount of specie in the south at the commencement of the war was about thirty millions in the banks and about fifty millions in currency.—Lost Cause, 421. As early as January, 1862, a dollar in gold was worth in Richmond one dollar and twenty cents in currency. In July, 1862, it was worth the same. Now, in January, 1863, one dollar in gold was worth three dollars and ten cents in currency. Remorseless speculators had succeeded in monopolizing and engrossing most of the entire stock of the necessaries and comforts of life, which they held at exorbitant prices. Even the nail factories were in the hands of a few speculators, who sold nails at exorbitant prices. There was also a monopoly of salt, which was sold at fifty cents per pound.—Lost cause, 427-8. Indeed one of the principal causes of the failure of the southern confederacy was speculation, both by monopolists and even the authorities, who sold cotton for greenbacks; thus depreciating and breaking down their own currency; as the people saw that the leaders had lost faith in their own money and that the cause of the Confederates was failing!

On the 4th of July, 1863, was fought the great battle of Gettysburg. Lee was compelled to fall back and retreated from Pennsylvania. He saved his artillery, with the exception of two or three guns, though he left twenty-five thousand small arms in the fields and woods. He crossed the Cumberland Mountains towards the Potomac, followed by Gen. Sedgwick. General French destroyed his pontoon train, at Falling Waters.—Headley vol. 2, page 207.

General Meade allowed Lee to escape and gave him time to cut timber and construct bridges to cross his army over the Potomac; when he could have captured his whole army. Yet the Republicans denounced McClellan the year before for not capturing Lee at about the same point, after Lee's retreat from the battle field of Antietam!—Headley vol. 2, pp. 208-9.

This is Republican honesty!

The Republicans employed the colored troops although it gave great offence to the north. For many of the northern soldiers did not want Negro equality. They knew that if the Negroes were made soldiers they would be made citizens. The Republicans told the country that the Negro soldiers were superior to the white soldiers, their object being to prepare the country for Negro equality. July 30, 1863, the President issued an order that no distinction should be made, in the exchange of prisoners on account of color.

Although the Republicans professed great love for the Negroes during the war, yet they were ill treated by the government agents. The Negroes complained that they were treated worse by the Northern authorities than they were by their masters. Many of them returned to their masters rather than endure the sufferings and hardships of the government camps! About Natchez they were reduced from 4000 to 2000, by exposure, filth, and disease brought on from various causes. In 1864, the report of Yoeman, President of the Western Sanitary Commission, as given in the New York Tribune shows the frightful condition of the great number of Africans scattered along the Mississippi from Cairo to Natchez. More than the barracoons of the African coast or the horrors of the middle passage, this shows an awful inhuman record of hunger and death.

The kidnapping of Negroes by members of the Loyal League, who made large fortunes by this inhuman practice of selling Negroes for cotton. Many northern officers went into raising cotton along the Mississippi and cheated the poor Negroes out of the fruits of their labor; yet, they were loyal. The Republicans had no more love for Africans than to merely use them for party purposes. They sacrificed the welfare of the Negro and the liberty of the country, honesty, honor and principles for office and power! The American people had from time to time denounced the despotism of the monarchs of Europe; now, strange to say, the administration had courted the despotic power of Russia, the oppressor of down-trodden Poland! The Russians were banqueted in New York, in 1863. The Republicans had stooped so low as to make an ally of Russia!

The great flood of "greenbacks," government paper currency, drove gold and silver out of circulation. The government issued postage currency as low as five cents. Every one in 1862, issued his own money. Barbers and saloon keepers issued scrip "good for one shave," or "good at this bar for one glass of beer." The government violated the constitution by making paper currency a legal tender. It was unjust to those, who lent money before the passage of this law, to make greenbacks a legal tender. This paper became so depreciated that one dollar in gold would buy $2.90 in greenbacks. This was a palpable swindle. This was robbing the creditor who lent his money in gold and now had to take depreciated currency; it also robbed the soldiers. One great cause of depreciation of the currency was occasioned by the blunders of northern Generals; and the intermeddling of the abolitionists, who drove the south to desperation for it was feared that the war would be prolonged until the public debt would be equal to that of Great Britain. Men of capital feared that the debt would not be paid. In 1863, the administration and Congress proposed to abolish the state banks and to establish United States Banks. For this purpose they legislated the state banks out of existence, by means of taxation.

All who spoke of the rights of the states, were denounced by the Radicals as traitors and copperheads. They held that the general government could swallow up the state governments. We give Jefferson's opinion on the rights of the States: "We should marshal the government into, 1st, the general Federal Republic for all concerns foreign and Federal; 2d, that of the state, for what relates to our own citizens exclusively."—Jefferson's Works vol. 7, p. 13.

But, what cared the Radicals for the opinions of either Jefferson or Washington? they followed the example of British statesmen and the bluelight Federalists! The old Federal and Whig party passed a high protective tariff; by this means the farmers were taxed to support the looms of New England. The Democratic party complained of this unjust measure. But the Radicals had the army and navy, the purse and the sword at their backs, and by means of arbitrary arrests drowned all opposition. In vain did the western papers complain that the east had oppressed the south and west. The Radicals claimed that it was for the benefit of the whole country that the people should be taxed to sustain New England and Pennsylvania. Those they could not intimidate were bought up and Congressmen were bought and sold like oxen in the shambles. Corruption and bribery were the order of the day. The Democrats were denounced for their opposition to the tariff. They were called traitors, rebels, and copperheads! We give Jefferson's opinion on the tariff:

"An equilibrium of agriculture, manufactures and commerce, is certainly becoming essential to our independence."—Jefferson's Works, vol. 5, p. 448. Thus we see that Thomas Jefferson considered agriculture as the most essential branch of industry. For all branches of industry depend on the prosperity of the farmers. But the Radicals who have followed the footprints of the Federalists, want to sacrifice the farmers to the interests of the manufacturers. Jefferson spoke of the policy of the Federalists in trying "to convert this great agricultural country into a city of Amsterdam."

The expense of the war had now assumed vast proportions. The people were alarmed at the expense of the war; but the Radicals reiterated Pitt's false doctrine that a "Public debt is a public blessing;" thus following in the wake of British Statesmen and American Federalists. They followed Hamilton's plan to make the public debt eternal. They issued bonds bearing interest in gold and some bearing compound interest. The ultimate design of the disciples of Hamilton has been to fund the public debt, the same as in England; so as to create a money king and afterwards a monarchy. We give Jefferson's opinion of a public debt:—

"I consider the fortunes of our Republic as depending, in an eminent degree on the extinguishment of the public debt.—Jefferson's Works vol. 5, p. 478. "We must not let our rulers load us with perpetual debt. We must make our election between economy and liberty or profusion and servitude." Jefferson's Works, vol. 7, p. 14.

Again he speaks of "emancipation of our posterity from that moral canker, it is an encouragement, fellow-citizens, of the highest order to proceed as we have begun in establishing economy for taxation." Jefferson's Works, vol. 8, p. 19.

CHAPTER XVII.

In the political campaign of 1863, the peace Democracy denounced the administration for employing Negro soldiers and suppressing the freedom of speech and of the free press, for suspending the Writ of Habeas Corpus and trial by jury. The unconstitutional acts of the administration were boldly denounced by the peace Democrats, through the press and at public meetings—for the people were, even now, tired of the war, in consequence of draft, military blunders, and the corruption of the government. The reign of terror inaugurated by Loyal Leaguers who were nothing less than the old "Wide-Awakes, who were Know-Nothings in disguise. The Loyal Leaguers became the nucleus of the "Grand Army of the Republic." The people called public meetings for the purpose of adopting some peace measures. The army was tired of the war and the corruption of army contractors and speculators. But the Republican party, who were adverse to peace, introduced a resolution in Congress, to the effect that no compromise should be made with rebels in arms. That the Republicans would not accept of any proposition short of an unconditional surrender of the Confederate Army and its leaders to the Federal authorities. This they ' well knew would never be accepted by the Confederate authorities, while they had a large army in the field and many strongholds in their possession. The truth of the matter is the Republicans did not want peace with the South until they had crushed out slavery and had put the Negro on terms of equality with the white man, until they had weakened the power of the South and the Democratic party, and had perpetuated the power of the Radicals. The administration and Congress having now the war power, the purse, and the sword, the loyal governors and the State Legislatures, threw off the mask and avowed their policy. The Republicans carried the election by force, fraud, and corruption even at the point of the bayonet, when necessary! Indeed, they were apt scholars. They followed Napoleon's plan of carrying the election by military force. They applied all the means used in England to corrupt or intimidate voters. Schenck carried the election in Maryland and Delaware, this year, at the point of the bayonet. Headley, vol. 2, p. 283.

By corruption, bribery, force, frauds, and military power, the Lincoln party carried the elections, this year, from Maine to Minnesota. After the result of this election was known, Lincoln wrote that "the crisis was past. The authorities at Washington now openly laid the constitution aside. They looked for precedents to the monarchs of Europe and imperial Rome. Although Vallandigham, of Ohio, the leader of the peace Democrats was arrested and banished beyond the Rebel lines, he was now allowed to get back and run for governor. For Lincoln and the Republican party wanted some pretext to connect the Democrats with the rebellion. Indeed they wanted to make the Democrats responsible for the war. They wanted to confound the Vallandigham Democrats with the rebels. This trick succeeded and helped to defeat the Democracy!—Headley vol. 2, 465. In 1862, while Cameron was secretary of war, he used the machinery of his office to make a fortune. He engaged in various speculations.

There were, at the commencement of the war, two railroad lines from New York to Washington; one direct through Philadelphia and the other by way of Harrisburg, which is the longer route by 80 miles. The bridges were burnt within the limits of Maryland at the breaking out of the rebellion. Cameron expended 14,000 dollars in repairing his own road, the other railroad company repaired its own bridges. This put 14,000 dollars into the pockets of Cameron's friends. He had the troops and supplies shipped over the road from Philadelphia, Harrisburg and Baltimore, a distance of one hundred miles longer than the other road. He amassed, while secretary of war, ten millions of dollars and for his pains and devotion to his country was made minister to Russia. With this vast fortune he was able to control the Pennsylvania Legislature!

Cameron placed in the hands of his pet, $2,000,000, to be used as this man might deem fit. A few days after this transaction, this pet drew a quarter of a million of dollars, and put 160,000 dollars of it in his own name, in a New York Bank, in the city of New York, and 90,000 dollars was put into the hands of another pet to meet such expenses as he should make. These were the competent and reliable agents of the secretary of war, Simon Cameron. Not even was the oath of office taken or any security given, by these Cameronian agents, to the government for the faithful performance of their official duties. This shows a gross, reckless and fraudulent expenditure of the public money; which helped to build monuments of debt. Cameron by shipping troops and supplies over his own road gained fifty per cent. profit in one year, which came out of the government. But, he was loyal.—App. Cong. Globe, 1861-2, pp. 131-2-3-4-5.

The secretary of the Navy gave his pet a commission for the purchase of vessels. To illustrate how the sales were conducted the *Daylight* and the *Dawn*, two vessels bought from the Secretary's "eminent merchants," one of them originally cost $45,000 and the other $55,000. They were chartered by the government till one of them realized $40,000, and the other $30,000. The government paying the expense of repairs and insuring them against perils. Then the secretary's pet purchased the two vessels; for the one he had paid what the vessel cost four years before, and for the other within $10,000 of what it originally cost. So the owner of the vessels gained $80,000 and the full cost of his vessels. The government agent received 2½ per cent on all sales. The more he gave for the vessels the greater the percentage. Thousands of cases of this description might be cited but this will suffice to show how the national debt was piled up. Besides the percentage, the agent had a salary of $70,000 per annum from the government.

Such wholesale plunder of the treasury is unknown in the annals of history!!—App. Cong. Globe 1861-2, pp. 135-6.

A New York Broker made the sum of $10,000, in the sale of a vessel, under this worthy agent. There was no question asked as to the quality of the vessel, but was the broker loyal—a Republican. In this fraudulent and corrupt manner the secretary of the navy gave a member of his own household the enormous sum of $95,000, in five months !!

Any Democrat who was bold enough to denounce this corruption of the government was pronounced disloyal and a traitor.—App. Cong. Globe, 1861-2, p. 136. Gen. Fremont got a grab from the treasury: in the purchase of arms. He gained in one transaction $51,225. He bought a lot of old Hall Carabines for $3,50 each and sold them to the government for the sum of $22,00 each.   This scheme of plunder gave him in all *Fifty-one-thousand* dollars.   But, he was loyal!—App. Cong. Globe, 1861-2, p. 136. The same General Fremont was the Republican Candidate for President, in 1856, and the Radical Candidate for President in 1864.   He, also, while in command at St. Louis made money in building worthless fortifications. This is Republican honesty—a premium for corruption.   What wonder that the Republicans wished to conceal from the people the true amount of the public debt.   For the people now found that a public debt was not a public blessing.

"We don't feel the war!" was the cry of Contractors and Speculators, in our large cities, while the country suffered from misery and the fearful havoc of war.   Such was the cry among those who made fortunes with marvelous rapidity and spent it in pleasure and extravagance.   They cared but little for the tears of the widow or the orphan.   While the wealth of the country was poured out, fortunes were made by the money-seekers. While brave fellows rushed in multitudes to defend the dear old flag, speculators had a rich field to make vast and rapid fortunes out of army clothing and subsistence contracts for provisions, mules, horses, railway conveyance, steamers, ships, coals, surgical instruments, drugs, and every thing to sustain or destroy life.   The government did not care much about quality or price but gave the whole thing up to some favorite individuals who made vast fortunes in a day.   Political and social friends and relatives were favored with information where there could be made a good "grab." Partisans, brothers, cousins, and brothers-in-law came in first for the biggest prizes.   Some of them made a hundred thousand dollars in one transaction! by merely signing their names!   They even made snug fortunes by the mere transfer of their contracts.   They cared nothing for the quality of the thing, so long as it bore the name.   Thus came this villainous shoddy —the refuse and sweepings of the shops, pounded, rolled, and glued, and hastily got up as clothing for the soldiers.   The shoddyites in a few months erected palatial residences, had splendid coaches, perfumed clothes and glistening silks.   Others made fortunes in old spavined horses and mules, and all this was accomplished by collusion and favoritism!

Now came the time for clearing out the refuse of the armories—even where some of the arms were returned by the ordnance department, yet, by bribery they would be accepted.   Hundreds of thousands of dollars were spent on worthless arms.   One merchant gained two millions of dollars in this speculation in one year.   Some coal-miners made such fortunes out of the government, that in a single year dividends amounted to two-thirds of its capital.   Men who were bankrupts a few months before suddenly could count their fortunes by millions.   This caused a mania for speculation, pervading the whole community.   The cry was, What is the price of gold to-day?

The sudden flow of wealth on contractors and speculators, brought on profusion never before seen in the country.   Stables were built of marble, costly furniture, clothes, and silks were imported in abundance.   Foreign luxury was the order of the day, men buttoned their waistcoats with diamonds, and women powdered their hair with gold and silver dust.   This had an injurious effect on the morals of the people.   This rage for wealth is fast taking hold of all classes—many, very many care little about the means of getting riches to spend in luxury.   This class certainly did not feel the war so long as there was a prospect of making money out of it—no one seemed to care for the country or for its welfare.   Any one who should speak against this waste of the people's money, was called a copperhead, traitor and rebel sympathizer—they could give thousands to partisan newspapers and stump speakers for denouncing those who were in favor of peace. Although we have incidentally spoken of arbitrary arrest we devote further space to this topic; during the reign of terror and the unconstitutional and dictatorial career of the administration no one was deemed safe from illegal arrest, who differed with the party in power, in politics or otherwise. The mere suspicion of being disaffected to the administration, was enough to be arrested and sent to some military prison, even without charges being preferred. In these evil days of discretionary power, under the tyrant's plea of "military necessity," to criticise the government or "Lincoln's policy," was punished with incarceration in a military dungeon. Mr. Seward held that to differ with the administration, was to oppose the Federal government. In this reign, Lincoln was the government; but when President Johnson differed with the Radicals, then "Congress was the government." These illegal and arbitrary arrests and imprisonments were made to crush all Democratic opposition; to break down the spirit of the people, so as to make them fit subjects for future military despotism and unconstitutional acts and to reduce the southern states to mere territories! During the first seven months of the war four hundred persons were arrested at the mere tinkle of Mr. Seward's "little bell." Did the founders of the government ever think that a mere secretary of state should assume powers, which even eclipsed the tyranny of the star-chamber during its worst days? Mr. Seward issued an order that the names of the parties arrested should not be published—enormous arrests were made in Kentucky, Missouri and Maryland. More than ten thousand persons were arrested by Seward's omnipotent "little bell." Thousands were doomed to remain in government bastiles without knowing the cause of their arrest. To prevent persons from inquiring into the cause of their arrest, Seward issued the following ominous order, that "the United States will not recognize any one as attorney for political prisoners, and will look *with distrust* upon all applications for release through such channels, and that such applications will be regarded as additional reason for declining to release the prisoners." Thus people were punished for inquiring why they were torn from their houses, families, and friends and shut up in military dungeons. Republicans called this liberty; and all who complained of such arrests were denounced as traitors, copperheads and rebel sympathizers —all this was done by a party that claimed to be the law and order party. Not in one single instance, was any of the thousands who were arrested brought to trial in the courts, or an accusation filed or an indictment found. In all these cases of arbitrary arrests, we have confined ourselves to those made in the *free states*. Democrats in the northern states, who had the manhood to criticise the policy of Lincoln and his officials were arrested for exercising their right of free speech. Indeed, during the war free speech was suppressed at the point of the bayonet!

Editors of newspapers, who differed with the administration were arrested upon spurious charges of not supporting the administration; "discouraging enlistments;" "writing treason;" "being a prominent Democrat;" "publishing treasonable articles;" the displeasure of the loyal authorities;" "publishing articles distasteful" to the Lincoln administration; "for speaking freely of the draft.

Democrats were incarcerated in the government bastiles merely for making Democratic speeches—on charges of "disloyalty"—on charge of sympathy with secession " — for cheering for Vallandigham — using seditious language "—"publicly expressing disloyal sentiments "—for being a newspaper correspondent—for condemning the policy of Lincoln—

for refusing to take the oath of allegiance—for publicly opposing Lincoln's administration—for disapproving of Lincoln's Emancipation proclamation—for saying that Lincoln's emancipation was "unwise, impolitic, and uncalled for"—for being seen to "smile over a rebel victory"—for not "praying for Lincoln"—for making speeches in favor of the Democratic party"—several persons were arrested and sent to prison without ever knowing the cause of their arrest—lawyers were arrested for merely prosecuting Republicans. Clergymen were seized at the altar, with prayer-book, in hand, while praying to their Maker, and dragged out of Church! Hon. C. L. Vallandigham was arrested by order of General Burnside, May 5, 1863, charged with "declaring disloyal sentiments and opinions." He was one of the leading members of Congress who opposed Lincoln's administration. He was tried by a military commission, while the courts of the country were open. He was found guilty, in direct violation of the Constitution of the United States. He was sentenced to be imprisoned in Fort Warren during the war. This sentence was commuted to banishment; a sentence unknown to the laws! Heretofore no one ever thought that the government would enforce such a vile act of despotism. This was, indeed, a revival of the alien and sedition laws with a vengeance, which had proved the political death of the John Adams blue-light Federal party; but under a worse system, for Adams and his blue lights had an act of Congress to give them color of power, authority; but the administration and its political friends had no law but that of the bayonet. For Thomas Jefferson and the Democratic party had swept the alien and sedition laws from the Statute books.

Rev. James L. Vallandigham of Delaware, was arrested, July 1863, on account of his name—men were arrested for merely having relations in the Rebel army! On the 13th September, 1861, the Maryland Legislature was arrested. In May, 1862, by mere order of General Dix, Judge Carmichael was assailed, while on the bench in open court, beaten and knocked down, and dragged from the court house bleeding and senseless, and sent to Fort La Fayette. For in the exercise of his judicial duties, he charged the grand jury of his country, that Lincoln had not authority to order arbitrary arrests. Ex-Governor Morehead, of Kentucky, without any charge was dragged from his bed, at night, and sent to Fort La Fayette. A newspaper called the *Kent Conservator*, was suppressed by order of General Lockwood for commenting on General Schenck's treatment of the women of Baltimore; The New York *Freeman's Journal* was suppressed and its editor McMasters sent to Fort La Fayette. Mahony, editor of the Dubuque *Herald*, was arrested merely for being a Democrat, and sent to the Capitol prison at Washington. The editor of the St. Louis *Christian Advocate* was arrested for publishing what was then called by the party in power, treasonable articles and the paper suppressed. It was deemed treason to differ with the administration! Several other papers were suppressed either by the government or the Republican mob. For, as in the time of Cromwell and the reign of terror in France, the mob and the government concluded to put down free speech and a free press!

G. W. Porter secretary of the board of trade, Baltimore, was arrested, in 1862, and sent to Fort La Fayette for repeating an account of one of McClellan's battles. The Police Commissioners of Baltimore were sent to Fort La Fayette, in 1861. Ex-Senator Gwin of California, was arrested, in 1861, at Panama, by General Sumner, and sent to Fort La Fayette, on charge of "publicly expressing disloyal sentiments." Thus, the administration crushed out all manner of opposition. What right had a general, merely on his own motion, to arrest outside of the United States, any one for words spoken? Several clergymen were arrested for refusing to pray for the President of the United States. The Rev. Robinson of Kentucky, was banished to Canada for not supporting the war. The administration had no scruples as to the manner of crushing out all opposition, Gibson, a prominent Democrat of Illinois, was arrested, in 1862, and sent to Cairo; thence to St. Louis and incarcerated. He was brought before the provost marshal and questioned as to what he thought of Lincoln's administration and if he thought that the President had violated the Constitution. Not giving satisfactory answers he was held in durance vile for three months.

Dr. Ross of Illinois was arrested, in 1862, for merely drawing his finger across his nose—others were imprisoned merely on the frivolous charge of "conspiring against the government." For being "secessionists." For having "secession proclivities," on charge of being "knights of the golden circle." For being "sons of liberty." And in many instances at the mere whim or caprice of the administration or the military authorities!

The judiciary of New York and Maryland have pronounced the illegal arrests of the President and his cabinet and of the northern generals unconstitutional! After the defeat of the administration, in the fall elections of 1862, the administration seeing that arbitrary arrest and usurpation were condemned by the popular vote released the prisoners in Forts Warren and La Fayette, among whom was a boy only sixteen years old, who had been arrested on mere suspicion. But, after the Republicans became again successful at the elections, by force, fraud, and corruption, they resumed the reign of terror and arrested and imprisoned on mere suspicion until the end of the war. The Radical reign was as tyrannical as the reign of terror in France, during the reign of the Red Republicans! Oh! how strange to behold Radicals, who, before the war, preached so much about free speech and free press, now, that they had the military power in their hands, mob, "lynch," or banish any one who did not support the war or who favored peace or who denounced the corruption of the party in power or who did not support emancipation, confiscation, devastation and negro equality.

The Radicals held various opinions. The New York *Tribune* said Jan. 22d, 1863, after the defeat of the Republicans and at the fall election in 1862. "If three months more of earnest fighting shall not serve to make a serious impression upon the rebels, if the end of that time shall find us no further advanced than its beginning—if some malignant fate has decreed that the blood and treasures of the nation shall ever be squandered in fruitless effort let us know our destiny, and make the best attainable peace." So Greeley and other Radicals could talk peace, disunion, or treason at pleasure; but if a Democratic paper should find fault with the administration it was suppressed and the Editor bastiled!

As the Radicals quoted Jefferson, freely, before the war, we give an extract from Jefferson on the freedom of the press:

"As to myself, conscious that there was no truth on earth which I feared should be known I have lent myself willingly to the support of a great experiment, which was to prove that the administration conducting itself with integrity and common understanding, cannot be battered down even by the falsehood of a licentious press. This experiment was wanting for the world to demonstrate the falsehood of the pretext that the freedom of the press is incompatible with order and government. I have never even contradicted the thousands of calumnies industriously propagated against myself. But the fact being once established that the press is impotent, when it lends itself to falsehood within the pale of truth, with that it is a noble institution equally the friend of science and civil liberty."—

Jefferson's Works vol. 5. p. 43–4. Again, he says in his letter to Washington :—

"No government ought to be without censors: and when the press is free no one ever will; if virtuous, it need not fear the fair operation of attack and defence. Nature has given to man no other means of sifting out the truth, either in religion, law or politics. I think it is honorable to the government neither to know, nor notice, its sycophants or censors, as it would be undignified and criminal to pamper the former and prosecute the latter." Jefferson's Works vol. 5. p. 13.

"Public duties more urgent press on the time of public servants, and the offenders have therefore been left to. find their punishment in the public indignation."—Jefferson's Works, vol. 8, p. 43. "Truth and reason have maintained their ground against false opinions in league with false facts, the press, confined to truth needs no legal restraint; the public judgment will correct false reasonings and opinions; and no other definite line can be drawn between the inestimable liberty of the press and its demoralizing licentiousness. If there be still inproprieties which this rule would not restrain, its supplement must be sought in the censorship of public opinion." —Jefferson's works vol. 8, p. 49. Did the administration and Congress follow the noble example of Thomas Jefferson towards the press ? Oh, no, but they followed the example of John Adams, whose disciples they were, and muzzled the press!

The following is from T. Pickering, Secretary of State under John Adams; July, 24, 1799:

"I shall give the paper" (a newspaper called the *Aurora*) to Mr. Rawle, and if he thinks it libellous, desire him to prosecute the Editor. I presume therefore that he (the editor of the *Aurora*) "is really a British Subject" (an Irishman) "and as an alien, liable to be banished from the United States."

"He is doubtless a United Irishman."—Works of Adams, vol. 9, pp. 3, 4. John Adams to the Attorney General, May 1800:

"I transmit you a copy of the resolutions of the senate of the United States passed in Congress on the 14th of this month, by which I am requested to instruct the proper law officers to commence and carry on a prosecution against William Duane, Editor of a newspaper called the *Aurora*, for certain false defamatory, scandalous, and malicious publications in the said newspaper of the 19th of Feb. last partly tending to defame the senate of the United States, and to bring them into contempt and disrepute and to excite against them the hatred of the good people of the United States. In compliance with this request, I now instruct you, gentlemen, to commence and carry on the prosecution accordingly."

"With great esteem, etc.,

"JOHN ADAMS."

—Works of Adams, vol, 9. p. 56.

John Adams followed in the footprints of the British government in its prosecutions for libel. The Republicans, during the war, went further than ever England or the Federalists, for Editors never got a trial. But, at the mere whim of the President, his Cabinet, Generals, and provost-marshals, democratic papers were suppressed and their Editors imprisoned. Democratic papers were excluded from 'the United States Mails by military orders. What wonder that the Radicals don't quote the writings of Jefferson!

CHAPTER XVIII.

The campaign of 1864, opened with vigor on the part of the administration, for it was evident that if the Union troops did not gain some decisive victories that Lincoln could not be re-elected. Banks failed in his Red River expedition. He went up that river to make a fortune out of cotton, but he got beautifully whipped. Sturgis was defeated at Guntown, so that the Confederate army was generally successful in the West, Charleston and Sumter defied the efforts of Gilmore, and Johnson was in the way of Sherman on his road to Atlanta. March 8th 1864, the President presented Grant with the commission of Lieutenant General; and on the 12th he was assigned to the command of all the armies of the United States. April 23th, 1864, the governors of Ohio, Illinois, Iowa, Wisconsin, and Indiana offered 85,000 men for 100 days.

July 13th 1864, General A. J. Smith defeated General Forrest at Tupelo in five different battles. The object of this raid was to cut the Mobile and Ohio Railroad. The battles lasted for five days, the Union troops fought with bravery and valor and completely defeated the confederates and cut up and destroyed a large portion of the railroad at this point, and then marched back to Memphis. Old England allowed her blockade runners to supply the Confederates with arms and ammunition; in 1864, the Crenshaw and Collier line of steamers made a practice of running the blockade. Indeed England since the commencement of the war did all in her power to aid the southern cause and to break up the Union. We turn to the army of the Potomac, where the Union troops suffered several defeats in consequence of the blunders of the administration in removing from command General McClellan, the only man who could cope with Lee. Before Grant took command of the army, he told the authorities at Washington that he would not take command unless he got full control of the campaign for be remembered that McClellan was defeated by the interference of the Washington authorities. Lincoln consented to give Grant control of the army provided that he would not be a candidate for President. He had made the same proposition to McClellan, but that soldier spurned his offer with high disdain. Grant accepted this offer and said to his friends that he did not want to be President—that he was a poor man. That he was sure of his salary as general. That without office he could not support his family. That if he should run for President, and get defeated that he had nothing to fall back upon for his support.

Grant had things his own way. He could march when he was ready. He was not ordered like other Commanders of the army of the Potomac, to march on a certain day. Thus, Grant was left free to carry out his own plans without interference of the Secretary of war or the politicians.— Headley vol. 2, p. 315. When the politicians requested Lincoln to control the actions of Grant, he said: "I have sent for Mr. Grant over the mountains —I have tried my plan long enough—let Grant have his own way." The people were now apprehensive that Lincoln could not put down the rebellion; and he knew that if something was not done to put it down he could not be re-elected. He knew that if Grant failed he could shift the whole responsibility on him. If on the other hand Grant should succeed it would give him another term of the Presidency. Indeed, it was feared that Lincoln not only wanted to be re-elected, but that he wanted to be President for life. (Beware of a third term.) Grant on being made commander-in-chief adopted the McClellan plan, to move two armies simultaneously on to Richmond and through Georgia.—Headley vol. 2, p. 287.

Soldiers were ordered to their regiments and supplies were ordered to the front by water and rail. Previous to the campaign of 1864, soldiers were scattered from Maine to Minnesota, and from New York to California. Now, Grant ordered even the sick soldiers in hospitals to be sent to the front as soon as they were able to march or do garrison duty. Soldiers who were detailed around posts and cities were also ordered to their commands. He called upon the states for 100 day men for garrison duty. Every soldier that could be spared from Fort Snelling to the Gulf of Mexico was sent to the front.

The Union army, in 1864, mustered one million of men.—Greeley's Am. Con. vol. 1, p. 759.—Lost Cause, 510–11.

Kilpatrick made a raid around Richmond with the bold intent of making one dash on the rebel capital to release the union prisoners. He failed in the bold enterprise. Grant's army about Richmond was estimated to be about two hundred thousand men. Grant sent Butler to capture Petersburg, and to destroy the south side railroad and then to march around Richmond until his left rested on the James, and form a junction with Grant's army.—Headley, vol. 2, p. 349.

Lee wanted but slight success to compel Grant to recross the Rapidan on the first day's battle of the Wilderness as he did Hooker.—Headley, vol. 2, p. 352. Grant had telegraphed to the Secretary of war, "I propose to fight it out on this line, if it takes all summer. But after the battle of the Wilderness he had to change his mind and adopt the McClellan plan.—Headley, vol. 2, p. 364.

May 9th 1864, Butler telegraphed to Grant and the press, that he had cut Beauregard's army in two. That General Grant would not be troubled with any more reinforcements from Beaureguard to Lee.—Headley, vol. 2, p. 369.

But notwithstanding this boast, Gen. Beauregard, on the 16th of May, 1864, made a dashing charge on Butler and compelled him to fall back on Bermuda Hundred, between the forks of the James and the Appomattox River, (Headley, vol. 2, p. 373.) Thus the boasting beast was "corked up." Butler was a "political general," he attempted to blow up Fort Fisher by exploding a ship filled with three hundred tons of powder.—Youth's History of the War, 353.

In the meantime Grant dashed against the fortifications of Spottsylvania in order to get to the North Anna, in sight of Lee's army. He was defeated and forced to move by the left flank.—Headley vol. 2, p. 383, towards Cold Harbor in order to cross the Chickahominy. Lee defeated him at Cold Harbor. Grant lost severely at both these places, Sigel had failed, in the Shenandoah valley; Gilmore had failed, and Grant stole away from Lee and crossed the James. The anxious inquiry was "what is next to be done."

Had the authorities at Washington allowed McDowell to reinforce Mc Clellan, in 1862, when the army of the Potomac was in sight of the spires of Richmond McClellan would have then taken Richmond and ended the war. Oh! what a waste of blood was sacrificed under Burnside, Pope, Hooker, and Grant, which could have been saved had the administration given McClellan his own way, and what men he wanted. All this waste of money and human gore was sacrificed for political purposes; to prevent the democracy from getting into power. Oh! what thousands of lives were lost—what a mountain of debt was accumulated—what lives lost in loathsome prisons and military hospitals—what suffering and agony—thousands of brave men met death in foul prisons.—Oh! what heartrending of parents on the death of their children—the tears of widows and orphans all shed to keep the Republicans in power—all shed to prevent the democracy from getting into power!! What a lesson for future generations. For be it remembered that all the lives that Grant sacrificed from the Rapidan to the James could be saved: had he followed McClellan's plan of moving his army on the James by water. For McClellan was right when he said that Washington was best defended at Richmond. Grant now found that he could not "fight it out on this line."

Grant thought that he could cut off Lee's communication with Richmond. We leave Grant pounding away in front of Petersburg and Butler digging his famous Dutch gap Canal, which he commenced Aug. 9, 1864. This canal was as great a failure as Grant's canal before Vicksburg! We turn to the western department. We find that Banks was defeated by Stonewall Jackson in the valley, and that he was defeated in his Red River expedition, which was made for cotton speculation; he having the sanction of both Stanton and Halleck. In this expedition he lost 8000 killed, wounded and prisoners, 35 pieces of artillery, 1200 wagons, one gunboat, 3 Transports and 20,000 stand of arms.—Lost Cause p. 498. Yet, strange to say he was made commander of the Gulf Department. But, he was loyal, he was not a democrat, he was in favor of Lincoln's policy! On the 5th of August 1864, Admiral Farragut took Mobile Bay, and Fort Gaines on the 8th and on the 10th Aug. 1864, Sherman's forces bombarded Atlanta, which soon fell and Sherman commenced his march to the sea. The fall of Mobile and the depredations of the Alabama on American commerce were the great naval events of the year 1864.

Although the Democrats had suffered a defeat in 1863 they now made a vigorous preparation for the campaign as early as the Spring, on a peace platform. For the people were tired of the war and the party in power, taxation and the draft, the tariff and the high prices of all the necessaries of life. The Republicans did all in their power to delude the people. They stopped for no law human or divine, which thwarted their ambition or stood in their way to power and plunder. And as the high price of gold was one of the causes of the high prices of provisions, they passed an act which made it penal for any one to sell or exchange for specie at more than ten days at the time and that over their own counters, yet gold went up to 290, notwithstanding this 'gold bill.' Peace meetings were now held everywhere denouncing military despotism, the draft and the policy of the administration and military blunders, corruption and custom-house frauds. The government used the military power to smother free speech and free press. Many newspapers were suppressed. The New York *World* and the *Journal of Commerce* were seized by order of General Dix, and the Chicago *Times* was threatened. Governor Seymour wrote to the district attorney of the county of New York to prosecute General Dix for suppressing the New York *World* and the *Journal of Commerce.*—Life of Seymour and Blair, p. 173. In some military districts Lieutenants took the grave responsibility of suppressing newspapers in their districts and of preventing their sale. The commander of every army and the commander of every post could say what papers could be read or excluded from the lines. Lincoln made some show of a desire to receive rebel peace commissioners; but it was all a political sham to delude the public—a mere electioneering trick. Colonel Jacques, a methodist clergyman of Illinois and a Mr. Kirks, self-constituted ambassadors got through the lines to Richmond, having private passes from the authorities at Washington and had an interview with Davis and his cabinet.

Early in July, 1864, Horace Greeley received a letter from W. C. Jewett, stating that prominent rebel commissioners would meet him at Niagara, Canada, respecting terms of peace. N. Saunders informed Greeley that Clay of Alabama, Holcombe of Virginia and himself would meet him on a mission of peace as soon as they had the necessary passes from Washington. That they would on these conditions go to Washington to confer with the President. Greeley replied that they could have safe passes to Washington if they could show authority from the Richmond government to treat of peace. This they could not do and Lincoln issued his famous proclamation "to all whom it may concern."

Thus ended the whole matter. This was a political trick on the part of the administration to disarm the peace party by a pretext that the administration wanted peace but that the South did not. The Republicans were not yet tired of the war. They had not yet established Negro equality, and they were feathering their own nests, and carrying out the doctrines and principles of the Federal party and making the way easy for the establishment of their model government the British Constitution.—Headley vol. 2, p. 463-4-5-6. The administration rejected peace measures from the South. In 1864, the peace party in the South, was on the increase: Governor Brown of Georgia gave some trouble to Jeff. Davis. He took a most decided and prominent stand for peace and state-rights. For this cause he was denounced by Davis.

CHAPTER XIX.

In the campaign of 1864, the whole people north and south were tired of the war. The soldiers who had volunteered in 1861, their term of enlistment had expired—they found from experience that the war was not altogether for the constitution and the Union but was also used for mere party purposes, favoritism and speculation—that a system of plunder had pervaded the whole army from Washington to the commanders of companies ! The people were not now willing to enlist, for they found that every one in power was for himself more than for the country. So the government had to give additional bounty for Veteran Soldiers, and as the rich Republicans did not want to fight for the country, although they were willing to accept contracts where they could make fortunes or take the office of Provost-marshal, in some country town where they could play "a petty Nero," so they raised bounties, in towns, cities, and counties. Republicans, who when the war broke out made war speeches and mobbed those who spoke of peace or compromise, now, when they were called upon to fight for the country and government, sulked back, and tried every device to avoid the draft. The doctors and provost-marshals made fortunes in taking bribes for exempting men from the draft, who were able-bodied men. Such was the commotion created by the draft that the Republicans sent even to Canada and Europe for substitutes for which they paid as high as two thousand dollars. Sharpers along the Canada frontiers smuggled over substitutes, who were even drugged and intoxicated by these rascals. Thus Canada furnished thousands of recruits for the Northern army.

So unpopular had the draft become, in 1864, that meetings were held to avoid it and to raise bounties and to encourage enlistments.

New England which had brought on the War as much as South Carolina by her political principles did not furnish her quota, but had more exemptions from the draft than any other section of the county. Such was the rage for substitutes, to avoid the draft, that military officers sold their men as substitutes. A colonel of a volunteer regiment, while his regimen was organizing in the city of New York, was put under arrest for thus defrauding the government by selling his men. It was shown that he had sold one hundred of his men to fill up the quota of a country town, for which he had received the sum of $7,800; other officers were found guilty of the same malpractices. It seems that the people were seized with a national mania for plunder, fraud, and corruption. For although millions of dollars were raised at the north by sanitary fairs; the soldiers got very little of it; the greater part being squandered by the officers, the christian commission and loafers around headquarters.

The administration not being able to get to the front one half of the five hundred thousand, which were called out. Indeed, had the war continued another year the north would not be able to put down the rebellion for volunteering had now "played out."—Headley, vol. 2, p. 463. Nothing now could get soldiers into the field but the draft or a bounty. The authorities at Washington had a particular spite against the city of New York, for being democratic, and the population being nearly foreigners, so they drafted more men out of New York city than its full quota—to drive the Germans and the Irish into the army, so as to save the Republican districts in the western part of the State. This caused the great riot of New York. The poor men all over the country found that they had to go and do the fighting while those who had money could stay at home, for medical men exempted for a bribe--each medical staff had a band of unprincipled, and greedy runners, who drummed up the parties who wanted exemption. These greedy cormorants preyed on the misfortunes of their fellowmen.

New York had furnished more men than any other state in the union in proportion to her population. Yet the authorities at Washington ordered the provost-marshal of New York to draft. The city of New York felt indignant at the course the Federal government was pursuing in drafting from the nine democratic districts, 83,729 men, while the nineteen western districts were to furnish but 39,626. In consequence of this outrage a violent riot broke out in New York. Governor Seymour and Bishop Hughes quelled the riot by addressing the mob; for this the governor was blamed by Greeley and the Republican party. Governor Seymour wrote to Lincoln to correct the statement of the Provost Marshal as his statement did not agree with that of the State Adjutant of New York. The correction was made and Lincoln and the war department allowed Gov. Seymour 13,000 men as an excess. For this Seymour was thanked by a Republican legislature (Life of Seymour and Blair, 132). Governor Seymour denounced arbitrary arrests and the unconstitutional acts of the Federal government. The New York agents appointed to take the soldiers' votes were arrested in Washington, without just cause, and the soldiers' votes given for McClellan and Seymour held back until after the election, and by this fraud Lincoln carried the state of New York. Foul play and the corruption of the ballot-box, were the favorite tricks of the Republicans.—Life of Seymour and Blair 194-5, 203, 188-89-90.

The great question of 1864-5, was how to escape the draft, various were the devices resorted to. The gutters were dragged for substitutes; even loyal Massachusetts brought negro slaves to the rescue. Massachusetts applied to the Southern states to get her a few colored soldiers to fill her quota—what became of the promise of Governor Andrews, that if "slavery were abolished the roads from Boston to Washington would be blocked with soldiers." Even the Radicals went further than any despot of Europe for they drafted into the army Catholic Priests. Priests were exempt from military duty even by Pagans! What wonder that deserters were leaving the army by thousands. Rebel soldiers were now deserting in great numbers. Traps were set in Europe to catch the poor immigrants on their arrival in this country—not a patriotic response from the wealthy. Yet they blamed the poor man for not enlisting. Republican papers had raised the mad accusation of "Cowardice." They spoke of "draft shifting." But, strange to say these Editors themselves would not shoulder a musket, even if the south should go out of the union, and Lee should invade Boston! These noisy and virulent agitators and fermenters of slaughter did nothing but preach since Lincoln called out 75,000 men till the close of the rebellion. But, to add to the suffering of the working people and to shelter Republicans from going to the front countless frauds were perpetrated in making out the draft. As the whole machinery was in their own hands they had no scruples in throwing the burden of the war from their own shoulders on the democrats and foreigners.

In consequence of this practice many claimed protection from foreign governments. The Radicals made great promises to the soldiers—they promised them land warrants which they failed to give! In order to carry the election by force, fraud and violence the Republican party instituted a reign of terror. The press was muzzled in the army; all military news was interdicted unless it was favorable to the party in power and the authorities at Washington. Newspapers that opposed the administration were silenced in this way. Many of the newspapers that were secretly opposed to the administration were silenced. They were under the terror of the mob and the government officials. What a strange affair was this. Thousands who a few years before the war, could not be made to believe that the freedom of speech or the press would be suspended, now, in their Fourth of July orations denounced all who claimed the freedom of speech as rebels and copperheads.

While the Republicans were indulging in their high-handed acts of despotism the democrats of the north supported Lincoln to put down the rebellion with men and money. Democrats poured out their blood to support the flag. Indeed, such was the rage for arrests that about 80,000 were made during the war. Thousands were dragged to prison without an opportunity of seeing their friends. They were not informed of the cause of the arrest. Detective police were not allowed to report to the press or to allow their books to be inspected. Oh, thou, reign of terror!!

The party that spoke and wrote so much about the freedom of speech and of the press were the first to strike it down when they got into power. Democrats while in power, never denied the people the right to criticise the acts of public servants—their motto was that the rulers were but the servants of the people. That governments were made for the people. The Republicans now held that the people were the servants of the rulers. That the people were made for the rulers! Before the advent of the Republicans into power, the Republican press teamed with vile and wicked abuse of James Buchanan: but, now, should any one say a word against Lincoln, he was either visited by the so called loyal mob, or incarcerated in some military dungeon. The same tyrants who made it treason to speak against Lincoln, abused Johnson, their own candidate, "for having a policy of his own" and for following the Constitution of his country. Democrats in Congress, by a vote of 54, thought to bring the matter of arbitrary proceedings before Congress but in vain. Democrats, who became disgusted with the arbitrary measures of the party in power, were opposed to Lincoln and opposed a formidable front in the presidential campaign of 1864. The Radicals made an effort to pave the way for church and state. Col. B. G. Farran, commanding at Natchez, issued an order requiring all pastors of churches to make public recognition of their allegiance to the government;

and to pronounce a prayer appropriate to the times, and expressive of a proper spirit towards the chief magistrate of the United States. The Bishop of Natchez, refused to comply with the order. He was arrested and sent beyond the lines and his Cathedral closed. A clergyman in central New York, wrote thirty letters in two months giving a list of such of his neighbors whom he wanted to have arrested. The President issued an order to the police to make arrests. They held the name of Democrat as equivalent to traitor, even it was enough to justify an arrest that the party was a democrat.—Lost Cause, 565.

Several other churches were closed and the pastors imprisoned for not praying for Lincoln, while the Radicals were preying on the country !

The reign of terror was so complete that Burnside issued an order, 1863, for sending Democrats and all who opposed the government beyond the Federal lines. That all copperheads, a name given to all who opposed Lincoln's administration, be tried as spies and traitors and on conviction to suffer death. The government had established a system of spies all over the country. The government had a list of 850 alleged sympathizers on the books in Washington, who were to be sent South on the least provocation. The United States had police detectives, during the war and persons embarking at American ports were thoroughly scrutinized. The government established a system of passports relative to vessels leaving the port of New York through Long Island Sound or Sandy Hook. The passengers and crews were searched. The department stationed a man-of-war at Throgs' Neck and one at Sandy Hook with orders to detain all American vessels and outgoing steamers and sailing crafts not provided with a pass from the United States Marshal. Orders were given to imprison in Fort Warren any person in whose possession contraband arms or correspondence were found. The marshal ordered the owners of vessels ·to exercise a rigid scrutiny over all persons going on board either as passengers or crew. This passport system was the result of a cabinet meeting. During this reign of terror women and little children were imprisoned for making some foolish remarks about the war, or for finding fault with Lincoln, or for uttering one word of sympathy for the South.

During the campaign of 1864, the press teamed with charges of Custom-House frauds. Even the rebels were supplied with arms and ammunitions of war from New York. Some of the Custom House officers were acting agents of blockade runners. Bonds were extracted from the Custom-House; investigations of those charges were not made in public, but in private, so as to hush matters up until after election as Mr. Stanton's own pets were alleged to be the guilty party. Frauds in the navy yard were perpetrated on the laboring men and clerks. The stream of corruption from Washington, as the fountain head, pervaded the whole country, and set an example of dishonesty. Lincoln (having made terms with both Grant and Chase that in consideration that the former would be made commander-in-chief of the whole union army and the latter chief justice of the United States they would not run for President) was nominated for President and Andrew Johnson of Tennessee for Vice-President. McClellan and Pendleton were nominated by the Democrats. Fremont was the champion of the Radicals.

The democrats were struggling for the constitution and the union while the Republicans were struggling for military power and for strengthening the powers of the Congress and the Executive, and destroying state rights. Indeed, it was the mark of a copperhead to speak of state rights—in some localities the unhappy individual, who spoke of supporting the constitution and state rights was mobbed by the so called loyal. The Republicans wanted, in this campaign, to extinguish the democratic party, for ever, by force, fraud, and the point of the bayonet. Indeed, whenever the Republican party was successful at the elections, it trampled on the constitution.

The democrats were unable to check the unconstitutional career of the Republicans. They were found step by step to sustain the war. The fury of the war party swept every thing before it of a political nature. The vast patronage of the administration bought up the avaricious and ambitious. The great number of officers and army contractors gave power to the administration. The democrats were beguiled at the commencement of the war by the skill and tact of Seward. They thought that the war would not last long.—Lost Cause, 561-2.

Seward said that the object of the war was to crush rebellion. That as soon as the rebel power was crushed the rebel states would be in the union. This was expressed by McClellan in his declaration, that "The union is the sole condition of peace—we ask no more." But as the war progressed the Radicals held that the rebel states could not come into the union unless themselves first abolished slavery!

The Fremont men claimed that the rebellion had destroyed slavery. That slavery should be abolished; rebels disfranchised; the rebel debt repudiated and Negro equality established North and South. The Republican papers teamed with the vilest and most shameful abuse of McClellan. They said that he was a military failure. They accused him of cowardice; that he was a traitor in open league with the rebels. That every vote for McClellan and Pendleton would be for Jeff Davis and the recognition of the Southern Confederacy. Governor Dennison of Ohio, said that McClellan was not removed by Lincoln for any doubt of his military talents but only because he thought the Democrats would make him their candidate in the coming election.

Seward, during this campaign consigned thousands to prison by the mere "tinkle of his little bell." Many said that the object of the war was to make Lincoln President. The Radicals said he had a right to it by divine authority. Seward said in his Auburn speech that the Republican party could not without injustice select any other candidate for President. That Lincoln had a vested right in the Presidency !

During the Presidential campaign of 1864, the confidential agents of Lincoln were all over the country giving the patronage of the government to gain support for the election of Lincoln. In St. Louis the Presidential patronage was freely offered to the Radicals if they would drop Fremont and take up Lincoln !

Union generals used the bayonet to obtain votes. Soldiers who would vote for Lincoln got furloughs and transportation to go home to vote the Republican ticket. Republican officials tampered with the soldiers in hospitals using intimidation to compel them to vote for Lincoln. They denounced the McClellan ticket as the rebel ticket. They would say to the poor sick soldiers, while in pain and misery, who were worn out from long and weary marches, exposure to heat, cold, hunger, and thirst, and who were now in the power of the doctors, if you vote for Lincoln you can have a furlough to visit your friends and families and free transportation, "but if you vote for McClellan you cannot have a furlough," and so soon as you are able we will send you back to your regiment. The poor soldiers thus on their beds of sickness, covered with wounds and the scars of war, were through fear of loss of life or limb compelled to vote for Lincoln; others would not vote at all. This will explain why so many soldiers voted the Republican ticket. The following is the vote of the 89th Illinois regiment for president in 1864.

For Lincoln - - - - - - - - - - - - 379
McClellan - - - - - - - - - - - - 15
Fremont - - - - - - - - - - - - 1

A soldier in the Louisville hospital who voted for Vallandigham, was court-martialed by General Boyle, and sentenced to lie in the guard-house for 21 days. He was made to stand on a barrel two hours every morning with a card on his back with the following inscription: "From God thou camest but to the devil shalt thou return." He had also to saw wood ten hours each day for twenty-one days. Soldiers on the Potomac were menaced with "ball and chain," shooting and hanging if they would vote for Vallandigham. The few votes put in by the Ohio soldiers for the democratic ticket were put in by stealth. Thousands of soldiers who had furloughs had written on them "to vote the Union ticket." The votes of thousands of soldiers who were dead for weeks were returned as Lincoln votes. Was there any chance for the democrats to elect McClellan? This was preserving the purity of the ballot box. McClellan's meetings were broken up by Republican mobs. The mails were opened and McClellan's correspondence examined, and when McClellan's friends complained to Lincoln he said, "let the friends of McClellan attend to their side of the election and I will attend to mine." Thus, by bribery, corruption, force, frauds, violence, power and patronage of the administration, Lincoln got every state except Delaware, Kentucky, and New Jersey.—Lost Cause 574.

CHAPTER XX.

Ever since the commencement of the war England displayed her Punic faith, as usual, towards the United States. It must be remembered that before the war, she encouraged the Abolitionists to agitate for the overthrow of slavery, which she knew would bring on a war between the North and South. For every man of common understanding knew that it would take rivers of blood to wipe out slavery! Now, when the most gigantic rebellion that the world ever saw, had threatened the overthrow of the government, the English Tory press at home, and even in Canada, aided the South. Every petty Canadian sheet preached a dissolution of the Union. England was so certain of the success of the Confederacy, that her Capitalists invested largely in Southern bonds. This shows that she was anxious to break up the Union. Her spies were all over the country plotting the overthrow of the Union. She had gone so far in her vile attempt to break up the Union, as to make a proposition to France to march two armies to aid the Confederates, at the same time. The English and French navies were to raise the blockade. England was to march an army from Canada into the Northern States, while France was to send an army from Mexico into Texas and Louisiana, and thus make a diversion in favor of the Confederates. France would not strike the first blow, she had no faith in her old enemy England, and wanted her to strike the first blow. Their mutual jealousies saved the United States from this contemplated invasion, which in all human probability would have proved the overthrow of the Lincoln government and the Union! The Canadian frontier, since the commencement of the war, was occupied by the rebels, who were plotting against the union. The confederates set on foot a plot to release twenty-five hundred rebel prisoners, on Johnson's Island, in Lake Erie, while the rebels in Canada were to burn Buffalo and other Lake cities.

In September 14th, 1864, John Y. Beall a rebel officer captured and destroyed two steamboats on the lakes, On the 19th Oct. 1864, Young with 40 men raided into the village of St. Albans, Vermont, fifteen miles from Canada, robbed the bank of 200,000 dollars and fired on the inhabitants killing one. They were tried in Canada and acquitted. The Tory authorities of Canada did not want to punish men they had encouraged to make war on the United States! There were rumors that the Confederates were plotting to burn hotels in New York! The southern cause was now on the decline, notwithstanding that the southern press had roused the falling spirits of the Confederates. Though Butler had failed in taking Fort Fisher by the novel means of blowing up a powder boat with several tons of gunpowder the Confederates were losing at every point. Price was driven out of Missouri and Sherman left Atlanta on the 16th Nov. 1864, southward on his march to the sea.

The south had denounced the mal-administration of Jeff Davis. His influence was on the wane. For a large party in the south had accepted the fall of the Confederacy as inevitable.—Lost Cause, 657. The south was now tired of the war and wished for peace. For the south had suffered wherever the northern army went, and though there was abundance in many parts of the country, other parts suffered from famine.

In Missouri, the property of all was depredated on by the Kansas raiders —men were called to their doors and shot. Several men who returned from the rebel army under the President's first proclamation of amnesty, were killed in cold blood. Houses were burned, horses stolen, and fields of grain laid waste, by men of boasted loyalty—men of doubtful loyalty, to avoid such infliction proclaimed themselves Radicals, even men who were in the rebel army, joined the League, and swore to drive out all who were not of the same party.

Jennison and his followers went forth from Kansas into Missouri and made themselves rich, in the name of God and liberty. They claimed to be in the service of the United States. Kansas Jayhawkers were mounted on stolen horses. They had no uniforms, but wore such clothing as they stole from the citizens. They wore red leggings. They were loud in proclaiming themselves "unconstitutional Union men." Any man who owned a good horse, house and property was condemned as a traitor or a copperhead and his property deemed lawful plunder, and himself hanged or compelled to flee for his life. They were sure to keep at a distance from armed men. They went about in small squads on their work of murder and plunder! They stole horses and if any resistance was offered the offender was left, in the modest language of Jim Lane "in the hands of the executioner." They cared little for truth, law or gospel, but they thought they were commissioned by heaven to commit all manner of crime.

A copperhead had no "rights which the Red Legs were bound to respect." The South had her bushwhackers, so that the southern people were robbed on all sides by friends and foes. Such is civil war. In some parts of the country it was thought modest to throw rotten eggs at democratic speakers; even buildings were set on fire because they were owned by democrats. Lee who now saw that the confederacy was falling to pieces and that the confederate army was deserting in great numbers, for thousands of the southern people were deluded with the fond hope that the war would last but a few months, now after years of hard fighting, they saw the Union army pushing the confederates before them; they despaired of the southern cause; they saw it was the lost cause.

In this extremity, Lee, in 1864, was in favor of enlisting Negroes into the Southern army. He also called on the authorities at Richmond to restore Johnson. But Davis carried both points against him. This was a fatal blunder on the part of the Richmond authorities to remove Johnson, and to put Hood in his place who failed in his insane attack on Nashville. Lee declined to be the commander-in-chief of the Confederate army, and was content to be the commander of the army of Virginia. The Legislature of Virginia was now besieged with every influence in favor of separate state negotiation with the Federal government for peace. Thousands in the South both in and out of the army wished for peace—desertions from both armies were very large. The Federal government offered as an inducement to rebel deserters, that they would be exempt from the draft, and as there were thousands of the working-men of the North who were induced to join the rebellion, now they thought that they would go North where there was good wages. Many of the Southern soldiers were working-men who had no property in the South, so they wanted peace.

In the campaign of 1865 Gen. Sheridan was victorious in the valley and was able to close in on Richmond. The shell of the Confederacy was broken, Sherman having made his famous march to the sea; and was now in rear of Lee: having cut off his communications with the interior. Lee's army about Petersburg and Richmond was about thirty thousand. This was kept a profound secret from the public; and newspapers were forbidden to publish anything pertaining to military affairs, but what came from the war office.—Lost Cause 680. Greeley's Am. Conf. vol. 2, p. 740.

April 2, 1865, Lee gave orders for the evacuation of Richmond, seeing that he could hold out no longer. This order was given and executed at night.

On the 6th of April, 1865, Sheridan's cavalry struck Lee's lines of retreat at Sailors' Creek, and after some hard fighting Lee surrendered to Grant, April 12, 1865.—Lost Cause, 703-711.

"April 9th, 1865.

"This done each officer and man will be allowed to return to his home, not to be disturbed by the United States authority so long as they observe their paroles and the laws in force where they may reside."

Signed by Grant and Lee.

Greeley Am. Conf. vol. 2, p. 744. April 14, 1865, Lincoln was assassinated by Booth—an attempt was made to assassinate Seward. President Johnson offered a reward of 100,000 dollars for the arrest of the offenders. May 10, 1865. David E. Harrold, George A. Atzeroth, Lewess Payne, Michael O'Laughlin, Edward Spangler, Samuel Arnold, Mary E. Surratt, and Samuel A. Mudd, were arrested on suspicion and tried by military commissioners as accomplices of Booth. Harrold, Payne, Mrs. Surratt and Atzeroth were found guilty and executed at Washington July 7, 1865. Mudd, Arnold, and O'Laughlin were imprisoned for life and Spangler for six months.—Headley vol. 2, p. 627-8.

Johnson surrendered to General Sherman. The Radicals were dissatisfied with the terms of surrender. They poured forth on Sherman the vilest of abuse. The Radical press accused him of treason. He was censured by that vile wretch the Secretary of war; who said he was acting without orders. That Sherman knew the purport of the telegram sent to Grant by the President for his guidance in negotiating with Lee. Sherman replied; "now I was not in possession of it, and I have reason to know that Mr. Stanton knew I was not in possession of it."

Halleck sent dispatches to the army not to obey Sherman. The Radicals wanted to blast the reputation and character of a noble and brave soldier, as they did that of McClellan, Porter and Buell. Stanton and his confederates were the vile marplots of the campaign. The war would have been over in one year but for their scheming and corruption!—Headley vol. 2, pp. 602–8.

They also blamed Sherman for Jeff Davis' escape. The Radical press claiming that he had got off with a fabulous sum of money. They strove to hold Sherman responsible for his escape. Sherman replied, "why did not Stanton order his arrest, instead of publishing to the world, through the newspapers that they wanted him arrested?" Thus giving him an opportunity to escape. Headley vol. 2, p. 603.

May 4, 1865, Dick Taylor surrendered to Gen. Canby: May 26 Kirby Smith surrendered; and on May 31st, Hood surrendered. Thus ended the most stupendous rebellion on record. After Lee's surrender the whole Confederacy came down tumbling. It appeared that all depended on Lee, for after his surrender the whole Confederate army became demoralized, and wanted to surrender, for the majority in the South thought that they would have all the rights they ever had under the constitution, except slavery, which seemed to be abandoned by all, as one of the results of the war. So the Confederates from the Potomac to the Rio Grande, laid down their arms. The people of the South did not dream that their States would be reduced to territories; their representatives turned out of the Halls of Congress; the Southern States put under the control of five military despots! They did not dream that the Congress would try to hurl from office the President of the United States before his term of office expired! That the Congress would try to put the power of the executive, the Supreme Court, and the State legislatures under the control of Congress. If the people of the South were aware of all this, would they have surrendered without further struggle? The Radicals should have carried out the terms of the surrender in good faith, for this surrender saved the lives of thousands.

During the war the Radical party made capital out of the treatment of Union prisoners of war. Yet the rebel commissioner Ould offered to exchange all the Union prisoners under his command. But Stanton would not accept of this offer, for he wanted to make political capital out of the misery and sufferings of poor Union soldiers in Andersonville prison—to make capital out of the "rebel barbarities." The southern generals did not want prisoners of war for they wanted clothing and provisions for their own soldiers. In August 1864 Commissioner Ould offered the Federal Agent General Mulford to deliver to him all the sick and wounded Federal prisoners without insisting upon an exchange of prisoners. He also informed General Mulford of the great mortality among the Federal prisoners, telling him to send transportation to the mouth of the Savannah River for the purpose of taking them away. This offer included the sick and the wounded at Andersonville and other prisons. Stanton and other authorities at Washington failed to attend to this matter, and so thousands of Union soldiers lost their lives, to please the wicked ambition of Stanton. Oh! on his head rests the blood of thousands of Union soldiers.—Lost Cause 627. The same offer was made to General Grant, Feb. 11th, 1865. "To rule is worth ambition even in hell." The Republicans would rule even if it cost the country oceans of blood, mountains of debt, and hills of slain.

CHAPTER XXI.

Immediately after the death of Mr. Lincoln, Andrew Johnson the Vice-President of the United States, was sworn in President, under the forms of the constitution of the United States. The Republicans interviewed him by several committees to find out his "policy." He said in reply that his policy was known to the country. That his speech in Congress against Jeff Davis was ample to show his policy and what his principles were. That he would make no change in his cabinet. He retained in office all the Lincoln men from Seward and Stanton, down to the country post-masters. This gave great satisfaction to the Republicans. This was a blunder for he should have removed the traitor Stanton. The Radicals said that Johnson would be more severe on the rebels, especially on Jeff Davis, than Lincoln would have been. Leading Radicals changed the rejoicings to grief and their laudation of Johnson to denunciation "so out of the same mouth cometh blessing and curses."

On the 29th of May, 1865, Johnson had declared by proclamation, that all restrictions on Trade were removed East of the Mississippi.

On May 29, 1865, the President granted a general amnesty to rebels, excepting the following classes of persons.

Foreign agents of the conferacy, those who left judicial stations under the United States to aid the rebellion; and military officers of the confederate army above the rank of colonel and all naval officers above the rank of Lieutenant, all who resigned seats in the United States Congress to aid the rebellion; all who resigned commissions in the army or navy of the United States to join the rebellion. All who were governors of the rebel states and some others were also excluded. It was proclaimed that all persons not thus excepted were entitled to a restoration of all property except slaves and in cases where proceedings have been instituted for the confiscation of the property of persons engaged in the rebellion.

Those claiming the benefit of this amnesty proclamation were required to take and subscribe the following oath:

"I ——— do solemnly swear (or affirm), in the presence of Almighty God, that I will henceforth faithfully support, protect, and defend the constitution of the United States and the Union of the States thereunder and I will, in like manner abide by, and faithfully support all the laws and proclamations which have been made during the existing rebellion with reference to the emancipation of slaves, so help me God."

December 7th, 1863, Lincoln issued an amnesty proclamation offering a free pardon to rebels on taking an oath to support the constitution of the United States, and also "to abide by and faithfully support all acts of Congress passed during the existing Rebellion having reference to slaves, so long and so far as not modified by decision of the supreme court." Exceptions were made of all who resigned seats in Congress. Federal judges or commissioned officers who resigned to take part in the rebellion, all officers of the rebel government; and all officers of the rebel army above the rank of colonel and all who treated Black soldiers and their officers" otherwise than lawfully as prisoners of war.—Greeley, Am. Conf. vol. 2, p. 539.

At the second secession of the thirty-eighth Congress, Feb. 1, 1865, the thirteenth amendment to the constitution was proposed in Congress:—That "neither slavery nor involuntary servitude, except as a punishment for crime whereof the party shall have been duly convicted, shall exist within the United States, or any place subject to their jurisdiction.

Congress shall have power to enforce this article by appropriate legisla
tion. The secretary of state December 18, 1865, by public notice, declared
that this amendment was adopted by the constitutional number of states.
Although the Republicans held that slavery was abolished by Lincoln's
proclamation of January 1, 1863. Yet, they now found that it could be
abolished only by the constitution of the United States! The President by
proclamation of May 29, 1865, provided for the reorganization of a constitutional government for North Carolina, and appointed Wm. H. Holden
provisional governor of the state. He provided that no person should be
an elector or eligible as a member of the state convention unless he took
the oath prescribed in the amnesty proclamation of May 29, 1865, and
unless he was a voter under the constitution and laws of South Carolina,
before May 20, 1861, the date of the ordinance of secession. The military
commander of the department was authorized to aid the provisional governor in enforcing said proclamation, and the Secretaries of the departments
were empowered to enforce the laws of the United States within the jurisdiction of North Carolina. In June 18, 1865, it was provided by proclamation for the reorganization of a constitutional government in Mississippi
and William L. Sharkey was appointed provisional governor. June 17,
1865, a provisional government was appointed for Georgia, and James
Johnson was appointed provisional governor; on the same day Andrew J.
Hamilton was appointed provisional governor of Texas. June 21, 1865,
Lewis E. Parsons was appointed provisional governor of Alabama. June 30,
1865, Benjamim T. Perry was appointed governor of South Carolina. June
13, 1865, William Marvin was appointed governor of Florida. All other
seceded states were organized precisely on the same footing as North
Carolina. October 12, 1865, the President by proclamation removed
martial law. December 1, 1865, he restored the Writ of Habeas Corpus,
and on September 1, 1865, all restrictions on trade were removed. Thus
we find that the war was now over, slavery was abolished by an amendment
to the constitution and it was supposed that the union was restored on the
fundamental principles of the constitution. The south had given up
slavery as one of the things of the past; and all conservatives, men North
and South thought that the Radicals would accept of Johnson's policy for
reorganizing the seceded states by giving them all their rights except
slavery which was now abolished.

The Republican State Conventions from Maine to California, in 1865, indorsed President Johnson's policy, Massachusetts and other States declared
for Negro suffrage and the payment of the public debt. Some of the other
States were silent on the subject as they feared it would defeat the party
in the coming election. The States lately in rebellion held elections under
President Johnson's proclamation; and elected members of Congress, State
Legislature, and State officers.

President Johnson sent the following message to Congress December 4th,
1865.

"The relations of the general government toward the four millions of inhabitants whom the war has called into freedom, have engaged my most
serious consideration. On the propriety of attempting to make the freedmen
electors by the proclamation of the Executive, I took, for my counsel, the
Constitution itself, the interpretation of that instrument by its authors and
their cotemporaries and recent legislature by Congress, when, at the first
movement toward independence, the Congress of the United States instructed
the several States to institute governments of their own, they left each state
to decide for itself the conditions for the enjoyment of the elective
franchise.

During the period of the confederacy, there continued to exist a very great diversity in the qualifications of electors in the several states; and even within a state a distinction of qualifications prevailed with regard to the officers who were to be chosen. The constitution of the United States recognizes these diversities when it enjoins that, in the choice of members of the House representatives of the United States, 'the electors in each state shall have the qualifications requisite for the electors of the most numerous branch of the state Legislature.' After the formation of the constitution, it remained, as before, the uniform usage for each state to enlarge the body of its electors according to its own judgment; and under this system, one state after another has proceeded to increase the number of its electors, until now universal suffrage, or something very near it, is the general rule. So fixed was this reservation of the power in the habits of the people, and so unquestioned has been the interpretation of the constitution, that, during the civil war, the late President never harbored the purpose—certainly never avowed the purpose of disregarding it: and in the acts of Congress during that period nothing can be found which, during the continuance of hostilities, much less after the close, would have sanctioned any departure by the executive from a policy which has so uniformly obtained. Moreover, a concession of the elective franchise to the freedmen, by act of the President of the United States, must have been extended to all colored men wherever found, and so must have established a change of suffrage in the Northern, Middle, and Western States, not less than in the southern and south-western. Such an act would have created a new class of voters, and would have been an assumption of· power by the President which nothing in the constitution or the laws of the United States would have warranted.

On the other hand, every danger of complaint is avoided when the settlement of the question is referred to the several states. They can, each for itself decide on the measure and whether it is to be adopted at once and absolutely, or introduced gradually and with conditions. In my judgment the freedmen, if they show patience and manly virtues, will sooner obtain a participation in the elective franchise through the states than through the general government, even if it had the power to intervene. When the tumult of emotions that have been raised by the suddenness of the social change shall have subsided, it may prove that they will receive the kindliest usage from some of those on whom they have heretofore most closely depended. But while I have no doubt that now, after the close of the war, it is not competent for the general government to extend· the elective franchise in the several states, it is equally clear that good faith requires the security of the freedmen in their liberties and their properties, their right to labor and their right to claim the just return of their labor. I cannot too strongly urge a dispassionate treatment of this subject, which should be carefully kept aloof from all party strife. We must equally avoid hasty assumptions of any natural impossibility for the two races to live side by side, in a state of mutual benefit and good will. The experiment involves us in no inconsistency; let us, then, go and make that experiment in good faith, and not be too easily disheartened. The country is in need of labor, and freedmen are in need of employment, culture, and protection, while their right of voluntary migration and expatriation is not to be questioned, I would not advise their forced removal and colonization; let us rather encourage them to honorable and useful industry, where it may be beneficial to themselves and to the country; and, instead of hasty anticipations of the certainty of failure, let there be nothing wanting to the fair trial of the experiment. The change in their condition is the substitution of labor by contract for the state of slavery. The freedman cannot fairly be accused of unwillingness to work, so long as a doubt remains about his freedom of choice in his pursuits, and the certainty of his receiving his stipulated wages. In this the interests of the employer and the employed coincide. The employer desires in his workmen spirit and alacrity, and these can be permanently secured in no other way, than if one ought to be able to enforce the contract, so ought the other.

The public interest will be best promoted if the several states will provide adequate protection and remedies for the freedmen. Until this is in some way accomplished, there is no chance for the advantageous use of their labor; and the blame of ill-success will not rest on them.

I know that sincere philanthropy is earnest for the immediate realization of its remotest aims; but time is always an element in reform. It is one of the greatest acts on record to have brought four millions of people to freedom. The career of free industry must be fairly opened to them; and then their future prosperity and condition must, after all, rest mainly on themselves. If they fall and so perish away, let us be careful that the failure shall not be attributable to any denial of justice. In all that relates to the destiny of the freedmen, we need not be too anxious to read the future; many incidents which, from a speculative point of view, might raise alarm will quietly settle themselves.

We give the President's message to show how far he differed with the party that elected him, in 1864. The majority of that party were in favor of what they called impartial suffrage, though only the most Radical proclaimed this before the Session of Congress of 1865-6; as they feared it would injure the party at the elections during the war. Now or never, they were determined to accomplish their long-cherished-aims. The reader will also bear in mind the opinions expressed by the President, in this message, as it will serve as a guide to the development of his policy.

Very little party spirit was displayed in the southern elections in 1865. Politics were indefinite. The South elected Representatives and senators to Congress, who applied for seats, at the session of Congress 1865-6, but they would not be admitted by the Republicans for they wanted to hold the two-thirds vote, in Congress, so as to be able to control the president and the Supreme Court. They wanted to retain the power of passing their favorite measures over the president's veto! For about this time they feared a collision with the president, for it was evident that he intended to make the Constitution his guide. They would sooner see the South out of the Union than to see the country governed by the constitution as it was!

The Republicans, having two-thirds of both Houses of Congress, were determined to carry out their long-cherished aims. They had now openly declared that Congress was Supreme. That the executive should be subservient to their dictation.

On Feb. 2, 1866, the senate passed the so called civil right's bill, by a vote of 38 Republicans against 9 Democrats. On March 13, 1866, the bill passed the House by a vote of 111 Republicans for, and 38 against it.

On the 27 March, 1866, the President sent the following veto message to the Senate:

"I regret that the bill which has passed both Houses of Congress, entitled, 'An act to protect all persons in the United States in their civil rights, and furnishes the means of their vindication,' contains provisions which I cannot approve consistently with my sense of duty to the whole people, and my obligations to the constitution of the United States. I am therefore constrained to return it to the Senate, the house in which it originated, with my objections to its becoming a law.

By the first section of the bill all persons born in the United States, and not subject to any foreign power, excluding Indians not taxed, are declared to be citizens of the United States, This provision comprehends the Chinese of the Pacific States. Indians subject to taxation, the people called Gypsies, as well as the entire race designated as Blacks, people of color, Negroes, Mulattoes, and persons of African blood. Every individual of these races, born in the United States, is by the bill made a citizen of the United States. It does not purport to declare or confer any other right of citizenship than Federal citizenship. It does not purport to give these classes of persons any status as citizens of the United States. The power to confer the right of state-citizenship is just as exclusively with the several states as the power to confer the right of Federal citizenship is with Congress.

The right of Federal citizenship thus to be conferred on the several excepted races before mentioned, is now, for the first time, proposed to be given by law. If, as is claimed by many, all persons who are native-born already are, by virtue of the constitution, citizens of the United States, the passage of the pending bill cannot be necessary to make them such. If, on the other hand, such persons are not citizens, as may be assumed from the proposed legislation to make them such, the grave question presents itself, whether, when eleven of the thirty-six states are unrepresented in Congress at the present time, it is sound policy to make our entire colored population and all other excepted classes citizens of the United States.

Four millions of them have just emerged from slavery into freedom. Can it be reasonably supposed that they possess the requisite qualifications to entitle them to all the privileges and immunities of citizens of the United States? Have the people of the several states expressed such a conviction? It may also be asked whether it is necessary that they should be declared citizens, in order that they may be secured in the enjoyment of the civil rights proposed to be conferred by the bill? Those rights are, by Federal as well as state laws, secured to all domiciled aliens and foreigners, even before the completion of the process of naturalization; and it may safely be assumed that the same enactments are sufficient to give like protection and benefit to these to whom this bill provides special legislation. Besides the policy of the government, from its origin to the present time, seems to have been that persons who are strangers to and unfamiliar with our institutions and our laws should pass through a certain probation at the end of which, before attaining the coveted prize, they must give evidence of their fitness to receive and to exercise the rights of citizens, as contemplated by the constitution of the United States. The bill, in effect, proposes a discrimination against large numbers of intelligent, worthy and patriotic foreigners, and in favor of the Negro to whom, after long years of bondage, the avenues to freedom and intelligence have just now been suddenly opened. He must of necessity, from his previous unfortunate condition of servitude, be less informed as to the nature and character of our institutions than he who, coming from abroad, has to some extent, at least, familiarized himself with the principles of a government to which he voluntarily intrusts life, liberty and the pursuit of happiness." Yet it is now proposed, by a single legislative enactment, to confer the rights of citizens upon all persons of African descent born within the extended limits of the United States, while persons of foreign birth, who make our land their home, must undergo a probation of five years, and can only then become citizens upon proof that they are of good moral character, attached to the principles of the constitution of the

United States, and well disposed to the good order and happiness of the same."

"The first section of the bill also contains an enumeration of the rights to be enjoyed by those classes, so made citizens, in every State and Territory in the United States. These rights are to make and enforce contracts, to sue the parties, and give evidence: to inherit, purchase, lease, sell, hold and convey, real and personal property; and to have full and equal benefit of all the laws and proceedings for the security of person and property as is enjoyed by white citizens. So, too, they are made subject to the same punishments, pains, and penalties in common with white citizens, and to no other. Thus a perfect equality of the white and colored races is attempted to be fixed by federal law in every State of the Union, over the vast field of State Jurisdiction covered by these enumerated rights. And in no one of these can any state ever exercise any power of discrimination between different races. In the exercise of state policy over matters exclusively affecting the people of each state it has frequently been thought expedient to discriminate between the two races. By the statutes of some of the states, northern as well as southern, it is enacted, for instance, that no white person shall intermarry with a negro or mulatto. Chancellor Kent says, speaking of the blacks, that marriages between them and the whites are forbidden in some of the States where slavery does not exist, and they are prohibited in all the slave-holding states, and when not absolutely contrary to law, they are revolting, and regarded as an offence against public decorum.

I do not say that this bill repeals state laws on the subject of marrriage between two races, for, as the whites are forbidden to intermarry with the blacks, the blacks can only make such contracts as the whites themselves are allowed to make, and therefore cannot under this bill enter into the marriage contract with the whites. I cite this discrimination, however, as an instance of the state-policy as to discrimination, and to inquire whether, if Congress can abrogate all state-laws of discrimination between the two races in the matter of real estate, of suits, and of contracts generally, Congress may not also repeal the state laws as to the contract of marriage between the races? Hitherto every subject embraced in the enumeration of rights contained in this bill has been considered as exclusively belonging to the states. They all relate to the internal police and economy of the respective states. They are matters which in each state concern the domestic condition of its people varying in each according to its own peculiar circumstances and the safety and well-being of its citizens. I do not mean to say that upon all these subjects they are not Federal restraints—as, for instance, in the state-power of legislation over contracts, there is a Federal limitation that no state shall pass a law impairing the obligation of contracts and, as to crimes, that no state shall pass an *ex post facto* law; and, as to money, that no state shall make any thing but gold and silver a legal tender. But where can we find a Federal prohibition against the power of any state to discriminate, as do most of them between artificial persons called corporations and natural persons, in their right to hold real estate. If it be granted that Congress can repeal all state-laws discriminating between whites and blacks in the subjects covered by this bill, why, it may be asked, may not Congress repeal, in the same way, all state-laws discriminating between the two races on the subjects of suffrage and office? If Congress can declare by law who shall hold lands, who shall testify, who shall have capacity to make a contract in a state, then Congress can by law also declare who, without regard to color or race, shall have the right to sit as a juror or as a judge, to hold any office, and, finally, to vote," in every State and Territory of the United States. As respects the Territories they come within the power of Congress, for as to them the law-making power is the Federal power; but as to the States, no similar provisions exist vesting in Congress the power to make rules and regulations for them.

"The object of the second section of the bill is to afford discriminating protection to colored persons in the full enjoyment of all the rights secured to them by the preceding section. It declares that any person who, under color of any law, statute, ordinance, regulation, or custom, shall subject, or cause to be subject any inhabitant of any state or Territory to the deprivation of any right secured or protected by this act, or to different punishments, pains or penalties, on account of such person having at any time been held in a condition of slavery or involuntary servitude, except as a punishment for crime, whereof the party shall have been duly convicted, or by reason of his color or race, than is prescribed for the punishment of white persons, shall be deemed guilty of a misdemeanor, and, on conviction, shall be punished by a fine not exceeding one thousand dollars, or imprisonment not exceeding one year, or both, in the discretion of the court. This section seems to be designed to apply to some existing or future law of a state or Territory which may conflict with the provisions of the bill under consideration. It provides for counteracting such forbidden legislation by imposing fine and imprisonment upon the Legislator who my pass such conflicting laws or upon the officers or agents who shall put or attempt to put them into execution. It means an official offence—not a common crime committed against law upon the persons or property of the Black race. Such an act may deprive the black man of his property, but not the right to hold property. It means a deprivation of the right itself, either by the state judiciary or the state legislature. It is therefore assumed that under this section members of state legislatures who should vote for laws conflicting with the provisions of the bill, that judges of the state courts who should render judgments in antagonism with its terms and that Marshals and Sheriffs who should, as ministerial officers, execute processes sanctioned by state laws, and issued by state judges in execution of their judgments, could be brought before other tribunals, and there subjected to fine and imprisonment for the performance of the duties which such state laws might impose. The legislation thus proposed invades the judicial power of the state. It says to every state court or judge, if you decide that this act is unconstitutional: if you refuse, under the prohibition of a state law, to allow a negro to testify: if you hold that over such a subject matter the state law is paramount, and, under color of a state law refuse the exercise of the right to the negro, your error of judgment, however conscientious, shall subject you to fine and imprisonment! I do not apprehend that the conflicting legislation which the bill seems to contemplate is so likely to occur as to render it necessary at this time to adopt a measure of such doubtful constitutionality.

In the next place, this provision of the bill seems to be unnecessary, as adequate judicial remedies could be adopted to secure the desired end, without invading the immunities of legislators, always important to be preserved in the interest of public liberty, without assailing the independence of the judiciary, always essential to the preservation of individual rights, and without impairing the efficiency of ministerial officers, always necessary for the maintenance of the public peace and order. The remedy proposed by this section seems to be, in this respect not only anomalous but unconstitutional: for the constitution guarantees nothing with certainty if it does not insure to the several states the right of making and executing laws in regard to all matters arising within their jurisdiction subject only to the restriction that, in case of conflict with the constitution and constitutional laws of the United States, the latter should be held to be the supreme law of the land.

"The third section gives the District Courts of the United States exclusive cognizance of all crimes and offences committed against the provisions of this act, and concurrent jurisdiction with the Circuit Courts of the United States of all civil and criminal cases affecting persons who are denied, or cannot enforce in the courts or judicial tribunals of the state or locality where they may be, any of the rights secured to them by the first section. The construction which I have given to the second section is strengthened by the third section, for it makes clear what kind of denial or deprivation of the rights secured by the first section was in contemplation. It is a denial or deprivation of such rights in the courts or judicial tribunals of the state. It stands, therefore, clear of doubt that the offence and the penalties provided in the second section are intended for the state judge, who, in the clear exercise of his functions as a judge, not acting ministerially but judicially, shall decide contrary to this Federal law. In other words, when a state judge, acting upon a question involving a conflict between a state law and a Federal law, and bound, according to his own judgment and responsibility, to give an impartial decision between the two, comes to the conclusion that the state law is valid and the Federal law invalid, he must not follow the dictates of his own judgment, at the peril of fine and imprisonment. The legislative department of the government of the United States thus takes from the judicial department of the states the sacred and exclusive duty of judicial decision, and converts the state judge into a mere ministerial officer, bound to decide according to the will of Congress.

"It is clear that, in states which deny to persons whose rights are secured by the first section of the bill any one of those rights, all criminal and civil cases affecting them will, by the provisions of the third section, come under the exclusive cognizance of the federal tribunals. It follows that if in any states which deny to a colored person any one of all those rights, that person should commit a crime against the laws of a state—murder, arson, rape, or any other crime—all protection and punishment through the courts of the state are taken away, and he can only be tried and punished in the Federal courts. How is the criminal to be tried if the offence is provided for and punished by Federal law, that law, and not the state law, is to govern? It is only when the offence does not happen to be within purview of Federal law that the Federal courts are to try and punish him under any other law. Then resort is to be had to the common law, as modified and changed by state legislation, so far as the same is not inconsistent with the constitution and laws of the United States, so that over this vast domain of criminal jurisprudence provided by each state for the protection of its own citizens, and for the punishment of all persons who violate its criminal laws, Federal law, whenever it can be made to apply, displaces state law.

The question here naturally arises from what source Congress derives the power to transfer to Federal tribunals certain classes of cases embraced in this section. The constitution expressly declares that the judicial power of the United States shall extend to all cases in law and equity arising under this constitution, the laws of the United States, and treaties made, or which shall be made under their authority: to all cases affecting ambassadors, and other public ministers and consuls: to all cases of admiralty and maritime jurisdiction: to controversies to which the United States shall be a party: to controversies between two or more states between a state and the citizens of another state, between citizens of different states, between citizens of the same state claiming land under grants of different states, and between a state, or the citizens thereof, and foreign states, citizens, or subjects. Here the judicial power of the United States is expressly set forth and defined; and the act of September 24, 1789, establishing the judicial courts of the United States, in conferring upon the Federal courts jurisdiction over cases originating in state tribunals is careful to confine them to the classes enumerated in the above recited clause of the constitution. This section of the bill undoubtedly comprehends cases and authorizes the exercise of powers that are not, by the constitution, within the jurisdiction of the courts of the United States. To transfer them to those courts would be an exercise of their authority well calculated to excite distrust and alarm on the part of all the states; for the bill applies alike to all of them—as well to those that have as to those that have not been engaged in rebellion. It may be assumed that this authority is incident to the power granted to Congress by the constitution, as recently amended, to enforce, by appropriate legislation, the article declaring that neither slavery nor involuntary servitude, except as a punishment for crime, whereof the party shall have been duly convicted, shall exist within the United States, or any place subject to their jurisdiction. It cannot, however, be justly claimed that, with a view to the enforcement of this article of the constitution, there is at present any necessity for the exercise of all the powers which this bill confers. Slavery has been abolished, and at present nowhere exists within the jurisdiction of the United States, nor has there been, nor is it likely there will be, any attempt to revive it by the people or the states. If, however, any such attempt shall be made, it will then become the duty of the general government to exercise any and all incidental powers necessary and proper to maintain inviolate this great constitutional law of freedom.

The fourth section of the bill provides that officers and agents of the Freedmen's Bureau shall be empowered to make arrests, and also that other officers may be specially commissioned for that purpose by the President of the United States. It also authorizes circuit courts of the United States, and the superior courts of the Territories to appoint, without limitation, commissioners, who are to be charged with the performance of quasi-judicial duties. The fifth section empowers the commissioners so to be selected by the courts to appoint in writing under their hands, one or more suitable persons from time to time to execute warrants and other processes described by the bill. These numerous official agents are made to constitute a sort of police, in addition to the military, and are authorized to summon a *posse comitatus*, and even to call to their aid such portion of the land and naval forces of the United States, or of the militia, as may be necessary to the performance of the duty with which they are charged. This extraordinary power is to be conferred upon agents irresponsible to the government and to the people, to whose number the discretion of the commissioners is the only limit, and in whose hands such authority might be made a terrible engine of wrong, oppression, and fraud. The general statutes regulating the land and naval forces of the United States, the militia, and the execution of the laws, are believed to be adequate for every emergency which can occur in time of peace. If it should prove otherwise, · Congress can at any time amend these laws in such a manner as, while subserving the public welfare, not to jeopard the rights, interests, and liberties of the people.

"The seventh section provides that a fee of ten dollars shall be paid to each commissioner in every case brought before him, and a fee of five dollars to his deputy or deputies, for each person he or they may arrest and take before any such commissioners," with such other fees as may be deemed reasonable by such commissioner." In general for performing such other duties as may be required in the premises, all these fees are to be paid out of the Treasury of the United States, whether there is a conviction or not, but in case of conviction they are to be recoverable from the defendant. It seems to me that under the influence of such temptations bad men might convert any law, however beneficent, into an instrument of persecution and fraud. "By the eighth section of the bill the United States courts, which sit only in one place for white citizens, must migrate with the marshal and the district attorney, and necessarily with the clerk, although he is not mentioned, to any part of the district upon the order of. the President, and there hold a court for the purpose of the more speedy arrest and trial of persons charged with a violation of this act, and there the judge and other officers of the court must remain, upon the order of the President, for the time therein designed.

"The ninth section authorizes the President, or such persons as he may empower for that purpose, to employ such part of the land or naval forces of the United States or of the militia, as shall be necessary to prevent the violation and enforce the due execution of his act.' This language seems to imply a permanent military force, that is always at hand, and whose only business is to be the enforcement of this measure over the vast region where it is intended to operate.

"I do not propose to consider the policy of this bill. To me the details of the bill seem fraught with evil. The white race and the black race of the south have hitherto lived together under the relation of master and slave—capital owning labor. Now, suddenly, that relation is changed, and, as to ownership, capital and labor are divorced. They stand now each master of itself. In this new relation, one being necessary to the other, there will be new adjustment, which both are deeply interested in making harmonious. Each has equal power in settling the terms, and, if left to the laws that regulate capital and labor, it is confidently believed that they will satisfactorily work out the problem. Capital, it is true, has more intelligence, but labor is never so ignorant as not to understand its own interests, not to know its own value, and not to see that capital must pay that value. This bill frustrates this adjustment. It intervenes between capital and labor, and attempts to settle questions of political economy through the agency of numerous officials, whose interest it will be to ferment discord between the two races; for as the breach widens their employment will continue, and when it is closed their occupation will terminate.

In all our history, in all our experience as a people, living under federal and state law, no such system as that contemplated by the details of this bill has ever before been proposed or adopted. They establish for the security of the colored race safe-guards which go infinitely beyond any that the general government has ever provided for the white race. In fact, the distinction of race and color is, by the bill, made to operate in favor of the colored and against the white race. They interfere with the municipal legislation of the state, with the relations existing exclusively between a state and its citizens or between inhabitants of the same state—an absorption and assumption of power by the general government which, acquiesced in, must sap and destroy our Federal system of limited powers, and break down the barriers which preserve the rights of the states. It is an other step, or rather stride, towards centralization and the concentration of all legislative powers in the national government. The tendency of the bill must be to resuscitate the spirit of rebellion, and to arrest the progress of those influences which are more closely drawing around the states the bonds of union and peace.

"My lamented predecessor, in his proclamation of the 1st January, 1863, ordered and declared that all persons held as slaves within certain states and parts of states therein designated were and thenceforth should be free, and, further, that the executive government of the United States, including the military and naval authorities thereof, would recognize and maintain the freedom of such persons. This guarantee has been rendered especially obligatory and sacred by the amendment of the constitution abolishing slavery throughout the United States. I, therefore, fully recognize the obligation to protect and defend that class of our people, whenever and wherever it shall become necessary, and to the full extent compatible with the constitution of the United States. Entertaining these sentiments, it only remains for me to say, that I will cheerfully co-operate with Congress in a measure that may be necessary for the protection of the civil rights of the freedmen, as well as those of all other classes of persons throughout the United States, by judicial process, under equal and impartial laws, in conformity with the provisions of the Federal constitution.

I now return the bill to the senate and regret that, in considering the bills and joint resolutions—forty-two in number—which have been thus far submitted for my approval, I am compelled to withhold my assent from a second measure that has received the sanction of both Houses of Congress." ANDREW JOHNSON, Washington, D. C. March 27, 1866.   April 6th, 1866, the senate passed this bill over the veto and on April 9 it passed the House, and was declared a law by the speaker.

The Freedmen's bureau bill, which passed the senate January 25, 1866, and the House Feb. 6, 1866, was vetoed by the President, but was passed over the veto by both Houses.

A second Freedmen's Bureau bill was passed by both Houses and vetoed by the President, but was passed over his veto by a two-thirds vote.

April 30th 1866, Mr. Stevens, from the joint select committee on reconstruction reported the first draft of the 14th amendment to the constitution of the United States.

It passed the senate, as amended June 8, 1866 by a vote of 33 Republicans; against the bill 11, (Democrats 7; Cowan, Doolittle, Norton, and Van Winkle, Unionists). It passed the House by 138 yeas (all Reps.) nays 36 (all demts.). June 16, 1866, the amendment was deposited in the state department and certified copies sent by the Secretary of the state to the state governors.

June 18, 1866, both Houses passed a resolution requesting the President to submit the adopted amendment. June 20, the Secretary of state notified the President that he had transmitted a copy of the bill to the state governors.   June 23, 1866, the President submitted the report of the Secretary of state to Congress, expressing at the same time to Congress, that he disapproved the said amendment.—Vide Cong. Globe on the civil rights, Freedmen's Bureau Bills and on the 14th Amendment.

The Legislatures of Connecticut, New Hampshire, Vermont, New Jersey, Tennessee and Oregon ratified the amendment in 1866. The Legislatures of Georgia, Alabama, North Carolina, South Carolina, Florida, and Texas rejected the amendment in 1866. Immediately on the reception of the President's veto the Radicals in and out of Congress poured forth on the President's head the vilest abuse known to denunciation.

The following is an extract from Johnson's Proclamation of April 2, 1866, announcing that the rebellion was over in the late rebel states.

"And whereas, by my proclamation of the thirteenth day of June last the insurrection in the state of Tennessee was declared to have been suppressed, the authority of the United States therein to be undisputed, and such United States officers as have been duly commissioned to be in the undisputed exercise of their official functions:

"And whereas there now exists no organized armed resistance of misguided citizens or others to the authority of the United States in the states of Georgia, South Carolina, Virginia, North Carolina, Tennessee, Alabama, Louisiana, Arkansas, Mississippi and Florida, and the laws can be sustained and enforced therein by the proper civil authority, State or Federal, and the people of the said states are well and loyally disposed, and have conformed or will conform in their legislation to the condition of affairs growing out of the amendment to the constitution of the United States, prohibiting slavery within the limits and jurisdiction of the United States:

And whereas, in view of the before recited premises, it is the manifest determination of the American people that no state of its own will, has the right or the power to go out of, or separate itself from, or be separated from the American Union, and therefore each state ought to remain and constitute an integral part of the United States:

"And whereas the people of the several before-mentioned states have, in the manner aforesaid, given satisfactory evidence that they acquiesce in this sovereign and important resolution of national unity:

"And whereas it is believed to be a fundamental principle of government that the people who have revolted, and who have been overcome and subdued, must either be dealt with so as to induce them voluntarily to become friends, or else they must be held by absolute military power or devastated so as to prevent them from ever again doing harm as enemies, which last-named policy is abhorrent to humanity and freedom:

"And whereas the constitution of the United States provides for constituent communities only as States and not Territories, dependencies, provinces or protectorates:

And whereas such Constituent States must necessarily be, and by the constitution and laws of the United States are made, equals and placed upon a like footing as to political rights, immunities, dignity, and power, with several states with which they are united:

And whereas the observance of political equality as a principle of right and justice is well calculated to encourage the people of the aforesaid states to be and become more and more constant and persevering in their renewed allegiance:

"And whereas standing armies, military occupation, martial law, military tribunals, and the suspension of the privilege of the Writ of Habeas Corpus are in time of peace, dangerous to the public liberty, incompatible with the individual rights of the citizen, contrary to the genius and spirit of our free institutions, and exhaustive of the national resources, and ought not therefore to be sanctioned or allowed except in cases of actual necessity, for repelling invasion or supressing insurrection or rebellion:

And whereas the policy of the government of the United States, from the beginning of the insurrection to its overthrow and final suppression, has been in conformity with the principles herein set forth and enumerated:

Now, therefore, I, Andrew Johnson President of the United States, do hereby proclaim and declare that the insurrection which heretofore existed in the States of Georgia, South Carolina, Virginia, North Carolina, Tennessee, Alabama, Louisiana, Arkansas, Mississippi, and Florida is at an end, and is henceforth to be so regarded."

The war department issued an order in relation to trials by military commissions.

"War Department, Adj. Gen. Office.
Washington, May 1, 1866.
General Orders, No 26."

"Whereas some military commanders are embarrassed by doubts as to the operation of the proclamation of the President, dated the 2d day of April, 1866, upon trials by military Courts-martial and military offences, to remove such doubts, it is ordered by the President that—

Hereafter, whenever offences committed by civilians are to be tried where civil tribunals are in existence which can try them, their cases are not authorized to be, and will not be brought before military courts-martial or commissions, but will be committed to the proper civil authorities. This order is not applicable to camp followers, as provided for under the 60th Article of war, or to contractors and others specified in Section 16, act of July 17, 1862, and Sections 1 and 2, act of March 2, 1863. Persons and offences cognizable by the rules and articles of war, and by the acts of Congress above cited, will continue to be tried and punished by military tribunals as prescribed by the Rules and Articles of war and acts of Congress, herein after cited, to wit:

Sixtieth of the Rules and Articles of war. All sutlers and retainers to the camp, and all persons whatsoever serving with the armies of the United States in the field, though not enlisted soldiers, are to be subject to orders according to the rules and discipline of war. By order of the Secretary of war: E. D. Townsend, Assistant Adjutant General.

The laws of suffrage in several states in 1865, the laws of Maine, Vermont, New Hampshire, Massachusetts and Rhode Island make no distinction in respect of color, as a qualification of voters, although in Rhode Island the law requires a property qualification of 134 dollars worth of real estate as a necessary qualification of a voter of foreign birth, and Massachusetts and Connecticut deny the right of suffrage to all who cannot read the constitution and the statutes in the English Language.

Indians, who are taxed, can vote in the following states, the New England States, Michigan, Wisconsin, California and Minnesota. Chinamen are expressly excluded from the benefit of suffrage in California, Oregon, and Nevada. Indiana, Michigan, Wisconsin. Minnesota, Oregon, Kansas and Illinois admit as voters those not yet citizens. The states of Connecticut, Colorado, Wisconsin, and Minnesota voted against negro suffrage in 1865.

An extract from President Johnson's speech at Washington, Aug. 18, 1866, showing the difference between himself and Congress:

"With the bill called the Freedmen's Bureau, and the Army placed at my discretion (laughter and applause), I could have remained at the Capital. With fifty or sixty millions of appropriations, with the machinery to be worked by my own hands; with my satraps and dependants in every township and civil district in the United States, where it might be necessary, with the Civil Rights bill coming along as an auxiliary (laughter) and all the other patronage of the government, I could have proclaimed myself dictator."—Sup. Cong. Globe, 1868, p. 99. Again, in the same speech, he spoke of the usurpation of Congress:

"We have seen Congress assuming to be for the Union when every step they took was to perpetuate dissolution, and make disruption permanent. We have seen every step that has been taken, instead of bringing about reconciliation and harmony, has been legislation that took the character of penalties, retaliation and revenge. I placed my foot upon the Constitution of my country as the great rampart of civil and religious liberty (applause) having been taught in early life, and having practiced it through my whole career to venerate, respect, and make the Constitution of my Fathers my guide through my public life."

" We have seen Congress organized: we have seen Congress in its advance. Step by step, it has gradually been encroaching upon constitutional rights and violating the fundamental principles of the government, day after day, and month after month. We have seen a Congress that seemed to forget that there was a constitution of the United States, that there were limits, that there were boundaries to the sphere or scope of legislation. We have seen Congress in a minority assume to exercise, and have exercised powers if carried out and consummated, will result in despotism or Monarchy itself. This is truth; and because I and others have seen proper to appeal to the country, to the patriotism and republican feeling of the country, I have been denounced. Slander after slander, vituperation after vituperation of the most vindictive character has made its way through the press. What has been my sin ? what has been your sin ? what has been the cause of your offending ? Because you dare to stand by the constitution of your fathers."

General Grant stood by the President, while he was making this speech—giving it his approval: yet the President was impeached for this offence, and Grant was made President.

The President denounced the Radical Congress in public speeches at Cleveland and St. Louis. While making a speech in Cleveland, Ohio, he was violently interrupted by a Radical mob.—The conduct of the Radicals on this occasion was disgraceful in the extreme.

In 1866, Alabama, Virginia, Louisiana, Florida, and Georgia held no general state elections, but a congressional election was held in Georgia.

In North Carolina, Worth the democratic candidate for governor defeated the Republican candidate Dockery, by a majority of 23,496. There was no election in South Carolina this year except to fill vacancies in the state legislature. Mississippi had no election this year except for district judges and county officers. Political matters in Arkansas, in 1866, were in a chaotic state and party lines were not well defined. The Radicals, (having been successful at the poles) made one more stride towards Federalism (in the language of Jefferson), they " wished to transform it " (the government) "ultimately into the shape of their darling model the English government; and in the meantime, to familiarize the public mind to the change, by administering it on English principles, and in English forms."

Jefferson's Works vol. 5, p. 257.

During the election of 1866 the Radicals held over the President's head the threat of impeachment. The people thought that this threat was made for political capital. That there would be no impeachment. The rank and file of the Republicans and the minor and local politicians had to follow the lead of their Radical masters. Sumner, Wade, Butler and others cracked their whips over them without mercy. Mr. Ashley, of Ohio, moved December 17, 1866, for a committee to investigate the acts of the President. This was done, so that the Radicals could place spies at the white House and pry into the secrets of the President. The Radicals were apprehensive that Johnson would turn them out of office and fill their places with his own friends. To guard against this, Congress passed the "Tenure of Office Bill." This bill was passed for two purposes, to keep the Radicals in office, and as a trap to ensnare the President; for they wanted some plausible pretext to oust him from office and to fill his place with their own instrument Ben Wade. They knew full well that this bill was unconstitutional, yet they trampled the constitution under their feet. They held that it was treason to speak of the constitution or the rights of the states. An othei object of the Radicals in passing this act was to compel the President to fill the highest offices with his enemies. This was the plan of the blue light Federalist. John Adams, in the last days of his power, attempted to fill the permanent offices with his friends so that his successor, Thomas Jefferson, would have to smart under officers who were his political and perhaps personal enemies.

"The last day of his political power (Adams), the last hours, and even beyond the midnight, were employed in filling all offices, and especially permanent ones, with the bitterest Federalists, and providing for me the alternative either to execute the government by my enemies, whose study it would be to thwart and defeat all my measures, or to incur the odium of such numerous removals from office, as might bear me down."—Jefferson's Works, vol. 5, p. 561.

The Radicals slipped into the bill making appropriations, passed March 2, 1867, a clause which deprived the President of his functions as commander-in-chief of the army under the constitution. Their object was to put the army, navy, and state militia under the control of Congress and their favorite generals. For the accomplishment of this usurpation they found a willing instrument in Stanton, the Secretary of war. We give sections 2 and 6 of this act.

Sec. 2. That the Headquarters of the general of the army of the United States shall be at the city of Washington; and all orders and instructions relating to military operations, issued by the President or the Secretary of war, shall be issued through the General of the Army, and in case of inability through the next in rank."

The General of the army shall not be removed, suspended, or relieved from command, or assigned to duty elsewhere than at said Headquarters, except at his own request, without the previous approval of the senate; and any orders or instructions relating to military operations issued contrary to the requirements of this section shall he null and void; and any officer who shall issue orders or instructions contrary to the provisions of this section shall be deemed guilty of a misdemeanor in office; and any officer of the army who shall transmit, convey, or obey any orders or instructions so issued, contrary to the provisions of this section, knowing that such orders were issued, shall be liable to imprisonment for not less than two nor more than twenty years, upon conviction thereof in any court of competent jurisdiction.

"Section 6. That all militia forces now organized or in service in either of the States of Virginia, North Carolina, South Carolina, Georgia, Florida, Alabama, Louisiana, Mississippi, and Texas, be fortwith disbanded, and that the further reorganization, arming, or calling into service of the said militia forces in any part thereof, is hereby prohibited under any circumstance whatever, until the same shall be authorized by Congress."—App. Cong. Globe, 1868, p. 210.

March the 2nd, 1867, Congress passed the first Reconstruction Bill which abolished the state governments in the ten southern states and divided them into five military districts. Each district was placed under the supreme control of a commanding General, who possessed both civil and military jurisdiction. Lieutenants from the office of the Freedmen's Bureau were clothed with civil power, and acted as judges and justices of the peace. These military officers were under the immediate control of Congress. On the 23rd March, 1867, the second Reconstruction Bill was passed. The fifth section of this bill made the majority of votes sufficient to ratify the so called constitutions. It also authorized the election of Congressmen. Generals of the army were authorized to remove all officers, who did not carry out the Reconstruction act, and to detail others in their places. They were authorized to remove all the officers of the provisional government. It made it unlawful for the President to detail the army and navy to support the provisional governments. It repealed all laws passed by the provisional governments. When it became known that the President had vetoed the Freedmen's bureau bill and the civil rights bill, the Radicals became frantic. They called the President a political apostate. They poured forth their wrath without stint on his head. He was called another Arnold! They exhausted their vocabulary of abuse and vile slang on him because he stood in their way in their attempt to trample upon the constitution; because he did not think proper to follow them beyond the pale of the constitution of Washington and the fathers of the revolution. The President saw that the Radicals had no settled policy. That they were every day drifting more and more to confusion and anarchy. That they had repudiated the wise teachings of Washington, Jefferson, Madison, Monroe and Jackson and that they were following such blind guides and fanatics, as Wendell Phillips and the whole restless fanatics of the country.

The following is an extract from the President's message Dec. 8th, 1867:

"That at this time there is no Union, as our fathers understood the term, and as they meant it to be understood by us. The Union which they established can exist only where all states are represented in both Houses of Congress; where one state is as free as an other to regulate its internal concerns according to its own will, and where the laws of the central government, strictly confined to matters of national jurisdiction, apply with equal force to all the people of every section. That such is not the present state of the Union is a melancholy fact."

"To me the process of reconstruction seems perfectly plain and simple. It consists merely in a faithful application of the constitution and laws. The execution of the laws is not now obstructed or opposed by physical force. There is no military or other necessity, real or pretended, which can prevent obedience to the constitution either North or South."

"There is therefore no reason why the constitution should not be obeyed, unless those who exercise its powers have determined that it shall be disregarded and violated."

In reference to the policy of Congress in its reconstruction measures he hints: "The mere naked will of this government, or of some one or more of its branches, is the only obstacle that can exist to a perfect union of all the states. In regard to the states lately in rebellion he said:

"It is clearly to my apprehension that the states lately in rebellion are still members of the national union. When did they cease to be so? The "ordinances of secession," adopted by a portion (in most of them a very small portion) of the citizens, were mere nullities. If we admit now that they were valid and effectual for the purpose intended by their authors, we sweep from under our feet the whole ground upon which we justified the war. Were those states afterward expelled from the union by the war? The direct contrary was averred by this government to be its purpose, and was so understood by all those who gave their blood and treasure to aid in its prosecution. It cannot be that a successful war, waged for the preservation of the union, had the legal effect of dissolving it. The victory of the nation's arms was not the disgrace of her policy; the defeat of secession on the battle field was not the triumph of its lawless principle. Nor could Congress, with or without the consent of the Executive do anything which would have the effect, directly or indirectly, of separating the states from each other. To dissolve the union is to repeal the constitution which holds it together, and that is a power which does not belong to any department of this government nor to all of them united."

"Congress submitted an amendment of the constitution to be ratified by the southern states, and accepted their acts of ratification as a necessary and lawful exercise of their highest function. If they were not states, or were states out of the union, their consent to a change in the fundamental law of the union would have been nugatory, and Congress in asking it, committed a political absurdity. The judiciary has also given the solemn sanction of its authority to the same view of the case. The Judges of the supreme court have included the southern states in their circuits, and they are constantly *in banc* and elsewhere, exercising jurisdiction which does not belong to them, unless those are states in the union." The right of the Federal government, which is clear and unquestionable, to enforce the constitution upon them implies the correlative obligation on our part to observe its limitations and execute its guarantees."

"Being sincerely convinced that these views are correct, I would be unfaithful to my duty if I did not recommend the repeal of the acts of Congress which place ten of the Southern States under the dominion of military masters. If calm reflection shall satisfy a majority of your honorable bodies that the acts referred to are not only a violation of the national faith, but in direct conflict with the Constitution, I dare not permit myself to doubt that you will immediately strike them from the statute-book."

"To demonstrate the unconstitutional character of those acts I need no more than refer to their general provisions. It must be seen at once that they are not authorized. To dictate what alterations shall be made in the Constitutions of the several states, to control the elections of state legislators and state officers, members of Congress and electors of the President and Vice-President, by arbitrarily declaring who shall vote and who shall be excluded from that privilege; to dissolve State Legislatures or to prevent them from assembling; to dismiss judges and other civil functionaries of the state, and appoint others without regard to state law, to organize and operate all the political machinery of the state; to regulate the whole administration of their domestic and local affairs according to the mere will of strange and irresponsible agents, sent among them for that purpose, these are powers not granted to the Federal government or to any one of its branches. "If the authority we desire to use does not come to us through the Constitution, we can exerercise it only by usurpation, and usurpation is the most dangerous of political crimes."

"The acts of Congress in question are not only objectionable for their assumption of ungranted power, but many of their provisions are in conflict with the direct prohibitions of the Constitution."

"It denies the *habeas corpus* and trial by jury. Personal freedom, property, and life, if assailed by the passion, the prejudice, or the rapacity of the ruler, have no security whatever. It has the effect of a bill of attainder, or bill of pains and penalties, not upon a few individuals, but upon whole masses."

"These wrongs, being expressly forbidden, cannot be constitutionally inflicted upon any portion of our people no matter how they may have come within our jurisdiction and no matter whether they live in States, Territories, or districts.

"I have no desire to save from the proper and just consequences of their great crime those who engaged in rebellion against the government, but as a mode of punishment the measures under consideration are the most unreasonable that could be invented. Many of these people are perfectly innocent. Many kept their fidelity to the Union untainted to the last; many were incapable of any legal offences; a large proportion even of the persons able to bear arms were forced into rebellion against their will."

But the acts of Congress confounded them all together in one common doom."

"The Blacks in the south are entitled to be well and humanely governed and to have the protection of just laws for all their rights of person and property. If it were practicable at this time to give them a government exclusively their own, under which they might manage their own affairs in their own way, it would become a grave question whether we ought to do so, or whether common humanity would not require us to save them from themselves." Speaking of the ignorance of the Blacks, he said that they are "so utterly ignorant of public affairs that their voting can consist in nothing more than carrying a ballot to the place where they are directed to deposit it."

"The transfer of our political inheritance to them would, in my opinion, be an abandonment of a duty which we owe alike to the memory of our fathers and the rights of our children."

"Of all the dangers which our nation has yet encountered none are equal to those which must result from the success of the efforts now making to Africanize the half of the country."

"Business in the south is paralyzed by a sense of general insecurity, by the terror of confiscation, and the dread of Negro supremacy."

"It cannot have escaped your attention that from the day on which Congress fairly and formally presented the proposition to govern the Southern States by military force with a view to the ultimate establishment of Negro supremacy, every expression of general sentiment has been more or less adverse to it. The affections of this generation cannot be detached from the institutions of their ancestors."

"It is true that cases may occur in which the executive would be compelled to stand on his rights, and maintain them regardless of all consequences. If Congress should pass an act which is not only in palpable conflict with the constitution, but will certainly, if carried out, produce immediate and irreparable injury to the organic structure of the government, and if there be neither judicial remedy for the wrong it inflicts nor power in the people to protect themselves without the official aid of their elected defender: if, for instance, the legislative department should pass an act even through all the forms of law to abolish a coördinate department of the government: in such a case the President must take the high responsibilities of his office, and save the life of the nation at all hazards."

"It is well and publicly known that enormous frauds have been perpetrated on the Treasury, and that colossal fortunes have been made at the public expense. This species of corruption has increased, is increasing, and if not diminished, will soon bring us into total ruin and disgrace." "The system, never perfected was much disorganized by the 'Tenure-of-office bill,' which has almost destroyed official accountability. The President may be thoroughly convinced that an officer is incapable, dishonest, or unfaithful to the constitution, but, under the law which I have named, the utmost he can do is to complain to the senate, and ask the privilege of supplying his place with a better man."

"A disordered currency is one of the greatest political evils. It has been asserted by one of our profound and most gifted Statesmen that of all the contrivances for cheating the laboring classes of mankind, none has been more effectual than that which deludes them with paper money. This is the most effectual of inventions to fertilize the rich man's fields, by the sweat of the poor man's brow. Ordinary tyranny, oppression, excessive taxation—these bear lightly on the happiness of the mass of the community compared with a fraudulent currency and robberies committed by depreciated paper. "It is one of the most successful devices in times of peace or war, expansions or revolution to accomplish the transfer of all the precious metals from the great mass of the people into the hands of the few."

"The expenses of the military establishment, as well as the number of the army, are now three times as great as they have ever been in time of peace." The President recommended the passage of such laws as would protect naturalized citizens in Europe, but especially in Great Britain. He said that England held that the allegiance of British subjects to the crown is indefeasible, and not to be absolved by our laws of naturalization. That British Judges cited the decisions of the Federal courts of the United States in support of their position. He called upon Congress to declare the national will on the subject of naturalization.

CHAPTER 23.

IMPEACHMENT OF PRESIDENT JOHNSON.

The first effort to impeach the President, began in the House of Representatives, by Mr. James M. Ashley, of Ohio, who moved, December 17, 1866, for the appointment of a Committee to inquire whether, "any acts have been done by any officers of the Government of the United States, which in contemplation of the Constitution, are high crimes or misdemeanors, and whether said acts were designed or calculated to overthrow, subvert, or corrupt the Government of the United States, or any department thereof." The resolution received yeas 90, and nays 49. It failed to receive *two-thirds vote* and was lost.

Benjamin F. Loan offered a resolution on Impeachment, January 7th, 1867. On the same day Mr. Kelso offered a similar resolution, and Mr. Ashley revived his resolution of 1866, which was referred to a Committee on Judiciary.

February 28, 1867, the Committee reported, notifying the succeeding Congress of the incompleteness of its labors.

Mr. Clark, on March 29, moved that the Committee should report the first day of the meeting of the House after the recess.

Meanwhile the Committee began to take evidence on February 6th, 1867, and continued to do so for several months.

November 25th, 1867, Mr. Boutwell from the Committee submitted a report of 1163 printed pages of evidence, and closing with a resolution "that Andrew Johnson be impeached for high crimes and misdemeanors." The Committee stood as follows: Against Impeachment–Messrs Wilson, Republican, of Iowa; Chairman: Woodbridge, Republican, of Vermont; Churchill, Republican, of New York; Marshall, Democrat of Illinois; and Eldridge of Wisconsin–5.

For Impeachment–Messrs, Boutwell, Republican, of Massachusetts, Williams, Republican, of Pennsylvania; Thomas, Republican of Maryland; and Lawrence, Republican, of Ohio–4.

On the 6th, December the Impeachment resolution was lost–The vote stood yeas, 57 (all Republican,) nays, 108, not voting 22 of those voting against the resolution 69, were Republicans. This result was attributed to the Republican losses in the election.

January 27th, 1868, the Impeachment was renewed by Mr. Spalding.

February 13, 1868, Thaddeus Stevens offered a resolution, before the Committee on reconstruction, to impeach President Johnson, which resolution was tabled by a vote of 6 to 3. This completed the second attempt to impeach the president.

On the 12th, of August, 1867, the President removed Stanton the Secretary of war, and appointed General Grant as Secretary of war *ad interim.* After the meeting of Congress, the President sent a message to the Senate giving his reasons for suspending Stanton. On January 13, 1868, the Senate refused to concur in the suspension, by a vote of 35 to 6.

This action of the Senate was officially communicated to General Grant, who thereupon January 14th, informed the President that his functions as Secretary of war *ad interim* ceased from the moment of the receipt of the notice from the Senate. Grant then turned over the office to Stanton. On the 22nd, of February 1868, Thaddeus Stevens, from the Committee on reconstruction, reported to the House a resolution which passed by a vote of 128 to 47, for impeaching the President, of high crimes and misdemeanors.

Feb. 21, 1868, the President issued an order for the removal of Stanton from the war department, and for the appointment of Gen. Thomas, as Secretary of war *ad interim.*

Thomas went with this order to Stanton and demanded possession of the office, books, and papers. In the meantime Mr. Sumner wrote a note to Stanton "to stick" on to the office.

Feb. 24, 1868, the House of Representatives resolved to impeach the President of The United States.

March, 3d, 1868, Articles of Impeachment were agreed upon by the House of Representatives, and on the 5th, they were presented to the Senate and read by the chairman of the managers, Mr. Bingham.

The following is a synopsis of the articles of impeachment:

$1st, Andrew Johnson, President of the United States, had violated the Tenure-of-office bill, of March, 2, 1867. The President was charged with the removal of Stanton and with the appointment of Gen. Thomas as Secretary of war *ad interim,* without the consent of the Senate.

2nd, He was also charged with a conspiracy for having violated the Conspiracy Act of July 31st, 1861, being an act to define and punish conspiracy. He was charged with the violation of the act of June 30th, 1868, for issuing all military orders through the Generals of the army.

3d, He was charged with making certain speeches, in the cities of Washington, Cleveland, and St. Louis. Another charge was, that he had attempted to bring the Congress of the United States into contempt.

That he had denied that the Thirty-Ninth Congress had the power to make amendments to the Constitution.

Another charge was, that the President had said that the Thirty-Ninth Congress was not the Congress of the United States.

John A. Bingham of Ohio; George S. Boutwell, of Mass; James F. Wilson, of Iowa; John A. Logan, of Illinois; Thomas Williams, of Pennsylvania; Benjamin F. Butler, of Mass.; and Thaddeus Stevens, of Pennsylvania; were elected managers to conduct the Impeachment.

March 13th, 1868, proclamation was made by the Sergeant-at-arms for the appearance of Andrew Johnson. Stanberry and Curtis entered an appearance for the President, and asked for forty days to put in an answer.

This motion was opposed by the managers who wanted to rush the trial through with rail road speed—with the same haste as an ordinary criminal case before a police Justice. Butler opposed the motion, and in a brutal, ungentlemanly and beastly manner, called the President a criminal. He said that there was great need to hasten the trial because the President was the Chief executive; that he could use the treasury, the army and the navy to overthrow the government, thus prejudicing public opinion against the President. Groesbeck, Nelson, and Evarts, subsequently appeared as Counsel for the President.

March 23, 1868, the President's answer was put in. The President claimed to have the power to remove Stanton under the act of Congress 1789,—That Stanton was appointed Secretary of war on the 15, Jan, 1862, by Abraham Lincoln, during his first term of office, to hold such office during the pleasure of the President. That the Respondent became President on the 15, April 1865, and that Stanton held his office during the pleasure of the Respondent. That on Aug, 5, 1867, he removed Mr. Stanton by the power invested in him by the Constitution and the Laws. So that he was responsible for the conduct of the Secretary of war. That he had notified the Senate thereof, on the 12, day of December, 1867. That he had authority to make said removal by the Act of Congress, Feb, 13, 1795. During the trial Butler displayed his usual arrogance and insolence towards the Chief Justice, the President's Counsel, and the witnesses.

He claimed that the Senate was not a Court; that it was not to be governed by law. The managers went back to old English black-letter learning—to old musty English law books, and the English parliament for their precedents.

They held that the high Court of Impeachment was bound by no law, neither statute nor common, but that the President should be tried, by common fame. They held, that popular opinion demanded the conviction of the President.

The managers further held the absurd idea, that Mr. Johnson was only serving out the remainder of Mr. Lincoln's term, and therefore that he could not remove Stanton; that Lincoln's term continued after his death. Butler in his speech, went over several American and English authorities which had no bearing on the case. He failed to make out even a plausible case against the President.

He assailed him in the vilest manner. He called him Judas Iscariot. He said, "By murder most foul he succeeded to the Presidency, and is the elect of an assassin to that high office." He said that the President was one of the conspirators. This was worthy of New Orleans "spoons."—The President was charged with want of decorum of speech. Butler also charged the President with advising and counseling the Legislature of the states lately in rebellion, to reject the 14th, amendment. This, indeed, was the sum of his sinning; he had differed with the party that elected him.

They charged the President with being a very bad and dangerous man —that he was a very dangerous person to remain the Chief magistrate of the nation—that he had obstructed the laws; that the managers considered him a great criminal; that he had trampled the laws under foot—that the reason for not granting him time for preparing his defense was that he was worse than an ordinary criminal. He was charged with advising the Legislature of Alabama to remain firm in its opposition to Congress on Reconstruction, and the 14th amendment, Freedman's bureau; and that he had advised the Legislature of South Carolina on the same subject.

The Counsel for the President held that the Tenure-of-office bill gave the President power to choose his own cabinet. That Stanton was not removed, that he was still in possession of the department of war. That it was at most an attempt to remove him as he did not obey the order of the President. That the President had the same right to construe the law, as Jackson had when he vetoed the bill, for chartering a United States Bank. Jackson said;

The Congress, Executive, and the Court must each for itself be guided by its own opinion of the constitution. Each public officer, who takes an oath to support the constitution, swears that he will support it as he understands it and not as it is understood by others. That he had the same right to remove Stanton that Lincoln had to remove Floyd, the

Secretary of war, and to appoint Holt. That he had power to re-move Stanton by the acts of congress 1787, 1795, 1792. That every President and Congress had participated in and acted under the con-struction given to the act of 1787, from Washington to Lincoln.

They held the tenure-of-office bill unconstitutional and that Stanton did not come within the law—That Stanton had no commission from Johnson nor from Lincoln after Lincoln's first term expired. That he was *merely* holding over at the pleasure of both Lincoln and Johnson. That consequently it made no difference whether the Senate was in ses-sion or not.

That the office was vacant and that the President had a right to ap-point a Secretary of war *ad interim*, until a new appointment was made and confirmed by the Senate.

That the tenure-of-office bill was unconstitutional and did not em-brace the case of Stanton. That the President acted from laudable and honest motives and was not guilty of any crime or misdemeanor.

That from the remarks made at the time of the passage of the tenure-of-office bill, it was manifest that it was not intended to embrace the Secretaries.

Honorable Lyman Trumbull, a leading Republican, in giving his opin-ion before the final vote was taken, said;

The question of the power to remove from office arose, at the first Congress, in 1787. That it was then recognized that the President had the right to remove all officers whose term was not fixed by the Consti-tution. That every President acted under this recognization down to 1867.

That this power was exercised when the Senate was in session, as well as during recess. He gave a long list of removals by Lincoln and other Presidents while the Senate was in session; he said that Stanton was only holding at the pleasure of the President. That Jackson, Van Buren, Tyler, Harrison, Polk, and Fillmore had made *ad interim* appointments during the session of the Senate. That his speeches were no ground for impeachment.

"He said painful as it is to disagree with so many political associates and friends, whose conscientious convictions have led them to a different result, I must, nevertheless, in discharge of the high responsibility un-der which I act, be governed by what my reason and judgment tell me is the truth, and the justice and the law of this case." To convict and depose the Chief Magistrate of a great nation when his guilt was not made palpable by the record, and for insufficient cause, would be fraught with far greater danger to the future of the country than can arise from leaving Mr. Johnson in office for the remaining months of his term, with powers curtailed and limited as they have been by re-cent Legislation.

Once set the example of impeaching a President, for what when the excitement of the hour shall have subsided will be regarded as insuffi-cient causes as several of those now alleged against the President were decided to be by the house of Representatives only a few months since, and no future President will be safe who happens to differ with a majority of the house, and two thirds of the Senate on any measure deem-ed by them important, particularly if of a political character blinded by partisan zeal. With such an example before them they will not scruple to remove out of the way any obstacle to the accomplishment of their purposes, and what then becomes of the checks and balances of the constitution, so carefully devised and so vital to its perpetuity ? They are all gone. In view of the consequences likely to flow from this day's proceedings, should they result in conviction on what my judgment tells me are insufficient charges and proofs, I tremble for the future of my Country. I cannot be an instrument to produce such a result, and at the hazard of the ties even of friendship and affection till calmer times shall do justice to my motives, no alternative is left me but the inflexible discharge of duty."

He was followed by Senators Grimes, Johnson, Fessenden and others, in very able and eloquent speeches in favor of acquitting the President.

Mr. Sumner made a disgraceful speech. He held that the President should be expelled the same as a member of Congress. That he should not have the benefit of doubt; that they should "catch at anything to convict the President and save the Republic; that he should be found guilty of getting drunk as well as for all political offences, especially for giving his support to slavery, for appointing rebels to office, for vetoing several acts of Congress. That he was guilty of inciting the New Orleans massacre; that he had given offices to rebels and had received them at the white house; that he had removed Sheridan, Pope, and Sickles who were military commanders in the five Kingdoms. He appealed to the usual party prejudices with all the passion and party rancor of a stump speaker.

The following is an extract from his speech ; "Here in the Senate we know officially how he has made himself the attorney of slavery, the usurper of Legislative powers, the violator of law, the patron of rebels, the helping hand of rebellion, the kicker from office of good citizens, the open bung-hole of the Treasury, the architect of the whiskey ring, the stumbling-block to all good laws by wanton vetoes, and then by criminal hindrances all these things are known here beyond question.

Johnson's cabinet recognized Gen. Thomas as Secretary of war *ad interim* which goes to show that they believed that the President had the right to remove Stanton.

When it was known that Senator Grimes, of Iowa, would vote for an acquittal, the Radicals, in the lobby, made a great noise, and used very insulting language toward the Senator. They made threatening demonstrations, and sang "Old Grimes is dead the poor old soul."

At the conclusion of Manager Bingham's speech he was loudly applauded in the galleries. The Chief Justice called for order, in vain. The galleries were ordered to be cleared, but the ruffians who made the disturbance refused to comply. The scene was the most disgraceful ever witnessed in Congress. It was necessary for the Sergeant-at-arms to use force to expel the disorderly Radical mob !

Chief Justice Chase acted, throughout the whole trial with firmness and dignity. He ruled according to law and justice, notwithstanding the threats of vengeance and impeachment made by the Radicals in and out of Congress. He was denounced as a traitor.

May 16, the Court voted on the eleventh article. The vote was 35 guilty ; and 19 not guilty.

The two third vote was wanting, and the Court adjourned to May 26. This verdict caused great rejoicing throughout the country. Meanwhile corrupt influences were attempted in vain to bear on the seven Republicans or as they were called "recreant" Senators, who were denounced as traitors by the Radical press. The house pretended to investigate the "corrupt means" used to influence these Senators to vote against the will of their party.

On the 26, a vote was taken on the second and third articles, which resulted the same as on the eleventh article. Guilty 35, not guilty 19. The Radicals, finding that they could not convict the President on these articles, voted for an adjournment. The Chief Justice entered Judgment of acquittal on the three articles voted upon, and the Senate, sitting as a Court of impeachment for the trial of Andrew Johnson, President of the United States, adjourned, *sine die*. On the same day Stanton communicated to the President his relinquishment of the war department, and left the same in the care of Assistant-Adjutant-General Townsend, and on the 29, of May the Senate confirmed Schofield (nominated by Johnson, April 23,) as Secretary of war. Stanton retired to private life covered with the curses of thousands of his countrymen. He was a tyrant of the blackest dye. He suffered thousands of brave soldiers to rot in military prisons. His name will be remembered only to be despised."

This ended the most villainous conspiracy of the Radicals to overthrow the constitution and perpetrate usurpation!

This was the political high water mark of Radical usurpation!!!

We conclude this chapter with the following extract from Washington, on usurpation.

"The spirit of encroachment tends to consolidate the powers of all the departments in one, and thus create, whatever the form of Government, a real despotism. * * * *

If, in the opinion of the people, the distribution or modification of the constitutional powers be in any particular, wrong, let it be corrected by amendments, *in the way which the constitution designates*. But let there be no change by usurpation, for though this in *one* instance may be the instrument of good, it is the *customary* weapon by which free Governments are destroyed. The precedent must always greatly overbalance, in permanent evil, any partial or transient benefit which the use can at any time yield."

Washington.

CONSTITUTION.

WE, the people of the United States, in order to form a more perfect union, establish justice, ensure domestic tranquillity, provide for the common defence, promote the general welfare, and secure the blessings of liberty to ourselves and our posterity, do ordain and establish this constitution for the United States of America.

ARTICLE 1.

SEC. 1. All legislative powers herein granted shall be vested in a congress of the United States, which shall consist of a senate and house of representatives.

SEC. 2. The house of representatives shall be composed of members chosen every second year by the people of the several states; and the electors in each state shall have the qualifications requisite for electors of the most numerous branch of the state legislature.

No person shall be a representative who shall not have attained to the age of twenty-five years, and been seven years a citizen of the United States, and who shall not, when elected, be an inhabitant of that state in which he shall be chosen.

Representatives and direct taxes shall be apportioned among the several states which may be included within this Union, according to their respective numbers, which shall be determined by adding to the whole number of free persons, including those bound to service for a term of years, and excluding Indians not taxed, three-fifths of all other persons. The actual enumeration shall be made within three years after the first meeting of the congress of the United States, and within every subsequent term of ten years, in such manner as they shall by law direct. The number of representatives shall not exceed one for every thirty thousand, but each state shall have at least one representative; and until such enumeration shall be made, the state of New Hampshire shall be entitled to choose three; Massachusetts eight; Rhode Island and Providence Plantations one; Connecticut five; New York six; New Jersey four; Pennsylvania eight; Delaware one; Maryland six; Virginia ten; North Carolina five; South Carolina five; and Georgia three.

When vacancies happen in the representation from any state, the executive authority thereof shall issue writs of election to fill such vacancies.

The house of representatives shall choose their speaker and other officers, and shall have the sole power of impeachment.

SEC. 3.   The senate of the United States shall be composed of two senators from each state, chosen by the legislature thereof, for six years; and each senator shall have one vote.

Immediately after they shall be assembled in consequence of the first election, they shall be divided, as equally as may be, into three classes. The seats of the senators of the first class shall be vacated at the expiration of the second year, of the second class at the expiration of the fourth year; and of the third class at the expiration of the sixth year, so that one-third may be chosen every second year; and if vacancies happen by resignation or otherwise, during the recess of the legislature of-any state, the executive thereof may make temporary appointments until the next meeting of the legislature, which shall then fill such vacancies.

No person shall be a senator who shall not have attained to the age of thirty years, and been nine years a citizen of the United States, and who shall not, when elected, be an inhabitant of that state for which he shall be chosen.

The vice-president of the United States shall be president of the senate, but shall have no vote unless they be equally divided.

The senate shall choose their other officers, and also a president *pro-tempore*, in the absence of the vice-president, or when he shall exercise the office of president of the United States.

The senate shall have the sole power to try all impeachments. When sitting for that purpose they shall be on oath or affirmation. When the president of the United States is tried, the Chief-justice shall preside; and no person shall be convicted without the concurrence of two-thirds of the members present.

Judgment in cases of impeachment shall not extend further than to removal from office, and disqualification to hold and enjoy any office of honor, trust or profit, under the United States; but the party convicted, shall nevertheless be liable and subject to indictment, trial, judgment and punishment, according to law.

SEC. 4. The times, places and manner of holding elections for senators and representatives, shall be prescribed in each state by the legislature thereof; but the congress may, at any time, by law make or alter such regulations, except as to the places of choosing senators.

The congress shall assemble at least once in every year, and such meetings shall be on the first Monday in December, unless they shall by law appoint a different day.

SEC. 5. Each house shall be the judge of the elections, returns, and qualifications of its own members; and a majority of each shall constitute a quorum to do business; but a smaller number may adjourn from day to day, and may be authorized to compel the attendance of absent members, in such manner and under such penalties as each house may provide.

Each house may determine the rules of its proceedings, punish its members for disorderly behavior, and with the concurrence of two-thirds, expel a member.

Each house shall keep a journal of its proceedings, and from time to time publish the same, excepting such parts as may in their judgment, require secrecy; and the yeas and nays of the members of either house on any question, shall, at the desire of one-fifth of those present, be entered on the journal.

Neither house during the session of congress, shall, without the consent of the other, adjourn for more than three days, nor to any other place than that in which the two houses shall be sitting.

SEC. 6. The senators and representatives shall receive a compensation for their services, to be ascertained by law, and paid out of the treasury of the United States. They shall, in all cases, except treason, felony, and breach of the peace, be privileged from arrest during their attendance at the session of their respective houses, and in going to, or returning from the same; and for any speech or debate in either house, they shall not be questioned in any other place.

No senator or representative shall, during the time for which he was elected, be appointed to any civil office under the authority of the United States, which shall have been created, or the emoluments whereof shall have been increased during such time; and no person holding any office under the United States, shall be a member of either house during his continuance in office.

SEC. 7. All bills for raising revenue shall originate in the house of representatives; but the senate may propose or concur with amendments as on other bills.

Every bill which shall have passed the house of representatives and the senate, shall, before it becomes a law, be presented to the President of the United States; if he approve, he shall sign it; but if not, he shall return it, with his objections, to that house in which it shall have originated, who shall enter the objections at large on their journal, and proceed to reconsider it. If, after such reconsideration, two-thirds of that house shall agree to pass the bill, it shall be sent, together with the objections, to the other house, by which it shall likewise be reconsidered, and if approved by two-thirds of that house, it shall become a law. But in all cases, the votes of both houses shall be determined by yeas and nays, and the names of the persons voting for and against the bill, shall be entered on the journal of each house respectively. If any bill shall not be returned by the president within ten days, (Sundays excepted,) after it shall have been presented to him, the same shall be a law, in like manner as if he had signed it, unless the congress by their adjournment prevent it's return, in which case it shall not be a law.

Every order, resolution, or vote, to which the concurrence of the senate and house of representatives may be necessary, (except on a question of adjournment) shall be presented to the President of the United States; and before the same shall take effect, shall be approved by him, or, being disapproved by him, shall be repassed by two-thirds of the senate and house of representatives, according to the rules and limitations prescribed in the case of a bill.

SEC. 8. The congress shall have power,

To lay and collect taxes, duties, imposts, and excises, to pay the debts and provide for the common defence and general welfare of the United States; but all duties, imposts, and excises shall be uniform throughout the United States:

To borrow money on the credit of the United States:

To regulate commerce with foreign nations, and among the several states, and with the Indian tribes:

To establish an uniform rule of naturalization, and uniform laws on the subject of bankruptcies throughout the United States:

To coin money, regulate the value thereof, and of foreign coin, and fix the standard of weights and measures:

To provide for the punishment of counterfeiting the securities and current coin of the United States:

To establish post-offices and post-roads:

To promote the progress of science and the useful arts, by securing for limited times, to authors and inventors, the exclusive right to their respective writings and discoveries:

To constitute tribunals inferior to the supreme court: To define and punish piracies and felonies committed on the high seas, and offences against the law of nations:

To declare war, grant letters of marque and reprisal, and make rules concerning captures on land and water:

To raise and support armies; but no appropriation of money to that use, shall be for a longer term than two years :

To provide and maintain a navy :

To make rules for the government and regulation of the land and naval forces :

To provide for calling forth the militia, to execute the laws of the Union, suppress insurrections, and repel invasions:

To provide for organizing, arming and disciplining the militia and for governing such part of them as may be employed in the service of the United States, reserving to the states respectively, the appointment of the officers, and the authority of training the militia according to the discipline prescribed by congress.

To exercise exclusive legislation in all cases whatsoever, over such district (not exceeding ten miles square) as may, by cession of particular states, and the acceptance of congress, become the seat of government of the United States, and to exercise like authority over all places purchased, by the consent of the legislature of the state in which the same shall be, for the erection of forts, magazines, arsenals, dockyards and other needful buildings : and

To make all laws which shall be necessary and proper for carrying into execution the foregoing powers, and all other powers vested by this constitution in the government of the United States, or in any department or officer thereof.

Sec. 9. The migration or importation of such persons as any of the states now existing shall think proper to admit, shall not be prohibited by the congress prior to the year one thousand eight hundred and eight, but a tax or duty may be imposed on such importation, not exceeding ten dollars for each person.

The privilege of the writ of *habeas corpus* shall not be suspended, unless when, in cases of rebellion or invasion, the public safety may require it.

No bill of attainder, or *ex post facto* law shall be passed.

No capitation or other direct tax shall be laid, unless in proportion to the census or enumeration herein before directed to be taken.

No tax or duty shall be laid on articles exported from any state. No preference shall be given by any regulation of commerce or revenue to the ports of one state over those of another; nor shall vessels bound to or from one state be obliged to enter, clear, or pay duties in another.

No money shall be drawn from the treasury, but in consequence of appropriations made by law; and a regular statement and account of the receipts and expenditures of all public money, shall be published from time to time.

No title of nobility shall be granted by the United States, and no person holding any office of profit or trust under them, shall, without the consent of congress, accept of any present, emolument, office, or title of any kind whatever, from any king, prince, or foreign state.

Sec. 10. No state shall enter into any treaty, alliance, or confederation; grant letters of marque and reprisal; coin money; emit bills of credit; make anything but gold and silver coin a tender in payment of debts; pass any bill of attainder, *ex post facto* law, or law impairing the obligation of contracts; or grant any title of nobility.

No state shall, without the consent of the congress, lay any imposts

or duties on imports or exports, except what may be absolutely necessary for executing its inspection laws; and the net produce of all duties
and imposts, laid by any state on imports or exports, shall be for the
use of the treasury of the United States, and all such laws shall be subject to the revision and control of the congress. No state shall, without the consent of congress, lay any duty of tonnage, keep troops or
ships of war in time of peace, enter into any agreement or compact with
another state, or with a foreign power, or engage in war, unless actually invaded, or in such imminent danger as will not admit of delay.

ARTICLE II.

Sec. 1. The executive power shall be vested in a President of the
United States of America. He shall hold his office during the term of
four years, and together with the vice-president, chosen for the same
term, be elected as follows:

Each state shall appoint in such manner as the legislature thereof
may direct, a number of electors, equal to the whole number of senators
and representatives to which the state may be entitled in the congress;
but no senator or representative, or person holding an office of trust or
profit under the United States, shall be appointed an elector.

The electors shall meet in their respective states, and vote by ballot for two persons, of whom one at least shall not be an inhabitant of
the same state with themselves. And they shall make a list of all the
persons voted for, and of the number of votes for each; which list they
shall sign and certify, and transmit sealed to the seat of the government
of the United States, directed to the president of the senate. The president of the senate shall, in the presence of the senate and house of representatives, open all the certificates, and the votes shall then be counted. The person having the greatest number of votes shall be the president, if such number be a majority of the whole number of electors appointed; and if there be more than one who have such majority, and
have an equal number of votes, then the house of representatives shall
immediately choose, by ballot, one of them for president; and if no
person have a majority, then from the five highest on the list, the said
house shall, in like manner, choose the president. But in choosing the
president, the votes shall be taken by states, the representation from
each state having one vote: a quorum for this purpose shall consist of
a member or members from two-thirds of the states, and a majority of
all the states shall be necessary to a choice. In every case, after the
choice of the president, the person having the greatest number of votes
of the electors, shall be the vice-president. But if there should remain
two or more who have equal votes, the senate shall choose from them,
by ballot, the vice-president.

The congress may determine the time of choosing the electors and the
day on which they shall give their votes, which day shall be the same
throughout the United States.

No person, except a natural born citizen, or a citizen of the United
States at the time of the adoption of this constitution, shall be eligible
to the office of president; neither shall any person be eligible to that
office, who shall not have attained to the age of thirty-five years, and
been fourteen years a resident within the United States.

In case of the removal of the president from office, or of his death resignation, or inability to discharge the powers and duties of the said office, the same shall devolve on the vice-president, and the congress may, by law, provide for the case of removal, death, resignation, or inability, both of the president and vice-president, declaring what officer shall then act as president, and such officer shall act accordingly, until the disability be removed, or a president shall be elected.

The president shall, at stated times, receive for his services a compensation, which shall neither be increased nor diminished during the period for which he shall have been elected: and he shall not receive within that period any other emolument from the United States, or any of them.

Before he enter on the execution of his office, he shall take the following oath or affirmation.

"I do solemnly swear(or affirm)that I will faithfully execute the office of president of the United States, and will, to the best of my ability, preserve, protect, and defend the constitution of the United States."

SEC. 2. The president shall be commander-in-chief of the army and navy of the United States, and of the militia of the several states, when called into the actual service of the United States, he may require the opinion in writing, of the principal officer in each of the executive departments, upon any subject relating to the duties of their respective offices; and he shall have power to grant reprieves and pardons for offences against the United States, except in cases of impeachment.

He shall have power by and with the advice and consent of the senate, to make treaties, provided two-thirds of the senators present concur, and he shall nominate, and by and with the advice and consent of the senate, shall appoint ambassadors, other public ministers, and consuls, judges of the supreme court, and all other officers of the United States whose appointments are not herein otherwise provided for, and which shall be established by law. But the congress may, by law, vest the appointment of such inferior officers as they think proper, in the president alone, in the courts of law, or in the heads of departments.

The president shall have power to fill up all vacancies that may happen during the recess of the senate, by granting commissions, which shall expire at the end of their next session.

SEC. 3. He shall, from time to time, give to the congress information of the state of the Union, and recommend to their consideration, such measures as he shall judge necessary and expedient: he may on extraordinary occasions, convene both houses, or either of them, and in case of disagreement between them, with respect to the time of adjournment, he may, adjourn them to such time as he shall think proper; he shall receive ambassadors and other public ministers; he shall take care that the laws be faithfully executed; and shall commission all the officers of the United States.

SEC. 4. The president, vice-president, and all civil officers of the United States, shall be removed from office on impeachment for, and conviction of, treason, bribery, or other high crimes and misdemeanors.

ARTICLE III.

SEC 1. The judicial power of the United States, shall be vested in one supreme court, and in such inferior courts as the congress may, from time to time ordain and establish. The judges both of the supreme and inferior courts, shall hold their offices during good behavior; and shall, at stated times, receive for their services a compensation which shall not be diminished during their continuance in office.

Sec. 2. The judicial power shall extend to all cases in law and equity, arising under this constitution, the laws of the United States, and treaties made, or which shall be made under their authority; to all cases affecting ambassadors, other public ministers, and consuls; to all cases of admiralty and maratime jurisdiction; to controversies to which the United States shall be a party; to controversies between two or more states, between a state and citizens of another state, between citizens of different states, between citizens of the same state claiming lands under grants of different states, and between a state, or the citizens thereof, and foreign states, citizens or subjects.

In all cases affecting ambassadors, other public ministers and consuls, and those in which a state shall be a party, the supreme court shall have original jurisdiction. In all the other cases before mentioned, the supreme court shall have appellate jurisdiction, both as to law and fact, with such exceptions and under such regulations as the Congress shall make.

The trial of all crimes, except in cases of impeachment, shall be by jury, and such trial shall be held in the state where the said crimes shall have been committed; but when not committed within any state, the trial shall be at such place or places as the congress may by law have directed.

Sec. 3. Treason against the United States shall consist only in levying war against them, or in adhering to their enemies, giving them aid and comfort. No person shall be convicted of treason unless on the testimony of two witnesses to the same overt act, or on confession in open court.

The congress shall have power to declare the punishment of treason; but no attainder of treason shall work corruption of blood, or forfeiture, except during the life of the person attainted.

ARTICLE IV.

Sec. 1. Full faith and credit shall be given in each state to the public acts, records, and judicial proceedings of every other state. And the congress may, by general laws, prescribe the manner in which such acts, records and proceedings, shall be proved, and the effect thereof.

Sec. 2. The citizens of each state shall be entitled to all privileges and immunities of citizens in the several states.

A person charged in any state with treason, felony, or other crime, who shall flee from justice, and be found in another state, shall, on demand of the executive authority of the state from which he fled, be delivered up, to be removed to the state having jurisdiction of the crime.

No person held to service or labor in one state under the laws thereof, escaping into another, shall, in consequence of any law or regulation therein, be discharged from such service or labor; but shall be delivered up on claim of the party to whom such service or labor may be due.

Sec. 3. New states may be admitted by the congress into this Union; but no new state shall be formed or erected within the jurisdiction of any other state, nor any state be formed by the junction of two or more states or parts of states, without the consent of the legislatures of the states concerned, as well as of the congress.

The congress shall have power to dispose of, and make all needful rules and regulations respecting the territory or other property belonging to the United States; and nothing in this constitution shall be so construed as to prejudice any claims of the United States, or of any particular state.

SEC. 4. The United States shall guarantee to every state in this Union a republican form of government, and shall protect each of them against invasion; and on application of the legislature, or of the executive, (when the legislature cannot be convened,) against domestic violence.

ARTICLE V.

The congress, whenever two-thirds of both houses shall deem it necessary, shall propose amendments to this constitution; or, on the application of the legislatures of two-thirds of the several states, shall call a convention for proposing amendments, which, in either case, shall be valid to all intents and purposes, as part of this constitution, when ratified by the legislatures of three-fourths of the several states, or by conventions in three-fourths thereof, as the one or the other mode of ratification may be proposed by the congress; *Provided*, That no amendment, which may be made prior to the year one thousand eight hundred and eight, shall in any manner affect the first and fourth clauses in the ninth section of the first article; and that no state, without its consent, shall be deprived of its equal suffrage in the senate.

ARTICLE VI.

All debts contracted and engagements entered into, before the adoption of this constitution, shall be as valid against the United States under this constitution, as under the confederation.

This constitution, and the laws of the United States which shall be made in pursuance thereof; and all treaties made, or which shall be made, under the authority of the United States, shall be the supreme law of the land; and the judges in every state shall be bound thereby; any thing in the constitution or laws of any state to the contrary notwithstanding.

The senators and representatives before mentioned, and the members of the several state legislatures, and all executive and judicial officers, both of the United States, and of the several states, shall be bound by an oath or affirmation, to support this constitution; but no religious test shall be required as a qualification to any office or public trust under the United States.

ARTICLE VII.

The ratification of the conventions of nine states, shall be sufficient for the establishment of this constitution between the states so ratifying the same.

Done in convention, by the unanimous consent of the states present, the seventeenth day of September, in the year of our Lord one thousand seven hundred and eighty-seven, and of the Independence of the United States of America, the twelfth. In witness whereof, we have hereunto subscribed our names.

GEORGE WASHINGTON, *President, and Deputy from Virginia.*

New Hampshire.—John Langdon, Nicholas Gilman.
Massachusetts.—Nathaniel Gorham, Rufus King.
Connecticut.—William Samuel Johnson, Roger Sherman.
New York.—Alexander Hamilton.
New Jersey.—William Livingston, David Brearly, William Patterson, Jonathan Dayton.
Pennsylvania.—Benjamin Franklin, Thomas Mifflin, Robert Morris, George Clymer, Thomas Fitzsimons, Jared Ingersol, James Wilson, Gouverneur Morris.
Delaware.—George Read, Gunning Bedford, Jun, John Dickinson, Richard Bassett, Jacob Broom.
Maryland.—James M'Henry, Daniel of St, Tho, Jenifer, Daniel Carroll.
Virginia.—John Blair, James Madison, Jun.
North Carolina.—William Blount, Richard Dobbs Spaight, Hugh Williamson.
South Carolina.—John Rutledge, Charles Cotesworth Pinckney, Charles Pinckney, Pierce Butler.
Georgia.—William Few, Abraham Baldwin.

Attest,   WILLIAM JACKSON, *Secretary.*

The conventions of a number of the states, having, at the time of their adopting the constitution, expressed a desire, in order to prevent misconstruction or abuse of its powers, that further declaratory and restrictive clauses should be added, congress, at the session begun and held at the city of New York, on Wednesday, the 4th of March, 1789, proposed to the legislatures of the several states twelve amendments, ten of which only were adopted. They are the ten first following:

AMENDMENTS TO THE CONSTITUTION.

ARTICLE I.

First Session, First Congress, March 4th, 1789.
Congress shall make no law respecting an establishment of religion, or prohibiting the free exercise thereof; or abridging the freedom of speech, or of the press; or the right of the people peaceably to assemble, and to petition the government for a redress of grievances.

ARTICLE II.

A well regulated militia being necessary to the security of a free state the right of the people to keep and bear arms, shall not be infringed.

ARTICLE III.

No soldier shall, in time of peace, be quartered in any house without the consent of the owner ; nor in time of war, but in a manner to be prescribed by law.

ARTICLE IV.

The right of the people to be secure in their persons, houses, papers, and effects, against unreasonable searches and seizures, shall not be violated ; and no warrants shall issue, but upon probable cause, supported by oath or affirmation, and particularly describing the place to be searched, and the persons or things to be seized.

ARTICLE V.

No person shall be held to answer for a capital or otherwise infamous crime, unless on a presentment or indictment of a grand jury, except in cases arising in the land or naval forces, or in the militia, when in actual service, in time of war or public danger ; nor shall any person be subject for the same offence to be twice put in jeopardy of life or limb ; nor shall be compelled, in any criminal case, to be a witness against himself, nor be deprived of life, liberty or property, without due process of law ; nor shall private property be taken for public use without just compensation.

ARTICLE VI.

In all criminal prosecutions, the accused shall enjoy the right to a speedy and public trial, by an impartial jury of the state and district wherein the crime shall have been committed, which district shall have been previously ascertained by law, and to be informed of the nature and cause of the accusation ; to be confronted with the witnesses against him ; to have compulsory process for obtaining witnesses in his favor ; and to have the assistance of counsel for his defence.

ARTICLE VII.

In suits at common law, where the value in controversy shall exceed twenty dollars, the right of trial by jury shall be preserved, and no fact tried by a jury shall be otherwise re-examined in any court of the United States, than according to the rules of the common law.

ARTICLE VIII.

Excessive bail shall not be required, nor excessive fines imposed, nor cruel and unusual punishments inflicted·

ARTICLE IX.

The enumeration in the constitution of certain rights, shall not be construed to deny or disparage others retained by the people.

ARTICLE X.

The powers not delegated to the United States by the constitution, nor prohibited by it to the states, are reserved to the states respectively, or to the people.

ARTICLE XI.

Third Congress, Second Session, December 2, 1793.
The judicial power of the United States shall not be construed to extend to any suit in law or equity, commenced or prosecuted against one of the United States by citizens of another state, or by citizens or subjects of any foreign state.

ARTICLE XII.

Eighth Congress, First Session, October 17, 1803.
The electors shall meet in their respective states, and vote by ballot for president and vice-president, one of whom, at least shall not be an inhabitant of the same state with themselves ; they shall name in their ballots the person voted for as president, and in distinct ballots the person voted for as vice-president ; and they shall make distinct lists of all persons voted for as president, and of all persons voted for as vice-president; and of the number of votes for each, which lists they shall sign and certify, and transmit sealed to the seat of the government of the United States, directed to the president of the senate ; the president of the senate shall, in the presence of the senate and house of representatives, open all the certificates, and the votes shall then be counted : the person having the greatest number of votes for president, shall be the president, if such number be a majority of the whole number of electors appointed ; and if no person have such majority, then from the persons having the highest numbers, not exceeding three, on the list of those voted for as president, the house of representatives shall choose immediately, by ballot, the president. But in choosing the president, the votes shall be taken by states, the representation from each state having one vote ; a quorum for this purpose shall consist of a member or members from two-thirds of the states, and a majority of all the states shall be necessary to a choice. And if the house of representatives shall not choose a president whenever the right of choice shall devolve upon them, before the fourth day of March next following, then the vice-president shall act as president, as in the case of the death or other constitutional disability of the president.
The person having the greatest number of votes as vice-president, shall be the vice-president, if such number be a majority of the whole number of electors appointed ; and if no person have a majority, then from the two highest numbers on the list, the senate shall choose the vice-president : a quorum for the purpose shall consist of two-thirds of the whole number of senators, and a majority of the whole number shall be necessary to a choice.
But no person constitutionally ineligible to the office of president, shall be eligible to that of vice-president of the United States.

ARTICLE XIII.

Sec. 1. Slavery abolished,—Neither slavery nor involuntary servitude except as a punishment for crime whereof the party shall have been duly convicted, shall exist within the United States, or in any place subject to their jurisdiction.

Sec. 2. Power of Congress.—Congress shall have power to enforce this article by appropriate legislation. (Declared adopted by the Secretary of state Feb. 18, 1865)

1 Abb, (U. S,) 28; 1 Dill, C. R. 248.

ARTICLE XIV.

Sec. 1. Who are citizens.—All persons born or naturalized in the United States, and subjects to the jurisdiction thereof, are citizens of the United States and of the state wherein they reside. No state shall make or enforce any law which shall abridge the privileges or immunities of citizens of the United States; nor shall any state deprive any person of life, liberty, or property without due process of law, nor deny to any person within its jurisdiction the equal protection of the law.

Sec. 2. Representatives, how apportioned,—Representatives shall be apportioned among the several states according to their respective numbers: counting the whole number of persons in each state, excluding Indians not taxed, but when the right to vote at any election for the choice of electors for President and Vice-President of the United States, representatives in Congress, the executive and judical officers of a state, or the members of the legislature thereof is denied to any of the male inhabitants of such state being twenty-one years of age, and citizens of the United States, or in any way abridge, except for participation in the rebellion or other crime, the basis of representation therein shall be reduced in the proportion which the number of such male citizens shall bear to the whole number of male citizens twenty-one years of age in such state.

Sec. 3. Eligibility to office, &c.—No person shall be Senator or Representative in Congress, or elector of President or Vice-President or hold any office civil or military, under the United States or under any state, who having previously taken the oath as a member of Congress or an officer of the United States, or as a member of any state legislature, or an executive or judical officer of any state, to support the constitution of the United States, shall have engaged in insurrection or rebellion against the same, or has given aid and comfort to the enemies thereof.

But Congress may by a vote of two thirds of each house remove such disability.

Sec. 4. Validity of public debt not to be questioned.—

The validity of the public debt of the United States authorized by law, including debts incurred for payment of pensions and bounties for services in suppressing insurrection or rebellion against the United States shall not be questioned. But neither the United States nor any State shall assume or pay any debt or obligation incurred in aid of insurrection or rebellion against the United States, or any claim for the loss or emancipation of any slave, but all such debts, obligations and claims shall be held illegal and void.

Sec. 5 That Congress shall have power to enforce by appropriate legislation the provisions of this article.

(Declared adopted by the Secretary of State, 28th of July, 1869.)

44 Alo. 367; Cal. 658; 1 Dill. C. R. 344.

ARTICLE XV.

Sec. 1. In regard to suffrage,—The rights of citizens of the United States to vote shall not be denied or abridged by the United States, or any State, on account of race or color, or previous condition of servitude.

Sec. 2. Congress shall have power to enforce this article by the appropriate legislation.

(Declared adopted by the Secretary of State, March 30, 1870.

NATIONAL PLATFORMS.

Before the nomination of Gen. Jackson by the Legislature of Tennessee, Candidates for President and Vice President were nominated by "Congressional Caucus", so that National conventions are of comparatively recent origin, as also party platforms.

U..S. Anti-masonic convention–

The United States Anti-masonic convention was held at Philadelphia in September, 1830, when the following resolution was adopted ; "Resolved, that it is recommended to the people of the United States, opposed to Secret Societies, to meet in convention on Monday the 26th day of September, 1831, at the city of Baltimore by delegates equal in number to their representatives in both houses of Congress, to make nominations of suitable candidates for the office of President and Vice-President, to be supported at the next election, and for the transaction of such other business as the cause of Anti-Masonry may require."

The Democratic convention met at Baltimore in May, 1832, when the following platform was adopted ;

" Resolved, that each state be entitled, in the nomination to be made for the Vice-Presidency, to a number of votes equal to the number to which they will be entitled in the electoral colleges, under the new apportionment in voting for President and Vice-President ; and that two-thirds of the whole number of the votes in the convention shall be necessary to constitute a choice."

The following resolution was adopted :

. " Resolved that it be recommended to the several delegations in this convention, in place of a general address from this body to the people 'of the United States, to make such explanation by address, report, or otherwise, to their respective constituents of the object, proceedings and result 'of them eeting, as they may deem expedient.

Henry Clay platform of 1831 :

" The political history of the union for the last three years exhibits a series of measures plainly dictated in all their principal features by blind cupidity or vindictive party spirit, marked throughout by a disregard of good policy, justice, and every high and generous sentiment, and terminating in a dissolution of the cabinet under circumstances more discreditable than any of the kind to be met with in the annals of the civilized world."

" On the great subjects of internal policy, the course of the President has been so inconsistent and vacillating, that it is impossible for any party to place confidence in his character, or to consider him as a true and effective friend.   By avowing his approbation of a judicious tariff, at the same time recommending to Congress precisely the same policy which had been adopted as the best plan of attack by the opponents of that measure; by admitting the constitutionality and expediency of internal improvements of a National character, and at the same moment negotiating the most important bills of this discription which were presented to him by Congress, the President has shown that he is either a secret enemy to the system, or that he is willing to sacrifice the most important national objects in a vain attempt to conciliate the conflicting interest, or rather adverse party feeling and opinions of different sections of the country."

The young men of the Clay party held a convention at the Capital May 11, 1832, when the following platform was adopted ;
" Resolved, that an adequate protection to American Industry is indispensable to the prosperity of the country ; and that an abandonment of the policy at this period would be attended with consequences ruinous to the best interests of the Nation."
" Resolved, that a uniform system of internal improvements, sustained and supported by the general government, is calculated to secure, in the highest degree, the harmony, the strength and the permanency of the Republic.
" Resolved, that the indiscriminate removal of public officers, for a mere difference of political opinion, is a gross abuse of power ; and that the doctrines lately boldly preached in the United States Senate, that "to the victors belong the spoils of the vanquished," is detrimental to the interests, corrupting to the morals, and dangerous to the liberties of the people of this country."

The Democratic convention which met at Baltimore, May 1835, unanimously nominated Van Buren for President.   No platform was adopted by this convention.

The Whig National convention met at Harrisburg, Pa. December 4, 1839, and nominated William Henry Harrison for President.   It adopted no platform.
A convention of abolitionists met at Warsaw, N. Y. Nov. 13, 1839. James G. Birney, of New York, and Francis J. Lemoyne, of Pa. were nominated for President and Vice-President. The following platform was adopted :
" Resolved, that in our judgment every consideration of duty and expediency which ought to control the action of Christian freemen, requires of the abolitionists of the U. S. to organize a distinct and independent political party, embracing all the necessary means for nominating Candidates for office and sustaining them by public suffrage."
A Democratic National convention met at Baltimore, May 5. 1840. The following platform was adopted :

"1. Resolved, that the Federal Government is one of limited pow-ers, derived solely from the constitution, ard the grants of power shown therein ought to be strictly construed by all the departments and agents of the government, and that it is inexpedient and danger-ous, to exercise doubtful constitutional powers."

"2. Resolved, that the constitution does not confer authority upon the general government the power to commence or carry on a general system of internal improvement."

"3. Resolved, that the constitution does not confer authority upon the Federal Government, directly or indirectly, to assume the debts of the several states, contracted for local internal improvements or other state purposes; nor would such assumption be just or expedient."

"4. Resolved, that justice and sound policy forbid the Federal Gov-ernment to foster one branch of industry to the detriment of another portion of our common Country—that every citizen and every section of the country has a right to demand and insist upon an ample protec-tion of persons and property from domestic violence or foreign aggres-sion."

"5. Resolved, that it is the duty of every branch of the government to enforce and practice the most rigid economy in conducting our pub-lic affairs, and that no more revenue ought to be raised than is required to defray the necessary expenses of the government."

"6. Resolved, that Congress has no power to charter a United States Bank, that we believe such an institution one of deadly hostility to the best interests of the country, dangerous to our republican institutions and the liberties of the people, and calculated to place the business of the country within the control of a concentrated money power, and a-bove the laws and the will of the people."

"7. Resolved, that Congress has no power under the constitution, to interfere with or control the domestic constitutions of the several states; and that such states are the sole and proper judges of every thing pertaining to their own affairs, not prohibited by the constitu-tion; that all efforts, by abolitionists or others, made to induce con-gress to interfere with the questions of slavery, or to take incipient steps in relation thereto, are calculated to lead to the most alarming and dangerous consequences, and that all such efforts have an inevita-ble tendency to diminish the happiness of the people, and endanger the stability and permanency of the Union, and ought not to be counte-nanced by any friend to our Political Institutions."

"8. Resolved, that the separation of moneys of the Government from banking institutions is indispensable for the safety of the funds of the government and the rights of the people.

"9. Resolved, that the liberal principles embodied by Jefferson in the Declaration of Independence, and sanctioned in the constitution, which makes ours the land of liberty and the asylum of the oppressed of every nation, have ever been cardinal principles in the democratic faith; and every attempt to abridge the present privilege of becoming citizens, and the owners of soil among us, ought to be resisted with the same spirit which swept the Alien and Sedition Laws from our statute book."

"Whereas, several of the states which have nominated Martin Van Buren as Candidate for the Presidency, have put in nomination differ-ent individuals as Candidates for Vice-President, thus indicating a di-versity of opinion as to the person best entitled to the nomination and whereas some of the said states are not represented in this convention, therefore,

"Resolved, that the convention deem it expedient at the present time not to choose between the individuals in nomination, but to leave the decision to their Democratic fellow-citizens in the several states, trusting that before the election shall take place, their opinions will become so concentrated as to secure the choice of a Vice-President by the Electoral College."

The Whig National convention met at Baltimore, May 1, 1844.

The following platform was adopted ;

" Resolved, that these principles may be summed as comprising a well regulated National Currency—a tariff for revenue to defray the necessary expenses of the government, and discriminating with special reference to the protection of the domestic labor of the country—the distribution of the proceeds from the sales of the Public Lands—a single term for the Presidency—a reform of executive usurpation—and generally such an administration of the affairs of the country, as shall impart to every branch of the public service the greatest practicable efficiency, controlled by a well-regulated and wise economy."

A Democratic National Convention met at Baltimore, May 27, 1844, when the following platform was adopted ;

" Resolved, that the proceeds of the Public Lands ought to be sacredly applied to the national objects specified in the constitution, and that we are opposed to the laws lately adopted and to any law for the distribution of such proceeds among the several states, as alike inexpedient in policy and repugnant to the constitution."

" Resolved, that we are decidedly opposed to taking from the President the qualified veto power by which he is enabled under restrictions and responsibilities amply sufficient to guard the public interest, to suspend the passage of a bill, whose merits cannot secure the approval of two-thirds of the Senate and House of Representatives until the judgment of the people can be obtained thereon, and which has thrice saved the American people from the corrupt and tyrannical domination of the Bank of the United States."

" Resolved, that our title to the whole of the Territory of Oregon is clear and unquestionable ; that no portion of the same ought not to be ceded to England or any other power ; and that the reoccupation of Oregon and the reannexation of Texas at the earliest practicable period are great American measures, which this convention recommends to the cordial support of the Democracy of the Union."

The Liberty party held a convention at Buffalo, August 30, 1843. James G. Birney was nominated for President, and Thomas Morris for Vice-President. The following platform was adopted ;

" Resolved, that human brotherhood is a cardinal principle of true

Democracy, as well as of pure christianity, which spurns all inconsistent limitations; and neither the political party which repudiates it nor the political system which is not based upon it, can be truly Democratic or permanent.

"Resolved, that the Liberty Party, placing itself upon this broad principle, will demand the absolute and unqualified divorce of the general Government from slavery, and also the restoration of equality of rights, among men, in every state where the party exists, or may exist.

"Resolved, that the Liberty Party has not been organized for any temporary purposes by interested politicians, but has arisen from among the people in consequence of a conviction, hourly gaining ground, that no other party in the country represents the true principles of American liberty, or the true spirit of the constitution of the United States.

"Resolved, that the Liberty Party has not been organized merely for the overthrow of slavery; its first decided efforts must, indeed be directed against slaveholding as the grossest and most revolting manifestation of despotism, but it will also carry out the principle of equal rights into all its practical consequences and applications, and support every just measure conductive to individual and social freedom.

"Resolved, that the Liberty Party is not a sectional party but a national party; was not originated in a desire to accomplish a single object, but in a comprehensive regard to the great interests of the whole country; is not a new party, nor a third party, but is the party of 1776 reviving the principles of that memorable era, and striving to carry, them into practical application.

"Resolved, that it was understood in the times of the declaration and the constitution, that the existence of slavery in some of the states, was a derogation of the principles of American Liberty, and a deep stain upon the character of the country, and the implied faith of the states and the Nation was pledged that slavery should never be extended beyond its then existing limits, but should be gradually, and yet at no distant day, wholly abolished by state authority.

Resolved, that the faith of the states and the Nation, thus pledged, was most nobly redeemed by the voluntary abolition of slavery in several of the states, and by the adoption of the ordinance of 1787, for the government of the Territory northwest of the river Ohio, then the only Territory in the United States, and consequently the only territory subject in this respect to the control of congress by which ordinance slavery was forever excluded from the vast regions which now comprise the states of Ohio, Indiana, Illinois, Michigan, and the Territory of Wisconsin, and an incapacity to bear up any other than freemen, was impressed on the soil itself.

Resolved, that the faith of the states and the Nation thus pledged, has been shamefully violated by the omission on the part of many of the states, to take any measures whatever for the abolition of slavery within their respective limits; by the continuance of slavery in the District of Columbia, and in the Territories of Louisiana and Florida; by the legislation of Congress; by the protection afforded by national legislation and negation to slaveholding in American vessels, on the high seas employed in the coastwise slave traffic; and by the extension of slavery far beyond its original limits, by acts of congress, admitting new slave states into the Union."

"Resolved, that the fundamental truths of the Declaration of Inde-

pendence, that all men are endowed by their Creator with certain inalienable rights, among which are life, liberty and the pursuit of happiness, was made the fundamental law of our National Government by
that amendment of the constitution which declares that no person shall
be deprived of life, liberty or property, without due process of law.

" Resolved, that we recognize as sound, the doctrine maintained by
slaveholding jurists, that slavery is against natural rights, and strictly
local, and that its existence and continuance rests on no other support
than state legislation, and not on any authority of Congress.

" Resolved, that the general government has under the constitution
no power to establish or continue slavery anywhere, and therefore that
all treaties and acts of Congress establishing, continuing or favoring
slavery in the District of Columbia, in the Territory of Florida, or on
the high seas, are unconstitutional, and all attempts to hold men as
property, within the limits of exclusive national jurisdiction ought to
be prohibited by law.

" Resolved, that the provision of the constitution of the United States,
which confers extraordinary political powers on owners of slaves, and
thereby constituting the two hundred and fifty thousand slaveholders
in the slave states a privileged aristocracy ; and the provision for the
reclamation of fugitive slaves from service are Anti-Republican in
their character, dangerous to the liberties of the people, and ought to
be abrogated.

" Resolved, that the practical operation of the second of those provisions is seen in the enactment of the act of congress respecting persons
escaping from their masters, which act, if the construction given to it
by the Supreme Court of the United States in the case of Prigg vs.
Pennsylvania, be correct, nullifies the habeas corpus acts of all the
states, takes away the whole legal security of personal freedom, and
ought therefore to be immediately repealed.

" Resolved, that the peculiar patronage and support hitherto extended to slavery and slaveholding, by the general government, ought to
be immediately withdrawn, and the example and influence of national
authority ought to be arrayed on the side of Liberty and Freedom.

" Resolved, that the practice of the general government, which pre-
vails in the slave states, of employing slaves upon the public works,
instead of free laborers, and paying aristocratic masters, with a view
to secure or reward political services, is utterly indefensible and ought
to be abandoned.

" Resolved, that freedom of speech, and of the press, and the right
of petition, and the right of trial by jury, are sacred and inviolable ;
and that all rules, regulations and laws, in derogation of either are oppressive, unconstitutional, and not to be endured by free people.

" Resolved, that we regard voting in an eminent degree, as a moral
and religious duty, which, when exercised, should be by voting for
those who will do all in their power for immediate emancipation.

" Resolved, that this convention recommend to the friends of liberty
in all those Free States where any inequality of rights and privileges
exists on account of color, to employ their utmost energies to remove
all such remnants and effects of the slave system.

" Whereas the constitution of these United States is a series of
agreements, covenants, or contracts between the people of the United
States each with all, and all with each ; and

" Whereas, it is a principle of Universal Morality, that the moral laws of the creator are paramount to all human laws; or, in the language of an apostle, that " we ought to obey God rather than men ;" and,

" Whereas, the principle of common law—that any contract, covenant, or agreement to do an act derogatory to natural right, is vitiated and annulled by its inherent immorality—has been recognized by one of the justices of the Supreme Court, of the United States, who in a recent case expressly holds that any contract, that rests upon such a basis is void, and

" Whereas, the third clause of the second section of the fourth article of the constitution of the United States, when construed as providing for the surrender of a Fugitive Slave, does rest upon such a basis, in that it is a contract to rob a man of a natural right—namely, his natural right to his own liberty, and is, therefore, absolutely void, therefore,

" Resolved, that we hereby give it to be distinctly understood by .nis nation and the world, that, as abolitionists, considering that the strength of our cause lies in its righteousness, and our hope for it in our conformity to the laws of God, and our respect for the rights of man, we owe it to the sovereign Ruler of the universe, as a proof of our allegiance to him, in all our civil relations and offices, whether as private citizens or as public functionaries sworn to support the constitution of the United States to regard and to treat the third clause of the fourth article of that instrument, whether applied to the case of a fugitive slave, as utterly null and void and consequently as forming no part of the constitution of the United States, whenever we are called upon or sworn to support it."

Resolved, that the power given to congress by the constitution, to provide for calling out the militia to suppress insurrection, does not make it the duty of the government to maintain slavery by military force, much less does it make it the duty of the citizens to form a part of such military force. When freemen unsheath the sword it should be to strike for Liberty, not for despotism.

Resolved. That to preserve the peace of the citizens, and secure the blessings of freedom, the Legislature of each of the Free States ought to keep in force suitable statutes rendering it penal for any of its inhabitants to transport, or aid in transporting from such state any person sought to be thus transported, merely because subject to the slave laws of any other state; this remnant of independence being accorded to the Free States, by the decision of the Supreme Court, in the case of Prigg vs. the state of Pennsylvania.

The Whig National Convention 1848 :

Resolved. That no candidate shall be entitled to receive the nomination of this convention for President or Vice-President, unless he has given assurances that he will abide by and support the nomination ; that if nominated he will accept the nomination; that he will consider himself the candidate of the Whigs, and use all proper influence to bring into practical operation the principles and measures of the Whig Party.

Resolved. That as the first duty of the representatives of the Whig party is to preserve the principles and integrity of the party, the claims of no candidate can be considered by this convention unless such candidate stands pledged to support, in good faith, the nominees and to be the exponent of the Whig Principles.

"Resolved. That the Whig Party, through its representatives here agrees to abide by the nomination of Gen. Zachary Taylor, on condition that he will accept the nomination as the candidate of the Whig Party, and adhere to its great fundamental principles—no extension of slave terntbry—no acquisition of foreign territory by conquest—protection to American industry, and opposition to executive usurpation."

"Resolved. That Gen. Zachary Taylor, of Louisianna, and Millard Fillmore, of New York, be, and they are hereby unanimously nominated as the Whig candidates for President and Vice-President of the United States."

"Resolved. That while all power is denied to Congress, under the constitution to control, or in any way interfere with the institution of slavery within the several states of this union, it nevertheless has the power and it is the duty of Congress to prohibit the introduction or existence of slavery in any territory now possessed, which may hereafter be acquired, by the United States." The convention failed to pass any of the above resolutions and ran Gen. Taylor without a platform.

The Democratic platform 1848.

"1st, Resolved. That the American Democracy place their trust in the intelligence, the patriotism, and the discriminating justice of the American people."

"2nd, Resolved. That we regard this as a distinctive feature of our political creed, which we are proud to maintain before the world, as the great moral element in a form of government springing from and upheld by the popular will; and we contrast it with the creed and practice of Federalism, under whatever name or form, which seeks to palsy the will of the constituent, and which conceives no imposture too monstrous for the popular credulity."

"3d, Resolved. Therefore, that entertaining these views the democratic party of this union, through the delegates assembled in general convention of the states, coming together in a spirit of concord, of devotion to the doctrines and faith of a free representative government and appealing to their fellow-citizens for the rectitude of their intentions, renew and assert before the American people, the declaration of principle, avowed by them, on a former occasion, when in general conventions they presented their candidates for the popular suffrage."

"Resolved. That it is the duty of any branch of the Government, to enforce and practice the most rigid economy in consulting our public affairs, and that no more revenue ought to be raised than is required to defray the necessary expenses of the Government, and for the gradual but certain extinction of the debt created by the prosecution of a just and necessary war, after peaceful relations shall have been restored. And that the results of Democratic Legislation, in this and all other financial measures upon which issues have been made between the two political parties of the country, have demonstrated to candid and practical men of all parties, their soundness, safety and reliability in all business pursuits.

"Resolved. That the proceeds of the Public Lands ought to be sacredly applied to the national objects specified in the constitution; and that we are opposed to any law for the distribution of such proceeds among the States, as alike inexpedient in policy and repugnant to the Constitution."

"Resolved. That we are decidely opposed to taking from the President the qualified veto powers, by which he is enabled, under restrictions and responsibilities amply sufficient to guard the public interests, to suspend the passage of a bill whose merits cannot secure the approval of two-thirds of the Senate and House of Representatives until the judgment of the people can be obtained thereon, and which has saved the American people from the corrupt and tyrannical domination of the Bank of the United States, and from a corrupting system of general internal improvements,"

"Resolved. That the war with Mexico, provoked on her part, by years of insult and injury, was commenced by her army crossing the Rio Grande, attacking the American troops and invading our sister state of Texas, and that upon all the principles of patriotism and the laws of Nations, it is a just and necessary war on our part in which every American citizen should have shown himself on the side of his country, and neither morally or physically, by word or by deed, have given ' aid and comfort to the enemy."

Resolved. That we would be rejoiced at the assurance of a peace with Mexico, founded on just principles of indemnity for the past and security for the future; but that while the ratification of the liberal treaty offered to Mexico remains in doubt, it is the duty of the country to sustain the administration and to sustain the country in every measure necessary to provide for the vigorous prosecution of the war, should that treaty be rejected."

"Resolved. That the officers and soldiers who have carried the arms of their country into Mexico, have crowned it with imperishable glory. Their unconquerable courage, their daring enterprise, their unfaltering perseverance and fortitude when assailed on all sides by innumerable foes, and that more formidable enemy—the disease of the climate—exalts their devoted patriotism into the highest heroism, and gives them a right to the profound gratitude of their country, and the admiration of the world."

"Resolved. That the Democratic National Convention of 30 States composing the American Republic, tender their fraternal congratulations to the National Convention of the Republic of France, now assembled as the free suffrage Representatives of the sovereignty of thirty-five millions of Republicans, to establish government on those eternal principles of equal rights for which their Lafayette and our Washington fought side by side in the struggle for our National Independence; and we would especially convey to them and to the whole people of France, our earnest wishes for the consolidation of their liberties, through the wisdom that shall guide their councils, on the basis of a Democratic Constitution, not derived from the grants or concessions of kings or dynasties, but originating from the only true source of political power recognized in the State of this Union; the inherent and inalienable rights of the people in their sovereign capacity to make and to amend their form of Government, in such manner as the welfare of the community may require."

"Resolved. That the recent development of this grand political truth, of the sovereignty of the people and their capacity and power for self Government, which is prostrating thrones and erecting Republics on the ruins of despotism in the old world ; we feel that a high and sacred duty is devolved, with increased responsibility, upon the democratic party of this country, as the party of the people, to sustain and advance among us, Constitutional Liberty, equality and fraternity, by continuing to resist all monopolies and exclusive Legislation for the benefit of the few at the expense of the many, and by a vigilant and constant adherence to those principles and compromises of the Constitution, which are broad enough and strong enough to embrace and uphold the Union as it was, the Union as it is, and the Union as it shall be, in the full expansion of the energies and capacity of this great and progressive people."

"Resolved. That a copy of these resolutions be forwarded through the American minister at Paris, to the National Convention of the Republic of France."

"Resolved. That the fruits of the great political triumph of 1844, which elected James K. Polk and George M. Dallas, President and Vice-President of the United States, have fulfilled the hopes of the Democracy of the Union in defeating the declared purposes of their opponents in creating a National Bank, in preventing the corrupt and unconstitutional distribution of the land proceeds from the common treasury of the Union for local purposes, in protecting the currency and labor of the country from the ruinous fluctuations, and guarding the money of the country for the use of the people by the establishment of the constitutional treasury; in the noble impulse given to the cause of Free Trade by the repeal of the tariff of 42 and the creation of the more equal, honest, and productive tariff of 1846, and that in our opinion it would be a fatal error to weaken the bands of a political organization by which these great reforms have been achieved and risk them in the hands of their known adversaries, with whatever delusive appeals they may solicit our surrender of that vigilance which is the only safe guard of liberty."

"Resolved. That the confidence of the Democracy of the Union, in the principles, capacity, firmness and integrity of James K. Polk, manifested by his nomination and election in 1844, has been signally justified by the strictness of his adherence to sound democratic doctrines, by the purity of purpose by the energy and ability which have characterized his administration in all our affairs at home and abroad; that we tender to him our cordial congratulations upon the brilliant success which has hitherto crowned his patriotic efforts and reassure him in advance that at the expiration of his Presidential term he will carry with him to his retirement, the esteem, respect, and admiration of a grateful country."

"Resolved. That this convention hereby present to the people of the United States, Lewis Cass, of Michigan, as the Candidate of the Democratic party for the office of President, and William O. Butler, of Kentucky, for Vice-President of the United States."

The Free Soil party 1848,—Buffalo platform.

Whereas, we have assembled in convention, as a Union of freemen, for the sake of freedom, forgetting all past political differences in a common resolve to maintain the rights of free labor against the aggressions of the slave power, and to secure free soil to a free people."

"And Whereas. The political conventions recently assembled at Baltimore and Philadelphia, the one stifling the voice of a great Constituency, entitled to be heard in its deliberations, and the other abandoning its distinctive principles for mere availability, have dissolved the National party organizations heretofore existing, by nominating for the Chief Magistracy of the United States, under the slaveholding dictation, candidates, neither of whom can be supported by the opponents of slavery extension without a sacrifice of consistency, duty, and self respect.

"And Whereas. These nominations so made, furnish the occasion, and demonstrate the necessity of the Union of the people under the banner of Free Democracy, in a solemn and formal declaration of their independence of the slave power, and of their fixed determination to rescue the Federal Government from its control ;

"Resolved. Therefore, that we, the people here assembled, remembering the example of our fathers in the days of the first Declaration of Independence, putting our trust in God for the triumph of our cause and invoking his guidance in our endeavors to advance it, do now plant ourselves upon the National Platform of Freedom, in opposition to the sectional platform of slavery."

"Resolved. That slavery in the several States of this Union which recognize its existence, depends upon the state laws alone which cannot be repealed or modified by the Federal Government, and for which laws, that Government is not responsible. We therefore propose no interference by Congress with slavery within the limits of any State."

"Resolved. That the proviso of Jefferson ; to prohibit the existence of slavery after 1800, in all the Territories of the United States, southern and northern; the votes of six states and sixteen delegates, in the Congress of 1784, for the proviso, to three States and seven delegates against it; the actual exclusion of slavery from the northwestern Territory, by the ordinance of 1787, unanimously adopted by the States in Congress; and the entire history of that period, clearly shows that it was the settled policy of the nation not to extend, nationalize or encourage, but to limit, localize, and discourage slavery ; and to this policy, which should never have been departed from, the Government ought to return."

"Resolved. That our fathers ordained the Constitution of the United States, in order, among other great National objects, to establish justice, promote the general welfare, and secure the blessings of liberty ; but expressly denied to the Federal Government, which they created, all Constitutional power to deprive any person of life, liberty, or property, without due legal process."

"Resolved. That in the judgment of this convention, Congress has no more power to make a slave, than to make a king; no more power to institute or establish slavery, than to institute or establish a monarchy; no such power can be found among those specifically conferred by the Constitution or derived by just implications from them.

"Resolved. That it is the duty of the Federal Government to relieve itself from all responsibility for the existence or continuance of slavery wherever the Government possesses Constitutional authority to legislate on that subject, and it is thus responsible for its existence."

"Resolved. That the true, and in the judgment of this convention, the only safe means of preventing the extension of slavery into Territory now Free, is to prohibit its extension in all such Territory by an act of Congress.

"Resolved. That we accept the issue which the slave power has forced upon us; and to their demand for more slave States, and more slave Territory, our calm but final answer is, no more slave States, and no more slave Territory. Let the soil of our extensive domains be kept free for the hardy Pioneers of our own land, and the oppressed and banished of other lands, seeking homes of comfort and fields of enterprise in the new world."

"Resolved. That the bill lately reported by the Committee of eight in the Senate of the United States, was no compromise, but an absolute surrender of the rights of the Non-Slaveholders of all the States; and while we rejoice to know that a measure which, while opening the door for the introduction of slavery into the Territories now free, would also have opened the door to litigation and strife among the future inhabitants thereof, to the ruin of their peace and prosperity, was defeated in the House of Representatives, its passage, in hot haste, by a Majority embracing several Senators who voted in open violation of the known will of their constituents, should warn the people to see to it, that their Representatives be not suffered to betray them. There must be no more Compromises with slavery: if made they must be repealed."

"Resolved. That we demand freedom and established Institutions for our brethern in Oregon, now exposed to hardships, peril and massacre by the reckless hostility of the slave power to the establishment of Free Government for Free Territories; and not only for them, but for our new brethern in California and New-Mexico."

"Resolved. It is due not only to this occasion, but to the whole people of the United States, that we should also declare ourselves on certain other questions of National Policy: therefore."

"Resolved. That we demand cheap postage for the people; a retrenchment of the expenses and patronage of the Federal Government; abolition of all unnecessary offices and salaries; and the election by the people of all civil officers in the service of the Government, so far as the same may be practicable."

"Resolved. That River and Harbor improvements, when demanded by the safety and convenience of commerce, with foreign nations, or among the several States are objects of National Concern, and that it is the duty of Congress, in the exercise of its Constitutional powers, to provide therefor."

"Resolved. That the free grant to actual settlers, in consideration of the expenses they incur in making settlements in the wilderness, which are usually fully equal to their actual cost, and of the public benefits resulting therefrom, of reasonable portions of the public lands under suitable limitations, is a wise and just measure of public policy, which will promote in various ways the interests of all the States of this Union, and we therefore recommend it to the favorable consideration of the American people."

"Resolved. That the obligations of honor and patriotism require the earliest practicable payment of the national debt, and we are therefore in favor of such tariff or duties as will raise revenue adequate to defray the necessary expenses of the Federal Government, and to pay annual installments of our debt, and the interests thereon."

"Resolved. That we inscribe on our banner "Free Soil, Free Speech, Free Labor, and Free Men," and under it we will fight on and fight ever, until a triumphant victory, shall reward our exertions.

The Whig National convention 1852,—Whig platform.

"The Whigs of the United States, in convention assembled, adhering to the great conservative principles by which they are controlled and governed, and now as ever relying upon the intelligence of the American people, with an abiding confidence in their capacity for self-government, and their devotion to the constitution and the Union, do proclaim the following as the political sentiments and determination for the establishment and maintenance of which their National organization as a party was effected."

"First. The government of the United States is of a limited character, and it is confined to the exercises of powers expressly granted by the constitution, and such as may be necessary and proper for carrying the granted powers into full execution, and that powers not granted or necessarily implied are reserved to the States respectively and to the people."

"Second. That the State governments should be held secure to their reserved rights, and the General Government sustained on its constitutional powers and that the Union should be revered and watched over as the palladium of our liberties.

"Third. That while struggling Freedom every where enlists the warmest sympathy of the Whig party, we still adhere to the doctrines of the Father of his Country as announced in his Farewell Address, of keeping ourselves free from all entangling alliances with foreign countries and of never quitting our own to stand upon foreign ground; that our mission as a republic is not to propagate our opinions, or impose on other countries our form of government, by artifice or force; but to teach by example, and show, by our success, moderation, and justice, the blessings of Self-government, and the advantage of Free Institutions."

"Fourth. That as the people make and control the government, they should obey its constitution, laws, and treaties as they would retain their self-respect, and the respect which they claim and will enforce from foreign powers."

"Fifth. Government should be conducted on principles of the strictest economy; and revenue sufficient for the expense thereof, in time, ought to be derived mainly from a duty on imports, and not from direct taxes; and on laying such duties sound policy requires a just discrimination, and, when practicable, by specific duties, whereby suitable encouragement may be afforded to American industry, equally to all classes and to all portions of the country; and economical ad-

ministration of the government, in time of peace, ought to be derived
from duties on imports, and not from direct taxation; and in laying
such duties, sound policy requires a just discrimination, whereby suitable encouragement may be afforded to American industry, equally to
all classes and to all parts of the country.

"Sixth. The constitution vests in Congress the power to open and
repair harbors, and remove obstructions from navigable rivers, whenever such improvements are necessary for the common defence, and for
the protection and facility of Commerce with foreign Nations, or among
the States—said improvements being in every instance National and
General in their character.

"Seventh. The Federal and State Governments are parts of one system, alike necessary for the common prosperity, peace and security, and
ought to be regarded alike with a cordial, habitual and immovable attachment. Respect for the authority of each, and acquiescence in the
just constitutional measures of each, are duties required, by the
plainest considerations of national, state, and individual welfare.

"Eighth. That the series of acts of the 32d Congress, the act
known as the Fugitive Slave law included are received and acquiesced
in by the Whig party of the United States as a settlement in principles
and substance of the dangerous and exciting questions which they
embrace; and, so far as they are concerned, we will maintain them,
and insist upon their strict enforcement, until time and experience shall
demonstrate the necessity of further Legislation to guard against the
evasion of the laws on the one hand and the abuse of their powers on
the other—not impairing their present efficiency; and we deprecate all
further agitation of the question thus settled as dangerous to our peace,
and will discountenance efforts, to continue or renew such agitation,
whenever, wherever, or however the attempt may be made; and we
will maintain this system as essential to the nationality of the Whig
party, and the integrity of the Union.

The Democratic platform—1852.

"Resolved. That it is the duty of every branch of the government
to enforce and practice the most rigid economy in conducting our public affairs, and that no more revenue ought to be raised than is required
to defray the necessary expenses of the Government, and for the
gradual but certain extinction of the public debt."

"Resolved. That Congress has no power to charter a National
Bank; that we believe such an Institution one of deadly hostility to
the best interests of the country; dangerous to our republican Institutions and the liberties of the people, and calculated to place the business of the country within the control of a concentrated money power,
and that above the laws and will of the people; and that the results of
Democratic legislation, in this and all other financial measures, upon
which issues have been made between the two political parties of the
country have demonstrated to candid and practical men of all parties,
their soundness, safety, and utility in all business pursuits."

"Resolved. That the separation of the moneys of the Government
from Banking Institutions, is indispensable for the safety of the funds
of the Government, and the rights of the people."

" Resolved. That the liberal principles embodied by Jefferson in the Declaration of Independence, and sanctioned in the constitution, which makes ours the land of liberty, and the asylum of the oppressed of every nation have ever been cardinal principles in the Democratic faith and every attempt to abridge their privilege of becoming citizens and the owners of the soil among us, ought to be resisted with the same spirit which swept the Alien and Sedition laws from our statute book.

"Resolved. That Congress has no power under the constitution to interfere with, or control the domestic institutions of the several states, and that such states are the sole and proper judges of everything appertaining to their own affairs, and not prohibited by the constitution; that all the efforts of the Abolitionists or others, made to induce Congress to interfere with questions of slavery or take incipient steps in relation thereto, are calculated to lead to the most alarming and dangerous consequences; and that all such efforts have an inevitable tendency to diminish the happiness of the people, and endanger the stability and permanency of the Union, and ought not to be countenanced by any friend of our political institutions. "

"Resolved. That the foregoing proposition covers, and is intended to embrace the whole subject of the Slavery agitation in Congress; and therefore, the Democratic party of the Union standing on its national platform, will abide by, and adhere to, a faithful execution of the acts known as the Compromise Measures settled by the last Congress—the act for the reclaiming fugitives from service or labor included; which act being designed to carry out an expressed provision of the constitution cannot with fidelity thereto be repealed, nor so changed as to destroy or impair its efficiency."

"Resolved. That the Democratic party will resist all attempts at renewing in Congress, or out of it, the agitation of the Slavery question, under whatever shape or color the attempt may be made."

"Resolved. That the Democratic party will faithfully abide by and uphold the principles laid down in the Kentucky and Virginia resolutions of 1792 and 1798, and in the report of Mr. Madison to the Virginia Legislature in 1799; that it adopts those principles as constituting one of the main foundations of its political creed and is resolved to carry them out in their obvious meaning and import."

"Resolved. That the war with Mexico * * * * and earnestly desire for her all the blessings and prosperity which we enjoy under Republican Institutions, and we congratulate the American people on the results of that war which have so manifestly justified the policy and conduct of the Democratic party, and insured to the United States indemnity for the past, and security for the future. "

"Resolved. That in view of the condition of popular institutions in the old world, a high and sacred duty is devolved with increased responsibility upon the Democracy of this country, as the party of the people, to uphold and maintain the rights of every state, and thereby the union of the states, and sustain and advance among them constitutional liberty, by continuing to resist all monopolies and exclusive legislation for the benefit of the few at the expense of the many, and by a vigilant and constant adherence to those principles and compromises of the constitution, which are broad enough and strong enough to embrace and uphold the Union as it is, and the Union as it should be, in the full expansion of the energies and capacity of this great and progressive people."

The Free Soil platform, 1852.

"Having assembled in National Convention as the Democracy of the United States, united by a common resolve to maintain right against wrong, and Freedom against Slavery; confiding in the intelligence, patriotism, and discriminating justice of the American people, putting our trust in God for the triumph of our cause, and invoking his guidance in our endeavors to advance it, we now submit to the candid judgment of all men the following declaration of principles and measures:

"1st. That governments deriving their just powers from the consent of the governed, are instituted among men to secure to all those inalienable rights of life, liberty, and the pursuit of happiness with which they are endowed by their creator, and of which none can be deprived by valid legislation, except for crime."

"2. That the true mission of American Democracy is to maintain the Liberties of the people, the Sovereignty of the States and the perpetuity of the Union, by the impartial application to public affairs, without Sectional discriminations of the fundamental principles of human rights, strict justice and an ecomonical administration."

"3. That the Federal Government is one of limited powers, derived solely from the constitution, and the grants of power therein ought to be strictly construed by all the departments and agents of the government, and it is inexpedient and dangerous to exercise doubtful constituional powers."

"4. That the constitution of the United States, ordained to form a more perfect Union, to establish justice and secure the blessings of Liberty, expressly denies to the General Government all power to deprive any person of life, liberty or property without due process of law; and therefore, the Government having no more power to establish slavery than to establish a monarchy should at once proceed to relieve itself from all responsibility for the existence of slavery, wherever it possesses constitutional power to legislate for its extinction."

"5. That, to the persevering, and importunate demands of the slave power for more Slave States, new Slave Territories and the nationalization of Slavery, our distinct and final answer is—no more Slave States, no Slave Territory, no nationalized Slavery, and no national Legislation for the extradition of Slaves."

"6. That Slavery is a sin against God, and a crime against man, which no human enactment nor usage can make right, and that Christianity, Humanity, and Patriotism alike demand its abolition."

"7. That the Fugitive Slave Act of 1850 is repugnant to the constitution, to the principles of the common law, to the spirit of Christianity and to the sentiments of the civilized world. We therefore deny, its binding force upon the American people, and demand its immediate and total repeal."

"8. That the doctrine that any human law is a finality, and not subject to modification or repeal, is not in accordance with the creed of the founders of our Government, and is dangerous to the liberties of the people."

"9. That the Acts of congress, known as the compromise measures of 1850, by making the admission of a sovereign State contingent upon the adoption of other measures demanded by the special interest of Slavery; by their omission to guarantee freedom in the free Territories; by their attempt to impose Unconstitutional limitations on the power of Congress and the people—to admit new States; by their provisions for the assumption of Five Millions of the State debt of Texas, and for the payment of Five Millions more, and the concession of a large Territory to the same State under menace, as an inducement to the relinquishment of a groundless claim, and by their invasion of the Sovereignty of the States and the liberties of the people through the enactment of an unjust, oppressive, and unconstitutional Fugitive Slave Law, are proved to be inconsistent with all the principles and maxims of Democracy, and wholly inadequate to the settlement of the questions of which they are claimed to be an adjustment."

"10.   That no permanent settlement of the Slavery question can be looked for except in the practical recognition of the truth that Slavery is sectional and Freedom national; by the total separation of the General Government from Slavery, and the exercise of its legitimate—and constitutional influences on the side of Freedom; and by leaving to the States the whole subject of Slavery and the extradition of fugitives from service."

"11.   That all men have a natural right to a portion of the soil; and that as the use of the soil is indispensable to life, the right of all men to the soil is as sacred as their right to life itself."

"12.   That the Public Lands of the United States belong to the People, and should not be sold to individuals nor granted to corporations, but should be granted in limited quantities, free of costs, to landless settlers."

"13.   That a due regard for the Federal constitutions, a sound administrative policy, demand that the funds of the General Government be kept separate from Banking institutions; that inland and ocean postage should be reduced to the lowest possible point; that no more revenue should be raised than is required to defray the necessary expenses of the public service, and to pay off the public Debt; and that the power and patronage of the Government should be diminished, by the abolition of all the unnecessary offices, salaries, and privileges, and by the election, by the people, of all civil officers in the service of the United States, so far as may be consistent with the prompt and efficient transaction of the public business."

"14.   That River and Harbor improvements, when necessary to the safety and convenience of commerce with foreign nations, or among the several States, are objects of national concern; and it is the duty of congress, in the exercise of its constitutional powers, to provide for the same."

"15.   That emigrants and exiles from the old world should find a cordial welcome to homes of comfort and fields of enterprise in the new; and every attempt to abridge their privilege of becoming citizens and owners of the soil among us, ought to be resisted with inflexible determination."

"16.   That every nation has a clear right to alter or change its own government and to administer its own concerns in such manner as may best secure the rights and promote the happiness of the people; and foreign interference with that right is a dangerous violation of the law of nations, against which all independent governments should protest, and endeavor by all proper means to prevent; and especialy is it the duty of the American government, representing the Chief Republic of the world, to protest against, and by all proper means to prevent the intervention of kings and emperors against Nations seeking to establish for themselves Republican or constitutional Government."

"17. That the Independence of Hayti ought to be recognized by our Government, and our commercial relations with it placed on the footing of the most favored nations."

"18. That as by the Constitution "the citizens of each State shall be entitled to all the priveleges and immunities of citizens in the several States," the practice of imprisoning colored seamen of other States, while the vessels to which they belong lie in port, and refusing the exercise of the right to bring such cases before the Supreme Court of the United States, to test the legality of such proceedings, is a flagrant violation of the Constitution, and an invasion of the rights of citizens of other States, utterly inconsistent with the professions made by the slaveholders, that they wish the provisions of the Constitution, faithfully observed by every State in the Union.

"19. That we recommend the introduction into all treaties hereafter to be negotiated between the United States and Foreign Nations, of some provision for the amicable settlement of difficulties by a resort to decisive arbitrations.

"20. That the Free Democratic Party is not organized to aid either the Whig or Democratic Wing of the great Slave Compromise Party of the Nation, but to defeat them both; and that repudiating and renouncing both, as hopelessly corrupt and utterly unworthy of confidence, the purpose of the Free Democracy is to take possession of the Federal Government, and administer it for the better protection of the rights and interests of the whole people.

"21. That we inscribe on our banner, Free Soil, Free Speech Free-Labor and Free Men, and under it we will fight on and fight ever until a triumphant victory shall reward our exertions.

"22. That upon this Platform the Convention presents to the American people as a candidate for the office of President of the United States, John P. Hale of New Hampshire, and as a candidate for the office of Vice-President of the United States, George W. Julian, of Indiana, and earnestly commend them to the support of all Freemen and all parties."

The Republican Platform—1856.

"This Convention of Delegates, assembled in pursuance of a call addressed to the people of the United States, without regard to past political differences or divisions, who are opposed to the repeal of the Missouri Compromise, to the policy of the present Administration, to the extension of Slavery into Free Territory; in favor of admitting Kansas as a Free State, of restoring the action of the Federal Government to the principles of Washington and Jefferson, and who purpose to unite in presenting candidates for the offices of President and Vice-President do resolve as follows ;

"Resolved. That the maintenance of the principles promulgated in the Declaration of Independence and embodied in the Federal Constitution, is essential to the preservation of our Republican institutions, and that the Federal Constitution, the right of the States, and the Union of the States, shall be preserved."

. "Resolved. That with our Republican fathers we hold it to be a self-evident truth, that all men are endowed with the inalienable right to life, liberty, and the pursuit of happiness, and that the primary object and ulterior designs of our Federal Government were, to secure these rights to all persons within its exclusive jurisdiction; that as our Republican fathers, when they had abolished Slavery in all our National Territory ordained that no person should be deprived of life, liberty, or property, without due process of law, it becomes our duty to maintain this provision of the Constitution against all attempts to violate it for the purpose of establishing Slavery in any territory of the United States by positive legislation prohibiting its existence or extension therein. That we deny the authority of Congress, or a territorial legislature, of any individual, or association of individuals, to give legal existence to Slavery in any territory of the United States, while the present Constitution shall be maintained."

"Resolved. That the Constitution confers upon Congress, sovereign power over the territories of the United States for their government, and that in the exercise of this power it is both the right and the duty of Congress to prohibit in the territories those twin relics of barbarism —Polygamy and Slavery.

"Resolved. That while the Constitution of the United States was ordained and established by the people in order to form a more perfect Union, establish justice, insure domestic tranquility, provide for the common defense, and secure the blessings of liberty, and contains ample provisions for the protection of the life, liberty and property of every citizen, the dearest constitutional rights of the people of Kansas have been fraudulently and violently taken from them—their territory has been invaded by an armed force—spurious and pretended legislative, judicial and executive officers have been set over them, by whose usurped authority, sustained by the military power of the government, tyrannical and unconstitutional laws have been enacted and enforced —the rights of the people to keep and bear arms have been infringed —test oaths of an extraordinary and entangling nature have been imposed, as a condition of exercising the right of suffrage and holding office— the right of an accused person to a speedy and public trial by an impartial jury has been denied—the right of the people to be secure in their persons, houses, papers and effects against unreasonable searches and seizures has been violated—they have been deprived of life, liberty and property without due process of law—that the freedom of speech and of the press has been abridged—the right to choose their representatives been made of no effect—murders, robberies and arsons have been instigated and encouraged, and the offenders have been allowed to go unpunished—that all these things have been done with the knowledge, sanction and procurement of the present Administration, and that for this high crime against the Constitution, the Union, and Humanity, we arraign the Administration, the President, his advisers, agents, supporters, apologists and accessories either before or after the facts, before the country, and before the world, and that it is our fixed purpose to bring the actual perpetrators of these atrocious outrages, and their accomplices, to a sure and condign punishment hereafter.

"Resolved. That Kansas should be immediately admitted as a State of the Union, with her present Free Constitution, as at once the most effectual way of securing to her citizens the enjoyment of the rights and privileges to which they are entitled; and of ending the civil strife now raging in her territory.

"Resolved. That the highwayman's plea that "might makes right" embodied in the Ostend circular, was in every respect unworthy of American diplomacy, and would bring shame and dishonor upon any government or people that gave it their sanction. .

"Resolved. That a railroad to the Pacific Ocean, by the most central and practicable route, is imperatively demanded by the interest of the whole Country, and that the Federal Government ought to render immediate and efficient aid in its construction and, as an auxiliary thereto the immediate construction of an emigrant route on the line of the railroad.

"Resolved. That appropriations by Congress for the improvement of rivers and harbors, of a national character, required for the accommodation and security of our existing commerce, are authorized by the Constitution, and justified by the obligation of government to protect the lives and property of its citizens."

<hr>

The American Platform—1856.

" 1. An humble acknowledgment to the Supreme Being, for his protecting care vouchsafed to our fathers in their successful Revolutionary struggle, and hitherto manifested to us, their descendents, in the preservation of the liberties, the independence, and the Union of these States.

" 2. The perpetuation of the Federal Union and Constitution, as the palladium of our civil and religious liberties, and the only sure bulwarks of American Independence.

" 3. *Americans must rule America ;* and to this end *native-born citizens* should be selected for all State, Federal, and Municipal offices of government employment, in preference to all others. *Nevertheless,*

" 4. Persons born of American parents residing temporarily abroad, should be entitled to all the rights of *native-born* citizens.

" 5. No person should be selected for political station (whether of native or foreign birth), who recognizes any allegiance or obligation of any description to any foreign prince, potentate or power, or who refuses to recognize the Federal and State Constitutions (each within its sphere) as paramount to all other laws as rules of political action.

" 6. The unqualified recognition and maintenance of the reserved rights of the several States, and the cultivation of harmony and fraternal good will, between the citizens of the several States, and to this end non-interference by Congress with questions appertaining solely to the individual States, and non-intervention by each State with the affairs of any other State.

" 7. The recognition of the right of native-born and naturalized citizens of the United States, permanently residing in any territory thereof, to frame their Constitution and laws, and to regulate their domestic and social affairs in their own mode, subject only to the provisions of the Federal Constitution, with the privilege of admission into the Union, whenever they have the requisite population for one representative in Congress; *Provided, always,* that none but those who are citizens of the United States, under the Constitution and laws thereof, and who have a fixed residence in any such Territory, ought to participate in the formation of the Constitution, or in the enactment of laws for the said Territory or State.

"8. An enforcement of the principles that no State or Territory ought to admit others than citizens to the right of suffrage, or of holding political offices of the United States.

"9. A change in the laws of naturalization, making a continued residence of twenty-one years, of all not heretofore provided for, are indespensable requisites for citizenship hereafter, and excluding all paupers, and persons convicted of crime, from landing upon our shores but no interference with the vested rights of foreigners.

"10. Opposition to any Union between Church and State; no interference with religious faith or worship, and no test oaths for office.

"11. Free and thorough investigation into any and all alleged abuses of public functionaries, and a strict economy in public expenditures.

"12. The maintenance and enforcement of all laws constitutionally enacted until said laws shall be repealed, or shall be declared null and void by competent judicial authority.

"13. Opposition to the reckless and unwise policy of the present Administration in the general management of our national affairs, and more especially as shown in removing "Americans," (by designation) and conservatives in principle, from office, and placing foreigners and ultraists in their places, as shown in a truckling subserviency to the stronger, and an insolent and cowardly bravado toward the weaker powers; as shown in reopening sectional agitation, by the repeal of the Missouri Compromise; as shown in granting to unnaturalized foreigners the right of suffrage in Kansas and Nebraska; as shown in its vacillating course on the Kansas and Nebraska question; as shown in the corruption which pervades in some of the departments of the Government; as shown in disgracing meritorious naval officers through prejudice or caprice; and as shown in the blundering mismanagment of our foreign relations.

"14. Therefore, to render existing evils, and prevent the disastrous consequences otherwise resulting therefrom, we would build up the "American Party" upon the principles therein before stated.

"15. That each State Council shall have authority to amend their respective Constitutions, so as to abolish the several degrees, and substitute a pledge of honor, instead of other obligations for fellowship and admission into the party.

"16. A free and open discussion of all political principles embraced in our platform.

The Democratic National Platform—1856.

"Resolved. That the American Democracy place their trust in the intelligence, the patriotism, and the discriminating justice of the American people.

"Resolved. That we regard this as a destinctive feature of our political creed, which we are proud to maintain before the world as a great moral element in a form of government springing from and upheld by the popular will, and we contrast it with the creed and practice of Federalism, under whatever name or form, which seeks to palsy the will of the constituent, and which conceives no imposture too monstrous for the popular credulity.

"Resolved. Therefore, that entertaining these views, the Democratic party of this Union, through their delegates assembled in general convention, coming together in a spirit of concord, of devotion to the doctrines and faith of a free representative government, and appealing to their fellow-citizens for the rectitude of their intentions, renew and re-assert before the American people, the declarations of principles avowed by them, when, on former occasions, in general conventions they have presented their candidates for the popular suffrage.

1. That the Federal Government is one of limited power derived solely from the Constitution, and the grants of power made therein ought to be strictly construed by all the departments and agents of the government, and that it is inexpedient and dangerous to exercise doubtful constitutional powers.

2. That the Constitution does not confer upon the general government the power to commence and carry on a general system of internal improvements.

3. That the Constitution does not confer authority upon the Federal Government, directly or indirectly, to assume the debts of the several States, contracted for local and internal improvements, or other State purposes, nor would such assumption be just or expedient.

4. That justice and sound policy forbid the Federal Government to foster one branch of industry to the detriment of another, or to cherish the interests of one portion of our common country; that every citizen and every section of the country has a right to demand and insist upon an equality of rights and priveleges, and a complete and ample protection of persons and property from domestic violence and foreign aggression.

5. That it is the duty of every branch of the government to enforce and practice the most rigid economy in conducting our public affairs, and that no more revenue ought to be raised than is required to defray the necessary expenses of the Government, and gradual but certain extinction of the public debt.

6. That the proceeds of the public lands ought to be sacredly applied to the National objects specified in the Constitution, and that we are opposed to any law for the distribution of such proceeds among the States, as alike inexpedient in policy, and repugnant to the Constitution.

7. That Congress has no power to charter a National Bank, that we believe such an institution of deadly hostility to the best interest of this country, dangerous to our Republican institutions and the liberties of the people, and calculated to place the business of the country with in the control of a concentrated money power and above the laws and will of the people, and the results of the Democratic legislation in this and all financial measures upon which issues have been made between the two political parties of the country, have demonstrated to candid and practical men of all parties, their soundness, safety and utility in all business pursuits.

8. That the separation of the money of the Government from banking institutions is indispensable to the safety of the funds of the Government and the rights of the people.

9. That we are decidedly opposed to taking from the President the qualified veto power by which he is enabled, under restrictions and responsibilities amply sufficient to guard the public interests, to suspend the passage of a bill whose merits cannot secure the approval of

two-thirds of the Senate and House of Representatives, until the judgment of the people can be obtained thereon, and which has saved the American people from the corrupt and tyrannical dominion of the Bank of the United States, and from the corrupting system of general internal improvements.

10. That the liberal principles embodied by Jefferson in the Declaration of Independence, and sanctioned in the Constitution, which makes ours the land of Liberty and the asylum of the oppressed of every nation, have ever been cardinal principles in the Democratic faith; and every attempt to abridge the privilege of becoming citizens and the owners of soil among us ought to be resisted with the same spirit which swept the alien and sedition laws from our "Statute books." *And whereas*, since the foregoing declaration was uniformly adopted by our predecessors in National Convention, an adverse political and religious test has been secretly organized by a party claiming to be exclusively American, and it is proper that the American Democracy should clearly define its relations thereto; and declare its determined opposition to all secret political societies, by whatever name they may be called.

"Resolved. That the foundation of this Union of States having been laid in, and its prosperity, expansion, and pre-eminent example of a free government, built upon entire freedom in matters of religious concernment, and no respect of persons in regard to rank, or place of birth, no party can justly be deemed national, constitutional or in accordance with American principles, which bases its exclusive organization upon religious opinions and accidental birth-place. And hence a political crusade in the nineteenth century, and in the United States of America, against Catholics and foreign-born is neither justified by the past history nor future prospects of the country, nor in unison with the spirit of toleration, and enlightened freedom which peculiarly distinguished the American system of popular government.

"Resolved. That we reiterate with renewed energy of purpose the well considered declarations of former conventions upon the sectional issues of domestic Slavery, and concerning the reserved rights of the States."

1. That congress has no power under the constitution to interfere with or control the domestic institutions of the several States, and that all such States are the sole and proper judges of everything appertaining to their own affairs not prohibited by the constitution; that all efforts of the Abolitionists or others made to induce congress to interfere with the questions of Slavery, or to take inefficient steps in relation thereto, are calculated to lead to the most alarming and dangerous consequences, and that all such efforts have an inevitable tendency to diminish the happiness of the people and endanger the stability and permacy of the Union, and ought not to be countenanced by any friend of our political institutions.

2. That the foregoing proposition covers and was intended to embrace the whole subject of Slavery agitation in congress, and therefore the Democratic party of the Union, standing on its national platform, will abide by and adhere to a faithful execution of the acts known as the Compromise measures settled by the congress of 1850: "the act for reclaiming fugitives from service or labor included; which act, being designed to carry out an express provision of the constitution, cannot, with fidelity thereto be repealed, or so changed as to destroy or impare its efficiency."

3. That the Democratic Party will resist all attempts at renewing in congress or out of it, the agitation of the Slavery question, under whatever shape or color the attempt may be made."

4. That the Democratic Party will faithfully abide by and uphold the principles laid down in the Kentucky and Virginia resolutions of 1797 and 1798, and in the report of Mr. Madison to the Virginia Legislature in 1799—that it adopts these principles as constituting one of the main foundations of its political creed, and is resolved to carry them out in their obvious meaning and import. And that we may more distinctly meet the issue on which a sectional party, subsisting exclusively on slavery agitation, now relies to test the fidelity of the people. North and South, to the constitution and the Union—

1. Resolved. That claiming fellow-ship with, and desiring Co-operation of all who regard the preservation of the Union under the Constitution as the paramount issue, and repudiating all sectional parties and platforms concerning domestic slavery, which seek to embroil the States and incite to treason and armed resistance to law in the Territories and, whose avowed purpose, if consummated, must end in civil war and disunion, the American Democracy recognize and adopt the principles contained in the organic laws establishing the Territories of Nebraska and Kansas embodying the only sound and safe solution of the slavery question, upon which the great national idea of the people of this whole Country can repose in its determined conservation of the Union, and non-interferences of Congress with slavery in the Territories or in the District of Columbia.

2. That this was the basis of the compromises of 1850, confirmed by both the Democratic and Whig parties in National convention, ratified by the people in the election of 1852, and rightly applied to the organization of the Territories in 1854.

3. That by the uniform application of the Democratic principle to the organization of Territories, and the admission of New States with or without domestic Slavery, as they may elect, the equal rights of all the States will be preserved intact, the original compacts of the constitution maintained inviolate, and the perpetuity and expansion of the union insured to its utmost capacity of embracing in peace and harmony, every future American State that may be constituted or annexed with a republican form of Government.

Resolved. That we recognize the right of the people of all the Territories, including Kansas and Nebraska, acting through the legally and fairly expressed will of the majority of the actual residents, and whenever the number of their inhabitants justifies it, to form a constitution with or without domestic Slavery, and be admitted into the union upon terms of perfect equality with the other States.

Resolved, finally. That in view of the condition of popular institutions in the old world (and the dangerous tendencies of sectional agitation, combined with the attempt to enforce civil and religious disabilities against the rights of acquiring and enjoying citizenship in our own land)' a high and sacred duty is involved with increased responsibility upon the Democratic Party of this country, as the party of the union, to uphold and maintain the rights of every State and thereby the union of the States—and to sustain and advance among us constitutional liberty, by continuing to resist all monopolies and exclusive legislation for the benefit of the few at the expense of the many, and by a vigilant and constant adherence to those principles and compromises of the constitution—which are broad enough and strong enough to embrace, and uphold the union as it was, the union as it is, and the union as it shall be—in the full expression of the energies and capacity of this great and progressive people.

1. Resolved. That there are questions connected with the foreign policy of this country which are inferior to no domestic question whatever. The time has come for the people of the United States to declare themselves in favor of free seas, and progressive free trade throughout the world, and, by solemn manifestations, to place their moral influences at the side of their successful example.

2. Resolved. That our geographical and political position with reference to the other states of this continent, no less than the interest of our commerce and the development of our growing power, requires that we should hold sacred the principles involved in the Monroe doctrine. Their bearing and import admit of no misconstruction, and should be applied with unbending rigidity.

3. Resolved. That the great highway which nature, as well as the assent of States most immediately interested in its maintenance has marked out for free communication between the Atlantic and the Pacific Oceans, constitutes one of the most important achievements realized by the spirit of modern times, in the unconquerable energy of our people, and the result would be secured by a timely and efficient exertion of the control which we have the right to claim over it, and no power on earth should be suffered to impede or clog its progress by any interference with relations that it may suit our policy to establish between our Government and the Government of the States within whose dominions it lies; we can under no circumstances surrender our preponderance in the adjustment of all questions arising out of it.

4. Resolved. That in view of so commanding an interest, the people of the United States cannot but sympathize with the efforts which are being made by the people of Central America to regenerate that portion of the continent which covers the passage across the interoceanic isthmus.

5. Resolved. That the Democratic Party will expect of the next Administration that every proper effort be made to insure our ascendency in the Gulf of Mexico, and to maintain permanent protection to the great outlets through which are emptied into its waters the products raised out of the soil and the commodities created by the industry of the people of our western valleys, and of the union at large.

Resolved. That the administration of Franklin Pierce has been true to Democratic principles, and therefore true to the great interests of the country; in the face of violent opposition, he has maintained the laws at home, and vindicates the rights of American Citizens abroad and therefore we proclaim our unqualified admiration of his measures, and policy."

Whig Platform,—1856.

"Resolved. That the Whigs of the United States, now here assembled, hereby declare their reverence for the constitution of the United States, their unalterable attachment to the National Union, and a fixed determination to do all in their power to preserve them for themselves and their posterity. They have no new principles to announce; no

new platform to establish; but are content to broadly rest—where
their fathers rested—upon the constitution of the United States, wishing no safer guide, no higher law.

Resolved. That we regard with the deepest interest and anxiety the
present disordered condition of our National affairs—a portion of the
country ravaged by civil war, large sections of our population embit-
tered by mutual recriminations; and we distinctly trace these calamities
to the culpable neglect of duty by the present national administration.

Resolved. That the Government of the United States was formed by
the conjunction in political unity of wide spread geographical Sections
materially differing not only in climate and products, but, in social and
domestic institutions; and that any cause that shall permanently array
the different Sections of the Union in political hostility and organized
parties founded only on geographical distinctions, must inevitably prove
fatal to a continuance of the National Union.

Resolved. That the Whigs of the United States declare, as a fundamental article of political faith, an absolute neccessity for avoiding
geographical parties. The danger so clearly discerned by the Father of
his Country, has now become fearfully apparent in the agitation now
convulsing the Nation, and must be arrested at once if we would preserve our constitution and our Union from dismemberment, and the
name of America from being blotted out from the family of civilized
nations.

Resolved. That all who revere the constitution and the Union must
look with alarm at the parties in the field in the present Presidential
Campaign—one claiming only to represent sixteen Northern States,
and the other appealing mainly to the passions and prejudices of the
Southern States; that the success of either faction must add fuel to the
flame which now threatens to warp our dearest interests in a common
ruin.

Resolved. That the only remedy for an evil so appalling, is to support a candidate pledged to neither of the geographical sections now
arrayed in political antagonism, but holding both in a just and equal
regard. We congratulate the friends of the Union that such a candidate
exists in Millard Fillmore.

Resolved. That without adopting or referring to the peculiar doctrine of the party which has already selected Mr. Fillmore as a candidate we look to him as a well-tried and faithful friend of the constitution and the Union, emiment alike for his wisdom and firmness, for his justice and moderation in our foreign relations—for his calm and pacific
temperament, so well becoming the head of a great Nation—for his devotion to the constitution in its true spirit—his inflexibility in executing
the laws; but, beyond all these attributes in possessing the one transcen-
dent merit of being a repretasentive of neither of the two sectional parties now struggling for political supremacy.

Resolved. That in the present exigency of political affairs, we are
not called upon to discuss the subordinate questions of administration
in the exercising of the constitutional powers of the government. It is
enough to know that Civil War was raging and that the Union was in
peril; and we proclaim the conviction that the restoration of Mr. Fillmore to the Presidency will furnish the best, if not the only means of
restoring peace." (Fillmore was also the candidate of the Know-noth
ings.)

Republican platform—1860. (Chicago platform.)

" Resolved that we, the delegated, representatives of the Republican electors of the United States, in convention, assembled in discharge of the duty we owe to our constituents and our country, unite in the following Declarations:

1. That the history of the nation, during the last four years, has fully established the propriety and necessity of the organization and perpetuation of the Republican party, and the causes which called it into existence are permanent in their nature, and now more than ever before demand its peaceful and constitutional triumph.

2. That the maintenance of the principles promulgated in the declaration of Independence and embodied in the Federal constitution "That all men are created equal; that they are endowed by their creator with certain inalienable rights; that among these are life, liberty and the pursuit of happiness; that to secure these rights governments are instituted among men deriving their just powers from the consent of the governed," is essential to the preservation of our Republican institutions; and that the Federal constitution, the rights of the States, and the Union of the States, must and shall be preserved.

3. That to the Union of the States this nation owes its unprecedented increase in population, its surprising development of material resources; its rapid augmentation of wealth, its happiness at home and its honor abroad; and we behold in abhorence all schemes for Disunion, come from whatever source they may; and we congratulate the country that no Republican member of congress has uttered or countenanced the threats of Disunion so often made by democratic members without rebuke, and with applause from their political associates; and we denounce those threats of disunion in case of a popular overthrow of their ascendency, as denying the vital principles of a free government and as an avowal of contemplated treason which it is the imperative duty of an indignant people sternly to rebuke and forever silence.

4. That the maintenance inviolate of the rights of the States, especially the right of each State to order and control its own domestic institutions according to its own judgment exclusively, is essential to that balance of powers on which the perfection and endurance of our political fabric depends; and we denounce the lawless invasion by armed force of the soil of any State or Territory, no matter under what pretext, as among the greatest of crimes.

5. Resolved. That the present Democratic Administration has far exceeded our worst apprehensions, in its measureless subserviency to the exactions of a sectional interest, as especially evinced in its desperate exertions to force the infamous Lecompton constitution upon the protesting people of Kansas; in construing the personal relation between master and servant to involve an unqualified property in persons; in its attempted enforcement everywhere, on land and sea, through the intervention of congress and of the Federal courts of the extreme pretentions of a purely local interest; and in its general and unvarying abuse of the power intrusted to it by a confiding people.

6. That the people justly view with alarm the reckless extravagance which pervades every department of the Federal Government; that a return to rigid economy and accountability is indispensable to arrest the systematic plunder of the public treasury by favored partisans; while the recent startling developments of frauds and corruptions at

the Federal metropolis, show that an entire change of administration, is imperatively demanded·

7. That the new dogma that the constitution, of its own force carries Slavery into any or all of the Territories of the United States is a dangerous political heresy, at variance with the explicit provisions of that instrument itself, with cotemporaneous exposition, and with legislative and judicial precedent; is revolutionary in its tendency and subversive of the peace and harmony of the country.

8. That the normal condition of all the the territory of the United States is that of freedom; that as our Republican Fathers, when they had abolished Slavery in all our national territory ordained that" no person should be deprived of life, liberty, or property, without due process of law," it became our duty, by legislation, whenever such legislation is necessary to maintain the provision of the constitution against all attempts to violate it; and we deny the authority of congress, of a territorial legislature, or of any individuals, to give legal existence to Slavery in any Territory of the United States.

9. That we brand the recent reopening of the African Slave-trade, under the cover of our national flag, aided by perversions of our judicial power, as a crime against humanity and a burning shame to our country and age; and we call upon congress to take prompt and efficient measures for the total and final suppression of that execrable traffic.

10. That in the recent vetoes by their Federal Governors, of the acts of the Legislatures of Kansas and Nebraska, prohibiting. Slavery in those Territories, we find a practical illustration of the boasted Democratic principle of non-intervention and popular sovereignty embodied in the Kansas—Nebraska bill and a demonstration of the deception and frauds involved therein.

11. Resolved, that Kansas, should, of right, be immediately admitted a State under the constitution recently formed and adopted by her people, and accepted by the House of Representatives.

12. That, while providing revenue for the support of the General Government by duties upon imposts, sound policy requires such an adjustment of these imposts as to encourage the development of the industrial interests of the whole country, and we commend that policy of national exchanges which secures to the working men liberal wages, to agriculture remunerating prices, to mechanics and manufacturers an adequate reward for their skill, labor, and enterprise, and to the nation commercial prosperity and independence.

13. That we protest against any sale or alienation to others of the Public Lands held by the actual settlers, and against any views of the Homestead policy which regards the settlers as paupers or suppliants for public bounty; and we demand the passage by congress of the complete and satisfactory Homestead measure which has already passed the House.

14. That the Republican party is opposed to any change in our Naturalization Laws or any State Legislation by which the rights of citizenship hitherto accorded to emigrants from foreign lands shall be abridged or impaired; and in favor of giving a full and efficient protection to the rights of all classes of citizens, whether native or naturalized, both at home and abroad.

15. That appropriations by congress for River and Harbor improvements of a national character, required for the accommodation and security of an existing commerce, are authorized by the constitution, and

justified by the obligations of Government to protect the lives and property of its citizens.

16. That a Railroad to the Pacific Ocean is imperatively demanded by the interest of the whole country that the Federal Government ought to render immediate and efficient aid in its construction, and that as preliminary thereto, a daily overland mail should be promptly established.

17. Finally, having thus set forth our distinctive principles and views we invite the co-operation of all citizens, however differing on other questions, who substantially agree with us in their affirmance and support.

———————

The Constitutional Union convention — 1860. Bell for President and Everett for vice President.

Constitutional Union platform — 1860.

Whereas, experience has demonstrated that platforms adopted by the partisan conventions of the country have had the effect to mislead and deceive the people and at the same time to widen the political divisions of the country, by the creation and encouragement of geographical and sectional parties; therefore,

Resolved. That it is both the part of patriotism and of duty to recognize no political principles other than *the constitution of the country the Union of the States and the enforcement of the laws* and that, as representatives of the constitutional Union, men of the country in national convention assembled, we hereby pledge ourselves to maintain, protect and defend, separately and unitedly, these great principles of public liberty and national safety, against all enemies at home and abroad, believing that thereby peace may once more be restored to the country, the rights of the people and of the States reestablished and the Government again placed in that condition, of justice, fraternity and, equality, which, under the example and constitution of our fathers, has solemnly bound every citizen of the United States to maintain a more perfect Union, to establish justice, insure domestic tranquility, provide for the common defense, promote the general welfare, and secure the blessings, of liberty to ourselves and our posterity.

———————

The Democratic National Convention met at Charleston, S, C, April 23, 1860. A rupture took place between the friends of Douglas and the extremists of the South—many of the Southern States withdrew from the convention, adjourned and met at Baltimore June 18, 1860, and nominated Douglas for President and Benj. Fitz-Patrick for Vice-President. Fitz-Patrick declined, and Herschel V. Johnson was nominated afterwards by the National Committee.

The Southerners nominated John C, Breckinridge for President and Gen, Joseph Lane for Vice-President.

DEMOCRATIC PLATFORM,—1860.

1. *Resolved*, That we, the Democracy of the Union, in Convention assembled, hereby declare our affirmance of the resolutions unanimously adopted and declared as a platform of principles by the Democratic Convention at Cincinnati, in the year 1856, believing that Democratic principles are unchangeable in their nature, when applied to the same subject matters; and we recommend as the only further resolutions the following:

2. *Resolved*, That it is the duty of the United States to afford ample and complete protection to all its citizens, whether at home or abroad, and whether native or foreign.

3. *Resolved*, That one of the necessities of the age, in a military, commercial. and postal point of view, is speedy communication between the Atlantic and Pacific States; and the Democratic Party pledge such Constitutional Government aid, as will insure the construction of a railroad to the Pacific coast, at the earliest practicable period.

4. *Resolved*, That the Democratic party are in favor of the acquisition of the Island of Cuba, on such terms as shall be honorable to ourselves and just to Spain.

5. *Resolved*, That the enactments of State Legislatures to defeat the faithful execution of the Fugitive Slave Law, are hostile in character, subversive of the Constitution, and revolutionary in their effect.

BRECKINRIDGE PLATFORM,—1860.

Resolved, That the Platform adopted by the Democratic party at Cincinnati be affirmed, with the following explanatory Resolutions:

First, That the Government of a Territory organized by an act of Congress, is provisional and temporary; and during its existence, all citizens of the United States have an equal right to settle with their property in the Territory without their rights, either of person or property, being destroyed or impaired by Congressional or Territorial Legislation.

Second, That it is the duty of the Federal Government, in all its departments, to protect when necessary the rights of persons and property in the Territories, and wherever else its Constitutional authority extends.

Third, That when the settlers in a Territory having an adequate population form a State Constitution in pursuance of law, the right of sovereignty commences, and, being consummated by admission into the Union, they stand on an equal footing with the people of other States; and the State thus organized ought to be admitted into the Federal Union, whether its Constitution prohibits or recognizes the institution of Slavery.

Fourth, That the Democratic party are in favor of the acquisition of the Island of Cuba, on such terms as shall be honorable to ourselves and just to Spain, at the earliest practicable moment.

Fifth, That the enactments of State Legislatures to defeat the faithful execution of the Fugitive Slave Law, are hostile in character, subversive of the Constitution, and revolutionary in their effect.

Sixth, That the Democracy of the United States recognize it as the imperative duty of this Government to protect the naturalized citizen in all his rights, whether at home or in foreign lands, to the same extent as its native-born citizens.

Whereas, one of the greatest necessities of the age, in a Political, Commercial, Postal and Military point of view, is a speedy communication between the Pacific and Atlantic coasts. Therefore, be it

Resolved, That the Democratic party do hereby pledge themselves to use every means in their power to secure the passage of some bill to the extent of the Constitutional authority of Congress for the construction of a Pacific Railroad from the Mississippi River to the Pacific Ocean, at the earliest practicable moment.

NATIONAL PLATFORMS OF 1868.

THE DEMOCRATIC PLATFORM.

The Democratic Party, in National Convention assembled, reposing its trust in the intelligence, patriotism, and discriminating justice of the people, standing upon the Constitution as the foundation and limitation of the powers of the Government, and the guarantee of the liberties of the citizen; and recognizing the questions of slavery and secession as having been settled for all time to come by the war or the voluntary action of the Southern States in Constitutional Convention assembled, and never to be renewed or reagitated, do with the return of peace demand;

First—Immediate restoration of all the States to their rights in the Union under the Constitution, and of civil government to the American people.

Second—Amnesty for all past political offences, and the regulation of the elective franchise in the States by their citizens

Third—Payment of the public debt of the United States as rapidly as practicable; all moneys drawn from the people by taxation, except so much as is requisite for the necessities of the Government, economically administered, being honestly applied to such payment; and where the obligations of the Government, do not expressly state upon their face, or the law under which they were issued does not provide, that they shall be paid in coin, they ought, in right and in justice, to be paid in the lawful money of the United States.

Fourth—Equal taxation of every species of property, according to its real value, including Government bonds and other public securities.

Fifth—One currency for the Government and the people, the laborer and the officeholder, the pensioner and the soldier, the producer and the bondholder.

Sixth—Economy in the administration of the Government; the reduction of the standing army and navy; the abolition of the Freedman's Bureau—and all political instrumentalities designed to secure negro supremacy; simplification of the system, and discontinuance of inquisitorial modes of assessing and collecting Internal Revenue, so that the burden of taxation may be equalized and lessened; the credit of the

Government and the currency made good ; the repeal of all enactments for enrolling the State militia into national forces in time of peace ; and a tariff for revenue upon foreign imports, and such equal taxation under the Internal Revenue laws as will afford incidental protection to domestic manufactures, and as will, without impairing the revenue, impose the least burden upon and yet promote and encourage the great industrial interests of the country.

Seventh—Reform of abuses in the administration, the expulsion of corrupt men from office, the abrogation of useless offices, the restoration of rightful authority to, and the independence of the executive and judicial department of the Government ; the subordination of the military to the civil power, to the end that the usurpation of Congress and the despotism of the sword may cease.

Eighth—Equal rights and protection for naturalized and native born citizens at home and abroad, the assertion of American nationality, which shall command the respect of foreign powers, and furnish an example and encouragement to people struggling for national integrity, constitutional liberty, and individual rights, and the maintenance of the rights of naturalized citizens against the absolute doctrine of immutable allegiance, and the claims of foreign powers to punish them for alleged crime committed beyond their jurisdiction.

In demanding these measures and reforms, we arraign the Radical party for its disregard of right and the unparalleled oppression and tyranny which have marked its career.

After the most solemn and unanimous pledge of both Houses of Congress to prosecute the war exclusively for the maintenance of the Government, and the preservation of the Union under the Constitution, it has repeatedly violated that most sacred pledge under which alone was rallied that noble volunteer army which carried our flag to victory. Instead of restoring the Union, it has so far as in its power, dissolved it, and subjected ten States, in time of profound peace, to military despotism and negro supremacy. It has nullified there the right of trial by jury ; it has abolished the *habeas corpus*, that most sacred writ of liberty ; it has overthrown the freedom of speech and the press ; it has substituted arbitrary seizures and arrests, and military trials and secret star-chamber inquisitions for the constitutional tribunals ; it has disregarded in time of peace the right of the people to be free from searches and seizures ; it has entered the post and telegraph offices, and even the private rooms of individuals, and seized their private papers and letters without any specific charge or notice or affidavit, as required by the organic law ; it has converted the American Capitol into a Bastile ; it has established a system of spies and official espionage to which no constitutional monarchy of Europe would now dare to resort; it would abolish the right of appeal on important constitutional questions to the supreme judicial tribunal, and threatens to curtail or destroy its original jurisdiction which is irrevocably vested by the Constitution, while the learned Chief-Justice has been subjected to the most atrocious calumnies, merely because he would not prostitute his high office to the support of the false and partisan charges preferred against the President. Its corruption and extravagance have exceeded everything known in history, and by its frauds and monopolies it has nearly doubled the burden of the debt created by the war. It has stripped the President of his constitutional power of appointment, even of his own Cabinet. Under its repeated assaults the pillars of the Government are rocking on their base, and should it succeed in November next and inaugurate its President, we will meet as a subjected and conquered people amid the ruins of liberty and the scattered fragments of the Constitution.

And we do declare and resolve, that ever since the people of the United States threw off all subjection to the British Crown, the privilege and trust of suffrage have belonged to the several States, and have been granted, regulated, and controlled exclusively by the political power of each State respectively, and that any attempt by Congress, on any pretext whatever, to deprive any State of this right, or interfere with its exercise, is a flagrant usurpation of power which can find no warrant in the Constitution, and if sanctioned by the people will subvert our form of government, and can only end in a single centralized and consolidated government, in which the separate existence of the States will be entirely absorbed and an unqualified despotism be established in place of a Federal Union of coequal States.

And that we regard the Reconstruction acts (so-called) of Congress, as such, as usurpations, and unconstitutional, revolutionary and void.

That our soldiers and sailors who carried the flag of our country to victory against a most gallant and determined foe must ever be gratefully remembered, and all the guarantees given in their favor must be faithfully carried into execution.

That the public lands should be distributed as widely as possible among the people, and should be disposed of either under the pre-emption of homestead lands, or sold in reasonable quanities, and to none but actual occupants, at the minimum price established by the Government. When grants of public lands may be allowed, necessary for the encouragement of important public improvements, the proceeds of the sale of such lands, and not the lands themselves, should be applied.

That the President of the United States—Andrew Johnson—in exercising the power of his high office in resisting the aggressions of Congress upon the constitutional rights of the States and the people, is entitled to the gratitude of the whole American people; and in behalf of the Democratic party we tender him our thanks for his patriotic efforts in that regard.

Upon this Platform the Democratic party appeal to every patriot, including the conservative element and all who desire to support the Constitution and restore the Union, forgetting all past differences of opinion, to unite with us in the present great struggle for the liberties of the people, and that to all such, to whatever party they may have heretofore belonged, we extend the right hand of fellowship, and hail all such co-operating with us as friends and brethren.

THE REPUBLICAN PLATFORM.

The National Republican Convention met at Chicago May 20, assumed the name of "The National Union Republican Party," and nominated General U. S. Grant, on the first ballot, as candidate for President, and Schuyler Colfax, of Indiana, on the fifth ballot, as candidate for Vice-President. May 21, the Convention adopted the following platform:

I.   We congratulate the country on the assured success of the reconstruction policy of Congress, as evinced by the adoption, in the majority of States lately in rebellion, of constitutions securing equal civil and political rights to all : and it is the duty of the Government to sustain those institutions and to prevent the people of such States from being re-admitted to a state of anarchy.

II.   The guaranty by Congress of equal suffrage to all loyal men at the South was demanded by every consideration of public safety, of gratitude, and of justice, and must be maintained ; while the question of suffrage in all the loyal States properly belongs to the people of those States.

III.   We denounce all forms of repudiation as a national crime ; and the national honor requires the payment of the public indebtedness in the uttermost good faith to all creditors at home and abroad, not only according to the letter but the spirit of the laws under which it was contracted.

IV.   It is due to the labor of the nation that taxation should be equalized and reduced as rapidly as the national faith will permit.

V.   The national debt, contracted as it has been for the preservation of the Union for all time to come, should be extended over a fair period for redemption ; and it is the duty of Congress to reduce the rate of interest thereon whenever it can be honestly done.

VI.   That the best policy to diminish our burden of debt, is to so improve our credit that capitalists will seek to loan us money at lower rates of interest than we now pay, and must continue to pay so long as repudiation, partial or total, open or covert, is threatened or suspected.

VII.   The Government of the United States should be administered with the strictest economy, and the corruptions which have been so shamefully nursed and fostered by Andrew Johnson call loudly for radical reform.

VIII.   We profoundly deplore the untimely and tragic death of Abraham Lincoln, and regret the accession to the Presidency of Andrew Johnson, who has acted treacherously to the people who elected him and the cause he was pledged to support ; who has usurped high legislative and judicial functions ; who has refused to execute the laws ; who has used his high office to induce other officers to ignore and violate the laws ; who has employed his executive powers to render insecure the property, the peace, liberty, and life of the citizen ; who has abused the pardoning power ; who has denounced the National Legislature as unconstitutional ; who has persistently and corruptly resisted, by every means in his power, every proper attempt at the reconstruction of the States lately in rebellion ; who has perverted the public patronage into an engine of wholesale corruption ; and who has been justly impeached for high crimes and misdemeanors, and properly pronounced guilty thereof by the votes of thirty-five Senators.

IX.   The doctrine of Great Britain and other European powers, that because a man is once a subject he is always so, must be resisted at every hazard by the United States as a relic of feudal times not authorized by the laws of nations, and at war with our national honor and independence.   Naturalized citizens are entitled to protection in all their rights of citizenship, as though they were native born ; and no citizen of the United States, native or naturalized, must be liable to arrest and imprisonment by any foreign power for acts done, or words spoken in this country: and if so arrested and imprisoned, it is the duty of the Government to interfere in his behalf.

X. Of all who were faithful in the trials of the late war, there were none entitled to more especial honor than the brave soldiers and seamen who endured the hardships of campaign and cruise, and imperilled their lives in the service of the country; the bounties and pensions provided by the laws for these brave defenders of the nation are obligations never to be forgotten; the widows and orphans of the gallant dead are the wards of the people—a sacred legacy, bequeathed to the nation's protecting care.

XI. Foreign immigration, which in the past has added so much to the wealth, development, and resources and increase of power to this Republic, the asylum of the oppressed of all nations, should be fostered and encouraged by a liberal and just policy.

XII. This convention declares itself in sympathy with all oppressed people struggling for their rights.

On motion of Carl Schurz, the following were added:

Resolved. That we highly commend the spirit of magnanimity and forbearance with which men who have served in the rebellion—but who now frankly and honestly co-operate with us in restoring the peace of the country, and reconstructing the Southern State governments upon the basis of Impartial Justice and Equal Rights, are received back into the communion of the loyal people; and we favor the removal of the disqualifications and restrictions imposed upon the late rebels in the same measure as their spirit of loyalty will direct, and as may be consistent with the safety of the loyal people.

Resolved, That we recognize the great principles laid down in the immortal Declaration of Independence as the true foundation of Democratic Government; and we hail with gladness every effort making these principles a living reality on every inch of American soil.

HORATIO SEYMOUR'S LETTER OF ACCEPTANCE.

GENTLEMEN:

UTICA, AUGUST 4.

When, in the City of New York, on the 11th of July, in the presence of a vast multitude, on behalf of the National Democratic Convention, you tendered to me its unanimous nomination as its candidate for the office of President of the United States, I stated that I had no words adequate to express my gratitude for the good will and kindness which that body had shown to me. Its nomination was unsought and unexpected. It was my ambition to take an active part, from which I am now excluded, in the great struggle going on for the restoration of good government, of peace and prosperity to our country. But I have been caught up by the whelming tide which is bearing us on to a great political change, and I find myself unable to resist its pressure. You have also given me a copy of the resolution put forth by the Convention, showing its position upon all the great questions which now agitate the country. As the presiding officer of that Convention, I am familiar with their scope and imports; as one of its members, I am a party to their terms. They are in accord with my views, and I stand upon them in a contest upon which we are now entering, and shall strive to carry them out in future, wherever I may be placed, in political or private life.

I then stated that I would send you these words of acceptance in a letter, as is the customary form. I see no reason, upon reflection, to change or qualify the terms of my approval of the resolutions of the Convention.

I have delayed the mere formal act of communicating to you in writing what I thus publicly said, for the purpose of seeing what light the action of congress would throw upon the interests of the country. Its acts since the adjournment of the convention show an alarm lest a change of political power will give to the people what they ought to have—a clear statement of what has been done with the money drawn from them during the past eight years. Thoughtful men feel that there have been wrongs in the financial management which have been kept from the public knowledge. The Congressional party has not only allied itself with military power, which is to be brought to bear directly upon the elections in many States, but it also holds itself in perpetual session, with the avowed purpose of making such laws as it shall see fit, in view of the elections which will take place within a few weeks. It did not, therefore, adjourn, but took a recess, to meet again if its partisan interests shall demand its re-assembling. Never before in the history of our country has Congress thus taken a menacing attitude towards its electors. Under its influence some of the States organized by its agents are proposing to deprive the people of the right to vote for Presidential electors, and the first bold steps are taken to destroy the rights of suffrage. It is not strange, therefore, that thoughtful men see in such action the proof that there is with those who shape the policy of the Republican party, motives stronger and deeper than the mere wish to hold political power; that there is a dread of some exposure which drives them on to acts so desperate and impolitic.

Many of the ablest leaders and journals of the Republican party have openly deplored the violence of congressional action, and its tendency to keep up discord in our country. The great interests of our Union demand peace, order, and a return to those industrial pursuits without which we cannot maintain the faith or honor of our government. The minds of business men are perplexed by uncertainties. The hours of toil of our laborers are lengthened by the costs of living made by the direct and indirect exactions of Government. Our people are harassed by the heavy and frequent demands of the tax-gatherer. Without distinction of party there is a strong feeling in favor of that line of action which shall restore order and confidence, and shall lift off the burdens which now hinder and vex the industry of the country. Yet at this moment those in power have thrown into the Senate Chamber and Congressional Hall new elements of discord and violence. Men have been admitted as Representatives of some of the Southern States, with the declaration upon their lips that they cannot live in the States they claim to represent without military protection. These men are to make laws for the North as well as the South. These men, who a few days since were seeking as suppliants that Congress would give them power within their respective States, are to-day the masters and controllers of the actions of those bodies. Entering them with minds filled with passions, their first demands have been that Congress shall look upon the States from which they come as in conditions of civil war;

that the majority of their populations, embracing their intelligence, shall be treated as public enemies; that military forces shall be kept up at the cost of the people of the North, and that there shall be no peace and order at the South save that which is made by arbitrary power. Every intelligent man knows that these men owe their seats in Congress to the disorder in the South; every man knows that they not only owe their present positions to disorder, but that every motive springing from the love of power, of gain, of a desire for vengeance prompts them to keep the South in anarchy. While that exists, they are independent of the wills or wishes of their fellow-citizens. While confusion reigns they are the dispensers of the profits and the honors which grow out of the government of mere force. These men are now placed in position where they cannot merely urge their views of policy, but where they can enforce them. When others shall be admitted in this manner from the remaining Southern States, although they will have in truth no constituents, they will have more power in the Senate than a majority of people of this Union living in nine of the great States. In vain the wisest members of the Republican party protested against the policy that led to this result. While the chiefs of the late rebellion have submitted to the results of the war, and are now quietly engaged in useful pursuits for the support of themselves and their families, and are trying by the force of their example to lead back the people of the South to the order and industry, not only essential to their well being, but to the greatness and prosperity of our common country, we see that those who, without ability or influence, have been thrown by the agitations of civil convulsion into positions of honor and profit, are striving to keep alive the passions to which they owe their elevation. And they clamorously insist that they are the only friends of our Union—a Union that can only have a sure foundation in fraternal regard and a common desire to promote the peace, the order, and the happiness of all sections of our land.

Events in Congress since the adjournment of the Convention have vastly increased the importance of a political victory by those who are seeking to bring back economy, simplicity, and justice in the administration of our national affairs. Many Republicans have heretofore clung to their party who have regretted the extreme of violence to which it has run. They have cherished a faith that while the action of their political friends has been mistaken, their motives have been good. They must now see that the Republican party is in that condition that it cannot carry out a wise and peaceful policy, whatever its motives may be. It is a misfortune not only to the country, but to a governing party itself, when its action is unchecked by any form of opposition. It has been the misfortune of the Republican party that the events of the past few years have given it so much power that it has been able to schackle the Executive, to trammel the Judiciary, and to carry out the views of the most unwise and violent of its members. When this state of things exists in any party, it has ever been found that the sober judgments of its ablest leaders do not control. There is hardly an able man who has helped to build up the Republican organization, who has not, within the past three years, warned it against its excesses, who has not been borne down and forced to give up his convictions of what the country called for; or, if too patriotic to do this, who has not been driven from its ranks. If this has been the case heretofore, what will be its action now with this new infusion of men who, without a decent respect for the views of those who had just given them their position, begin their legislative career with calls for arms, with demands that their States shall be regarded as in a condition of civil war, and with a declaration that they are ready and anxious to degrade the President of the United States, whenever they can persuade or force Congress to bring forward new articles of impeachment.

The Republican party, as well as we, are interested in putting some check upon this violence. It must be clear to every thinking man that a division of political power tends to check the violence of party action and to assure the peace and good order of society. The election of a Democratic Executive and a majority of Democratic members to the House of Representatives would not give to that party organization the power to make sudden and violent changes, but it would serve to check those extreme measures which have been deplored by the best men of both political organizations. The result would most certainly lead to that peaceful restoration of the Union and re-establishment of fraternal relationship which the country desires. I am sure that the best men of the Republican party deplore as deeply as I do the spirit of violence shown by those recently admitted to seats in Congress from the South. The condition of civil war which they contemplate must be abhorrent to every right thinking man.

I have no mere personal wishes which mislead my judgment in regard to the pending election. No man who has weighed and measured the duties of the office of President of the United States, can fail to be impressed with the cares and toils of him who is to meet its demands. It is not merely to float with popular currents, without a policy or a purpose. On the contrary, while our Constitution gives just weight to the public will, its distinguishing feature is that it seeks to protect the rights of minorities. Its greatest glory is that it puts restraints upon power. It gives form and force to those maxims and principles of civil liberty for which the martyrs of freedom have struggled through ages. It declares the right of the people : " To be secure in their persons, houses and papers against unreasonable searches and seizures. That Congress shall make no law respecting an establishment of religion or the free exercises thereof, or abridging the freedom of speech or of the press, or the right of the people to petition for the redress of grievances. It secures the right of a speedy and public trial by an impartial jury."

No man can rightfully enter upon the duties of the Presidential office unless he is not only willing to carry out the wishes of the people, expressed in a constitutional way, but is also prepared to stand up for the rights of minorities. He must be ready to uphold the free exercise of religion. He must denounce measures which would wrong personal or home rights, or the religious conscience of the humblest citizen of the land. He must maintain, without distinction of creed or nationality. all the privileges of American citizenship.

The experience of every public man who has been faithful to his trust teaches him that no one can do the duties of the office of President unless he is ready not only to undergo the falsehoods and abuse of the bad, but to suffer from the censure of the good who are misled by prejudices and misrepresentation. There are no attractions in such positions, which deceive my judgment, when I say that a great change is going on in the public mind. The mass of the Republican party are more thoughtful, temperate, and just than they were during the excitements which attended the progress and close of the civil war. As the energy of the Democratic party springs from their devotion to their cause and not to their candidates, I may with propriety speak of the fact that never in the political history of our country has the action of any like body been hailed with such universal and widespread enthusiasm as that which has been shown in relation to the position of the National Democratic Convention. With this the candidates had nothing to do. Had any others of those named been selected, this spirit would have been, perhaps, more marked. The zeal and energy of the conservative masses spring from a desire to make a change of political policy, and from the confidence that they can carry out their policy.

In this faith they are strengthened by the co-operation of the great body of those who served in the Union army and navy during the war. Having given nearly sixteen thousand commissions to the officers of that army, I know their views and wishes. They demand the Union for which they fought. The largest meeting of these gallant soldiers which ever assembled was held in New York, and indorsed the action of the National Convention. In words instinct with meaning, they called upon the Government to stop in its policy of hate, discord and disunion, and in tones of fervid eloquence they demanded the restoration of the rights and liberties of the American people.

When there is such accord between those who prove themselves brave and self-sacrificing in war, and those who are thoughtful and patriotic in council, I cannot doubt we shall gain a political triumph which will restore our Union, bring back peace and prosperity to our land, and will give us once more the blessings of a wise, economical and honest Government.

I am, Gentlemen, truly, yours, &c.,
HORATIO SEYMOUR.
To Gen. G. W. Morgan, and others, Committee, &c., &c.

GENERAL GRANT'S LETTER OF ACCEPTANCE.
WASHINGTON, JUNE 1.

To J. R. Hawley, President of the National Union Republican Convention:

In formally accepting the nomination of the National Union Republican Convention of the 21st, of May, it seems proper that some statement of views beyond the mere acceptance of the nomination should be expressed.

The proceedings of the Convention were marked with unusual moderation and patriotism, and I believe express the feelings of the great mass of those who sustained the country through its recent trials. If elected to the office of President of the United States, it shall be my endeavor to administer all the laws in good faith, with economy, and with a view of giving peace, quiet and protection everywhere.

In times like the present it is impossible or at least eminently improper, to lay down a policy to be adhered to, right or wrong, through an administration of four years. New political issues not foreseen are constantly arising, to the views of the public, and old ones are constantly changing, and a purely administrative officer should be left free to execute the will of the people. I always have respected that will, and always shall. Peace and universal prosperity is its sequence and with economy of administration, will lighten the burden of taxation, while it constantly reduces the national debt. Let us have peace.

With great respect,
Your obedient servant,
U. S. GRANT.

NATIONAL PLATFORMS OF 1872.

THE DEMOCRATIC PLATFORM.

Adopted by the National Democratic Convention at Baltimore, July, 1872.

We, the Democratic electors of the United States in convention assembled, do present the following principles, already adopted at Cincinnati, as essential to just government.

First: We recognize the equality of all men before the law, and hold that it is the duty of government in its dealings with the people to mete out equal and exact justice to all, of whatever nativity, race, color or persuasion, religious or political.

Second: We pledge ourselves to maintain the union of these States, emancipation, and enfranchisement, and to oppose any reopening of the questions settled by the Thirteenth, Fourteenth, and Fifteenth amendments to the constitution.

Third: We demand the immediate and absolute removal of all disabilities imposed on account of the rebellion, which was finally subdued seven years ago, believing that universal amnesty will result in complete pacification in all sections of the country.

Fourth: Local self-government, with impartial suffrage, will guard the rights of all citizens more securely than any centralized power. The public welfare requires the supremacy of the civil over the military authority, and freedom of person under the protection of the habeas corpus. We demand for the individual the largest liberty consistent with public order; for the State, self-government, and for the nation a return to the methods of peace and the constitutional limitations of power.

Fifth: The Civil Service of the government has become a mere instrument of partisan tyranny and personal ambition, and an object of selfish greed. It is a scandal and reproach upon free institutions, and breeds a demoralization dangerous to the perpetuity of republican government. We therefore regard such thorough reforms of the Civil Service as one of the most pressing necessities of the hour, that honesty, capacity, and fidelity constitute the only valid claim to public employment, that the offices of the government cease to be a matter of arbitrary favoritism and patronage, and that public station become again a post of honor. To this end it is imperatively required that no President shall be a candidate for re-election.

Sixth: We demand a system of federal taxation which shall not unnecessarily interfere with the industry of the people, and which shall provide the means necessary to pay the expenses of the government economically administered, the pensions, the interest on the public debt, and a moderate reduction annually of the principal thereof, and, recognizing that there are in our midst honest but irreconcilable differences of opinion with regard to the respective systems of protection and free trade, we remit the discussion of the subject to the people in their Congress Districts, and to the decision of the Congress thereon, wholly free of executive interference or dictation.

Seventh: The public credit must be sacredly maintained, and we denounce repudiation in every form and guise.

Eighth: A speedy return to specie payments is demanded alike by the highest considerations of commercial morality and honest government.

Ninth; We remember with gratitude the heroism and sacrifices of the soldiers and sailors of the republic, and no act of ours shall ever detract from their justly-earned fame for the full reward of their patriotism.

Tenth: We are opposed to all further grants of lands to railroads or other corporations. The public domain should be held sacred to actual settlers.

Eleventh: We hold that it is the duty of the government, in its intercourse with foreign nations, to cultivate the friendship of peace, by treating with all on fair and equal terms, regarding it alike dishonorable either to demand what is not right, or to submit to what is wrong.

Twelfth: For the promotion and success of these vital principles and the support of the candidates nominated by this convention, we invite and cordially welcome the co-operation of all patriotic citizens, without regard to previous affiliations.

THE REPUBLICAN PLATFORM.

Adopted by the National Republican Convention at Philadelphia, June, 1872.

The Republican Party of the United States, assembled in National Convention in the city of Philadelphia, on the 5th and 6th days of June, 1872, again declares its faith, appeals to its history, and announces its position upon the questions before the country:

First: During eleven years of supremacy it has accepted with grand courage the solemn duties of the time. It suppressed a gigantic rebellion, emancipated four millions of slaves, decreed the equal citizenship of all, and established universal suffrage. Exhibiting unparalleled magnanimity, it criminally punished no man for political offences, and warmly welcomed all who proved their loyalty by obeying the laws and dealing justly with their neighbors. It has steadily decreased, with a firm hand, the resultant disorders of a great war, and initiated a wise policy toward the Indians. The Pacific Railroad and similar vast enterprises have been generally aided and successfully conducted; the public lands freely given to actual settlers; immigration protected and encouraged, and a full acknowledgment of the naturalized citizens' rights secured from European powers. A uniform national currency has been provided: repudiation frowned down: the national credit

sustained under most extraordinary burdens, and new bonds negotiated at lower rates; the revenues have been carefully collected and honestly applied. Despite the annual large reductions of rates of taxation,
the public debt has been reduced during Gen. Grant's presidency at the
rate of $100,000,000 a year. A great financial crisis has been avoided,
and peace and plenty prevail throughout the land. Menacing foreign
difficulties have been peacefully and honorably compromised, and the
honor and the power of the nation kept in high respect throughout the
world. This glorious record of the past is the parties best pledge for the
future. We believe the people will not intrust the government to any
party or combination of men composed chiefly of those who have
resisted every step of this beneficial progress.

Second : Complete liberty and exact equality in the enjoyment of all
civil, political, and public rights should be established and effectually
maintained throughout the Union, by efficient and appropriate State and
federal legislation. Neither the law nor its adminstration should admit
of any discrimination in respect of citizen by reason of race, creed, col-
or, or previous condition of servitude.

Third : The recent amendments to the national Constitution should
be cordially sustained, because they are right, not merely tolerated because they are law, and should be carried out according to their spirit
by appropriate legislation, the enforcement of which can be safely
trusted only to the party that secured those amendments.

Fourth : The national government should seek to maintain an honorable peace with all nations, protecting its citizens everywhere, and sym-
pathizing with all people who strive for greater liberty.

Fifth : Any system of the Civil Service under which the subordinate
positions of the government are considered rewards for mere party zeal,
is fatally demoralizing; and we, therefore, favor a reform of the system
by laws, which shall abolish the evils of patronage, and make honesty,
efficiency, and fidelity the essential qualifications for public position,
without practically creating a life tenure-of-office.

Sixth : We are opposed to further grants of the public lands to corporations and monopolies, and demand that the national domain be set
apart for free homes for the people.

Seventh : The annual revenues, after paying the current debts, should
furnish a moderate balance for the reduction of the principal, and the
revenue, except so much as may be derived from a tax on tobacco and
liquors, be raised by duties upon importations, the duties of which
should be so adjusted as to aid in securing remunerative wages to labor,
and promote the industries, growth, and prosperity of the whole country.

Eighth : We hold in undying honor the soldiers and sailors whose
valor saved the Union ; their pensions are a sacred debt of the nation,
and the widows and orphans of those who die for their country are entitled to the care of a generous and grateful people. We favor such
additional legislation as will extend the bounty of the government to
all our soldiers and sailors who were honorably discharged, and who in
the line of duty became disabled, without regard to the length of service
or the cause of such discharge.

Ninth : The doctrine of Great Britain and other European powers
concerning allegiance—"Once a subject always a subject"—having
at last, through the efforts of the Republican party, been abandoned, and
the American idea of the individual's right to transfer his allegiance

having been accepted by European nations, it is the duty of our government to guard with jealous care the rights of adopted citizens against the assumption of unauthorized claims by their former government; and we urge the continual and careful encouragement and protection of voluntary immigration.

Tenth: The franking privilege ought to be abolished, and the way prepared for a speedy reduction in the rate of postage.

Eleventh: Among the questions which press for attention is that which concerns the relations of capital and labor, and the Republican party recognize the duty of so shaping legislation as to secure full protection and the amplest field for capital, and for labor the creator of capital, the largest opportunities, and a just share of the mutual profits of these two great servants of civilization.

Twelfth: We hold that Congress and the President have only fulfilled an imperative duty in their measures for suppression of violent and treasonable organizations in certain lately rebellious regions, and for the protection of the ballot-box, and therefore they are entitled to the thanks of the nation.

Thirteenth: We denounce repudiation of the public debt in any form or disguise as a national crime. We witness with pride the reduction of the principal of the debt and of the rates of interest upon the balance, and confidently expect that our excellent national currency will be perfected by a speedy resumption of specie payments.

Fourteenth: The Republican party is mindful of its obligation to the loyal women of America, for their noble devotion to the cause of freedom. Their admission to wider fields of usefulness is received with satisfaction, and the honest demands of any class of citizens for additional rights should be treated with respectful consideration.

Fifteenth: We heartily approve the action of Congress in extending amnesty to those lately in rebellion, and rejoice in the growth of peace and fraternal feeling throughout the land.

Sixteenth: The Republican party propose to respect the rights reserved by the people to themselves as carefully as the powers delegated by them to the state and to the federal government. It disapproves of the resort to unconstitutional laws for the purpose of removing evils by the people to either the State or national government.

Seventeenth: It is the duty of the general government to adopt such measures as will tend to encourage American commerce and shipping.

Eighteenth: We believe that the modest patriotism, the earnest purpose, interference with rights not surrendered by the sound judgement, the practical wisdom, the incorruptible integrity and the illustrious services of Ulysses S. Grant have commended him to the heart of the American people, and with him at our head we start to-day upon a new march to victory.

THE ORIGINAL

ARTICLES OF CONFEDERATION.

TO ALL TO WHOM THESE PRESENTS SHALL COME.

We, the undersigned Delegates of the States affixed to our Names send greeting.

WHEREAS the Delegates of the United States of America in Congress assembled, did, on the fifteenth Day of November, in the Year of our Lord one thousand seven hundred and seventy-seven, and in the second Year of the Independence of America, agree to certain Articles of Confederation and perpetual Union between the States of New Hampshire, Massachusetts Bay, Rhode Island and Providence Plantations, Connecticut, New York, New Jersey, Pennsylvania, Delaware, Maryland, Virginia, North Carolina, South Carolina and Georgia, in the Words following, viz:—

Articles of confederation and perpetual Union between the States of New Hampshire, Massachusetts Bay, Rhode Island and Providence Plantations, Connecticut, New York, New Jersey, Pennsylvania, Delaware, Maryland, Virginia, North Carolina, South Carolina and Georgia.

ARTICLE I.   The Style of this Confederacy shall be "The United States of America."

ART. II.   Each State retains its Sovereignty, Freedom, and Independence, and every Power, Jurisdiction, and Right, which is not by this Confederation expressly delegated to the United States in Congress assembled.

ART. III.   The said States hereby severally enter into a firm League of Friendship with each other, for their common Defence, the Security of their Liberties, and their mutual and general Welfare; binding themselves to assist each other, against all Force offered to, or Attacks made upon them, or any of them, on Account of Religion, Sovereignty, Trade, or any other Pretence whatever.

ART. IV.   The better to secure and perpetuate mutual Friendship and Intercourse among the People of the different States in this Union, the free Inhabitants of each of these States, Paupers, Vagabonds, and Fugitives from Justice excepted, shall be entitled to all Privileges and immunities of free citizens in the several States; and the people of each State shall have free Ingress and Regress to and from any other State, and shall enjoy therein all the Privileges of Trade and Commerce, subject to the same Duties, Impositions, and Restrictions as the Inhabitants thereof respectively, provided that such Restrictions shall not extend so far as to prevent the Removal of Property imported into any State, to any other State of which the Owner is an Inhabitant; provided also, that no Imposition, Duties, or Restriction shall be laid by any State, on the Property of the United States, or either of them.

If any Person guilty of, or charged with Treason, Felony, or other high Misdemeanor in any State, shall flee from Justice, and be found in any of the United States, he shall, upon Demand of the Government or executive Power of the State from which he fled, be delivered up and removed to the State having Jurisdiction of his Offence.

Full Faith and Credit shall be given in each of these States to the Records, Acts and Judicial Proceedings of the Courts and Magistrates of every other State,

ART. V. For the more convenient Management of the general Interests of the United States, Delegates shall·be annually appointed, in such Manner as the Legislature of each State shall direct, to meet in Congress on the first Monday in November, in every Year; with a Power reserved to each State, to recal its Delegates, or any of them, at any Time within the Year, and to send others in their Stead, for the Remainder of the Year.

No State shall be represented in Congress by less than two, nor by more than seven Members, and no Person shall be capable of being a Delegate for more than three Years in any Term of six Years; nor shall any Person, being a Delegate, be capable of holding any Office under the United States, for which he, or another for his Benefit, receives Salary, Fees, or Emolument of any Kind.

Each State shall maintain its own Delegates in a Meeting of the States, and while they act as Members of the Committee of the States.

In determining Questions in the United States, in Congress assembled, each State shall have one Vote.

Freedom of Speech and Debate in Congress shall not be impeached or questioned in any Court, or Place out of Congress, and the Members of Congress shall be protected in their Persons from Arrests and Imprisonments, during the Time of their going to, and from, and attendance on Congress, except for Treason, Felony, or Breach of the Peace.

ART. VI. No State, without the Consent of the United States in Congress assembled, shall send any Embassy to, or receive any Embassy from, or enter into any Conference, Agreement, Alliance, or Treaty with any King, Prince, or State; nor shall any Person holding any Office of Profit or Trust under the United States, or any of them accept of any Present, Emolument, Office, or Title of any Kind whatever from any King, Prince, or foreign State; nor shall the United States in Congress assembled, or any of them, grant any Title of Nobility.

No two or more States shall enter into any Treaty, Confederation, or Alliance whatever between them, without the Consent of the United States in Congress assembled, specifying accurately the Purposes for which the same is to be entered into, and how long it shall continue.

No State shall lay any Imposts or Duties, which may interfere with any Stipulations in Treaties, entered into by the United States in Congress assembled, with any King, Prince, or State, in pursuance of any Treaties already proposed by Congress, to the Courts of France and Spain.

No Vessels of War shall be kept up in Time of Peace by any State, except such Number only, as shall be deemed necessary by the United States in Congress assembled, for the Defence of such State, or its Trade; nor shall any Body of Forces be kept up by any State, in Time of Peace, except such Number only, as in the Judgment of the United States, in Congress assembled, shall be deemed requisite to garrison the Forts necessary for the Defence of such State; but every State shall always keep up a well-regulated and disciplined Militia, sufficiently armed and accoutred and shall provide and constantly have ready for Use, in public Stores, a due Number of Fieldpieces and Tents, and a proper Quantity of Arms, Ammunition and Camp-equipage.

No State shall engage in any War without the Consent of the United States in Congress assembled, unless such State be actually invaded by Enemies, or shall have received certain Advice of a Resolution being formed by some Nation of Indians to invade such State, and the Danger is so imminent as not to admit of a Delay, till the United States in Congress assembled can be consulted: nor shall any State grant Commissions to any Ships or Vessels of War, nor Letters of Marque or Reprisal, except it be after a Declaration of War by the United States in Congress assembled, and then only against the Kingdom or State and the Subjects thereof, against which War has been so declared, and under such Regulations as shall be established by the United States in Congress assembled; unless such State be infested by Pirates, in which Case Vessels of War may be fitted out for that Occasion, and kept so long as the Danger shall continue, or until the United States in Congress assembled shall determine otherwise.

ART. VII. When land Forces are raised by any State for the Common Defense, all Officers of or under the Rank of Colonel shall be appointed by the Legislature of each State respectively, by whom such Forces shall be raised, or in such Manner as such State shall direct; and all Vacancies shall be filled up by the State which first made the Appointment.

ART. VIII. All Charges of War, and all other Expenses that shall be incurred for the common Defence or general Welfare, and allowed by the United States in Congress assembled, shall be defrayed out of a common Treasury, which shall be supplied by the several States, in Proportion to the Value of all Land within each State, granted to or surveyed for any Person, as such Land and the Buildings and Improvements thereon shall be estimated, according to such Mode as the United States in Congress assembled shall from Time to Time direct and appoint.

The Taxes for paying that Proportion shall be laid and levied by the Authority and Direction of the Legislature of the several States, within the Time agreed upon by the United States in Congress assembled.

ART. IX. The United States in Congress assembled shall have the sole and exclusive Right and Power of determining on Peace and War, except in the Cases mentioned in the sixth Article—of sending and receiving Ambassadors—entering into Treaties and Alliances, provided that no Treaty of Commerce shall be made, whereby the Legislative Power of the respective States shall be restrained from imposing such Imposts and Duties on Foreigners, as their own People are subjected to, or from prohibiting the Exportation or Importation of any Species of Goods or Commodities whatsoever—of establishing Rules for deciding, in all Cases, what Captures on Land or Water shall be legal, and in what Manner Prizes taken by land or naval Forces in the Service of the United States shall be divided or appropriated—of granting Letters of Marque and Reprisal in Times of Peace—appointing Courts for the Trial of Piracies and Felonies committed on the high Seas—and establishing Courts for receiving and determining finally Appeals in all Cases of Captures, provided that no Member of Congress shall be appointed a Judge of any of the said Courts.

The United States in Congress assembled shall also be the last Resort on Appeal in all Disputes and Differences now subsisting, or that hereafter may arise between two or more States, concerning Boundary, Jurisdiction, or any other Cause whatever ;, which Authority shall always be exercised in the Manner following. Whenever the legislative or executive Authority, or lawful Agent of any State in controversy with another, shall present a Petition to Congress, stating the Matter in Question, and praying for a Hearing, Notice thereof shall be given by Order of Congress to the legislative or executive Authority of the other State in Controversy, and a Day assigned for the Appearance of the Parties by their lawful Agents, who shall then be directed to appoint, by joint Consent, Commissioners or Judges to constitute a Court for hearing and determining the Matter in Question; but if they cannot agree, Congress shall name three Persons out of each of the United States, and from the List of such Persons each Party shall alternately strike out one, the Petitioners beginning, until the Number shall be so reduced to thirteen; and from that Number not less than seven, nor more than nine Names, as Congress shall direct, shall in the Presence of. Congress be drawn by Lot, and the Persons whose Names shall be drawn, or any five of them, shall be Commissioners or Judges, to hear and finally determine the Controversy, so always as a major Part of the Judges who shall hear the Cause shall agree in the Determination : and if either Party shall neglect to attend at the Day appointed, without showing Reasons which Congress shall judge sufficient, or being present shall refuse to strike, the Congress shall proceed to nominate three Persons out of each State, and the Secretary of Congress shall strike in behalf of such Party absent or refusing; and the Judgment and the Sentence of the Court to be appointed, in the Manner before prescribed, shall be final and conclusive; and if any of the Parties shall refuse to submit to the Authority of such Court, or to appear or defend their Claim or Cause, the Court shall nevertheless proceed to pronounce Sentence, or Judgment, which shall in like Manner be final and decisive; the Judgment or Sentence and other Proceedings being in either Case transmitted to Congress, and lodged among the Acts of Congress, for the Security of the Parties concerned: provided that every Commissioner, before he sits in Judgment, shall take an Oath, to be administered by one of the Judges of the Supreme or Superior Court of the State where the Cause shall be tried, "*well and truly to hear and determine the Matter in Question, according to the best of his Judgment, without Favor, Affection, or Hope of Reward;*" provided also that no State shall be deprived of Territory for the benefit of the United States.

All Controversies concerning the private Right of Soil .claimed under different Grants of two or more states whose Jurisdictions, as they may respect such Lands, and the States which passed such Grants are adjusted, the said Grants or either of them being at the same Time claimed to have originated antecedent to such Settlement of Jurisdiction, shall, on the Petition of either party to the Congress of the United States, be finally determined as near as may be in the same Manner as is before prescribed for deciding Disputes respecting territorial Jurisdiction between different States.

The United States in Congress assembled shall also have the sole and exclusive Right and Power of regulating the Alloy and Value of Coin - struck by their own Authority, or by that of the respective States—fix- ·

ing the Standard of Weights and Measures throughout the United States —regulating the Trade and managing all Affairs with the Indians, not Members of any of the States, provided that the legislative Right of any State within its own Limits be not infringed or violated—establishing and regulating Post-Offices from one State to another, throughout all the United States, and exacting such Postage on the Papers passing through the same as may be requisite to defray the Expenses of the said Office--appointing all Officers of the land Forces, in the Service of the United States, excepting regimental Officers—appointing all the Officers of the naval Forces, and commissioning all Officers whatever in the Service of the United States—making Rules for the Government and Regulation of the said land and naval Forces, and directing their Operations.

The United States in Congress assembled shall have Authority to appoint a Committee, to sit in the Recess of Congress, to be denominated "a Committee of the States," and to consist of one Delegate from each State; and to appoint such other Committees and civil Officers as may be necessary for managing the general affairs of the United States under their direction to appoint one of their Number to preside, provided that no Person be allowed to serve in the Office of President more than one year in any term of three Years; to ascertain the necessary Sums of Money to be raised for the Service of the United States, and to appropriate and apply the same for defraying the public Expenses--to borrow Money, or emit Bills on the credit of the United States, transmitting every half Year to the respective States an Account of the sums of Money so borrowed or emitted—to build and equip a Navy—to agree upon the Number of land Forces, and to make Requisitions from each State for its Quota, in proportion to the Number of white Inhabitants in such State; which Requisitions shall be binding, and thereupon the Legislature of each State shall appoint the regimental officers, raise the Men, and clothe, arm, and equip them in a soldier-like Manner, at the expense of the United States; and the officers and Men so clothed, armed and equipped, shall march to the Place appointed and within the Time agreed on by the United States in Congress assembled; but if the United States in Congress assembled shall, on consideration of circumstances, judge proper that any State should not raise men or should raise a smaller number than its Quota and that any other State should raise a greater Number of Men than the Quota thereof, such extra Number shall, be raised, officered, clothed, armed, and equipped in the same Manner as the Quota of such State, unless the Legislature of such State shall judge that such extra Number cannot be safely spared out of the Same, in which Case they shall raise, officer, clothe, arm, and equip as many of such extra Number as they judge can be safely spared. And the Officers and Men so clothed, armed and equipped shall march to the place appointed, and within the Time agreed on by the United States in Congress assembled.

The United States in Congress assembled shall never engage in a War, nor grant Letters of Marque and Reprisal in Time of Peace, nor enter into Treaties or Alliances, nor coin Money, nor regulate the Value thereof, nor ascertain the Sums and Expenses necessary for the Defence and Welfare of the United States, or any of them, nor emit Bills, nor borrow Money on the Credit of the United States, nor appropriate Money, nor agree upon the Number of Vessels of War, to be built or purchased, or the Number of land or sea Forces to be raised nor appoint a Commander in chief of the Army or Navy, unless nine States assent to the same, nor shall a Question on any other point, except for adjourning from Day to Day bedetermined, unless by the Votes of a Majority of the United States in Congress assembled.

The Congress of the United States shall have Power to Adjourn to any Time within the Year, and to any place within the United States so that no Period of Adjournment be for a longer Duration than the Space of six Months; and shall publish the Journal of their Proceedings Monthly, except such parts thereof relating to Treaties, Alliances, or Military Operations, as in their Judgment require Secrecy; and Yeas and Nays of the Delegates of each State on any Question shall be entered on the Journal, when it is desired by any Delegate; and the Delegates of a State, or any of them, at his or their Request, shall be furnished with a Transcript of the said Journal, except such Parts as are above excepted, to lay before the Legislature of the several States.

ART. X. The Committee of the States, or any nine of them, shall be authorized to execute, in the Recess of Congress, such of the Powers of Congress as the United States in Congress assembled, by the Consent of nine States shall from Time to Time think expedient to vest them with; provided that no Power be delegated to the said Committee, for the Exercise of which, by the Articles of Confederation, the Voice of nine States in the Congress of the Untited Sates assembled is requisite.

ART. XI. Canada acceding to this Confederation, and joining in the Measures of the United States, shall be admitted into and entitled to all the Advantages of this Union; but no other Colony shall be admitted into the Same, unless such Admission be agreed to by nine States.

ART. XII. All Bills of Credit emitted, Moneys borrowed, and Debts contracted by, or under the Authority of Congress, before the Assembling of the United States, in pursuance of present Confederation, shall be deemed and considered as a Charge against the United States for Payment and Satisfaction whereof, the said United States, and the Public Faith are hereby solemnly pledged.

ART. XIII. Every State shall abide by the Determinations of the United States in Congress assembled on all Questions which by this Confederation are submitted to them. And the Articles of this Confederation shall be inviolably observed by every State, and the Union shall be perpetual; nor shall any Alteration at any Time hereafter be made in any of them, unless such Alteration be agreed to by a Congress of the United States, and be afterwards confirmed by the Legislatures of every State.

And whereas it hath pleased the great Governor of the World to incline the Hearts of the Legislatures we respectively represent in Congress to approve of and to authorize us to ratify the said Articles of Confederation and perpetual Union; KNOW YE, that we, the undersigned Delegates, by virtue of the Power and Authority to us given for that Purpose, do by these Presents, in the Name and in behalf of our respective Constituents fully and entirely ratify and confirm each and every of the said Articles of Confederation and perpetual Union and all and singular the Matters and Things therein contained: and we do further solemnly plight and engage the Faith of our respective Constituents, that they shall abide by the Determinations of the United States in Congress assembled, on all Questions which by the said Confederation are submitted to them: and that the Articles there-

of shall be inviolably observed **by the** States we respectively represent, and that the Union **shall** be perpetual.

In **witness whereof,** we have hereunto set our Hands in Congress.
Done at Philadelphia in the State of Pennsylvania, the ninth Day of
July in the Year of our Lord one thousand seven hundred and seventy
eight, and in the third Year of the Independence of America.

On the Part and Behalf of the State of New Hampshire.

JOSIAH BARTLETT,   JOHN WENTWORTH, Jun., August 8, 1778.

On the Part and Behalf of the State of Massachusetts Bay.

JOHN HANNOCK, ELBRIDGE GERRY, JAMES LOVELL,
SAMUEL ADAMS, FRANCIS DANA, SAMUEL HOLTEN.

On the Part and Behalf of the State of R. I., and Providence Plantations.

WILLIAM ELLERY, HENRY MARCHANT, JOHN COLLINS.

On the Part and Behalf of the State of Connecticut.

ROGER SHERMAN, OLIVER WOLCOTT, ANDREW ADAMS.
SAMUEL HUNTINGTON, TITUS HOSMER,

On the Part and Behalf of the State of New York.

JAS. DUANE, FRA. LEWIS, WM. DUER, GOUV. MORRIS.

On the Part and Behalf of the State of New Jersey.

JNO. WITHERSPOON, Nov. 26, 1778.   NATH SCUDDER, do.

On the Part and Behalf of the State of Pennsylvania.

ROBT. MORRIS, JONA. BAYARD SMITH, JOS, REED, 22d July, 1778.
DANIEL ROBERDEAU, WILLIAM CLINGAN,

On the Part and Behalf of the State of Delaware.

THOS. M'KEAN, Feb. 13, 1779   NICHOLAS VAN DYKE.
JOHN DICKINSON, May 5th, 1779

On the Part and Behalf of the State of Maryland.

JOHN HANSON, March 1, 1781.   DANIEL CARROLL, do.

On the Part and Behalf of the State of Virginia.

RICHARD HENRY LEE, THOMAS ADAMS, FRANCIS LIGHTFOOT LEE.
JOHN BANISTER,   JNO. HARVIE,

On the Part and Behalf of the State of North Carolina.

JOHN PENN, July 21st, 1778. CORNS. HARNETT, JNO. WILLIAMS.

On the Part and Behalf of the State of South Carolina.

HENRY LAURENS, JNO. MATHEWS, THOMAS HEYWARD, Jun.
WILLIAM HENRY DRAYTON, RICHARD HUTSON.

On the Part and Behalf of the State of Georgia.

JNO. WALTON, 24th July, 1778. EDWD. TELFAIR, EDW. LANGWORTHY.

[*Note.*—From the circumstance of delegates from the same state having signed the
Articles of Confederation at different times, as appears by the dates, it is probable
they affixed their names as they happened to be present in Congress, after they had
been authorized by their constituents.]

UNITED STATES GOVERNMENT.

December 20. 1874.

THE EXECUTIVE.

ULYSSES S. GRANT, of Illinois, *President of the United States*.........Salary $50,000
HENRY WILSON, of Massachusetts, *Vice-President of the United States.*   "   10,000

THE CABINET.

HAMILTON FISH, of New York, *Secretary of State*.......................Salary $10,000
BENJAMIN H. BRISTOW, of Kentucky, *Secretary of the Treasury*......   "   8,000
WILLIAM W. BELKNAP, of Iowa, *Secretary of War*...................   "   10,000
GEORGE M. ROBESON, of New Jersey, *Secretary of the Navy*...........   "   10,000
COLUMBUS DELANO, of Ohio, *Secretary of the Interior*.................   "   10,000
EDWARD PIERREPONT, of New York, *Attorney-General*...............   "   10,000
MARSHALL JEWELL, of Connecticut, *Postmaster-General*.............   "   10,000

THE JUDICIARY.

SUPREME COURT OF THE UNITED STATES.

MORRISON R. WAITE, of Ohio, *Chief Justice*....................Salary $10,500
NATHAN CLIFFORD, of Maine, *Ass., Justice.* | STEPHEN J. FIELD, of Cal., *Ass., Justice.*
NOAH H. SWAYNE, of Ohio,   "   " | WILLIAM M. STRONG, of Pa.,   "   "
SAMUEL F. MILLER, of Iowa,   "   " | JOSEPH P. BRADLEY, of N. J.,   "   "
DAVID DAVIS, of Illinois,   "   " | WARD HUNT, of N. Y.,   "   "
Salary of Associate Justices, $10,000. ; Court meets first Monday in Dec. at Washington.

MINISTERS TO FOREIGN COUNTRIES.

ENVOYS EXTRAORDINARY AND MINISTERS PLENIPOTENTIARY,

Country.	Capital.	Ministers.	Salary.	Appointed.
Austria—Hungary	Vienna	John Jay, N. Y.	$12,000	1868
Brazil	Rio Janeiro	James R. Partridge, Md.	12,000	1871
Chili	Santiago	Cornelius A. Logan, Kansas.	10,000	1873
China	Pekin	Benjamin P. Avery, Cal.	12,000	1874
France	Paris	Elihu B. Washburne, Ill.	17,500	1869
Great Britain	London	Robert C. Schenck, Ohio.	17,500	1870
Italy	Rome	George P. Marsh, Vt.	12,000	1861
Japan	Yedo	John A. Bingham, Ohio.	12,000	1873
Mexico	Mexico	John W. Foster, Indiana.	12,000	1873
Peru	Lima	Francis Thomas, Md.	10,000	1872
Germany	Berlin	J. C. Bancroft Davis, Mass.	17,500	1874
Russia	St. Petersburg		17,500	
Spain	Madrid	Caleb Cushing, Va.	12,000	1874

MINISTERS RESIDENT.

Argentine Republic	Buenos Ayres	Thomas O. Osborn, Ill.	7,500	1874
Belgium	Brussels	J. Russell Jones, Ill.	7,500	1869
Bolivia	La Paz	Robert M. Reynolds, Ala.	7,500	1874
Cent. American States	San Jose	George Williamson, La.	10,000	1873
Denmark	Copenhagen	M. J. Cramer, Ky.	7,500	1870
Ecuador	Quito		7,500	
Greece	Athens	J. Meredith Read, Pa.	7,500	1873
Hawaiian Islands	Honolulu	Henry A. Peirce, Mass.	7,500	1869
Netherlands	Hague	Chas. T. Gorham, Mich.	7,500	1870
Portugal	Lisbon	Benjamin Moran	7,500	1874
Sweden and Norway	Stockholm	C. C. Andrews, Minn.	7,500	1869
Switzerland	Berne	Horace Rublee, Wis.	7,500	1869
Turkey	Constantinople	George H. Boker, Penn	7,500	1870
Uruguay & Paraguay	Montevideo	John C. Caldwell, Mo.	10,000	1874
U. S. of Columbia.	Bogota	Wm. L. Scruggs, Ga.	7,500	1873
Venezuela	Caracas	Thomas Russell, Mass.	7,500	1874

MINISTERS RESIDENT AND CONSULS GENERAL.

Hayti	Port-au-Prince	E. D. Bassett, Pa.	7,500	1869
Liberia	Monrovia	J. Milton Turner, Mo.	4,000	1871

THE STATES OF THE UNION.—State Governments.

STATES. (38)	CAPITALS.	GOVERNORS.	Term Expires.	Sal'ry.	Legislatures Meet.	State Elections.
Alabama	Montgomery	*George S. Houston*	Nov. 1878	$4000	3 M. Nov.	Tu. aft. 1 M. Nov.
Arkansas	Little Rock	*Augustus H. Garland*	Jan. 1877	3500	1 Tu.a.2M. Nov.	Tu. aft. 2 M. Nov.
California	Sacramento	Newton Booth	Dec. 1875	7000	1 M. Dec.	1 Wed. Sept.
Connecticut	Hartford	*Charles R. Ingersoll*	May, 1876	2000	1 W. May	1 Monday, April.
Colorado	Denver	Edward M. McCook				
Delaware	Dover	*John P. Cochran*	Jan. 1879	1333	*1 Tu. Jan.	Tu. aft. 1 M. Nov.
Florida	Tallahassee	*Marcellus L. Stearns*	Jan. 1877	3500	1 Tu. Jan.	Tu. aft. 1 M. Nov.
Georgia	Atlanta	*James Milton Smith*	Jan. 1877	4000	*2 W. Jan.	1 Wed. Oct.
Illinois	Springfield	John L. Beveridge	Jan. 1877	2500	*1 M. Jan.	Tu. aft. 1 M. Nov.
Indiana	Indianapolis	*Thomas A. Hendricks*	Jan. 1877	3000	*1 W. Jan.	2 Tuesday, Oct.
Iowa	Des Moines	Cyrus C. Carpenter	Jan. 1876	2500	*2 M. Jan.	2 Tuesday, Oct.
Kansas	Topeka	Thomas A. Osborn	Jan. 1877	3000	2 Tu. Jan.	Tu. aft. 1 M. Nov.
Kentucky	Frankfort	*Preston H. Leslie*	Sept. 1879	5000	1 M. Dec.	Monday, Aug.
Louisiana	New Orleans	William Pitt Kellogg	Jan. 1877	8000	1 M. Jan.	1 Monday, Nov.
Maine	Augusta	Nelson Dingley Jr.	Jan. 1876	2500	1 W. Jan.	2 Monday, Sept.
Maryland	Annapolis	*James B. Groome*	Jan. 1876	4500	*1 W. Jan.	Tu. aft. 1 M. Nov.
Massachusetts	Boston	William Gaston	Jan. 1876	5000	1 W. Jan.	Tu. aft. 1 M. Nov.
Michigan	Lansing	John J. Bagley	Jan. 1877	1000	*1 W. Jan.	Tu. aft. 1 M. Nov.
Minnesota	St. Paul	Cushman K. Davis	Jan. 1876	3000	1 Tu. Jan.	Tu. aft. 1 M. Nov.
Mississippi	Jackson	*Adelbert Ames*	Jan. 1876	3000	1 Tu. Jan.	Tu. aft. 1 M. Nov.
Missouri	Jefferson City	*Charles H. Hardin*	Jan. 1877	6000	*W. Jan.	Tu. aft. 1 M. Nov.
Nebraska	Lincoln	Silas Garber	Jan. 1877	1000	Tu. a. 1 M. Jan.	2 Tuesday, Oct.
Nevada	Carson City	*L. R. Bradley*	Jan. 1879	6000	*Last M. Jan.	Tu. aft. 1 M. Nov.
New Hampshire	Concord	*James A. Weston*	Jun. 1877	1000	1 W. June	2 Tuesday, March.
New Jersey	Trenton	*Joseph D. Bedle*	Jan. 1877	3000	2 Tu. Jan.	Tu. aft. 1 M. Nov.
New York	Albany	*Samuel J. Tilden*	Jan. 1877	10000	1 Tu. Jan.	Tu. aft. 1 M. Nov.
North Carolina	Raleigh	Curtis Brogden	Jan. 1877	6000	3 M. Nov.	1 Thursday, Aug.
Ohio	Columbus	*William Allen*	Jan. 1876	4000	*2 M. Jan.	2 Tuesday, Oct.
Oregon	Salem	*Lafayette F. Grover*	Sept. 1878	1500	*2 M. Sept.	1 Monday, June.
Pennsylvania	Harrisburg	John F. Hartranft	Jan. 1876	5000	*1 Tu. Jan.	Tu. aft. 1 M. Nov.
Rhode Island	Newp't.&Provid.	Henry Howard	May, 1876	1000	May & Jan.	1 Wed. April.
South Carolina	Columbia	Daniel H. Chamberlain	Jan. 1877	4000	4 M. Nov.	Tu. aft. 1 M. Nov.
Tennessee	Nashville	*James D. Porter, jr.*	Jan. 1878	3000	1 M. Oct.	Tu. aft. 1 M. Nov.
Texas	Austin	*Richard Coke*	Jan. 1878	5000	*1 W. Oct.	1 Tuesday, Sept.
Vermont	Montpelier	Asahel Peck	Oct. 1876	1000	*1 W. Oct.	1 Tuesday, Sept.
Virginia	Richmond	*James L. Kemper*	Jan. 1878	5000	1 W. Dec.	Tu. aft. 1 M. Nov.
West Virginia	Charleston	*John J. Jacob*	Mar. 1877	2700	2 Wed. Jan.	Tu. aft. 1 M. Nov.
Wisconsin	Madison	*William R. Taylor*	Jan. 1876	5000	1 W. Jan.	Tu. aft. 1 M. Nov.

Territories.	Capitals.	Governors.
Alaska	Sitka	Not organized.
Arizona	Tucson	A. P. K. Safford.
Dakotah	Yankton	John L. Pennington.
Idaho	Boise City	Thos. W. Bennett.
Indian	Tahlequah	Not Organized.
Montana	Virginia City	Benj. F. Potts.
New Mexico	Santa Fe	Marsh Giddings.
Utah	Salt Lake City	S. B. Axtell.
Washington	Olympia	Elisha P. Ferry.
Wyoming	Cheyenne	John A. Campbell.

*Biennial Sessions and Elections. Democrats in *Italic*.

Popular Vote for President from 1852 to 1860.

STATES.	1852			1856			1860			
	Scott, Whig.	Pierce, Dem.	Hale, F. Soil.	Fremont, Rep'n.	Buck'n, Dem.	Fillmore, Am'n.	Lincoln, Rep'n.	Doug'se, Dem.	Breck. Dem.	Bell. Un'n.
Alabama	15038	26881			46739	28552		13651	48831	27825
Arkansas	7404	12173			21910	10787		5227	28732	20094
California	35057	40626	100	20691	53365	36165	39173	38516	34334	6817
Connecticut	30057	33249	3160	42715	34965	2615	43692	15522	14641	3291
Delaware	6293	6318	62	308	6044	6175	3815	1023	7347	3864
Florida	2875	4318			6358	4833		367	8543	6437
Georgia	16660	34705			56578	42228		11590	51889	42886
Illinois	64934	80597	9966	96189	105348	37444	172161	160215	2404	3913
Indiana	80001	95340	6929	94375	118670	22386	139033	115609	12295	5306
Iowa	15856	17763	1604	43954	36170	9180	70409	55111	1048	1763
Kentucky	57068	53906		314	74642	67416	1364	25451	83143	66058
Louisiana	17255	18647			39080	20709		7625	22681	22931
Maine	32543	41609	8030	67379	39080	3325	62811	20693	6368	2046
Maryland	35060	44620	54	281	39115	47460	3294	6966	42482	41760
Massachusetts		44569	29073	108190	39240	19626	106533	34372	3509	22331
Michigan	33859	41842	7237	71762	82136	1660	88480	65087	905	405
Minnesota					35446		22069	11920	748	62
Mississippi	17548	26876			35446	24195		3283	40707	25040
Missouri	29984	38353			58164	48624	17028	58901	31317	58372
New Hampshire	16147	29997	6695	38345	32789	422	37519	25881	2112	441
New Jersey	38556	44305	350	28338	46943	24115	84324	62801		
New York	234882	262083	25329	276007	195878	124604	362646	312510		44900
North Carolina	39058	39744			48240	36986		2701	48339	12194
Ohio	152526	169220	31682	187497	170874	28126	231610	187232	11405	12194
Oregon							5270	3951	3806	183
Pennsylvania	179974	198568	8525	147310	230710	82175	268090	16765	178871	12776
Rhode Island	7626	8735	644	11467	6680	1675	12244	7107		183
Tennessee	68698	67018			73638	64178		11350	64709	69274
Texas	4995	13655			31108	15639		6849	47548	16438
Vermont	22173	13044	9621	39661	10569	545	33808	6509	218	1969
Virginia	68572	73858		291	89706	60310	1029	16290	74323	74681
Wisconsin	22240	33658	8814	66000	52843	870	86101	65021	889	161
Total.....	1380076	1601474	156695	1341264	1838169	874534	1866352	1376957	847763	590631

Popular Vote for President from 1864 to 1872.

STATES.	1864 McClel. Dem.	1864 Lincoln. Rep.	1864 Dem. maj'y	1864 Rep. maj'y	1868 Seym'r Dem.	1868 Grant. Rep.	1868 Dem. maj'y	1868 Rep. maj'y	1872 Greeley. Lib'l.	1872 Grant. Adm.	1872 Liberal maj'y	1872 Adm. maj'y
Alabama					73908	76366		4278	79444	90272		10828
Arkansas					19078	22112		3034	37927	41373		3446
California	43841	62134		18293	54077	54583		506	40718	54020		13502
Connecticut	42285	44691		2406	47392	50595		3043	45880	50638		4788
Delaware	8767	8155	612		10980	7623	3357		10206	11115		909
Florida									15427	17763		2336
Georgia					102722	57134	45588		76356	62650	13906	
Illinois	158730	189496		30766	199143	250000		51160	184938	241944		67006
Indiana	130233	150422		20189	166980	176648		9668	163632	186147		22515
Iowa	49530	89075		39479	74040	120399		46359	71196	131566		60370
Kansas	3691	16441		12750	13600	31048		17058	32970	67048		34078
Kentucky	64301	27786	36515		115890	39566	76324		99995	88766	11220	
Louisiana					80225	33263	46962		57063	71663		14634
Maine	44211	61803		17592	42460	70453		28093	27087	61422		32335
Maryland	32739	40153		7414	62257	30438	31919		67687	60760	927	
Massachusetts	48745	126712		77997	59408	136477		77069	134672	133472		74212
Michigan	74604	91521		16917	97069	128550		31481	78355	138455		60100
Minnesota	17375	25060		7685	28076	43545		13470	35117	55117		20694
Mississippi									47288	82175		34887
Missouri	31678	72750		41072	65628	86960		21332	151434	119196	32238	
Nebraska					5439	9729		4250	7812	18329		10517
Nevada	6594	9826		3232	5218	6480		1262	6236	8413		2177
New Hampshire	32871	36400		3529	31224	38191		6967	31424	37168		5744
New Jersey	68024	60723	7301		83001	80131	2870		76456	91656		15200
New York	361986	368745		6749	429883	419883	10000		440736	440736		53455
North Carolina					84601	96769		13168	70094	94769		24675
Ohio	205568	265154		59586	238606	280223		41617	244321	281852		37531
Oregon	8457	9888	1431		11125	10961	164		7730	11819		4089
Pennsylvania	276316	296391		20075	313382	342280		28898	212041	349588		137548
Rhode Island	8470	13692		5222	6348	12993		6445	5329	13665		8336
South Carolina					45237	62301		17064	22703	72290		49587
Tennessee					26129	56628		34499	94391	85655	8736	
Texas									66500	47406	19094	
Vermont	13321	42419		29098	12045	44167		32122	10927	41481		30354
Virginia									91654	93468		1814
West Virginia	10438	20153		12714	20306	29175		8869	29451	32315		2864
Wisconsin	65884	82458		17574	84707	108857		24150	86177	104997		18520
Total.	1808725	2216067	44428	431710	2709613	3015071	21718	529643	2834079	3597070	86030	849021

Lincoln's majority over McClellan, 407,342; Grant's over Seymour, 305,458; Grant's over Greeley, 762,991.

UNION PLATFORM.—1864.

THE National Convention which assembled at Baltimore on the 7th of June, 1864, and there nominated ABRAHAM LINCOLN for re-election as President, with ANDREW JOHNSON as Vice-President, adopted and presented to the American people the following:

Resolved, That it is the highest duty of every American citizen to maintain against all their enemies the integrity of the Union, and the paramount authority of the Constitution and laws of the United States; and that, laying aside all differences of political opinion, we pledge ourselves as Union men, animated by a common sentiment, and aiming at a common object, to do everything in our power to aid the Government in quelling by force of arms the rebellion now raging against its authority, and in bringing to the punishment due to their crimes the rebels and traitors arrayed against it.

Resolved, That we approve the determination of the Government of the United States not to compromise with rebels, nor to offer any terms of peace except such as may be based upon an "unconditional surrender" of their hostility and a return to their just allegiance to the Constitution and laws of the United States, and that we call upon the Government to maintain this position and to prosecute the war with the utmost possible vigor to the complete suppression of the Rebellion, in full reliance upon the self-sacrifice, the patriotism, the heroic valor, and the undying devotion of the American people to their country and its free institutions.

Resolved, That, as Slavery was the cause, and now constitutes the strength of this rebellion, and as it must be always and everywhere hostile to the principles of republican government, justice and the national safety demand its utter and complete extirpation from the soil of the republic; and that we uphold and maintain the acts and proclamations by which the Government, in its own defense, has aimed a death-blow at this gigantic evil. We are in favor, furthermore, of such an amendment to the Constitution, to be made by the people in conformity with its provisions, as shall terminate and forever prohibit the existence of Slavery within the limits of the jurisdiction of the United States.

Resolved, That the thanks of the American People are due the soldiers and sailors of the Army and Navy, who have periled their lives in defense of their country, and in vindication of the honor of the flag; that the nation owes to them some permanent recognition of their patriotism and valor, and ample and permanent provision for those of their survivors who have received disabling and honorable wounds in the service of the country; and that the memories of those who have fallen in its defense shall be held in grateful and everlasting remembrance.

Resolved, That we approve and applaud the practical wisdom, the unselfish patriotism, and unswerving fidelity to the Constitution and the principles of American liberty, with which Abraham Lincoln has discharged, under circumstances of unparalleled difficulty, the great duties and responsibilities of the Presidential office; that we approve and indorse, as demanded by the emergency and essential to the preservation of the nation, and as within the Constitution, the measures and acts which he has adopted to defend the nation against its open and secret foes; that we approve especially the Proclamation of Emancipation, and the employment as Union soldiers of men heretofore held in Slavery; and that we have full confidence in his determination to carry these and all other constitutional measures essential to the salvation of the country into full and complete effect.

Resolved, That we deem it essential to the general welfare that harmony should prevail in the National councils, and we regard as worthy of public confidence and official trust those only who cordially indorse the principles proclaimed in these resolutions, and which should characterize the administration of the Government.

Resolved, That the Government owes to all men employed in its armies, without regard to distinction of color, the full protection of the laws of war; and that any violation of these laws or of the usages of civilized nations in the time of war by the Rebels now in arms, should be made the subject of full and prompt redress.

Resolved, That the foreign immigration, which in the past has added so much to the wealth and development of resources and increase of power to this nation, the asylum of the oppressed of all nations, should be fostered and encouraged by a liberal and just policy.

Resolved, That we are in favor of the speedy construction of a Railroad to the Pacific.

Resolved, That the National faith, pledged for the redemption of the Public Debt, must be kept inviolate; and that for this purpose we recommend economy and rigid responsibility in the public expenditures, and a vigorous and just system of taxation; that it is the duty of every loyal State to sustain the credit and promote the use of the National Currency.

Resolved, That we approve the position taken by the Government that the people of the United States never regarded with indifference the attempt of any European power to overthrow by force, or to supplant by fraud, the institutions of any republican government on the western continent, and that they view with extreme jealousy, as menacing to the peace and independence of this our country, the efforts of any such power to obtain new footholds for monarchical governments, sustained by a foreign military force, in near proximity to the United States.

DEMOCRATIC PLATFORM.—1864.

The Democratic National Convention which gathered at Chicago on the 29th of August, and presented the names of GEORGE B. McCLELLAN for President, and GEORGE H. PENDLETON for Vice-President, agreed on and adopted the following:

Resolved, That in the future, as in the past, we will adhere with unswerving fidelity to the Union under the Constitution, as the only solid foundation of our strength, security, and happiness as a people, and as a framework of government equally conducive to the welfare and prosperity of all the States, both Northern and Southern.

Resolved, That this Convention does explicitly declare, as the sense of the American People, that, after four years of failure to restore the Union by the experiment of war, during which, under the pretense of a military necessity of a war power higher than the Constitution, the Constitution itself has been disregarded in every part, and public liberty and private right alike trodden down, and the material prosperity of the country essentially impaired, justice, humanity, liberty, and the public welfare, demand that immediate efforts be made for a cessation of hostilities, with a view to an ultimate Convention of all the States, or other peaceable means to the end that at the earliest practicable moment peace may be restored on the basis of the Federal Union of the States.

Resolved, That the direct interference of the military authority of the United States in the recent elections held in Kentucky, Maryland, Missouri, and Delaware, was a shameful violation of the Constitution, and the repetition of such acts in the approaching election will be held as revolutionary, and resisted with all the means and power under our control.

Resolved, That the aim and object of the Democratic party is to preserve the Federal Union and the rights of the States unimpaired; and they hereby declare that they consider the Administrative usurpation of extraordinary and dangerous powers not granted by the Constitution, the subversion of the civil by military law in States not in insurrection, the arbitrary military arrest, imprisonment, trial, and sentence of American citizens in States where civil law exists in full force, the suppression of freedom of speech and of the press, the denial of the right of asylum, the open and avowed disregard of State rights, the employment of unusual test-oaths, and the interference with and denial of the right of the people to bear arms, as calculated to prevent a restoration of the Union, and the perpetuation of a government deriving its just powers from the consent of the governed.

Resolved, That the shameful disregard of the Administration to its duty in respect to our fellow-citizens who now and long have been prisoners of war in a suffering condition, deserves the severest reprobation, on the score alike of public interest and common humanity.

Resolved, That the sympathy of the Democratic party is heartily and earnestly extended to the soldiery of our army, who are and have been in the field under the flag of our country; and, in the event of our attaining power, they will receive all the care and protection, regard and kindness, that the brave soldiers of the Republic have so nobly earned.

THE MONROE DOCTRINE.

WE copy from the Seventh Annual Message of Mr. Monroe, dated December 2, 1823:

"It was stated, at the commencement of the last session, that a great effort was then making in Spain and Portugal to improve the condition of the people of those countries, and that it appeared to be conducted with extraordinary moderation. It need scarcely be remarked that the result has been, so far, very different from what was then anticipated. Of events in that quarter of the globe, with which we have so much intercourse, and from which we derive our origin, we have always been anxious and interested spectators. The citizens of the United States cherish sentiments the most friendly in favor of the liberty and happiness of their fellow-men on that side of the Atlantic. In the wars of the European powers, in matters relating to themselves, we have never taken any part, nor does it comport with our policy so to do. It is only when our rights are invaded or seriously menaced, that we resent injuries or make preparation for our defense. With the movements in this hemisphere we are of necessity more immediately connected, and by causes which must be obvious to all enlightened and impartial observers. The political system of the allied powers is essentially different in this respect from that of America. This difference proceeds from that which exists in their respective governments. And to the defense of our own, which has been achieved by the loss of so much blood and treasure, and matured by the wisdom of their most enlightened citizens, and under which we have enjoyed unexampled felicity, this whole nation is devoted. We owe it, therefore, to candor, and to the amicable relations existing between the United States and those powers to declare, that we should consider any attempt on their part to extend their system to any portion of this hemisphere as dangerous to our peace and safety. With the existing colonies or dependencies of any European power we have not interfered, and shall not interfere. But with the governments who have declared their independence, and maintained it, and whose independence we have, on great consideration, and on just principles, acknowledged, we could not view any interposition for the purpose of oppressing them, or controlling in any other manner their destiny, by any European power, in any other light than as the manifestation of an unfriendly disposition toward the United States. In the war between these new governments and Spain, we declared our neutrality at the time of their recognition, and to this we have adhered, and shall continue to adhere, provided no change shall occur, which in the judgment of the competent authorities of this Government, shall make a corresponding change on the part of the United States indispensable to their security. The late events in Spain and Portugal show that Europe is still unsettled. Of this important fact no stronger proof can be adduced than that the allied powers should have thought it proper, on a principle satisfactory to themselves, to have interposed by force in the internal concerns of Spain. To what extent such interposition may be carried, on the same principle, is a question to which all independent powers, whose governments differ from theirs, are interested—even those most remote, and surely none more so than the United States. Our policy in regard to Europe, which was adopted at an early stage of the wars which have so long agitated that quarter of the globe, nevertheless remains the same, which is, not to interfere in the internal concerns of any of its powers; to consider the Government, *de facto,* as the legitimate Government for us; to cultivate friendly relations with it, and to preserve those relations by a frank, firm, and manly policy; meeting, in all instances, the just claims of every power, submitting to injuries from none. But in regard to these continents, circumstances are eminently and conspicuously different. It is impossible that the allied powers should extend their political system to any portion of either continent without endangering our peace and happiness; nor can any one believe that our Southern brethren, if left to themselves, would adopt it of their own accord. It is equally impossible, therefore, that we should behold such interposition, in any form, with indifference. If we look to the comparative strength and resources of Spain and those new Governments, and their distance from each other, it must be obvious that she can never subdue them. It is still the true policy of the United States to leave the parties to themselves, in the hope that other powers will pursue the same course."

NOTE.

[See Chapter vii., pp. 60—64.]

THE thirteen colonies derived their titles through grants (charters) from the crown, purchases from the Indians, the right of occupancy and vacancy (3 Kent's Comm., pp. 481—488; Vol. I., pp. 271-2). The United States derive their title to the public lands as follows :

"The whole territory north of the river Ohio, and west of the State of Pennsylvania, extending northwardly to the northern boundary of the United States, and westwardly to the Mississippi, was claimed by Virginia, and that State was in possession of the French settlements of Vincennes and Illinois, which she had occupied and defended during the revolutionary war. The States of Massachusetts and Connecticut claimed all that part which was within the breadth of their respective charters; and the State of New York had also an indeterminate claim to the country. The United States have obtained cessions from the four States, and thus acquired an indisputable title to the whole." * * "The State of Connecticut reserved a tract on lake Erie, bounded on the south by the 41st degree of North latitude, and extending westwardly one hundred and twenty miles from the western boundary of the State of Pennsylvania. The cessions of Massachusetts and New York included an insulated tract, commonly called ' the triangle,' lying on lake Erie, west of the State of New York, and north of that of Pennsylvania; and which has since been sold by the United States to Pennsylvania."

"North Carolina has ceded to the United States all her vacant lands beyond the Alleghany chain of mountains, within the breadth of her charter, that is to say, between the 35th degree and 36th degree, 30 minutes of North latitude, the last parallel being the southern boundary of the States of Virginia and Kentucky. That territory, which now forms the State of Tennessee, was, however, subject to a great variety of claims described in the Act of cession. And Congress has, by the Act of April 18, 1806, ceded to the last mentioned State the claim of the United States to all the lands east of a line described in the Act, leaving the lands west of that line still liable to satisfy such of the claims secured by the cession from North Carolina as cannot be located in the eastern division."

"South Carolina and Georgia were the only States which had a claim to the lands lying south of the 35th degree of North latitude. By the cessions from those two States, the United States have acquired the title of both to the tract of country now forming the Mississippi territory, extending from the 31st to the 35th degree of latitude, and bounded on the West by the river Mississippi, and on the East by the river Chatahouche, and by a line drawn from a place on that river, near the mouth of Uchee creek, to Nickajack, on the river Tennessee." * * " Cessions having thus been obtained from all the States claiming any part of the ' public lands,' it is now immaterial, so far as relates to those States, to examine the foundations of their respective titles." * * (Lands in West Florida, that portion of territory between the 31st degree and about 32d degree, 30 minutes of latitude) "appears therefore to have been acquired, not by any of the States as lying within its boundaries, but by the United States as part of West Florida, and for the benefit of the whole Union." * * " In several instances the same land will be found to have been purchased from different tribes, the purchase not being considered complete until all their conflicting claims have been acquired." * * See the volume of Land Laws, compiled in virtue of a resolution of Congress, of the 27th of April, 1810. Laws of the United States (published 1815) Vol. I., p. 452.

"The treaties with foreign nations by which territory has been acquired, or which relate to boundaries, are those of 1783 and 1794 with Great Britain, of 1795 with Spain, and of 1803 with France," and of 1848 with Mexico. See treaty with Great Britain, respecting the N. E. boundary, signed at Washington by Lord Ashburton and Mr. Webster, ratified by the Senate, August 20, 1842. Laws of the United States (published 1815) Vol. I. p. 435.

For the mode of passing a title of lands from a State to the United States, we insert the following :

An Act of the Legislature of the State of New York was read in Congress, 7th of March, 1780, which was certified as follows :

"*State of New York*, ss. :

I do hereby certify, that the aforegoing is a true copy of the original Act, passed the 19th of February, 1780, and lodged in the Secretarie's office.

ROBERT HARPUR,

Deputy Secretary of State."

"The delegates for the State of New York executed in Congress the following Act or declaration, to wit :

To all people who shall see these presents, we James Duane, William Floyd, and Alexander M. Dougall, the underwritten delegates for the State of New York in the honorable Congress of the United States of America, send greeting :

Whereas, it is stipulated as one of the conditions of the cession of territory, made for the benefit of the United States by the Legislature * *

In testimony whereof, etc.

JAMES DUANE,   [L. S.]
WM. FLOYD,   [L. S.]
ALEXANDER M. DOUGALL. [L. S.]

Sealed and delivered in presence of

CHARLES THOMSON,
CHARLES MORSE,
EBENEZER SMITH."

"The foregoing being executed, the delegates aforesaid, in virtue of the powers vested in them by the Act of their Legislature above recited, proceeded and executed in due form in behalf of their State, the following instrument, viz. :

To all who shall see these presents, we James Duane, William Floyd and Alexander M. Dougall, the underwritten delegates, etc. * *

In testimony, etc.

JAMES DUANE,   [L. S.]
WM. FLOYD,   [L. S.]
ALEXANDER M. DOUGALL. [L. S.]

Sealed and delivered in presence of

CHARLES THOMSON,
CHARLES MORSE,
EBENEZER SMITH."

Journals of Congress, March 1, 1781, Laws of Congress (published 1815) Vol. I, pp. 467—469.

See cessions of lands from the States of Virginia, Massachusetts, Connecticut, South Carolina, and Articles of agreement and cession of land or territory between the United States and the State of Georgia.

ANALYSIS.

CHAPTER I.—Page 5.

Colony of Virginia—French and Spanish settlements—New England—London company—Plymouth—First Government of Virginia—Puritans—Church of England—Tithes—Parishes—Slavery—Church and State—Penal laws—Normans and Saxons—Right of suffrage—Carolinas—Maryland settled—Lord Baltimore—Irishmen—Liberty of conscience—Delaware settled—New York settled—Military governors—Holland Dutch—English rule—New Jersey settled—Quakers and Dutch—Pennsylvania settled—Swedes—Proprietary governors—Suffrage—Georgia settled.

CHAPTER II.—Page 9.

Passengers in the Mayflower—New Plymouth—Clergy elected—The Puritans a joint stock company—Town meeting—All power in the people—All officers elected by the people—Vote by ballot—The people sovereign—English laws repudiated—Property qualification—Religious test—Judicial sanction of British common law—Public schools—Plymouth united with Massachusetts—The authority of the Church of England repudiated—Marriage—Laws against Quakers—Rhode Island—Roger Williams—Liberty of conscience—No toleration—Witchcraft.

CHAPTER III.—Page 17.

Town meeting—Parish—Town officers—Schools—Vacancies and resignations in offices—County officers—Vacancies and resignations—Removal from office—Property qualification.

CHAPTER IV.—Page 22.—State Government.

Judiciary—Church and State—Compulsory education—Naturalization laws—Oath of objuration—Aliens—Natural born Citizens—Alien enemy—Alien purchaser—Alien sueable—Allegiance—Naturalization—State laws—State sovereignty—English courts—Native born—Free speech and free press—Martial law—Banishment—Property qualification—Resignation—Oath of office—Legislative powers—Territorial government.

CHAPTER V.—Page 36.—The Federal Government.

Restriction on States—Recall of delegates in Congress—Reserved powers—Express powers—Co-ordinate powers—Checks and balances—Veto—Judiciary—Conflict of authority—Limitation of power—Unconstitutional laws—Congress—Electors—Vacancies and Resignation—Impeachment—Oath of office—Revenue—Restriction on the powers of the States—Jury—Common law—Commerce—President—Presidential elections—Contested elections—Treaties—Removal from office—Appointments—Public lands—Neutrality laws—Courts-martial—Insurrection—Executive—State rights—Suit between two States—Jurisdiction—Taxation—Railroads—Banks—Legal tender—State laws.

CHAPTER VI.—Page 50.

Foreigners—Alien laws—Ten dollars taxes on emigrants—Mayor Clark's letter against emigration—Report of Council—14 years residence before naturalization—Jefferson—21 years before naturalization—Laws against emigration—Pre-emption laws.

OPINIONS OF THE PRESS.

A CONSTITUTIONAL HISTORY OF THE UNITED STATES,

By P. Cudmore, Counsellor at Law,

"Mr. Cudmore . . . has prepared an exceedingly serviceable compendium of the constitutional laws of the United States. He has gathered into his book in convenient form nearly every thing that materially affects the legal relations of the people of the country and of the various States constituting the Union. The book opens with a brief account of the various colonies that took part in the war of 1776, and emerged from the struggle as the United States of North America. The crown grants and regulations, under which these colonies were founded, are succinctly stated, and the steps intelligently marked by which they passed from comparative vassalage to independence.

"The theory upon which our present government was founded, and the distribution of power between the States, counties and towns, is concisely, but lucidly, explained. The history of parties that have from time to time contested for the control of the government, is traced with candor and accuracy, and the fundamental law, as it stands to-day, is placed in proper and instructive relief.

"The book . . . is of unmistakable value, and we commend it as a work of reference to students of American law, politics and history."—*Brooklyn Daily Eagle.* (N. Y.)

"This work covers the entire history of the progress of civil government in this country from its first settlement down to 1868, with a concise review of the development of constitutional law in each State in the United States. The facts are briefly and clearly stated, and their relations illustrated in general by brief quotations from the writings of prominent constitutional lawyers and essayists, including Jefferson, Madison, Hamilton, Adams, De Tocqueville and others. A vast amount of research has been expended in the collection of these references, which, in connection with a number of important public documents, will render the work of great value as a book of reference."—*New York Evening Express.* (N. Y.)

"The whole forms a very acceptable and useful book for reference, containing much valuable information in a form that renders it easy of access. A concise history of the colonies and of the formation of the different States is given, with the main features in the constitution of each; the plan of the general government, and the constitution of the United States as it now stands, with chapters on the naturalization laws, soldiers' bounty, land grants, homestead laws, etc.; a short history of the rebellion, and the various platforms of the national conventions of all parties, from the first convention till the present time, besides many other extracts and tables of historical importance and interest."—*The Irish American.* (N. Y.)

"Mr. Cudmore . . . has condensed in an able manner, into the limits of a single volume, a colonial, general and constitutional History of the United States, which will prove an invaluable hand-book to the political student. The volume is a digest of the speeches and writings of the framers of the Constitution, and many of the most eminent jurists and statesmen the country has produced. It gives numberless judicial decisions of interest and importance, and also the platforms of all the political parties that have ever existed. The department devoted to Colonial History and Civil Government will be found especially interesting."—*The Argus.* (Jersey City, N. J.)

"Those who wish to understand the structure of the government, both State and Federal, will find this a very useful reliable manual, of facts and reference."—*New York Star.* (N. Y.)

"Throughout the entire work, the untiring energy, clear judgment and good taste of the author are clearly discernible. . . . No library should be without a copy of it."—*Sunday Democrat.* (N. Y.)

"This work is evidently the result of much patient accumulation of legal, political and historical material, bearing on the object of the author, which has been to condense into one volume the colonial, general and constitutional history of the United States."—*Manhattan and De La Salle Monthly.* (N. Y.)

"This is a very compact and useful publication for the lawyer, editor, statesman and public man of any kind, for it has an array of political and historical facts that renders it especially desirable for all who must, in brief compass, understand our political history, . . . it is really a most valuable publication, and to the editor, writer and public man of any kind, it is especially desirable."—*New York Day-Book.* (N. Y.)

"The Civil Government of the States, and the constitutional history of the United States, is the title of an able and exhaustive treatise on Government."—*St. Louis Dispatch.*

"No man who desires to be an intelligent and effective political writer, speaker, or public servant should be without a copy of it. . . . Its condensation also is remarkable. What information it contains is truly in a nutshell and yet it is co-extensive with the history of the country."—*St. Louis Times.*

" . . . It may be reasonably conjectured that he possesses a talent for condensation that Montesquieu might have envied."—*Catholic World.* (N. Y.)

"We earnestly recommend all lovers of the great American Republic to supply themselves with copies of the work, and become familiar with its contents."—*Western Watchman.* (St. Louis, Mo.)

"The politician will find much valuable information in this work."—*Dubuque Telegraph.* (Iowa.)

"It is a compendium brim full of information nowhere else to be found, and as an accurate history and book of reference it fills a space in American literature long needed."—*Anti-Monopolist.* (St. Paul, Minn.)

"A number of important public documents will render the work of great value as a book of reference."—*The Chicago Pilot.* (Ill.)

"He shows considerable research."—*Western Journal of Education.* (Chicago, Ill.)

"A vast amount of labor and research, has been expended in the preparation of the book."—*Faribault Republican.* (Minn.)

"It is certainly a very valuable work, and does Mr. Cudmore great credit."—*Faribault Democrat.* (Minn.)

"To a student of the political history of his country, this book is invaluable. . . . The opinions of Madison, Jefferson, Adams, De Tocqueville, and other eminent authorities, requiring a vast amount of research, have been examined in its preparation. This is a book that should be in every farmers' club and grange library, as well as in the library of private individuals."—*Prairie Farmer.* (Chicago, Ill.)